Also by Julie Corbin

TELL ME NO SECRETS
WHERE THE TRUTH LIES
DO ME NO HARM
NOW THAT YOU'RE GONE

What Goes Around

Julie Corbin

MULHOLLAND
BOOKS
HODDER

First published in ebook in Great Britain in 2016 by Hodder & Stoughton
An Hachette UK company

1

This Mulholland paperback edition first published in 2017

A CIP catalogue record for this title is available from the British Library

Paperback ISBN 978 1 473 65973 5
eBook ISBN 978 1 444 75403 2

Typeset in Plantin Light by Palimpsest Book Production Limited, Falkirk,
Stirlingshire

Printed and bound by Clays Ltd, St Ives plc

Hodder & Stoughton policy is to use papers that are natural, renewable
and recyclable products and made from wood grown in sustainable forests.
The logging and manufacturing processes are expected to conform to the
environmental regulations of the country of origin.

Hodder & Stoughton Ltd
Carmelite House
50 Victoria Embankment
London EC4Y 0DZ

www.hodder.co.uk

For Helen Lewis, great friend and fellow reader

Prologue

It was her son who found her body. Something she would never have wanted. If she'd been given the choice she would have said, 'Let me die in my bed, aged eighty-five with those I love beside me. Let us linger over memories that make us smile, practise our goodbyes, give and take last hugs.'

But that wasn't how it was.

He opened the front door with a shove and tipped into the hallway, kicking a shoe onto the bottom stair. He took an apple from his bag, then dropped the bag onto the floor and shuffled one-handed through the letters on the hall table, wasting precious time (he realised afterwards). He even held up a letter to the light, for no reason except that he didn't recognise the writing and the envelope looked like it might be see-through. It wasn't.

He chewed another bite of apple, juice bursting into the corners of his mouth. His eyes roamed until he spotted a flyer with gold and orange writing proclaiming that the Indian restaurant in the high street was under new management. 'Twenty per cent off in the first week!' he called out. 'We should get a carry-out tonight.' He paused, cocking his head at the silence. 'Mum?'

The house had a quietness to it that didn't feel right. He took a few steps along the hallway and held his breath, listening. He knew his mum was in because he'd texted her just an hour ago.

'Mum!' he called out again. She could be asleep on her bed of course, except that she never slept in the daytime. 'It's me!'

He moved around on his tiptoes, just in case she was asleep. He checked the living room first. There was a half-empty mug on the mantelpiece. He picked it up; the coffee was stone cold. He put it down again and left the apple beside it. He sat down on the sofa and switched on the TV (more time-wasting for him to curse himself with later). He scrolled through the channels, spending less than a second on each.

Kitchen next. And there she was, lying on the floor in front of the window. A deep cut sliced across her forehead, the blood meandering towards the wall and pooling against the skirting board. Her right arm was twisted underneath her, bendy as a pipe cleaner. Her eyes stared straight ahead but were unseeing; her mouth hung open.

He absorbed all this in a fractured second as he ran towards her, crashing down onto the floor beside her. 'Jesus! Fuck! Mum! Help! *Help!*' he bawled, fear hoarsening his voice. 'Help! Help us!'

1. Ellen

Thursday evening, quarter to eight, and I'm standing outside on the meeting room steps. A dull light filters through the opaque windowpanes and the murmur of voices is just audible beyond the closed doors. I'm in two minds whether to go inside or make a run for it. Last week's group left me feeling like I spent far too much time talking about myself and I have no clear recollection of what I said. For over an hour I seemed to do most of the talking – *My name is Ellen and I was mugged* – then I spent a further half an hour huddling round with the other people there, drinking cups of tea and munching on custard creams. I woke up the next morning feeling uneasy about what I might have said and the feeling has stuck with me all week, like the half-recollection of a drunken mistake.

It occurs to me that I don't want to risk it happening again, so I turn my back on the meeting room and hurry across the road towards a cafe. It's been raining since mid-afternoon. The gutters stream with fast-flowing water and my umbrella is useless against the wind that blows me sideways, spraying me with monster drops of rainwater; I'm drenched in seconds.

Inside the cafe is warm, steam rising off people's bodies and off the deep fat fryers. The room smells of fish and chips and the pungent tang of vinegar. I climb up onto a free stool in front of a long, narrow table that faces the window. Waterlogged pavements, goose-grey sky, streetlights illuminating brave pedestrians struggling against the wind and the rain – it feels good to be indoors.

'Changed your mind?'

I swivel round towards a group of three people sitting along from me – two women and one man. Fish supper leftovers congeal in front of them: tomato ketchup smeared across the dinner plates, crispy ends of chips and silver fish skin dotted through the sauce.

'We saw you standing over the road.' It's one of the women who's talking. 'You looked like you were deciding whether or not to go inside.' She holds out her hand. 'You're Ellen?' I nod, recognising them from last week's meeting. 'I'm Trish.' She gestures to her right and left. 'This is Pam and Francis.'

I shake her hand and try to smile at the three faces staring at me but this is the last thing I need. I would have kept on walking but for the rain. Bloody Edinburgh weather. Now I'm stuck talking to them.

'We're heading across to the hall,' Trish says, standing up. 'You going to join us?'

'Not tonight.' I smile properly this time, relieved that they're leaving. 'But thank you for the offer.'

'Are you sure? We could walk in together.' Trish gives a knowing laugh. 'Makes it much easier.'

I start rummaging in my bag, hoping they'll see I'm busy and get the message to leave me alone. I know they're only trying to help but their interest feels intrusive.

'Pam and I will help put out the chairs,' I hear Trish say to Francis. 'Maybe you could . . .'

I don't catch the end of her sentence because she lowers her voice. I'm feeling hot suddenly. Hot and anxious. I find my mobile and begin to scroll through the photographs. I took two dozen of them this morning. I always start in the kitchen before working my way through the rest of the rooms in the house. The hob: all six switches are in the off position. The oven: the same. I photographed every socket in each of the rooms, all of them plug-free. I—

'Ellen.' Francis reaches across and touches my arm just above the elbow. It makes me jump. 'I'm not meaning to be pushy.' He's looking towards the door and I can tell he feels he's drawn the short straw being left with me. 'I'm going across now.' He pulls his wallet out of his trouser pocket and signals to the waitress at the other end of the counter, her order pad and pencil slack in her hand as she chats to a customer. He glances back at me. 'See you there?'

'Not tonight.'

'Sure?'

I drag my attention away from the photos to give him an explanation. 'Thing is Francis, I'm a bit of a fraud. It wasn't even a bad mugging. It was a couple of kids. They couldn't have been more than twelve or thirteen. They grabbed my bag but I hung on tight, and then they ran off.'

I'm telling the truth. There was no great drama. It was a fairly half-hearted mugging but nevertheless it was enough to push an already anxious me deeper into a free-floating anxiety that never quite leaves me. It's a cliché, isn't it? But as soon as a couple of things go wrong, you get the overwhelming feeling that life is slipping out of your control, that fate's cruel hand has you in its grasp and it's only a matter of time before the hand tosses you carelessly towards the drain.

'You said last week that the mugging was the final straw,' Francis tells me.

'I did?'

'You talked about your husband.' He pauses before saying, 'And about how anxious you've become recently.'

That makes me wince. 'I have a horrible feeling I said far too much at last week's meeting.' Air pushes into my lungs and I stand up, feel the pulse in my neck pick up pace. 'You probably know more about me than my close family do.' I search his face to see whether I'm right but he's not giving anything more away. (What did I say? Did I rant and rave about the bitch who stole my life? Did I mention that Tom had left me to seek, in his words, 'greater intimacy and friendship'? That I spent weeks oscillating between shock and tears, and that now I am a basket case of checking and checking and yet more checking, over and over like a stuck record?)

The waitress comes across and Francis settles his bill, then gathers up his coat and umbrella. 'Can I get you anything?' the waitress says to me, her pen poised above her pad.

'No, thank you.' I reach for my bag just as Francis is heading outside, follow him out onto the street and shout after him, 'Wait! I'm going to come to the meeting. It's the lesser of the evils. I'll only sit here chewing my nails, worrying about what I said last week.'

'You shouldn't worry.' He raises an umbrella that's large enough and sturdy enough to shelter us both and not be overwhelmed by the strength of the wind and rain. 'We're all in the same boat. That's the whole point of the group.'

We fall into step and jog across the road, hopping over the rush of water in the gutters. We're through the doors and into the meeting hall before I can catch my breath. Trish and Pam have arranged the chairs in a circle and almost half of them are already taken. Several people look up at us as we come into the room and Sharon, the police liaison officer who runs the group, calls out, 'Welcome! Glad you've both made it.'

I walk to the far side of the circle and sit beside a young woman, a girl really, with pale skin, huge grey eyes and curly, faded-red hair piled up on her head. On my other side is a man of about sixty wearing a thick woollen jumper of the sort I associate with hardy fishermen. The girl I don't remember having seen before but the man has been here every Thursday evening for the last five weeks and I have yet to hear him speak.

I slide my coat onto the back of the chair and look around the circle, taking a few seconds to catch my breath. The age range must be from about eighteen to eighty and there are both men and women. Some of them are timid, limbs held close to their bodies as they avoid catching anyone's eye, while others are straight-backed and open-faced, communicating their encouragement to relax – we're all friends here.

Except that we're not friends. Our common denominator is an unusual one – we are all victims of crime: a motley crew of the sad and the frightened. Some crimes are serious, chillingly so, hence the reason I came to the meetings for four weeks before I had the nerve to say anything, the crime against me being minor by anyone's reckoning.

Trish and Pam are both to my left while Francis is opposite me. His metal chair scrapes across the faded wooden floor with a high-pitched screech as he rearranges it to sit down on. Our eyes meet and he smiles encouragingly. Slowly, my brain makes connections and I find myself half-remembering his story – *My name is Francis and someone tried to kill me.*

Could he have said that?

'So shall we get started?' says Sharon. There's a
murmur of assent from half of the group. 'We have a
couple of newcomers here tonight.' She gestures towards
a man sitting close to Trish and to the girl beside me.
'No pressure, but if either of you would like to introduce
yourselves then please know that you'll be made welcome.'
The girl nods; the man is staring fixedly at the floor.
'The rules of the group are simple. This is a safe space
where we listen and support one another. Confidentiality
is adhered to within the group.' She smiles round at us
all. 'So . . . who would like to begin?'

'I would,' the girl on my left says at once. She is sitting
on her hands and her legs are shaking. 'I'm Gemma and
I need help.' She leans forward. 'I'm here because our
house was burgled and it's had a bad effect on my mum
and dad.' She tells us about what happened to her family.
The details aren't as harrowing as some people's are,
but I can see that for her, this event has been a water-
shed. 'And I just think . . . well, I just think that there
are three types of people.' She ticks them off on her
fingers. 'Those who make things happen, those who
watch things happen and those let things happen to
them.' She pauses. 'I'm tired of feeling like a victim and
just letting things happen to me. As a family we do that
and I've had enough. I want to take charge.' There are
tears in her eyes as she sits back and inhales tense breaths.
We all clap and then Sharon asks whether anyone has
anything to offer.

There follows a few minutes of people supporting her
with praise and with advice, and during that time I drift
off into my own thoughts, worried that I didn't look
properly at the photographs, and that makes me doubt
my checks. Beads of sweat break out on my scalp. I try
to visualise the photographs. The switches on the hob

were definitely in the off position. I'm sure of it. I'm—

'Ellen.' Gemma is pulling at my sleeve. She points along the circle to where Trish is staring at me expectantly.

'I was just asking how you've been doing this week, Ellen?' Trish says and everyone's eyes are suddenly upon me.

'I've been . . . fine, thanks.'

She nods. 'Only, last week you were—'

'I barely remember what I said last week,' I say quickly, my tone flat.

'You mentioned some obsessions,' Trish reminds me. 'You'd been taking photos and—'

'Fire.' It's another voice, a man with long hair tied back in a ponytail. 'You're afraid of your house going on fire.'

An anxiety tremor begins in my toes and travels up my legs, all the way to my skull where it sets up an insistent thrumming. Gemma takes my arm. I think she's saying something but I don't know what. All at once I'm on my feet, lurching towards the door and out into the rain. The cold and the wet hit me hard and force a shiver right through me.

Then a coat goes round my shoulders – my coat – and my arms are pushed inside the sleeves. We're going across the road again – myself and Francis – and into the cafe, straight into the same seats we vacated just thirty minutes before.

'You go back to the group,' I tell him, waving him aside. The thrumming in my ears has lessened and my vision is clearing. 'Please go.' He's holding my bag and I seize it from him.

'Will you wait here?' he says. 'I know that Sharon will be concerned.'

'I'll wait.' I give him my look-at-me-I'm-fine-now smile. 'I'm a private person, that's all. Talking about myself goes against the grain.'

'And there's nothing wrong with that.' He moves to the door. 'Just wait, okay?'

I nod but in truth I have no intention of waiting. As soon as I've checked my mobile I intend to head home and never show my face at the meetings again. I scroll through the morning's photos, checking the times they were taken, satisfied that it was just before I left the house. I check each photo once, twice, three times, ignoring the hand that's raised in the back row of my mind, reminding me that none of this is rational, in fact it's utterly nonsensical. I have read the statistics. Fires aren't started by plugs being left in. Fires are started by dropped cigarettes and unattended fat fryers, by a toppled candle or the lint in the tumble dryer catching alight.

But I am beyond the point of being able to be reassured by the sensible and so I keep checking. Before I left the house this afternoon I photographed every socket in each of the rooms, for evidence that all of them are plug-free. This morning I even took the time to number each of the sockets with a black marker pen – nineteen in all – just in case I have any doubts about which one is which.

When I've checked the photographs for the third time, I feel calmer and make ready to leave before the meeting breaks up and I have half a dozen well-meaning people descending on the cafe.

'So what can I get you?' The waitress is all smiles. I can see that it's automatic for her. She's tired, she's fed up, she probably has another hour of work to get through but still she has her game face on.

'Nothing,' I say, standing up. 'I'm just leaving.'

The rain has lessened to a weak drizzle and I run to the bus stop, relieved to have made my escape. I climb upstairs on the bus and plonk myself down at the front to watch the city lights stretch ahead of me. The bus crosses the Royal Mile and then heads down the Mound, the castle cresting the rock to my left. I make a concerted effort to count my blessings: I have my children, Ben and Chloe, and a sweet-natured granddaughter called Molly; I have my lovely dad close by; I have a house to live in and a job I enjoy; my body is healthy; I have limbs that work and eyes that see and enough food in my belly to keep me from hunger.

You have a major problem, the voice in my head insists. And it's getting worse. A month ago you didn't need to take photographs. A month before that you could leave for work having checked the whole house just the once. Where will you be in another month?

This unknown quantity terrifies me, dragging at my peace of mind like a boulder tied to my ankle, pulling me underwater, knocking the air and the happiness out of me.

My mobile rings and I glance at the name. *For fuck's sake! Leave me alone!* I let the call go to voicemail and don't listen to the message until ten minutes later when I'm walking home. 'I'm sorry, Ellen. I should have stepped in. I think perhaps you felt threatened?' Sharon's tone is apologetic. 'You know, group work doesn't suit everyone. Perhaps one-to-one sessions would be better for you? I can recommend some therapists, if you like?' She pauses. 'Tell you what, I'll text you their names and numbers and you can make up your own mind. But do come back to the group if you feel it will help you.'

One-to-one therapy has never appealed to me; I don't

seek undivided attention because it makes me feel uncomfortable. But when her text arrives, I glance at the names and immediately my breath catches in my throat. One of the names is familiar to me and it causes the blood to pulse at my temples. It hadn't occurred to me that *she* would be one of the recommended therapists so it's a shock to see her name there.

Leila Henrikson.

I remember Ben telling me that she was running her psychotherapy practice from the house – my house – Maybanks. The home I spent years restoring. My children were born there, learned to walk there, talk there, milestones reached and surpassed within the walls of a family home that seemed to celebrate along with us, and all this brought painfully, abruptly, to a halt when Leila Henrikson set her sights on Tom. In a matter of months, I was out and she was in.

She holds dinner parties in my kitchen. She enjoys the benefits of my hard work: the restored fireplaces, the stained-glass door panels that I learned to make at an evening class, the tiled hallway that my dad and I worked on one Easter holiday. She basks in the sunshine of the south-facing garden. She sleeps in my bed, with my husband lying beside her.

Heat warms my cheeks as anger builds inside me and then, out of nowhere, the germ of an idea presents itself to me.

What if?

What if I were to choose her as my therapist, give a false name and get myself back inside my home? I could gain her trust, make her see me as a human being rather than just the discarded ex-wife who's no longer up to scratch.

Ben has told me how important her therapy practice

is to her, how much she values her ability to help people. She would be ashamed of herself, then, wouldn't she? After I'd confronted her, after I'd made her see how much damage she'd done. A trusted health professional who behaves with such obvious disregard for another human being – how would she square that with her principles?

The thought of biting back, of orchestrating an act of revenge, brings me a bitter pleasure. And later, when I'm in bed, I turn off the bedroom light and lie back on the pillow, enjoying a brief let-up from worry and fear as I stare beyond the shadows on the ceiling into a world where we play by my rules, and my rules dictate fairness and respect. Leila Henrikson has wilfully stolen from me. She has taken my husband. She has moved into my home. And she deserves to be right royally punished for it.

I concoct a scenario where she is made to feel small, weak, beaten. I play around with the idea, imagine her humiliated, in tears, mascara running down her face, her cheeks an ugly, blotchy red. She would beg my forgiveness – but I wouldn't give it to her. I would show no mercy. I might even slap her.

And then as my thinking crowns a dizzy, revengeful peak, so it begins to fall back to earth and my confidence falls with it. Me? Is someone like me capable of humiliating a woman like Leila? Capable of taking a woman like her to task? A woman who could steal another woman's life without shame or regret?

I turn over in bed, discounting the whole idea as ridiculous. I'm not that sort of person. I'm someone who plays by the rules, doesn't deceive, doesn't wilfully set out to hurt someone.

And more to the point, she'd recognise me. Of course she would.

She would, wouldn't she?

1. Leila

David has started calling me again, three times already this week, and just when I finally have my life in order:

Tom and I are living together – check.

Alex has completed his first year at university and scraped a pass in all of his exams – even economics – miracle! – check.

I'm finally living in a property – Maybanks, grey stone Victorian villa – where I have the room to practise psychotherapy without having to travel, no arm-and-a-leg costs, no having to kowtow to another therapist's idea of what makes up a therapeutic environment. My space. My way – check.

And then David has to raise his head again. A phone call, on Sunday evening, in the middle of me trying to make Tom's children feel welcome. When I saw his name flash up on the screen I considered ignoring him, but I knew that would only make him double his persistence.

There was no 'hello', no 'how's it going?', just, 'It's important I see you,' he said, his tone strangely formal.

'David, hi,' I said. 'How are you?' I had drunk three glasses of prosecco and realised my voice was raised. I pulled the door shut behind me and stood in the pantry. 'Where are you?'

'In Edinburgh. We need to talk.'

'Okay, sure . . . David.' I couldn't help but sigh. 'What do you need to talk about?'

'What do you think?'

'Let's not talk about the past again. We don't have to keep going back there, you know?'

'Yes, we do,' he said. 'You're a therapist, for God's sake! You know how damaging this stuff can be long-term.' He continued on for several minutes, telling me what he wanted, what he needed, and I listened because I'm his sister and that's what I do.

I agreed to meet him. I know that I'll need to make some effort, prove my sincerity, in order to win him round to my way of thinking, but I've been doing that for years after all. Three o'clock this afternoon in the cafe at the Portrait Gallery. I met him there eighteen months ago when he returned from his extended trip to India. He likes the scones – date and walnut – no cream, but lots of butter and jam.

Before I go I have a full morning of clients and I check through the names in my diary while I'm having breakfast: Susan, a divorcee with abandonment issues, Alison and Mark who are wrestling with infertility, and Tobias, a long-term client who was sexually abused as a child.

'Three clients this morning?' Tom says, looking over my shoulder.

'Yes, and then afterwards I'm going into town.' I take a last bite of toast. 'I have a meeting about the class I'll be teaching next year.'

'Will you be able to collect my suit from the dry-cleaners?' he says.

'I'll ask Katarina to go.'

Tom shakes his head.

'Why can't Katarina do it?' I say.

'She's likely to lose it.' He picks up a car magazine from the rack and takes a seat opposite me. 'She only has to leave it on the bus or on a park bench. The girl is barely conscious.'

He has a point. Katarina is a dreamy girl, distant, sometimes sullen. I don't think she's taken to life with us. She spends many an evening Skyping her family at home in the Czech Republic, probably wishing herself back there. 'Maybe so,' I admit. 'But I've known worse.'

'I don't understand why we need to have her living with us,' Tom says. 'Why not simply have someone in to clean a couple of times a week?'

'Because we have the room and in the long run I think it saves us money.'

Tom doesn't comment but his opinion is written all over his face. It's that look, the one I first noticed when we'd been seeing each other for almost six months and I asked him why he hadn't left his wife yet. It was our first argument and it had shaken my trust in him. I glimpsed a rigidity, an intractability that I didn't like. We were having lunch in Harvey Nichols and he was already moody in case we bumped into people who knew him. His expression was cloudy and intense as if a storm was about to break. He moved his hand off the table when I stretched mine out to him. He told me that he was waiting until his son had completed his Highers and his father-in-law had recovered from an operation. The family didn't need any more drama. 'Any more drama' – that's exactly how he put it.

'Maybe you're right about Katarina.' I kiss him, starting just beneath his ear and working towards his lips. I feel him relax and he kisses me back. He's a better kisser than any man I've ever met. He makes me feel dizzy, heady, girlish even. 'I can stop at the dry-cleaners,' I say, pulling back for air. 'I'll have time.'

'You're an angel,' he says. 'It's my dinner suit. I'll need

it for my trip to London.' He slides his hand between my legs. I'm already wet from the kissing, the lining of my mouth tingles, my body is showing me it's keen to keep going but my mind is already preoccupied with the day ahead.

'Katarina might come in.' I take his hand, kiss his fingers and stare down at my crotch and then his, lick my lips. 'Let's save ourselves for this evening.'

He groans as if wounded but I can see that in reality he enjoys being denied. He stands up and I follow him to the front door. 'Please have a word with her, Leila.' He trails his index finger along the length of my spine from my neck to my arse. 'It's surely only a matter of time before she crashes the Mini or breaks something expensive.'

'You're right. I will.' I wait until he's climbed into his car and I wave him off before walking through the house, into the back garden. The sun is weak, obstinate grey clouds obscuring the heat and light. I walk across the patio and onto the wet grass that's cold on my bare feet; I shiver but don't stop walking.

The garden is divided into three distinct sections, which I like because it means I can't be seen smoking from the house. People perceive smoking as a weakness because any intelligent, informed adult would give up if she could, wouldn't she? Ergo, if such an adult continues to smoke, she must be weak, addicted, needy, and all the bad things that those traits imply.

Bollocks.

At the bottom of the garden, behind the wild rose bushes, is a well-placed garden hut, and inside the hut, paint pots and varnish hide my stash of tobacco and cigarette papers. I'm not succumbing to temptation. I'm succumbing to want. Some people would say there's no point in drinking kale and avocado smoothies if I ruin it with a cigarette. My internal sensor tells me different. My internal sensor tells me that smoking is nothing. Smoking is the lesser of all the evils. Better to be a smoker than an alcoholic or a sex addict. You don't do my job and get hysterical about a minuscule dose of nicotine and a pinch of tar. Everyone is entitled to kindness. I say that to my clients often enough and it's true. A life of strict denial is no life at all.

So be kind to yourself – smoke the hell out of a cigarette if that's what you want to do and fuck the naysayers.

I roll two cigarettes expertly between thumb and forefinger, then light the end and inhale.

Bliss.

I smoke one after the other and spend a prolonged minute relishing the rush of nicotine before I refocus my mind for the day ahead.

Clients first. The appointments are scheduled on the hour and are fifty minutes long; the ten minutes in between I spend writing notes on the previous client and then reminding myself of the needs of the client who is about to arrive. I enjoy my job. I'd even go so far as to say I love my job because I'm able to make a difference. If that sounds trite then I make no apologies for that. The fact of the matter is that I am skilled in my work. I'm able to guide my clients from a point of distress to a point of resolution. How can that not be special?

I stroll back through the garden, running my fingers over bushes and flowers, and think about Tom's wife Ellen, a woman I've never met and don't care to. I lack curiosity where she is concerned. I'm clear in my own mind that Ellen is part of Tom's past and not part of our future. Tom has told me very little about her and I haven't asked because the details aren't for me to know.

That said, occasionally I can't help but consider Ellen, because it was Ellen who designed and maintained the garden. Chloe and Ben told me this on Sunday when they noticed the changes their father and I are making. Ben seemed disappointed, but Chloe was visibly angry, even when I assured her that we are simply tidying the garden up, pruning back some of the wildness to introduce more light. Chloe's mood remained surly throughout the meal and she left early – Ben went with her, saying he needed to 'be somewhere' – and Tom asked me to 'just leave them be'.

I didn't want to leave them be. I would have preferred to talk it over. Chloe and Ben are adults, and they need to understand that their dad has moved on and that perhaps they should move on too. I held my tongue though, because Tom has been careful where Alex is concerned, not often interfering in my relationship with my son even though Alex is frequently rude to him. Alex hasn't taken to Tom, just as Tom's children haven't taken to me. We are becoming a blended family and there will be teething problems. It's only to be expected.

I clear the breakfast dishes off the table just as Katarina comes into the kitchen wearing her garish dressing gown and an expression of benign self-pity.

'Good morning, Katarina,' I say.

'Good morning, Leila.' She gives me a weak smile.

'I need you to do something for me today.'

'I am cleaning the bathrooms today,' she says, dropping bread into the toaster. 'I am washing the floors.'

'That's great. Thank you.' I smile. 'But I'd also like you to walk to the dry-cleaners in the high street and collect Tom's suit.'

A suspicious frown brings her prominent eyebrows into collision. 'I don't know this.'

'Yes, you do!' I encourage. 'You came with me last week. We stopped at the bank and then we went into the baker – the one with the green lettering across the glass.' I pause to make space for her to reply. She fills it with a weighty silence. 'Do you know where I mean?' I say.

Her face is completely blank. She isn't even trying to remember. I don't have time to walk to the dry-cleaners myself and it's impossible to park in the high street. Double yellow lines stretch along its length and further, into the side streets where traffic wardens swoop out of nowhere like pigeons to a picnic. What's more, the walk would do Katarina good. There is more than one layer of puppy fat hiding in the folds of the dressing gown.

'Katarina?'

She doesn't reply. She's busy helping herself to a large dollop of butter to spread over her toast. If Katarina were my daughter, I'm sure I'd have developed strategies to cope with her, but three months isn't time enough for a full-scale assault on the girl's personality. I grab a pen and paper. 'This is the address,' I tell her, writing quickly. 'If you really can't remember where it is then use the map icon on your phone.' I push the paper across the breakfast bar towards her. 'Clean up the kitchen. I'll be in my consulting room. My first client arrives in twenty minutes.'

I can feel her watching me as I leave the room. I expect that if I had eyes in the back of my head I would see her scowling.

The space I've remodelled for my therapy rooms is not part of the original house but an extension built on in the nineties. There is a connecting door from the kitchen that leads into the waiting area, also accessible from the outside so that my clients don't need to come through the house. The waiting area leads into a large room with windows overlooking the back garden. I can't help but smile whenever I walk in here. This space used to be Tom's study and it was a dark, arguably dismal room with magnolia walls, patterned curtains in three tones of beige and ugly, mismatched furniture. As soon as I moved in I asked Tom whether he would be willing to relinquish the space. 'It's everything I've ever wanted,' I told him. 'A perfect space to see clients.'

'Not possible I'm afraid, darling,' he told me. 'It's been my study for ever. I couldn't move from here.'

It took me three months of persuading, most of which took place in the bedroom – roleplay, massages, hand-cuffs and vibrators, attending to his every desire like a high-class hooker – before he softened towards the idea.

'Well . . . I guess I could let you have the room,' he said. 'Chloe doesn't need a bedroom here any more. I can move my study in there. It's important for you to get your business off the ground.'

Result.

I had Tom's study completely redecorated in a lilac shade, transforming the walls from dead and dirty to warm and inviting. The carpets are now a cappuccino woollen blend. The curtains were replaced by swish, modern blinds, and concealed lighting has replaced an old standard lamp. Two chairs and a sofa are covered in a rich yellow fabric that reminds me of a Tuscan orchard, branches bending under the weight of ripe lemons.

The answermachine light is flashing and I play back the message that was left in the small hours.

'Hello, my name is Mary, Mary McNeil, and I need to see a therapist.' Short pause. 'I was given your name by Sharon, a police liaison officer. I have been attending her group therapy for victims of crime but . . . And well . . .' Longer pause. 'I have developed . . . anxiety. I was mugged. But it didn't start there.' A nervous cough. 'I wonder whether you might give me a call back?'

2. Ellen

I wake up in the morning and instantly remember – last night, the phone call. Recollection has me covering my face with the duvet. I called Leila Henrikson. I left a message on the answermachine. I'd been doing my checks – again – the front door lock, every socket in the house, the hob. I was sneaking about in the dark, frustrated with myself and my inability to control my compulsion, when I decided to act. (Okay, so I'd been drinking – a very large gin and tonic – no ice, no lemon and more gin than tonic.) It was two in the morning but that didn't stop me. I lifted the phone and I called her. As I was keying in the numbers, I knew I was calling the separate phone line into Tom's study but that didn't stop me either. I didn't try to disguise my voice but I did use my middle and my maiden name. And I remember everything I said with a startling clarity. I told her I was anxious and that I'd been mugged. I asked her to call me back and then I returned to bed feeling powerful, feeling like I was taking the battle right to her door.

Now I'm not so sure. I shower and get dressed, my anxiety levels climbing with the passing of every minute. It's barely a year since Leila Henrikson took my husband and my home, and I'm still trying to get my head and my heart around it, and to have some cockamamie idea that I can seize back control?

'Jesus, Ellen,' I say out loud. 'Talk about making things more difficult for yourself.'

I picture Tom and Leila listening to the answermachine message and having a laugh. 'What's she playing at?' they'll say to one another. 'Is she for real?'

I try to put a lid on my anxiety by losing myself in more checking – the front door, every socket in the house, the knobs on the cooker – over and over again. This preoccupies me, soothes me even, as it silences the ever-critical, ever-fearful voice inside my head.

I now live in a house a third of the size of Maybanks, a property that has been rented out for fifteen years and is desperately in need of a facelift. Most of the paintwork is chipped, the carpets intermittently stained, and the kitchen units are seventies Formica in a lurid shade of orange. I signed the lease for a year with an option for another year, a reasonably priced, interim solution until the divorce is finalised, but I'm not sure I can live here for much longer. There is a fusty, mouldy smell about the place and no matter how much I clean, I can't get the smell out of the air. I've spoken to the landlord but he refuses to acknowledge it, despite the fact that everyone else who comes here smells it too. I've even had my dad investigate the drains but the job was beyond him.

I check and recheck for over an hour and then I decide to bake. Ben is home for the university holidays – still asleep in his room – and school's broken up, so I now have eight weeks off teaching. Almost two months without having to cope with reluctant teenagers and overworked colleagues. I'm left to my own devices and the thought is terrifying. Keeping busy is the answer. I'd set aside this time for tackling my anxiety and for trying to get to grips with the divorce paperwork – who knew how much time that would take up? Certainly not me. The paperwork I will get round to, but fixing my psyche is tougher and so in the meantime, I'll bake.

Twenty-eight years of marriage means that I've accumulated more kitchen equipment than I know what to do with. I packed up what I needed – Tom had neither shopped nor cooked, nor, in fact, taken much of an interest in anything I bought for the house – and brought it with me. I also took every photograph, and everything the children had made and given to us, from knitted egg cosies to misshapen pots. (Most of it is still in boxes in the hallway.) Tom made no objection – he was never the photographer and because his profession occupied most of his waking hours, we were used to him missing family occasions. For weeks at a time he flew down to London on the early-Monday morning plane and returned late Friday evening, only to spend the weekend reading through briefs and catching up on sleep. Often my parents were greater players in the children's lives than he was. That's not to say we didn't have more than our share of good times – we did – but remembering those times only makes me sad for what I no longer have.

I find mixing bowls and weighing scales, a measuring jug and wooden spoons, and then all the ingredients to make a steak pie for tea and some date slices for snacking on. Ben is always hungry and Chloe's bound to pop in at some point. I'll give her some baking to take home with her.

I've made the steak pie and am weighing out the oats for the date slices when my mobile rings. It's her – the uber-bitch, as Ben calls her. I recognise the number – Maybanks' second phone line. The one I called last night. The one that is a dedicated phone line into Tom's study.

'Hello, am I speaking to Mary?'

'Yes.'

'My name is Leila Henrikson.' Her tone is confident, bordering on strident. 'You called me last night with a view to beginning therapy?'

'Yes.'

'Why don't we meet for a first appointment and see whether I'm able to help you?'

I drop the baking tray on the floor and the metallic clang makes me jump. I let go of the phone too and have to scrabble around on the floor to retrieve it.

'Mary? Are you still there?'

My cheeks are a flame of embarrassment. 'Yes . . . sorry.'

'So let's see . . .' I hear the turning of pages. 'When are you free?'

'I'm a teacher,' I say, holding the phone tightly with both hands. 'I've broken up for the summer.'

'I have a vacancy at 2 p.m. on Tuesday. How does that suit you?'

'That suits me fine,' I say.

'Great.' She proceeds to give me directions to Maybanks, the house I spent hours, days, weeks, months, years turning into a home. The home I lived in for twenty-eight what I thought were happy years for all of us. The home I could locate with my internal, automatic pilot even if I was blindfolded and dumped on the outskirts of Edinburgh.

I end the call and stand perfectly still. She doesn't know who I am! I say this out loud, my tone disbelieving. I laugh into the empty room, amazed that this is possible. I have thought about her for hours at a time, wondering what she's like, hating her, wishing her ill. I have imagined her being struck down by cancer or hit by a car. In my saner, quieter moments, when I don't wish her dead but

I do wish her to be forced out of her loved-up bubble, I have contemplated waiting until Tom is at work, then turning up at the door to give her a piece of my mind. This would be reasonable for a woman in my position, expected even, but I've never done it, not because I'm spineless, but because I'm not one for confrontations. I've always believed it better not to act in anger but to manage situations, subtly steer the ship a few degrees to the left or the right. I'd spent twenty-eight years managing Tom's moods, after all, so I had the practice.

And now I feel as if the universe is giving me a nudge. What should I do? Keep the appointment? Begin therapy? Bide my time until either I'm found out or I choose to reveal myself?

I accept that it's just about feasible she would be unfamiliar with my maiden name and my voice, but will she recognise me in person? She might, but then again she might not, because even if she's seen photographs of me, I've changed a lot over this last year – I've had my hair cut shorter and coloured several shades darker, the grey strands dyed a deep chestnut. I've comfort-eaten my way up two dress sizes, weight settling everywhere, including my face, altering its contours and profile.

The house I now live in is a mile away from Maybanks but in city terms, a mile is a fair distance. I live in a different neighbourhood, on a separate bus route, served by an alternative row of local shops. I have never so much as glimpsed Tom on the street or in his car and I only know what Leila looks like because Ben has shown me a photograph of her online – her profile on LinkedIn. She looks professional, poised, accomplished. To protect my sanity, I've tried to extract myself from thoughts of them as a couple, and when the divorce settlement comes through, I've been planning to relocate to south of the city, closer to my work.

And if I turn up at her – *my* – door and she doesn't recognise me in person, doesn't twig that I'm Tom's wife, then am I brave enough to deceive her? To talk about what's happened to me, to lay the blame firmly at the other woman's door. As a therapist, she'll surely have to be empathetic. And when I have her on side, I'll tell her that she is the other woman, the home-wrecker, the husband-stealer. See how she squares *that* with her professional integrity. If nothing else it will unsettle her and that will be a small victory to me, and the very thought of managing such a coup makes me smile. Leila Henrikson and me, face to face. The mind does more than boggle – it seethes, schemes, sets fire to the imagination.

I am still sitting on the sofa mulling over the possi-bilities when the front door opens. 'It's only me!' Chloe calls out, appearing seconds later. 'How's it going?' She kisses me on the cheek. 'Is my lazy brother up yet?'

'Not yet, no.' I stand up, and hug her tight. 'Where's Molly?'

'Playing with her wee friend Cara from school. I've just dropped her off. And Jack's off to Aberdeen to work for a couple of days.'

'You want a cuppa?' She nods, and goes over to make it herself. 'And look.' I hold up the steak pie I've just made. 'This is for tea tonight. Plenty for you and Molly and Granddad.'

'Great, Mum.' She fills the kettle at the sink, settles it on the base and plugs it in. 'What's this?' She points at the black marker-pen numbers I've written on the sockets.

'The landlord. He numbered them for some reason.

I'm not sure why.' The lie is out of my mouth in a flash. I don't usually lie to Chloe but I'm not ready to talk about my OCD. I feel ashamed and frustrated enough as it is. I don't want it all out in the open because then it becomes doubly real, a topic for family discussion, Chloe and Ben, sotto voce in the hallway while I make tea, 'How has she been this week? Does she seem okay to you? Do you think she's getting better?'

They've had enough to worry about over the past year and I'm not going to add to their burden, which is why I've been trying to sort myself out by going to the group meetings. For now it's my secret, and I'd like it to stay that way but Chloe is a nurse and the clock is ticking. At any minute she could notice how anxious and obsessive I've become and she will insist on helping me – kindly, considerately, but without any let-up.

'You know the patient I was telling you about the other day? The one with the hernia?' Chloe says. 'Well, she happened to be talking about her marriage break-up and it got me thinking about you and Dad.' She hands me a mug of tea. 'And don't take this the wrong way, Mum, but I think that sometimes you let people take advantage of you.'

'Biscuit?' I hold the tin out towards her.

'No thanks.' She gives a brief shake of her head. 'Mum, I want to talk to you. Properly. Seriously.'

My hands begin to shake. I put the biscuit tin and my mug down on the coffee table and sit myself on the sofa.

'Have you signed the divorce papers yet?' she says, sitting opposite me.

'No.' I frown at her. 'Everything takes ages, you know how it is with lawyers.'

'I think you should negotiate a better deal.'

'I'm fine with what's being drawn up.' That isn't entirely true and she picks up on it at once.

'You're not, Mum,' she states baldly. 'And I think that's because you've allowed Dad to have everything his own way.'

So this is where we're headed. I've tried very hard not to get my children involved in the nuts and bolts of my marriage break-up. Tom was often an absent father but he was a good dad (mostly) when he was around and I haven't wanted them taking sides. 'Well . . . I don't think I did.'

'I've had an idea,' she says quickly.

'Chloe . . .' I make a weary face.

'Just hear me out.' She pauses, her expression intent, and I nod my agreement for her to continue. 'Why don't you talk to Granddad? Jack and Molly and I will have our own place soon – we've almost saved our deposit – and Granddad will be on his own and he's not going to like that. He thrives on company. You know he does. You could afford to stay in Maybanks if you lived together. You could sell his place and set up a granddad flat at the side of the house where Dad had his study.'

'But Granddad loves his house! And I'm only on a teacher's salary, remember, so—' I stop and think for a moment. 'What do you mean Dad *had* his study?'

'You should be getting maintenance from Dad. He earns a fortune! Why aren't you asking for more money?'

The penny drops. I was picturing Leila using Tom's phone but I hadn't for one moment thought that Tom would have completely given up his study. 'Does she practise her therapy from Dad's study?'

'Mum—'

'Chloe?'

She nods, reluctant to upset me. 'They had the decorators in.' She sighs. 'It's no longer the gloomy old den it once was. It's all prettified and smart.'

'He loved his study!' I reel back. 'When I think of the evenings I spent in there with him, discussing cases, helping him organise his files, acting as judge and jury.'

'I know. You were such a help to him. And remember at weekends? I played with my dolls on the armchair and Ben ran a train track under the desk.' She sighs. 'Happy times.' Her expression is wistful and it makes my heart contract. 'Dad's changed, Mum. He's changed a lot. He's using my old bedroom as a study now.'

That explains why he didn't hear my voice on the answermachine. It was no longer his domain. Luckily for me, otherwise I would have been rumbled immediately. 'He must really love her,' I say, as if it's only just dawning on me, the crack in my voice there for us both to hear.

'I know how this must hurt, Mum,' Chloe says.

'It's nothing, Chloe. I'm fine.' I suddenly remember that I haven't unplugged the kettle and I jump to my feet as if stung. 'I think I'll get started on Ben's breakfast. He'll be awake in a minute. You know he's always starving!' I make an attempt at a laugh and fuss about the work surfaces, touching this and that, before pulling the plug from the socket.

'Are you worried about the electricity?'

I glance over my shoulder and see Chloe watching me. 'No. Why would I be?'

'Well, if the landlord is marking the sockets it might be because there's something wrong with them. Do you want me or Jack to have a word with him?'

'No! I'm perfectly capable of talking to the landlord myself.' I hold up a hand. 'Not that I don't appreciate your concern.' She's watching me, her arms folded. The kitchen is small and I feel hemmed in. 'Maybe I'll start Ben's breakfast later.' I go to sit down again but she's blocking my way. 'What is going on with you?' I say.

'For fuck's sake, Mum! I wish you would at least try!'

'What on earth?' I step away from her, shocked; Chloe rarely swears.

'*You* should be in Maybanks, not *them*. You haven't fought hard enough!'

'I couldn't . . . It's . . . it's . . . been a lot to come to terms with.'

'Okay! So it's been tough! But it happened, and now you need to take some power back from Dad. He's bullying you. He's bullying you into accepting less than you're entitled to.' She paces around in front of me. 'Don't get me wrong, I love Dad, but the way he's been behaving lately makes me ashamed.' Her tone is loaded with emotion. 'Why should you be the one to leave Maybanks when it was Dad who was in the wrong? Why, Mum? Why you not him?'

'You know I thought the house was going to be sold.'

'Exactly. But it wasn't, was it? He moved her in. And now a whole year has gone by but there's still time for you to get a fairer deal.' She takes a breath. 'You're perfectly entitled to ask for a change in the agreement.' She stares around the room and then back at me. 'I hate seeing you living here. It's practically a slum.'

'Chloe.' I smile, hoping that she's running out of steam at last. 'It's not that bad.'

'There's damp in the bathroom. The shower barely works.'

'That's better n—'

'The awful smell! And now the electricity's playing up!'

I turn away from her fierce expression and close my

eyes. I don't want to think about any of this. I don't want to think about this house and I don't want to think about the moment when I heard that Tom had moved Leila into Maybanks. At that point I was still imagining that we might get back together but then it became patently obvious that he'd moved on, spectacularly so. Whenever I think about it now, it feels like a dark, dank void and if I walk too close I'll be sucked back into all the misery and pain. I can trace the onset of my anxiety back to that point. I started losing sleep, crying without warning; and then the obsessive checking began.

'Mum?'

I sigh. 'Chloe . . .'

'I know you, and I know Dad,' she says with conviction. 'And it's plain to see you're getting a raw deal.' She starts pacing again, picking up letters and magazines and putting them down. 'You did everything in that house and now they're living there benefiting from all your hard work. It was stupid of you to leave. You should have dug in your heels.'

'Okay, I hear you, Chloe.' I throw out my arms in surrender. 'I hear you,' I repeat.'

'Good.' She folds her arms, nodding. 'I'm glad I've got through to you.'

'But why are you bringing this up now?' I say puzzled.

'Because time's running out. Ben and I were there on Sunday and . . .' She rubs her forehead. 'It was . . .'

'For Dad's birthday?'

She nods. 'And I just . . . I just thought that . . .' Her eyes fill with tears. 'Soon it's going to be too late. The house will be theirs and our whole childhood will be spoiled.'

'Chloe, your childhood can't be spoiled.'

I hug her and try to persuade her otherwise, but she's

having none of it and when she leaves I have no option but to admit to myself that she's right. I have been too passive. I should never have given up Maybanks but Tom's infidelity was like a punch to the stomach. I thought he was happy with our marriage. I thought that, despite our differences, he loved me and valued the life we had built together. When he announced he was in love with another woman I buckled under the betrayal. For the first few months I was constantly on the back foot, my broken heart unable to cope with the conveyer belt of solicitor's letters, arrangements to be made, documents to be signed, assets to be divided. Tom's solicitor was like a bull terrier, constantly biting at my heels, and the only way I could stop the biting was to agree to give Tom what he wanted.

And what do I feel about Tom now? It's a question I often ask myself, and as time goes by my feelings change. At first, I loved him still, I even hoped he might come back to me, but as the weeks rolled into months, love has been replaced with anger. It's not a hot, fiery anger. It's a simmering anger. Dispassionate. Patient.

Broken hearts mend and mine is well on the way to being whole again but that doesn't mean I don't want to hit back at him, at them, at her – mostly her. I read somewhere that women are especially good at two things: love and revenge. Well, now that the love has died, I'm left with the revenge. I'll go to see Leila, the therapist, the woman he loves, the woman I hate. I'll make myself heard. I might even do more than that. What better way to get back at Tom than to target his new woman?

2. Leila

'Is there anything to eat?'

I've finished with my morning clients and have come into the kitchen. Alex looks as if he has just rolled out of bed. His eyes are puffy and his hair is sticking up. He's wearing boxer shorts and a T-shirt that says, 'Go F**k Yourself.' The fridge door is open and he's staring inside.

'Have you had a shower?' I say.

'Katarina's cleaning the bathroom.' He scratches his crotch. 'She says she'll be a while yet.'

'You could use the en suite.'

'Tom had a go at me last time I did that.' He reaches for the milk.

'That's because you left such a mess.' When he moves to one side, I pull open the vegetable drawer and take out an avocado and a bag of spinach. 'Would you like a smoothie?'

'Not if it's green.'

'You'd be doing your body a favour.' I peel and stone the avocado and drop it into the blender. 'I haven't heard you playing your guitar for a couple of days.'

'Yeah, well . . .' He's staring at the cereal boxes – a choice of two equally healthy mixes; I can see that neither appeals. 'Why can't you buy sugary cereals like normal people?'

'You were doing really well with your guitar.'

'And you would know?'

'Didn't I hear you playing a Bon Jovi song last week? Sounded good to me.'

'It's four chords. A monkey could play it.' He gives a heavy sigh. 'Both these cereals taste like shit.'

'Alex . . .'

'Yeah, I know. Sugar is evil.' He takes a bowl from the cupboard and bangs it down on the work surface. 'Long live maple syrup.'

I cram handfuls of baby spinach into the blender and top it up with coconut water. 'Have you signed up for summer tuition?' I say. 'You just scraped a pass in economics, remember.'

'Like I could forget with you going on about it every five minutes.' He finally chooses a cereal and tips a huge portion into a bowl. 'There's loads of time.'

'Until there isn't.'

'Don't start nagging me.'

'I'm not nagging you.' While the blender motor runs, I look through the window and see next door's cat walking along the brick wall that separates our properties. The cat has a bird in his mouth and when he reaches the magnolia tree he steps daintily down through the branches and drops onto the ground. He starts to chew on the bird. He is holding the body with one paw and ripping it to pieces with his teeth, his movements economical and skilful. I stop the motor and bang on the window but he doesn't even look up.

'What's going on?' Alex says.

'Next door's cat.' I join Alex at the breakfast bar with my smoothie. 'Killing birds again. I'm going to speak to Tom about cutting down the magnolia tree, might stop the cat coming into our garden.'

'Uh-oh!' He widens his eyes. 'Ben and Chloe won't

like that.' He adds milk into his bowl. 'You'll have a repeat of Tom's birthday.' He snorts into his cereal. 'Hashtag mystepchildrenhateme.'

'You could learn a lot from Tom's children, Alex.' I swallow a mouthful of smoothie. 'They are focused on their studies.'

He doesn't reply but his body language is indignant and his wrist knocks against the bowl, hard enough for toasted oats and splashes of milk to spill over the edge.

'You don't agree?' I say.

He leans back in his seat and crosses his arms. 'Well, Chloe was pregnant at eighteen so you can't be talking about her. So it must be the mighty *Ben*. With his A stars and his eighty per cent average.'

'He works hard,' I say.

'Unlike me, you mean?' He throws his spoon down and it skids across the breakfast bar. 'Never quite good enough for you, Mum, am I?'

'You know how much I love you, Alex. And that means I want what's best for you.'

He stands up. 'You're full of shit, Mum.' He stares at me, his expression hateful. 'You really are.'

I follow him into the hallway. 'Don't walk away when we're talking!'

'*We're* not talking.' He takes the stairs two at a time '*You* are.'

'Do *not* slam the—'

He slams his door and at once Katarina appears at the top of the stairs. She's wearing yellow rubber gloves and is holding the toilet brush. 'I am sorry. I am finished nearly.'

'It doesn't matter. I'm going out now,' I tell her. 'Don't forget Tom's suit.'

I take my bag and umbrella from the porch and walk

round the side of the house. The cat is still there. He glances up at me, blinking clear, green eyes. We stare at each other; he breaks eye contact first and then he uses his paw to pull the dead, dismembered bird in towards him. I step forward, slowly. He is preoccupied with his kill and makes the mistake of letting me get close enough to extend my foot and kick his huge, furry body up into the air. He gives a startled, shrieking meow and claws his way up the wall, grabbing for a branch on the magnolia tree and finding enough purchase to scrape his way to the top and back over the wall into his own garden. The remains of the bird are scattered across the flagstones; tiny, bloody intestines gleam scarlet as they drape across a broken wing.

I revolve the ankle of my kicking foot; the sudden exertion has set up an ache in the muscle. When I turn round Katarina is standing there, toilet brush still in her hand. 'What?' I say.

'I was . . .' She dithers, staring up at the sky and then back at the ground, frowning. I've a feeling she wants to tell me off and it makes me smile.

'Another job for you,' I tell her, pointing to the bird and then walking past her to my car. 'Use the outside brush and dustpan. They're kept in the garden hut. Not the ones from the kitchen!' I call back to her.

She's standing at the front of the house staring at me as I drive away. Tom's right; she really is quite gormless. But she is also an excellent cleaner, and she's cheap, so I can forgive her anything. She keeps the house clean and fresh and, literally, smelling of roses and that is important to me. Godliness I can do without, but cleanliness is a must. I know it's a hangover from my childhood; I hate all signs of death and decay even if it's only drooping buds in a vase or a yellowed leaf hanging from the stem of a plant.

As I drive up Dundas Street, my thoughts move on to my brother David. He'll be on his way to meet me at the gallery cafe. He's my only sibling – and half-sibling at that. I was six when he was born and within days of his birth, I was enchanted by him. He was a dreamy-eyed, sweet-cheeked boy who didn't so much cry as squeak, and only when he was hungry. He loved me talking to him. His eyes would widen and sometimes he would gasp as if everything I told him he then imagined and lived along with me. He was my right-hand man, my go-to, my confidant.

My father was long gone but David's dad stuck around for that first year. His name was Mal and he was a loud, cheery layabout, often drunk, but essentially good-natured. He had time for me. He would scoop me up onto his shoulders, make me scream and grab for his hair, which was thick and lush as a bear's pelt.

For a short time we were a proper family and I felt proud to be out in the park, the four of us – mother, father, girl and baby boy just like in the storybooks.

I watched my mother lose Mal's interest, piece by painful piece when a few months after David was born she took to her bed like an invalid. I tried to persuade her up and out of bed, but she turned her face away from me and no amount of cuddling or enthusiasm could persuade her downstairs. I knew what she had to do to keep us all together – she had to get up and get on with it, get dressed, shop, make a meal, wear lipstick, smile at Mal and let him join her in bed instead of shouting at him to sleep on the sofa.

This had been going on for two months when I made a passing comment to my teacher. 'My mum doesn't get up any more,' I said.

'Why's that, Leila?'

'She's not well, Miss Foster, so I look after baby David. I can make scrambled eggs and mashed potatoes.'

'By yourself?'

'Yes, Miss Foster.' I was painting a picture and I remember finishing off the sun with a flourish before adding, 'Sometimes I can't get baby David out of the bath because he's too slippy.'

By the time I returned home from school my mother was downstairs, sitting on the sofa. Our family doctor, Dr Morgan, and a social worker were there too. I don't remember anything they said to me because in my chest there was a flutter of happy butterflies. Mummy was up and about! She was smiling and talking normally. She had baby David on her knee and was giving him a bottle. She loved us again!

When the doctor and the social worker left, my mother smacked me so hard that the tops of my legs stung for days. She dragged me upstairs to my bedroom and threw me on the bed, then she dropped baby David into his cot. He got such a fright that he started screaming and it took me ages to settle him. She wedged a chair against the door so that I couldn't get out, not even when I needed to pee, so I tried to wee in one of David's empty bottles and it made a mess on the carpet.

When Mal came home from work, after my mum had gone to bed, I listened at the bedroom door. I heard him switch on the television and then I heard the sizzle of frying bacon, the smell drifting upstairs and making my mouth water. I tried to shout to him but the sound that came out of my mouth was barely a whisper because I didn't want to wake baby David and I certainly didn't want to wake my mum.

When I woke up in the morning, I was lying on the floor by the door. The chair was gone, so I was able to get to the bathroom and press a flannel on my stinging legs. At school, Miss Foster asked me if everything was better at home and I said, 'Yes, Miss Foster,' smiling so that all of my teeth showed and I looked like the happy girl in the advert for Fairy Liquid. 'Thank you, Miss Foster.'

Mal left us before David was even walking. He went off with Cathy, the woman from the corner shop, who had puffy hair and kissy lips. I stole from her shop for a year after that – usually just penny sweets, but often I was bold enough to stand in front of her and show her the milk bottle and the loaf of bread – hold them up, one in each hand like two prize-winning cups – and then walk out the door. She never stopped me. She didn't bloody dare. She knew I occupied the moral high ground, not just because she'd stolen Mal but because the whole neighbourhood knew about my mother. They knew she didn't get out of bed. They knew I was the person doing all the looking after. Some of the neighbours helped me. They would carry the heavy shopping bags or buy David and me ice creams. When Dr Morgan came back to visit us I told him that Mummy was getting up now and that she was cooking proper meals. I knew he didn't believe me, but if he left a message for the social worker to come back again then she never received it.

Mal came round every so often but Mum would shout abuse from upstairs. I'd make him a mug of tea, find a saved biscuit from the cupboard and encourage David to show off his latest skills, but Mum's voice was insistent – a bellowing of swear words, creatively strung together – and after ten minutes Mal would look apologetic and say, 'Sorry, Leila Mae and little Dave.' He'd kiss us on our foreheads and walk backwards through the door, waving as he went.

Soon after David's second birthday Mal and Cathy emigrated to Benidorm to run an English pub. Postcards and Christmas cards told us they had found their calling. We had an open invitation to stay with them. I imagined David and me getting on a plane – he'd have to be out of nappies – and when we arrived in Spain Mal would be waiting for us, suntanned and grinning. We'd stay in a whitewashed apartment above the pub and the sound of happy drunks would lull us to sleep. After a few days Mal would tell us that we were never going home. Mum would be okay with that because we'd be by the seaside and that's what she wanted for us, and before long we'd be speaking Spanish and calling Mal and Cathy Mum and Dad.

Needless to say, we never made it out there. When Gareth, Mum's third and final live-in partner, came to stay with us the postcards stopped and we forgot all about Mal and his out-of-this-world promises. Gareth filled all the free spaces in our lives with his weirdness and cruelty, but to this day I make no effort to recall any of those memories – not because I can't but because I deliberately choose not to.

I have a quick meeting at the university to discuss the class I'll be teaching over the coming year (Crisis, Meaning and Failure) and then I find a parking space close to the Portrait Gallery and hurry along the pavement. I'm smiling as I walk and when I spot David my heart lifts. He's sitting at a corner table, reading a newspaper. 'Hello you,' I say.

'Sis.' He stands up and stretches across the table to hug me. He feels thinner than he did the last time we hugged. I feel the edges of bone, shoulder blades and collarbone and strips of rib.

'Are you eating enough?' I say.

'I am.' He puffs out his chest. 'No need for you to worry on that score.'

'You're growing a beard?'

'Isn't everyone?'

Tom isn't, but I'm not about to mention that. David knows very little about Tom and Tom knows absolutely nothing about David.

'Control is an illusion, Sis,' he says as if he can read my thoughts.

'Shall I get us some afternoon tea?'

'Just a scone for me.'

'Coming up.' I go to the counter and choose a couple of scones, some butter and jam and two pots of tea. I feel David's eyes on me. He is watching me walk, interact with the staff, hand over my debit card. When I return to the table he has cleared his newspaper away and is sitting with his hands clasped. He means business. But first there's the small talk: the weather, the throng of tourists, the posters for this year's festival.

And then I say, 'I was thinking about Mal just now.'

David nods. 'I saw him, you know.'

'You did?' I'm surprised. 'When?'

'A few months ago.'

'In Benidorm?'

He nods again. 'He's doing okay. So is Cathy. They asked me to send you their love.'

I give a short laugh. 'It's a bit late for that.' I incline my head, unforgiving. 'We needed their love back then, not now.'

'People make mistakes. Parents make mistakes, don't they? Isn't that what happens?' He laughs. 'They fuck you up, your mum and dad.'

'They don't have to.'

'You would know.' He raises his eyebrows at me. 'You're a parent and you're a therapist. Perfect combination, no?'

'David.' I glance down into my teacup, then back at my brother. 'About what you said to me on the phone.'

'Yes.' He pushes his plate aside and leans forward. 'Let's talk about what I said.'

We lock eyes. Seconds tick by. We neither blink nor breathe and then I say, 'You know why you can't stay with me.'

'Because you can't trust me?'

'Because I need to keep things simple for Alex.' I take a breath. 'I wasn't just thinking about Mal when I drove here – I thought about Gareth too, briefly, and—' David goes to speak and I hold up my hand to stop him. He is always in a rush to take charge and I can't allow that. 'Wait, please. Listen to me.' He sits back, his expression half-pleading, half-guarded. I wait. I hold eye contact with him, not speaking until his expression relaxes back to neutral. 'Life is shit for lots of people, David. Life is sad and tiresome and unlucky but we're not those people. We have what we've always had.' I clasp his hand across the table. 'Each other.' I smile, let my words sink in before adding, 'But that doesn't mean I can always give you what you want.'

'You don't have to. Not any more.' His answering smile is almost a smirk. 'I've been to a therapist.'

'You have?' I let go of his hand. 'You've always said that didn't appeal to you.'

'I changed my mind.' He watches my face. 'Why aren't you pleased? I thought you'd be pleased. You should be pleased!'

'Of course.' I look down at the table while I compose myself. 'I'm surprised, that's all.'

'She's helping me to be real and truthful.'

'She? Does she practise in Edinburgh?' I keep my tone light. 'Do I know her?'

'No.'

'Will you tell me her name?'

'Why? So you can discuss me behind my back?' His eyes challenge mine. 'Your pathetic, fucked-up brother who had the breakdown.'

I start back, appalled. 'How could you even think that of me?' I shake my head, then place my hand on my chest. 'I have your best interests at heart, David. You know I do.'

'That isn't enough any more, Leila.' He drums his fingers on the table. 'I'm changing. I'm seeing things differently. And I want to keep seeing things differently.' He nods, convincing himself. 'I want that more than anything. I want to peel back all the layers until I get to the truth.'

'Okay.' My pulse is racing. 'I understand that. But please . . . slow down. We worked hard to escape Gareth and you need to be very careful if you choose to revisit that time.'

He shakes his head, emphatic. 'I want to face my demons.'

'Easier said—'

'I know! I know! But . . .' His eyes glow as if there is a fire within. 'Fuck, Leila! We did stuff back then—'

'Don't.' I hold my hand up for the second time. 'So we did things that don't square well with the people we've become but . . .' I shrug, then say quietly, 'Really, David, so what?'

'So what?' He laughs. 'So everything!'

'I don't agree.'

'Because you're afraid to agree.' He slaps his right

hand on the table as he says this. 'You're afraid, Leila. Just admit it!'

'That's not true. I'm not afraid. I've grown to accept myself despite everything I've done and everything that's happened to me.'

'To us.'

'To us,' I acknowledge.

'And you'd deny me the same?'

'I'm not denying you anything. I'm trying to help you to see that you could open up a whole Pandora's box of grief.' I exhale a long breath. 'And I'm also saying that I'm not coming on the journey with you.'

He tugs at his beard while he thinks about this, hard enough to pull his lower lip into a pout. 'What have you told Tom about your childhood?' he says.

'Nothing much.'

'He doesn't ask?'

'No.'

'But Tom must be special enough for you to confide in, surely? You've never moved in with a man before.'

'I've lived with three men,' I say.

'But that was different, they moved in with you. And then when you'd had enough, they were gone pretty quickly.' He laughs, deliberately trying to keep it light. 'What's Tom got that they didn't?'

'It's not just about him.' I shrug. 'It's also about timing and the fact that I'm not getting any younger. And, as an added bonus, he has the perfect house where I'm able to base my practice.'

'And Alex? What does he know about his mother's past?'

'Nothing.'

'And his father?'

'I've told you already, David.' Gareth's face looms up

before me and I shiver. 'As far as Alex is concerned his father left when he was young.'

'You think it's fair to keep his paternity a secret from him?'

'Under the circumstances? Most definitely.' I lean across the table, my voice low. 'If you want to revisit our childhood then that's up to you, but as I've just made clear, you have to leave me out of it.'

'How can I?' He throws his arms out. 'What happened to me happened to you!'

'Do not stalk me, David.' I stand up. 'Not like before.'

'Geez!' He laughs. 'Call a spade a shovel why don't you.'

'I mean it.'

'Leeds wasn't stalking.' He stands up too. 'That was a brother trying to spend time with his sister.'

'Well, I forbid you to do it again.'

'You forbid it?'

'Yes, I forbid it.' The air between us grows thick and unyielding. I gather my bag and jacket into my arms. 'You have to respect my space.'

'I can do whatever the fuck I want.' His tone is dismissive. 'You're not my keeper.'

I glance over his right shoulder to where the exit door is being held open by the doorman. 'How long are you going to be in Edinburgh?'

'Another few weeks.'

'Please don't contact me again.' I walk towards the exit and don't look back.

3. Ellen

'So what have you got to tell me?' my dad says.

'What do you mean?'

'Chloe told me she was round at yours this morning.'

'The sockets?' I blush, wondering whether he can see right through me to the anxiety I have about the house going on fire, my mind tormenting me with images: flames licking around the light switches, settling into sofas and chairs, roaring along the hallway, flashing light and heat towards me, making hot, grey ash out of everything in its path.

'Sockets? What sockets? I'm talking about the house!'

'The house?'

'Earth to Ellen.' He waves his hand in front of my startled eyes. '*This* house.' He points down at the floor. 'My house, belongs to you, not to me. We can sell up and get you back into Maybanks if that's what you want.'

'Dad!' I wave his words aside, relieved he hasn't guessed my secret shame. 'Don't be daft!'

'Grannie, Grannie, Grannie!' Molly rushes into the room and stops in front of me, grinning and pulling at the corners of her mouth with her fingers. 'Look!'

'Where's your tooth?' I pretend to be shocked.

'It fell out.' She hops around on one foot, propelling her arms to balance herself. 'The fairy will bring me a pound!'

'Come wash your hands, Molly!' Chloe calls from the bathroom. 'Grannie has tea ready.'

Molly grabs my hand and swings round, my arm being pulled this way and that as she swivels and sways.

'Molly!' Chloe calls again.

'I'll be back in a minute, Grannie,' Mollie says, her upturned face golden as if she's been touched by sunshine. 'For my mashed potatoes.' She skips off. 'Coming, Mummy!'

'I don't mind moving, you know,' my dad says. 'It's worth thinking about, Ellen.'

'You love this house, Dad.'

'Aye, but I love you more, and—' he lowers his voice '—I'd be happy to stuff it to that bastard of a husband of yours.'

I smile. 'Now there's reason enough.'

'Think about it, Ellen,' he says, giving me one of his significant looks. 'You can't change the wind but you can adjust the sails.'

A couple of years ago when my mum died, Dad needed to be closer to family so Tom and I bought the house for him to live in. It's only a short distance to the centre of Edinburgh and is perfect for him; the shops are outside his front door and there's plenty going on for the over-seventies. Chloe, Jack and Molly have been living with him for almost three years now as it's walking distance to Jack's work, and my dad loves the company. Officially speaking, his house is part of the marriage assets and my solicitor advised me that because of this I'm entitled to less than half the value of Maybanks. The idea of teaming up with my dad and selling his property to keep Maybanks had never occurred to me before Chloe raised it, and despite my dad also bringing it up now, I still don't give it much thought.

We all sit down to tea and have a happy hour of laughing and eating. At the end of the meal, as we're leaving the table, my dad farts and we all shout at him at once. 'Dad!' 'Granddad!' 'Grandpops!'

'It's a poor backside that never rejoices!' he says. Molly clutches her hands over her mouth and giggles.

I gather up the plates and Chloe takes them from me. 'Let me do that, Mum,' she says. 'I know Ben's itching to get home.'

I look across at Ben, who's already on his feet. 'Not meaning to rush you, Mum, but I need to get back.' He holds out his hand. 'You got the car keys?'

'You want to drive?' I say, trying not to let him see how much my heart sinks.

'Definitely. I could do with the practice.'

We say our goodbyes and go outside. I reluctantly give him the keys and he climbs in at the driver's side, grinning. 'Can't wait to pass my test.'

'Have you booked it yet?' I fasten my seatbelt and wave to Molly, who is standing at the living room window blowing kisses.

'I was waiting for Dad to give me the money. He said he'd give it to me for my birthday but you know what he's like; he might not follow it through.'

'If he doesn't then I'm sure I can find at least half for you.' I look over my shoulder and into the street behind us. I can already feel the onset of anxiety cramping my neck muscles. It's not that Ben's a bad driver but my OCD kicks in with any activity that is potentially dangerous, especially when it's out of my control. 'You're okay this side.' He pulls out into the road and slowly changes up the gears. 'Talking of birthdays,' I say, distracting myself with conversation. 'Chloe said you were both round at Dad's on Sunday.'

'We were, but we didn't have that good a time.'

I inhale a quick breath and say loudly, 'You're too close to the kerb!'

'We ended up leaving early.' He corrects the steering. 'The uber-bitch was doing her hostess-with-the-mostess thing and then—'

'Remember to look in the mirror before you signal.'

'—Dad went into one of his moods.'

'Why?' I ask, briefly closing my eyes against the traffic.

'He thinks everyone should constantly be doing something worthwhile. It's a crime to watch TV or be in bed after seven in the morning.'

'But he must have been pleased with your exam results?'

'He was, to be fair. He wasn't getting at me. They were both having a go at her son Alex.'

Ben has mentioned this before – the fact that her son falls short of expectations. 'He gets it in the neck a lot?'

'All the time. Although it's not so much Dad who's on his case as Leila. She treats him like he's about twelve.'

'Be careful at this junction,' I say. 'Right turns aren't easy here.' He waits his turn, then manoeuvres carefully around the oncoming traffic. 'What do you think of Alex?' I ask.

'He's okay. But we don't really have anything in common. He's into stuff I'm not into.'

'Like what?' I use a tissue to wipe the sweat from my forehead.

He hesitates before saying, 'He does a lot of drugs.'

'Crikey! Your dad won't like that.'

'They haven't sussed it. They're always nagging him but they don't really know how he spends his time. They're too busy getting loved up with each other.'

I flinch.

He glances across at me. 'Sorry, Mum.'

'It's okay.'

It isn't okay. The thought of Tom making love to another woman still hurts – but not as much as it did. It's a short, sharp pain that wears off in an hour or so. I don't take it into my bed and into my sleep the way I used to.

What makes me feel better, though, is the thought of them arguing. It won't take long for the gloss to wear off their relationship if her son is causing problems. I know Tom – he has very little patience with teenagers. We had two motivated, intelligent, hardworking children and still he regularly found fault with them. Chloe's pregnancy at eighteen – a contraceptive failure – made him furious, especially when she wouldn't agree to a quick abortion. He refused to speak to her for weeks, despite the fact that she'd been going out with Jack for a year. They were clearly committed to each other and they still are.

I go to bed at eleven thirty but I'm up again within the hour. My nightly ritual is exhausting. Every night it's the same. I wake up fearful and jittery, my heart pounding and a feeling of dread washing through me. My main fear is of the house going on fire but I also check that the taps are properly off and the front door is locked. I even go into Ben's room, creeping around with a torch like a burglar. Fortunately Ben is a deep sleeper and so he doesn't see his mother in her nightie on her hands and knees, double- and triple-checking sockets. When I've checked once, I check again and then a third time. It allows me to go back to bed calmer, still concerned, but calm enough to fall asleep.

Next day Sharon, the police liaison officer, calls to find out how I'm doing. As soon as I hear her voice I picture myself running out of the meeting and across the road, closely followed by Francis. And I remember promising myself that I'd never put myself through group meetings again.

'I haven't heard from you so I just wanted to check that you're okay?' she says. I tell her I am and then she tells me that Trish asked her for my mobile number. 'I didn't want to give it to her without asking you first.'

'Why does she want it?'

'She said that she was with Pam and Francis and that they bumped into you in the cafe over the road from the hall. She's concerned they pressured you into coming to the meeting.'

'They didn't. Not really.' I think about that evening: the embarrassment, the anxiety, the running away. 'Please tell her I'm fine.'

'Will do.' She reads me some times and dates of upcoming group meetings. 'Do you think you'll come along?'

'You know, Sharon, I don't think I will, but thank you for the therapists' names you gave me. I am beginning one-to-one therapy.' *With my ex-husband's mistress.*

'That's good news,' she says.

'It is,' I agree. 'It really is.'

'Oh, and I have your scarf here,' she says. 'You dropped it when you left.'

'Did I?'

'It's a blue one, cashmere.'

'That sounds like mine, right enough. I haven't missed it yet but I would quite like it back.'

'I could post it to you?'

'Thank you.'

'Let me know how the therapy goes, won't you?' she says.

I tell her I will. I'm dying to get there; Tuesday can't come quickly enough. Every time my mobile rings I think it's the uber-bitch ringing to cancel. She's realised who I am and I won't get the chance to confront her after all. Tom will tell his solicitor (a colleague of his) and within twenty-four hours I'll have received a letter quoting some law and threatening me with a court order.

But that doesn't happen. Tuesday comes and I walk the mile back to my old house. Edinburgh is known as the windy city, and not for nothing. A brisk breeze is whipping up from the Firth of Forth and that gives me the excuse I need to pull my coat in close to my body and keep my head down. The weight gain and the change in hairstyle and colour must surely help and I wear clothes I never wore when I lived here.

I need to be on the lookout to avoid being spotted by a neighbour. Most of them will be at work, but there's Mrs Patterson, who lives next door and takes a stroll after lunch in the large, grassy, tree-lined square that the houses surround. The dog-walkers congregate there in the morning, and later on when the children come out of school there might be a game of football.

Tom is almost never home at this time of day. He'll be ensconced in his office in the New Town, a plush, luxurious suite of rooms where junior members of staff run around after him. Tuesday is bin collection day, and I know a couple of the workers by name, but I don't see any sign of the truck. Ben is in Stirling with a friend and Chloe is at work. I've never met Alex so it won't matter if I bump into him.

When I reach the square I walk on the opposite side of the road to Maybanks, my head down. I even change the length of my stride in case my walking style gives me away. Concentrating on not being noticed preoccupies me, but still I feel an almost overwhelming urge to turn round and retreat with my tail between my legs.

I don't, though. I let the battle wage inside me and just keep on walking, reminding myself that this is what I want. To face her. To play along. To confront her. And then to leave, knowing that I've pushed back, regained some ground, shown strength of character.

I can't wait to see my house. I haven't been back to the street since I left almost a year ago. I knew that if I came back it would make me sad, so I avoided it. I met the neighbours who were my friends in cafes up town rather than returning to the street and being confronted with the home I could no longer have.

My throat feels like barbed wire. I swallow and wince, and when I catch sight of Maybanks I feel a pull inside my chest. The first thing I'm reminded of is how special the house is. It's a large, stand-alone Victorian villa. Unlike many of the houses in this neighbourhood, Maybanks isn't symmetrical. On the right of the house there's a square turret that we used as a tiny library and reading room, and on the left is an old-fashioned conservatory that sits, one floor up, on top of the kitchen. I filled the room with cacti, over a hundred of them. Occasionally I bought them from the garden centre but mostly they were cuttings from friends. Every afternoon the room is flooded with sunlight and the cacti flourish, flower, grow beyond the scope of their pots. I loved spending time pottering in there, Molly and me, rearranging and attending to the cacti.

The second thing I notice is that the box hedge has been trimmed to within an inch of its life. I can see this from the end of the street, a good twenty yards away. In fact, as I draw closer I notice that this radical pruning goes for most of the plants in the garden. Someone has run amok with the clippers. It makes me fear for how much Maybanks has been changed inside, as I expect Leila has cut me and my influence out of the house too.

The middle section of the road is cobbled, many of the stones rubbed almost flat by weather and cars. As I cross the street I remember frequently catching my heel in the gaps between the cobbles. One night in particular, when Tom and I had been out to dinner, I broke a heel getting out of the taxi and walking to the kerb. We'd had a tricky year: my dad had had an operation for a slipped disc and was laid up for a few months and Ben was doing his Highers. Tom was tired of coming home and finding me still at Dad's, even although his tea was always ready for him to warm up, and he was convinced that Ben wasn't working hard enough. Tom was distant with me – as ever assuming that I took any side but his, when in fact I saw us as a family who stuck together. That evening we'd been to a charity dinner and had fun dancing and mixing with friends. I felt sexy and confident in a blue silk dress and strappy sandals. Tom wore his dinner suit with a blue tie and cummerbund to match my dress. At times throughout the evening I watched him, pleased to see that he was happy at last, and I told myself that if every now and then he was moody and bad-tempered then it wasn't the end of the world. Marriage is a lifelong commitment and nobody ever told me it would be easy.

He kissed me under the streetlamp and carried me up to bed. We were laughing when we got to the top of the stairs and when we made love I felt as if we were closer than we had been in years. I remember being convinced that this was the beginning of the good times. We'd reached the end of the down curve in the cycle of up-and-down that happens to everyone, and we were now on the climb. That's what I naively thought.

A week later he told me he was leaving me. He'd been having an affair for more than six months. I was no longer the woman he was in love with. She gave him the sort of intimacy that he needed. What made it worse was that he held my hand as he told me, breaking the news as sensitively as he could, telling me he would always be fond of me, acknowledging my skills as home-maker and mother. He didn't want to hurt me and he knew that ultimately I would thank him for leaving. 'You know what a selfish git I can be,' he said. 'Honestly Ellen, I'm sure most people feel you're far too good for me.'

'But I love you!' I cried out. 'Tom! Please!'

I begged. I pleaded. I think I even threatened suicide.

Memories.

Bitter, painful memories.

I go through the front gate and to the left of the house where the extension is grafted onto the side. Once Tom's office, it's now Leila's space, this made clear by a polished brass sign that says 'Leila Henrikson MA, UKCP accred-ited psychotherapist'. The magnolia tree that shelters against the grey stone wall has been carelessly hacked, the branches ragged and stunted.

He who hesitates is lost, I say to myself, and so I don't hesitate; I ring the bell and wait. But my heart is banging against my ribcage and I know at once that I have to turn and run. I have to run and keep running because this is fate-tempting insanity and I'm bound to end up the loser.

As I turn away, I hear the door open.

'Mary?'

I freeze.

'Mary McNeil?'

I focus on the end of the driveway, willing my legs to

move, but they won't. I try to lift my feet but I'm rooted
to the spot. I hear her come down the step behind me.
Her hand touches my shoulder. 'Won't you come inside?'

I slowly swivel my head and upper body towards her.
'Miss Henrikson?' I say, her name poison on my tongue.

'Call me Leila.'

'Leila.' I stare at her. I am face to face with the woman
who wrecked my life. She has a small forehead. Her eyes
are high and almond-shaped; her cheekbones prominent.
Her hair is long and sleek with a few deliberate curls
and has the rich, black sheen that only comes with regular
visits to a salon. She smiles. She has the look of a woman
who is comfortable in her skin.

I don't smile. I wait. I'm waiting for her to recognise
me. Waiting not breathing. My mouth is dry; my pulse
is racing. I expect her to frown, draw back, point at me
– 'Have we met?' Her frown will deepen. 'Ellen? You're
Ellen.' She will look shocked and then slightly panicked.
She'll demand that I leave.

'I've been looking forward to meeting you,' she says.

My legs collapse at the knees and I almost fall but at
least I can move my feet now so I lean up against the
brickwork and stare down at the ground.

'Please don't be anxious, Mary.' Her hand is on my
back. 'I know that coming for therapy is a huge step and
I promise that you'll leave feeling much better than you
do now.'

I turn my face towards her again. She flicks her hair
back over her shoulder, tilting her head as if she's in a
TV ad, and I feel a welcome surge of hate against this
woman who is inviting me into my own home. She thinks
she belongs in Maybanks. She thinks *I'm* the visitor.

I stand up straight. 'Sorry,' I say. 'I'm not sure what
came over me.'

'Never apologise, Mary,' she says. 'You have nothing to apologise for.'

I smile. Genuinely. Because I have the feeling she might regret that statement.

'Let's go inside.' She opens the door wide.

I nod. And then I follow her into my house.

3. Leila

I'm not worried about David. But my intuition tells me that I should be. There was something different about him today – a determination that I don't remember seeing before. Normally he wants my reassurance, a maternal interest that realigns him, reminding him that he is loved and cherished.

And I do love him. But I have Alex to consider, so I can't take a trip down memory lane and face up to what we did back then because it would ruin my here and now. I'm a mother; I need to focus on the present and the future. David should see that. And he will. Although I asked him not to contact me again, I don't expect him to take any notice of my request and so, if necessary, I'll meet with him again before he leaves Edinburgh. He can tell me about his therapy and I'll listen. We'll come to an understanding and then all will be well for another year or more.

I park the car and instantly spot the cat loitering on the flagstones trying to sniff out the remains of his kill. Katarina has cleared the dead bird away and all that's left is a faint bloodstain. I dump my handbag in the porch and go into the kitchen to fill a bucket with cold water. 'What are you doing?' Alex says. He's still wearing his boxers and T-shirt and has an open can of Diet Coke in his hand.

'Taking action,' I say.

Alex trails behind me as I go back outside. When the water hits the cat, he squeals and jumps three feet up into the air, a cartoon cat, all four legs splayed. He meows and wails like a creature possessed, then he scarpers to the bottom of the garden, knocking over a wooden chair on the way. 'Scaredy-cat!' I shout and can't help but smile.

'Fuck, Mum!' Alex is behind me. 'What did the cat ever do to you?'

'Go to the garden hut and get the chainsaw,' I tell him, rolling up my sleeves.

'What?' His eyes are wild. 'Are you going to kill it?'

'Don't be ridiculous! I'm not going to follow him over the wall, am I?' I pull a few of the creamy flowers off the magnolia tree and drop them into the empty bucket. 'I'm going to saw the higher branches off this tree.'

'Don't you think you should ask Tom first?' Alex says, grinning. I can see that this excites him; he's wired for a good time.

'Just get the chainsaw.'

'Bad-ass!' He runs off down the garden and is back in a few moments with the saw. I take it from him, steady my feet on the ground and pull the cord. At first the motor struggles to get going, fires and dies almost at once. On the fifth try it catches. I rev it a couple of times and then hold the machine above my head height to start cutting at the branches.

'Woo-hoo!' Alex shouts, leaping up and down and clapping like a nine-year-old.

I manage to saw into four branches before my arms are aching and I have to stop. 'Let me do it!' Alex shouts. He's unsteady on his feet and when I hand him the chainsaw he lurches to one side, laughing. An alarm bell sounds in my head. I watch him lift up the saw, carrying it like a gun, brandishing it in the air as if he's playing a game, and I know that I'm right to be worried.

'Okay, give it back to me.' My voice is stern. I'm sure he's exhibiting signs of drug use: overexcited, loud, problems balancing – I've seen my son like this before. I hold out my hand and he retreats away from me.

'I can do it!' He sidesteps me and I grab his arm. 'Just fuckin' leave me, woman!' He turns the chainsaw in my direction, half-pretending, half-not.

I slap him hard across the face and it shocks him into dropping the chainsaw onto the grass. 'Bitch!' he shrieks.

I shake his shoulders and his head snaps up. 'You little shit!' I say, my voice low. 'Don't think I don't know what you've been up to. You've been taking drugs again, I know you have, so there's no point denying it and I am warning you—' I stop. The menacing tone I'm using is familiar to my ears but it shouldn't be coming out of my mouth.

Breathe, Leila. Breathe.

I remind myself that this isn't me. This isn't the person I am. This isn't the sort of parent I am.

I take another breath and then I release him.

I smooth his T-shirt across his chest and kiss his cheek. 'Have a shower.' I kiss his other cheek. 'We'll talk later.' I pat his shoulders and gently push him away from me towards the house. He goes off without a peep, his eyes wide and scared, too shocked to know what to say or do. He hasn't been brought up like me, after all. I have only hit him three times over his nineteen years and he's yet to work out how to react.

I rub the back of my hand over my forehead and temples. Shit, shit, shit. 'That wasn't me,' I whisper into the air. 'I don't behave that way.'

I'm disappointed with myself. I aim to always parent

consciously, but like any mother, I have my triggers. Drug-taking is one of them – in Alex's case he loses all sense of himself and becomes glassy-eyed and moronic. I've been down this road before with him and it's not happening again.

There's a sound above me and when I look up, I see Katarina watching from the upstairs window, her body leaning against the pane, palms flat against the glass as if she's trapped inside the room. I point to the fallen branches on the ground and then to the furthermost end of the garden where we keep the brown bin for garden waste, then I go into the kitchen to prepare dinner.

My heart is racing. The teenage girl inside me wants to punch someone's lights out. Punch, kick, scratch. Gouge. Dismember.

I take a knife from the block and slice into a red pepper, rhythmically and with more force than required, until the pepper is shredded into too-thin strips that I immediately empty into the bin.

Stop, Leila.

Just stop.

An old trick. I take a mirror from my handbag and stare at my face. I don't see the lines, the lips pale without lipstick, a small smudge of mascara under my right eye. I stare into my own eyes and wait. I wait for the glimmer of me – the grown-up me, the considered me, the me I've cultivated over the last twenty years – and when I see that glimmer I latch onto it and it grows. I reconnect with myself in the colour of my own eyes and the teenage ghost loosens her grip.

The radio fills the kitchen with music, easy-listening tunes, not to relax me but to reassure Alex and Katarina that I've calmed down now. I chop another pepper into perfect strips. Reassured, I tackle a third – perfect – and then the green beans.

I'm scrubbing the new potatoes when Katarina arrives at my elbow. 'Do you want me help?'

'My help,' I say, automatically correcting her English.

'My help,' she repeats, her smile tentative.

'Did you clear up the branches?' I ask her.

'Yes, and I collect Tom's suit. I put it in the wardrobe.'

'Thank you.'

'I fuckin' hate fish,' Alex mumbles, as he edges into the kitchen, his eyes on the tray of salmon waiting to go into the oven. 'You know I do.'

'Please don't swear, Alex.' I dry my hands and stand beside him. 'You smell lovely and clean!' I kiss his cheek and wrap him up in a hug.

'Too tight!' He pulls away, frowning.

'Katarina, why don't you go through to the living room and watch the news?' I say, smiling brightly.

She glances at Alex. I can see she's unsure whether she should leave him alone with me.

'It's good for your English.' I take hold of her shoulders and propel her towards the front of the house. 'Alex and I will prepare dinner.'

I come back into the kitchen and close the door behind me. Alex is standing with his ankles and arms crossed, his head dipping down onto his chest. I stand in front of him and wait for him to look up. When he does, he peers at me through the flop of hair that curtains his eyes.

'What is it you've taken?'

He sighs and rubs his cheeks. 'Nothin'. Just what everyone takes.'

'Dope? Skunk? Pills of some sort? What?'

'Something I got from Harry.' He looks sheepish. 'I

won't take it again. I promise. It makes me feel spaced out.'

'I was hoping you'd learned your lesson, Alex.' I pitch my head at an angle so that I can see up into his eyes. 'After last year.'

'I've said I won't take it again! Don't start on me! Fuck!'

He slopes off and I follow him to the kitchen door, catching hold of his arm. 'I will be keeping an eye on you,' I say quietly. 'And you will eat with Tom and me this evening.'

He yanks his arm away and leaves the room. I return to the chopping board and pick up the knife. I press the tip of the blade into the end of my finger, just until the skin yields and a blob of blood settles on the surface like a raindrop on a leaf. Then I lick it.

Katarina has eaten and is in her room when Tom comes home from work. I hand him a single malt in a crystal glass, two ice cubes clinking together in the base. 'How was your day?' I ask, leaning in for a kiss, my breasts brushing against his sleeve.

'Productive. Getting to grips with the brief.' He lets the whisky roll around in his mouth as he looks me up and down. 'You've been gardening?' He reaches forward and removes a petal of magnolia flower from my hair, a petal I had deliberately left there so that he could make just such a gesture.

'Tidying up a little.' I shrug it off as if it was nothing. 'Alex helped too.'

'Did he?' He nods and has another swig of whisky. 'That's good.'

Tom has yet to properly get to know Alex and that makes life, if not exactly difficult, then slightly tiresome;

and so, if an opportunity arises, I like to spin the wheel in Alex's favour.

'Were you able to collect my suit?'

'I was.' I smile into his neck and weave sleepy kisses on the softness around his throat. 'It was tricky getting parked but I managed it.'

'What would I do without you?' he says, sounding genuinely amazed, as if I'd just performed a feat that was well beyond the scope of the average human being. I don't feel even remotely guilty lying to him. Most relationships are sustained, strengthened even, by tiny, insignificant lies that ensure one party feels loved while the other party gains control. As long as the power see-saws between the couple, always fluid, never stuck, then balance is maintained. (Ideally, of course, a couple should never see-saw. They should walk hand-in-hand, neither competitive nor combative, but since when has life ever been ideal?)

I call Alex downstairs for supper, but just as we sit down, the doorbell sounds. 'I'll get it,' Tom says, dropping his napkin on the table and heading for the front door.

Alex's eyes snap to mine when we hear the high-pitched voice of Mrs Patterson, our neighbour. I make out the words 'cat' and 'wall' and 'soaking wet'. I pass Alex the pepper grinder. 'Add a squeeze of lemon, too,' I say. 'Brings out the flavours.'

I can't hear what Tom is saying but his tone is polite and friendly and before long he has Mrs Patterson laughing. 'I'm not sure what all that was about,' he says when he returns to the table. 'Apparently her cat arrived home drenched and terrified. Came over our wall.'

'How strange,' I say. I catch Alex's eye and wink. He stifles a smile. Conspiracy makes us friends again.

'So I hear you helped in the garden today, Alex?' Tom says, pouring us both a glass of wine.

'Just a bit,' Alex mumbles.

'Now, if you won't blow your own trumpet, then I will,' I say. I rest my free hand on Tom's knee. 'I wasn't strong enough to wield the chainsaw so Alex helped me.' I take a sip of wine – crisp, fruity Sauvignon Blanc that I swirl inside my mouth. 'And he cleared up afterwards.'

'Good for you,' Tom says, smiling at Alex. He begins to tell him about his time as a fruit picker in East Anglia. 'Paid my way through university. There's something to be said for hard, physical work. Especially at your age when you have the strength and flexibility.'

Alex manages not to look dismissive and Tom moves on to talking about his day. He's working on a high-stakes case involving money laundering and multiple murders by the sort of gangsters most people believe exist only on TV dramas. Alex is genuinely gripped by what Tom is telling him. 'But why don't the police arrest them?' he says. 'If everyone knows they did it.'

'Insufficient evidence,' Tom says. 'Let me tell you how it works.'

It's good to see my son relaxed and it's good to see Tom acknowledging Alex's opinion and chatting to him without the need for me as a mediator. But after a few minutes, I begin to feel uneasy and I steer the conversation onto sport, because Alex is just a bit too interested in the details of the crime and I don't think it's healthy. There will always be the spectre of his father lurking at the back of my mind – but, while DNA loads the gun, surely it doesn't have to fire it. Nurture is key and I am nurturing Alex as best I can.

I sit back with my glass of wine and watch them both getting on at last. Tom is at his best when he is conversing about a subject he's sure of (in this case, Scotland's rugby team and their scrum tactics) and his enthusiasm is infectious. I admire successful men. That's one of the things I know about myself – I couldn't be with a man who wasn't successful. Tom is at the top of his profession, a barrister in much demand who can name his price. Many of his cases are tried in London but he is powerful enough to make instructing solicitors and researchers come north of the border until the actual trial date.

I believe romantic love is mostly transactional. We can all pretend otherwise. We can all wax lyrical about soul-mates and one-man-for-one-woman and meant-to-be foolishness. We can all be teary-eyed when we hear of serendipity bringing lovers together. But truthfully, when it comes down to it, this belief is a deceit. Time wears away the unconditional aspects of romantic love until it becomes a simple equation of what each partner offers the other – sex, money, companionship, intellectual stim-ulation, social opportunities, friendship, loyalty, a shared life . . . and so on. The equation needs to be balanced. I speak as one who knows. I spent five years specialising in couples therapy and so I've seen how it pans out for people. There's nothing worse than feeling consistently short-changed as the long march of year in and year out takes its toll.

Tom offers me money – in the shape of this house, an annexe for me to practise in – and social opportu-nities. He has a large cast of friends that reads like a *Who's Who* of Edinburgh society. We go to events and he shows me off like a prize. He's proud to have me on his arm and he isn't threatened by the fact that I am able to hold my own with his, mostly male, friends.

And what do I offer Tom? I offer him exciting sex and a shared life. It's a cliché, but traditional men like

Tom are mostly about their cock and their stomach. All the other good things that a woman might have to offer come as a bonus, not a necessity.

I believe that for women, being sexy is a choice. Women withhold their sexiness because they feel the man doesn't deserve them and I think that's short-sighted. Play the long game, encourage him to try harder, tease him and make sure you've pre-positioned whatever you want in return, and that it's ready to tip onto your lap. It's about management and it's about preparation. I've always used underwear, sex toys, hooker's tricks – whatever it takes to keep a man's interest until he has lost mine. My interest usually wanes first: I have never been left – I've aimed high but still I've never been left.

Tom needs validation. He's not a man who can ever be allowed to feel as if he's being taken for granted. His ego is too fragile for that. And, in truth, he's easy enough to please. His desires sit squarely in the middle of normal: a double shift – morning and evening sex, a willingness to give with enthusiasm, variety thrown in once a week. (No imagination required – sex manuals tell you everything you need to know.)

This evening he's in the mood to satisfy me, kissing, licking and sucking until he's made me come, and then he falls asleep next to me, neatly, on his side. He's always asleep in seconds and I envy him that. He is a man who, untroubled by his past, lives very squarely in the present. Me, on the other hand, I'm struggling to settle. Despite the evening going well, I'm concerned about Alex but I reassure myself that as long as I'm vigilant, he will be fine.

My brother, though, I do worry about because I hate to see him hurt. He's going through a process of change, and change inevitably brings disruption. He's never wanted to go to therapy before but now that he's going, I'm well aware of what that could mean. I went to therapy myself as part of my training. It was a prerequisite for my qualification – seek to know yourself before you seek to guide others, see how it feels to be in therapy. Dig, dig deeper. My therapist was, and still is, Maurice van Burren, a patient, intuitive man who encouraged me to see beyond my own carefully constructed self-deception.

When Maurice and I first met, he was most interested in exploring my childhood, the formative years, not so called for nothing.

'Tell me about your mother,' he said.

'My mother.' I pictured her lying in her bed, greasy-haired, hunched under multiple blankets like a woman three times her age, believing she was ill, unloved, abandoned. I pictured her shouting at Mal, flecks of spit landing on his cheek; he was a man lacking in ambition but otherwise perfectly adequate. She was the problem, not him.

'She was weak,' I told Maurice. 'She believed her own self-serving delusions. She had no fight. No sense of herself and what she could achieve. She thought she was owed love from those around her. She expected attention and support but she rarely gave anything back. She was one of life's passengers.'

Silence. My words hang in the air. Harsh-sounding and judgemental. And as an adult I stand by them because it's not for me to understand my mother.

'Was that what you saw and felt as a child?' Maurice said.

'No. As a child I thought she was . . .' I paused to travel back in time and find the little girl. I felt myself shrink as I re-inhabited her body, her small hands dexterous enough to make tea and change nappies. Her legs that could only run so fast – sixty-five seconds to the corner shop, and baby David left alone in his crib while she counted out the change. Then running back home, plastic bag banging against her legs, breathless with anxiety in case baby David had choked to death or somehow found his way out of his cot and ended up in the fire.

But although my body felt smaller, my heart felt larger, stretching like an ever-expanding balloon. 'I thought my mother was beautiful,' I told Maurice. 'When she smiled, my ribcage would swell. When she was sad, I thought it was my fault.'

Maurice inclined his head. 'You felt it was your job to make her happy?'

'When she was happy, I was happy. How could I not have seen it as my job?'

It was a few weeks later that we progressed to talking about siblings.

'One sibling,' I told him. 'David. He was born when I was six.'

More silence . . . an essential component of therapy. Allow the words to hover in the air to be considered and reconsidered. 'He saved my life,' I said. 'I was never jealous of him.' I smiled. 'He gave me purpose.'

'How so?' Maurice asked me.

'I thought about him constantly. What would I give him for tea? Did he need to see the doctor for his cough? Was it time to toilet-train him? And as he grew older, I listened to him read, practise his tables, learn the world's capitals. I was the goalie to his striker. I was the giver of treats and the taker of his pain.'

'All of this a parent's responsibility, surely?'

'David was always on my mind. And that was a good thing because when Gareth came along—' I shifted in my seat '—I needed to keep my thoughts busy elsewhere.'

'Elsewhere?'

'Gareth moved in when I was eight. He took over the house.' I stared past Maurice and out into his back garden, where one of his granddaughters sat on a blanket on the grass while his wife hung up washing. 'I didn't want him occupying my head too.'

It was almost a year before I allowed Maurice to return to the subject of Gareth. I poured the truth out over four sessions and knew I'd never revisit it again. It informed my adulthood but it didn't need to define me. Except that sometimes it did.

What would Maurice make of my behaviour this afternoon? First the cat and then Alex. And all because David wants to revisit our childhood. Trouble is, I know what I'd be telling David if I was his therapist. I would be encouraging him to talk, to rant, to rail against the misery and the injustice. And I'd encourage him to be truthful with the people who were there when he was a child. 'Your sister doesn't want you to speak the truth?' I would say. 'Well, she needs to understand that this isn't about her – this is about you.'

That's what I'd be telling him.

4. Ellen

I hand her my coat and walk into the therapy room, looking around me as if this is the first time I've been in here, and in a way it is, because Tom's study has been completely remodelled. The doors and windows are where they've always been but otherwise the space is unrecognisable. The walls are a muted lilac and the furniture is comfortable and expensive. The new furniture, carpets and blinds are plush and modern and straight out of a high-end showroom.

'Do take a seat, Mary,' Leila says. She's wearing a red and cream patterned shirt-dress and cream wedge sandals, no tights, her legs smooth and subtly tanned.

I sit down on a yellow armchair and she sits down opposite me. There is a glass of water and an open box of tissues on the table next to me. The room is cleaner and neater than it ever was before, but gone is all sense of the personal. This room used to be stuffed to the gunnels with all of sorts of souvenirs and memorabilia, some would say clutter. Tom had shelves and shelves of textbooks and journals, and an assortment of possessions he'd gathered over the years: old photographs, a brass cigarette case that belonged to his granddad, a large wooden Labrador that sat by the door for everyone's hand to blindly reach out and stroke, awards he'd won, a rugby ball from a winning match and so on. I wonder what's happened to all his stuff and then I remember

Chloe telling me he's using her old bedroom as his home office.

'I need to take a few details from you,' Leila says. 'And also to let you know of my charges.' She hands me a piece of thick, expensive paper – £55 for a fifty-minute session. Cancellation charges apply. 'Do you have private health insurance?' she asks.

'I don't.' I make a growling sound that I try to disguise by clearing my throat. 'And my problem isn't serious enough for me to get help on the NHS.' I focus my gaze on the paper on my lap. I can't look at her because I don't know what will happen if I do.

'You're feeling anxious at the moment?' she says.

I swallow down the urge to reach across and slap her smug face.

'There's no rush,' she says. 'I want you to feel that this is a safe space.'

A safe space? This room has been more than just a safe space. This room has been somewhere I have spent hours of my married life. The first fifteen years we lived here, when Tom was building his career, I would put the children to bed and then join him in here. We would share cocoa or a brandy, depending on whether he was in court the next day. He would tell me about his latest case, practise his opening address in front of me, run his logic past me. I was often a pretend juror, an everywoman, his link with the general public. But that wasn't all. We frequently made love in here. We conceived Ben on the sofa, both of us giggling as the springs squeaked along with our rhythm.

'Whenever you're ready,' Leila says.

'I'd rather . . .' I fold the paper and slide it into the back pocket of my jeans. 'Please continue.'

'You've been to your GP?'

'He gave me some antidepressants.' I stare at the floor and cough into my fist. 'I stopped taking them because they didn't make any difference.'

'And how long were you on them?'

'Six months.'

She asks for my GP's name and address and then she asks for my address. I haven't thought about this in advance and I make the snap decision not to give her my address but to give her my dad's instead – which, seconds after I've said it, I realise might be just as much of a giveaway if she knows anything about the divorce agreement.

'And have you been in therapy before?' she says.

'No.' I cross and uncross my legs. 'I tried to go once but my husband didn't want to.'

'You wanted to attend couples therapy?'

'I did. My husband was having an affair and I thought it might help us.' I feel brave enough to look up at her. I expect to see recognition on her face. I expect to see her draw back from her note-taking and realise who I am, but she doesn't. She's either an incredible actress or she really has no idea who is sitting in front of her.

'Is that when your symptoms started?'

'Yes. And then I was mugged – it wasn't serious but it was the final straw. I went to a support group but that didn't really suit me and—'

I stop talking because I have a sudden skin-crawling sensation. I reposition myself in my chair but it doesn't help. Forgetting my reserve and being frank with the very woman who is the root cause of all my problems feels perverse. I haven't thought this far ahead because I hadn't really expected to get this far.

She lays her paper and pen to one side and gives me her full attention, her expression sympathetic. 'You said on the phone that you are suffering from anxiety and obsessive compulsion.' I nod. 'Would you like to tell me a little bit about that?'

I glance around the room, stalling for time, wondering how I can possibly open my mouth and talk to her as if this is a perfectly normal situation.

'For example,' she says. 'How does the anxiety manifest itself?'

Think, Ellen, think. The penny isn't dropping for her. She's not going to show me the door. I can do and say whatever I want. I can lead her on and then reveal my true identity exactly when it suits me. I am in control of this.

'The time we spend together is for you to use as you wish,' Leila says. 'I'm here to listen to everything you tell me without judgement.'

'Without judgement?'

She nods.

And then I stare through the window, into the back garden. For a second I'm stunned. I blink and blink again.

The oak tree is gone. The oak tree that stood there for over a hundred years, that added a stately permanence to the garden, shade to lie under, branches to climb, space to nurture children's imaginations. Chloe was seven and Ben was a newborn when my dad came round to build the tree house. Chloe was wearing yellow shorts, a sparkly top and red wellie boots and was beside herself with excitement. She ran around fetching and carrying tools while I nursed the baby.

It wasn't elaborate; it was a rudimentary tree house. The floor was made from the tops of two discarded coffee tables that my dad had found in a skip and the roof was partly open, partly covered with an old tent.

The project lasted the whole weekend and after it was finished Chloe played in it for years. Even when she was a teenager she'd go up there to read or sleep or gaze up through the branches and the leaves to the sky. I now understand what she meant when she told me her childhood was being destroyed. She is being thoroughly removed from the house. Yes, she's an adult, but she's still Tom's child and this has always been her family home, from the moment she was born in the downstairs bathroom, an unexpectedly quick and easy birth that caught us all by surprise, to her twenty-fourth birthday party that we held in the garden just days before Tom announced that he was having an affair.

I experience an acute sense of betrayal on Chloe's behalf. How could Tom have allowed this woman to do this? What about Molly, his granddaughter? When Molly was born, hadn't we said to one another that as soon as she was able to use the ladder to climb up to the tree house, she'd spend many a happy afternoon up there? Just as her mum had done.

And now the tree is gone. Completely. And in its place there is decking and a square hot tub with a green plastic cover.

In the tick-tock of that one shocking minute, I make up my mind to do two things. Firstly, to get back into my house before she destroys everything that makes it unique. And secondly, to make her feel sorry for what she's done. This isn't just about a tree; this is about more than that – it's about taking what isn't yours to take and then wilfully destroying it.

Leila sits with her ankles crossed and says nothing. I know of people who've gone to therapy and cried for the whole session, filling the silence with tears. The tissues next to my chair are strategically placed. I'm sure Leila is anticipating my tears. I expect she sees me as a typical middle-aged woman who has lost her husband because she doesn't understand him or isn't exciting enough in bed.

Well fuck her. She wants me to talk? Then I'll talk.

'I have a fear of the house going on fire,' I say quickly. 'I don't know why. It's not rational. It's ridiculous, in fact. I've always been a slightly anxious person but never as bad as this. Not until my husband and I separated. I've gradually gone downhill. Worrying about everything. And, well . . . He has a very aggressive solicitor and I've been bullied into agreeing to things I didn't want to agree to.'

I pause. She seems to feel no compunction to fill the silence so I continue. I tell her that leaving the house isn't simple any more. I tell her about taking photographs, every day, and about how this is beginning to rule my life.

She nods.

'And then I have to check that the front door is locked. I do that several times in the evening and even wake up in the middle of the night to do it again. And to check the sockets. And often I check the car too, to make sure the handbrake is on.'

I pause. More silence. So I continue. I tell her that I'm a teacher and that before school broke up for the summer, my anxiety was beginning to impact on my work. 'I teach chemistry and I now worry about my lab going on fire, so leaving for the day involves me double- and triple-checking gas and electricity points. I make sure the chemicals are locked up and the equipment is securely shelved. I leave the classroom and when I'm halfway along the corridor I go back and check again and then again. Soon my colleagues will notice and I don't know what I'll say to them.'

I hear the muffled vibration of a phone ringing. It's coming from Leila's pocket. She doesn't lose her focus but keeps her understanding gaze fixed very firmly on me.

'That's it, really,' I say. 'I think I'm reaching a critical point.' I sit back in the seat. 'That's why I'm here. To get help before it completely disables me.'

I stare at her and she stares back. Then she slowly nods. 'Thank you for sharing your thoughts and feelings with me, Mary,' she says. 'I can see that you have a lot to talk about.' She gives me a soft, encouraging smile. 'You deserve to be listened to.' She pauses to let this sink in. 'It's often the case that when we experience a major life event, such as a separation, then our feeling of safety, our trust in the world and in ourselves also feels threatened.' Her tone oozes empathy like sweet sap from a maple tree. 'Sometimes we are forced to confront old emotions, ones we have never dealt with before, and this can be frightening.'

She's lost me now. I wonder whether she means that the anxiety lies deeper than Tom leaving me?

'I can offer you two alternative therapies,' she says. 'I am trained as a Jungian therapist.' I nod. 'Are you familiar with Jungian therapy?'

'No, not really. I saw a film about Jung and Freud a few years ago.' In the cinema, with Tom. He hadn't wanted to come but I'd persuaded him and I think that on the walk home we were even holding hands. 'Recalling dreams seemed to feature . . .' I trail off.

'Jungian analysis is a depth psychology, or psychology of the unconscious. Dream interpretation is integral.'

'Right.' I nod as if I fully understand what she means.

'Jungian therapy is a fairly long-term commitment.'

'How long?' I say.

'A year, possibly more.'

'That's too long, I think . . .' *I'll be done with you long before that.* 'And I'm not sure I can afford it.'

'I'm also trained to deliver CBT – cognitive behavioural therapy. CBT would be a course of six or eight treatments – you can always return for more if you need a top-up – and essentially it's a therapy that helps you manage your problems by changing the way you think and behave.'

'That sounds more like what I'm looking for.'

She goes on to tell me that CBT works by breaking down the problem into smaller, more manageable parts, and at that point, I tune out because I have an excuse to stare at her – really stare – and I am free to think my own thoughts. She has long, piano player's fingers and shiny, blue nails. She uses her right hand when she speaks, her hand moving through the air, dipping and weaving to enhance the meaning of the words, her blue nails catching and reflecting the light. Her lips are full, scarlet lipstick defining their shape. This is the woman who is sleeping with my husband, the woman who seduced a married man and has the barefaced cheek to move into the family home. The woman who is too full of her own importance, too fond of her own voice, too blatantly conceited to see I am deceiving her.

Tom is a kisser. I imagine their tongues colliding and their limbs dragged round each other. I imagine her sitting astride him and him urging her on. I imagine her worshipping at the temple of his cock, endlessly pleasing him, like a paid whore.

I hate her. I hate her for her easy confidence and her selfishness. I hate her for the fact that she has so effortlessly acquired Maybanks. And I hate her for not even knowing who I am. How unimportant I must be to her. How eminently disposable.

'There are exercises for you to practise and we'll discuss how you get on with them at the following session.' She gives me her calm, encouraging smile. A smile that's meant to relax me, and I'm sure it works with most people because she's good at her job. I can see that. 'How does that sound?'

'Perfect,' I acknowledge. 'I think I will really benefit from being honest with you.'

We spend the next thirty minutes discussing 'exposure therapy', which in simple terms seems to mean facing my fears. She talks me through exercises that I will need to practise at home. At first I listen with only half an ear but then I realise that what she's telling me might actually help, so I concentrate properly.

'If you do the exercises then I expect you will notice the effects quite quickly,' she says.

'I'm not the worst case you've ever come across then?' I ask her.

'No, not even close.'

When she shows me out I pause to admire the rigorously tamed flower border. Verbascum, lupins and mallow no longer tumble against the wall in a rainbow of colours but stand to attention in regimented rows. I distinctly remember planting each flower, down on my hands and knees, dirt caking my palms and clotting under my fingernails. 'Beautiful flowers,' I say. 'Are you the gardener?'

'I do my best,' she says, utterly without shame. 'I always wanted to live in this area. I was brought up further south.' She points vaguely over her shoulder.

'Thank you for today,' I say. 'See you next week.'

I'm seething as I walk home. And it feels good to

seethe. It feels good to seethe, to plot and to hate. Leila Henrikson has it coming. And I feel the justified anger of betrayed women everywhere urging me on to revenge.

I call my solicitor to make an appointment and when I finish the call I breathe deeply, fuelled by anger. My anxiety has been replaced by a vivid sense of purpose. I was wrong to make way so easily. I should have dug in my heels like Chloe said and I'm lucky to be given a second chance. It has taken me a year to get here but now that I'm back on my own doorstep, I'm not going to give in again. Retreating was a reflex – like someone poking you with a stick; first you recoil but then – you grab the stick.

And now, at last, I'm grabbing the stick.

I scroll though my phone and delete the photos of the sockets – all two dozen of them – and then I call my dad. 'Are you serious about selling up so that we can combine forces?'

'You bet I am,' he says.

'Okay, Dad.' I smile up at the cloudy sky and use anger to breathe fire into my words. 'Let's do it.'

4. Leila

My new client Mary McNeil is in the room when my mobile rings. I have it on silent but the vibration is obvious enough to distract her and I'm annoyed with myself for not switching it off. It rings three more times but each of those times I'm talking and so Mary doesn't notice. The first meeting with a new client is an important one to gauge what will be the best therapeutic approach; different strokes for different folks – not everyone is suited to Jungian therapy, much as I love it myself. There is a depth and a simplicity to the Jungian model that I find inspiring. I certainly wouldn't be the person I am today without it.

When Mary leaves I use the five minutes before Alison and Mark arrive to take notes that will trigger my memory next time I see her. I have the sense that she has a lot to say, that she is both anxious and lacking in confidence. She looked worn out and chronically tired, which doesn't surprise me bearing in mind her OCD, although after her reflective five minutes when she stared out into the garden, I noticed steel in her expression and that bodes well for her recovery. Her description of her symptoms is a typical story and it appears to be the break-up with her husband that has precipitated this anxiety. I don't sense any underlying issues. She sustained a marriage for almost thirty years, holds down a responsible job and has raised a family. I expect her to do well with CBT provided she is motivated enough to practise the exercises. I look forward to working with her. Clients like Mary provide a welcome balance to my long-term clients who often need therapy for years to untie the knot of childhood patterns. We are all shaped by our early childhood experiences, our biases and behaviours set and then hardened over time. My sense is that Mary's childhood was a nurturing one. Not everyone is so lucky.

I lock away Mary's notes and then I check my phone. I've already guessed the calls will be from David so I'm not surprised when I see that the four missed calls are indeed from him. Twice he's left messages but I don't listen to them and I don't call him back either. This is a pattern I'm familiar with because David has been behaving this way for years. I hear nothing from him for months on end and then he spends a week or two contacting me every day, expecting me to drop everything and devote all my time to him.

I switch off my phone and prepare for Alison and Mark. They have been attending as a couple for three months. After years of trying for a baby they have given up on IVF and are deciding whether or not to adopt. They are working hard to move forward and the fifty minutes is often punctuated with anger and tears from Alison and a stiff resilience from Mark.

I know it's going to be an intense session when Alison begins by saying, 'I don't feel like I know Mark any more. In fact, I wonder whether I've ever known him. I think I've always imagined that Mark is a better person than he actually is.' She sits back on the sofa after she says this, her expression defiant. Mark is at the other end of the sofa, his arms folded against her as she stares along at him. 'Nothing?' she says. 'You have nothing to say to that?' Mark still doesn't respond and Alison turns challenging eyes towards me. With couples therapy I have to resist taking on the role of referee, so I don't say anything either. Alison closes her eyes and rests her head back. I watch her shoulders drop and her limbs relax on the sofa as if she's falling asleep.

A minute passes before Mark says to me, 'Sorry about that. We've had a difficult week. Alison works hard; she's tired. And when she's tired she gets angry—'

'Apologising for me now?' Alison's eyes snap open. 'Like I'm some badly behaved teenager!'

He shakes his head, in a pretence of tolerance. 'You're always so dramatic.'

'I wonder why that is?' she says.

'It's important not to speak in anger.'

'Like you, you mean?' She snorts with laughter. 'You're the angriest person I know. You just hide it well.'

This is an astute observation and I hope that Mark will address it but he doesn't.

'I love you, Alison,' he says. 'And I want us to adopt a baby.'

Alison's head drops onto her knees and her body shakes. At first I think she's crying but when she sits up straight again, I see she's laughing.

'I have to tell you, Leila,' she says. 'That once upon a time Mark loved me because I was dynamic and hard-working. Now he finds me tired and angry. Yesterday he accused me of lying when I said I enjoyed my job. I do enjoy my job. I complain about it sometimes, but doesn't everyone?' She throws out her arms, her expression questioning. 'He told me he knows when I'm not being truthful because I have a certain look on my face. He's constantly defining the way I am and if I tell him otherwise he doesn't believe me.'

She looks to Mark for a response but he has tuned

out. He is quietly smiling to himself as if he's remembering something amusing.

'This is him all over,' Alison says. 'He presses my buttons and then just drifts off as if it's got nothing to do with him.' She stands up and walks behind the sofa. 'I'm married to a man who says he loves me but his love feels like control.' She pulls at the collar of her blouse. 'It strangles me.' She walks backwards and forwards several times, then sits down again. 'So what do you think I should do, Leila?'

I wait a few seconds before I reply in case Mark wants to add anything. My personal feeling is that their relationship has run its course. They seem to be forever torturing one another with accusations and counter-accusations. If I was her, I'd have cut and run some time ago. But I'm the last person to question the ties that bind us so I keep my opinion to myself. 'Alison, you know I can't tell you what to do,' I say. 'Therapy is a safe space to explore loss, to recognise behaviour patterns and to resist the urge to blame each other.' I pause long enough to take a slow breath. 'All I can do is help you both to articulate your feelings so that you can come to the decision that's right for you, as individuals and as a couple.'

This falls on deaf ears and Mark says to me, 'All I want is for Alison to be happy.'

'For fuck's sake!' Alison throws her head back and adds sharply, 'Shut up about me and talk about yourself!'

There follows thirty-five minutes of wrangling and I do my best to steer them away from reproach and towards reflection. It's subtle work but it's a process I'm skilled at. Towards the end of the fifty minutes they are almost listening to each other – and then the session ends.

'Same time next week?' Mark says.

'Of course,' I reply.

As they leave the room Alison's hand tentatively reaches for Mark's and I hear them discuss what they're going to eat for dinner that evening. I close the door behind them and immediately listen to David's two messages. 'We really need to talk, Leila.' Pause. 'Call me.' Followed five minutes later by, 'I'm going out for a walk. Meet me in the Botanic Gardens?'

The message was left over an hour ago so I call him to check he'll still be there. We arrange to meet in the cafe and I drink a glass of water and then head off. It's only a five-minute journey in the car so I'm there in no time.

'It's looking beautiful out there,' I say, finding him at a table by the far wall. 'Especially the wildflower garden.' He is dressed in a suit and his hair is tidy, his beard trimmed. 'You look very smart.'

'I went for an interview today.'

'Oh? You didn't tell me you were looking for a job.'

'John Lewis. It seemed to go well.'

'I thought you were only staying in Edinburgh for another couple of weeks?'

'I changed my mind.'

My heart is able to do strange things where David is concerned, it's able to sink and soar at the same time. Sink because of the trouble he could cause me and soar because he's my brother and despite all our differences I love him.

'You're doing a lot of that these days, changing your mind.' I stand up. 'I'm gasping for a cuppa.'

'It's waitress service.'

'I'll just go to the loo quickly, then. If the waitress arrives, order for me.'

The loo is downstairs and I head off almost at a run.
I feel chilled, as if I've just passed through one of those
industrial freezers. I examine my face in the mirror; my
lips have lost all their colour and I look panic-stricken.
I stare into the black of my eyes and see myself reflected
back at me, my grown-up self not my teenage self. The
teenage Leila Mae would have known how to deal with
this. She was resourceful.

'Stop it!' I whisper to my reflection. 'You're overreacting.'

He's cornering me, is the thought that comes back to
me.

'He's not,' I whisper. 'David has never been your
adversary and he never will be.'

David will bring Gareth back into our lives. The fallout
from that will destroy me.

I shiver and step away from the mirror. My peace of
mind relies on me moving forward, always moving
forward, never dwelling, never standing still.

When I went through therapy I had the decency not
to inflict myself on David. I worked through the wreckage
of our childhood with Maurice my therapist and no one
else. David needs to do the same. He needs to leave me
out of his process. I take my make-up out of my bag
and add colour to my cheeks and lips, then return to
the table determined to be strong with him.

'I've ordered us tea and cake,' he says. 'I wasn't sure
whether you wanted anything to eat.'

'I'll have a small slice.' I take a deep breath and smile
at him. 'So where are you living?'

'A shared flat in Gorgie.'

'Is it nice?'

'Not especially. But it'll do for now.'

'It's all happening so fast, David! I only saw you a
couple of days ago.'

'I was hoping that if I stick around we could see more of one another.'

'Okay.'

'Perhaps I could even meet Tom.'

'Perhaps.'

The waitress brings our order and we both sit back while she places everything on the table. We hold eye contact throughout but it doesn't help me to feel less anxious because I've never been able to work out what David is thinking. His feelings, on the other hand, are written all through his body language – tension concentrates in his fingers, they move constantly as he shreds a napkin and arranges the pieces in a pile next to his left hand – but his plans? His intentions? His thoughts? They remain impenetrable.

'So how's Tom?'

'He's good.'

'Is he married like all your other men?'

'He's getting divorced.'

'He left his wife for you?'

'His marriage was already over bar the actual separation.'

'And is he good with Alex?'

'Of course. He's a parent himself. He has two children of his own – Chloe and Ben. And a granddaughter called Molly.' I pour our tea and push both pieces of cake towards David. 'I'll just have the small end of the fruit cake.' I scoop some into my mouth and watch as he takes a forkful of Victoria sponge.

'I've never kept a relationship going beyond three months,' he says.

'Why do you think that is?'

'I don't know.' He sighs. 'Maybe because I'm unlovable.'

'Nobody's unlovable, David. But sometimes we might push people away. We don't mean to but we do.'

'Do you?'

'I don't think so, but then I was in therapy for years as part of my training and I still see my therapist once a month. I never forget that I'm a work in progress. We all are.'

We lapse into silence for a minute. I sip my tea and David eats more cake.

'Our childhood wasn't easy,' he says.

'You're right.'

'Have you let go of it?'

'Mostly.'

'Leila.' He leans forward. His expression is animated. 'I want to confront Gareth.'

I nod. 'I understand that. But remember we agreed to put Gareth behind us.'

'An unspoken agreement maybe but—'

'It wasn't unspoken,' I counter. 'I distinctly remember us discussing it.'

That makes him hesitate. He finishes the cake and then says, 'Who does Alex think his dad is?'

He already knows the answer to this but I tell him again. 'I told Alex his father was a man I loved but had lost touch with. That was when he was about ten. He hasn't asked me since then.'

'Do you think it was good to lie?'

'Of course it wasn't good to lie! But he was ten years old. Do you think I should have told him the truth?'

'I could have helped you break it to him.'

'I would never have agreed to that! Truth can destroy people.'

'If I had known . . .' He shakes his head and pushes the plate away. 'I just . . . I've wasted years! Years and fucking years. Gareth's cruel, crazy shit . . . and it's like I'm just waking up. I've let stuff hold me back and— Fuck, Leila!'

'David, I understand. I do.' His eyes are full of tears. He's my little brother and I want to comfort him. 'When you begin therapy, you experience an opening-up and it feels both good and bad, especially if you've felt trapped or stuck for some time. You want to instantly act upon it, take a short cut, jump forward to where you want to be.' I look around the room for inspiration and find it in a poster about world ecosystems. 'It's like you've glimpsed a new way of being, but as yet the picture is incomplete. Just imagine that there's an elephant behind a curtain and you're only allowed to view a small section of the elephant and what you see is its trunk and nothing else. You won't have a sense of the whole beast. You haven't seen the tiny tail or the huge ears. So if you were to act on that understanding you would be limited. Do you see what I mean?'

'You're saying I should wait until I see the whole elephant?'

'Yes. Exactly. You need to be patient. You will have realisations and you'll want to act upon them at once, but you mustn't.'

A muscle twitches on the right side of his face, pulling at the corner of his mouth. I gently touch his cheek and he leans into my hand to rest his face in the cup of my palm. We sit like this for a moment and then our attention is caught by a group of young children jostling for seats at the table next to us. 'I'm so sorry!' a young mother says as her son elbows me in his rush to sit down. 'He's overexcited.'

'No problem. We were just leaving.' I stand up. 'We'll give you some more space.'

David and I hug and agree to meet again soon, and this time I watch him as he walks away. Three times he turns round and we both wave. He is reluctant to leave me and part of me is reluctant to let him go. My maternal instinct was activated at such a young age and I feel the pull of that now. I want to run after him, invite him home, care for him like I used to.

But I can't, because I know that giving him too much sympathy will validate his choices, and David is on a trajectory that will cause a shitstorm of pain. The can of worms he wants to open will bring our stepfather crawling out and I need to protect Alex, and also myself. I think about how I can do this on the drive home but don't come up with anything – and then the answer presents itself, via Katarina of all people. She is lurking in the hallway when I come in the front door. 'Is everything okay?' I say.

'I need to talk you, please.'

'To you,' I say. I drop my keys on the hall table. 'What about?'

'Alex.'

'What about Alex?'

She hesitates, then visibly swallows down her nerves. 'He is drink and drugs. Too many.'

I walk towards her and she backs away as if she expects me to hit her. 'What makes you say that?'

'I see him. He behave . . . strange. And now he is on bed.'

We both go upstairs – I'm rushing because I'm afraid of what I might find. I push open his bedroom door and am met by the malty smell of spilt beer. Alex is wearing jeans and a T-shirt and is lying face down on his bed, crashed out like a felled tree. At first I think he might be unconscious and panic rises inside me like vomit. 'Alex! Alex!' I shake him repeatedly and he makes no sound until finally his arm comes up to push me away and he mumbles a string of incoherent sounds.

Katarina is watching me, her hand over her mouth. 'We call ambulance?'

'No,' I say. 'Unfortunately, we've been down this road before. He needs to sleep it off, that's all.' I rearrange his limbs and manoeuvre him into the recovery position so that if he's sick, he won't inhale it.

'I will clean up mess,' she says. She picks up the fallen beer bottle and goes to fetch a cloth.

I look down at my son and feel the heavy weight of irritation piggyback a mother's love. 'Okay, Alex,' I say out loud. 'It's rehab for you.'

Two birds, one stone.

A timely solution.

5. Ellen

I walked away from my first therapy session feeling angry but strangely elated. I was waiting for it all to go wrong, for me to be ejected from the house with a flea in my ear, but it never happened. Instead, I left Maybanks with a fresh perspective. I realised that while my anxiety was linked to Tom leaving me, I was making it worse by being so passive. A whole year of going along with whatever he said, bending in the face of his demands. And look where it had got me – out of my home, short of money and anxiety-ridden.

The absence of the oak tree has been enough to catapult me from anxiety to anger. The therapy is already working . . . Not in the way that Leila intended it to, but here I am, with a gear shift that I'm convinced will reverse the slide in my mental state. I am going to be well again. I say this to myself a couple of times, standing in front of the mirror.

I am going to be well again.

I am going to be well again and I am going to live in Maybanks again.

I watch my lips as I say this. I see the light in my eyes and I know that it's true.

Going back inside my home made me remember how much the house is mine. A house is just a house until it's a home, and all my love and effort went into the very walls of the place. We bought it when we were newly married and hard up. An elderly couple had lived there for decades and the house needed complete modernisation. We didn't have the money at first. It took us five years to afford to have it rewired and the heating installed. With my dad's help, I learned how to save us money on hiring tradesmen. I was a dab hand with a drill, I could tile, I could change the washers on the taps and wield a paintbrush, hang wallpaper and build shelves.

Tom was establishing his career and, apart from the times I joined him in his study, he was often pre-occupied. His work was important, that was a given, so I rarely complained. Once I mentioned Tom's lack of attention to my parents and my mother reacted at once. 'He's an important man!' She was scandalised. 'You should feel lucky to be married to a man who is such a good provider.'

I could see her point but still I often felt like a single parent, sensing at times that he used his work to avoid being with the family. So as the months went by I adapted. I got on with the job of raising Chloe and Ben, and when Ben was six I went back to teaching. We were a happy unit of three, and when Tom was between cases and we were a family of four, we were happier still.

Now I glimpse a possible future where I am living with my dad in Maybanks and my children and Molly visit regularly: Sunday lunches, laughter and games, Molly playing on the grass. The tree house is gone but we can build her a playhouse towards the rear of the garden, a hideaway for her to call her own.

I'm impatient to get on with my plans and I can't wait for my solicitor to get back to me, but I'm even more keen for Tuesday to come round again. As a therapist Leila was sound. As a woman, she needs to pay for being a home-wrecker and I worry that my resolve will lessen as the days go by and I'll return to being overwhelmed by anxiety again.

I'm not wrong. Within twenty-four hours, anxiety creeps up on me, stealthy as a cat. A permanent change will take a while, it will take practice, I tell myself, as I rush to check the sockets again. Everything is fine – of course it is – but it takes time for my body to catch up, my pulse racing and my breathing ragged.

I make myself a cup of tea and decide not to unplug the kettle but to practise the exposure therapy Leila described to me. Usually I can't relax and enjoy a cup of tea if I know that the kettle is still plugged in. Leila instructed me to sit it out, write down what I'm feeling, let the anxiety build but don't be a slave to the feeling – watch it, as if it's something separate from me, because when it reaches a peak, the anxiety will simply recede again without me doing anything.

I'm working through this process when the doorbell rings. I'm glad of the distraction and go to answer it at once. A man I don't immediately recognise is standing on my doorstep, under an umbrella, the rain dripping off the spokes of the brolly and down his sleeve. 'Hi, Ellen.' He holds my blue scarf out towards me and I take it from him. It's the one that I left at the group meeting and it prompts me into realising who he is.

'Francis. Hi.' I smile. 'Thank you.'

'Sharon was going to post it but I offered to drop it off – I was passing your door anyway.'

'That's kind of you.'

'No worries.' He gives me a brief wave. 'Sorry to have disturbed you.'

He walks off along the path, and I watch a gust of wind blow rain underneath his umbrella. It feels mean not to invite him in. 'Hold on, Francis!' I call out. 'Would you like to shelter from the rain until this shower passes through?'

'Well . . .' He glances up at the sky towards a patch of clear weather in the distance. 'Maybe just five minutes?'

'Of course. Come in.'

He leaves his umbrella and coat in the porch and follows me along the hallway, manoeuvring his way past the boxes. 'I don't normally come to this part of town but I've been visiting my mum in the hospice.'

'I'm sorry,' I say. 'Is she very ill?'

He nods. 'She has cancer but she's not in any pain. And the staff are fantastic.' He stares off into the middle distance. 'They really are. She's kept very comfortable.'

'I'm just having a cup of tea. Would you like to join me?'

'That would be great.' He rubs his hands together. 'I could do with the warming up.' He looks around the room. 'I'm not disturbing you, though?'

'Not at all. To be honest I'm glad of the interruption.'

'How come?'

'I've started seeing a therapist and I'm learning cognitive behaviour therapy. So far I've managed not to unplug the kettle. Five minutes and counting.' I glance at my watch. 'Hang on. We've been talking for two minutes thirty-three seconds so that makes it close to eight minutes and counting.'

He cheers. 'Well done you!'

'It's early days but—' I let out a laboured breath '—I'm hopeful.'

'And so you should be,' he says.

'Have a seat and I'll make us some tea.'

He's easy to talk to. The afternoon slips into early evening in a flow of relaxed conversation. We talk about everything from our childhoods – mine spent in the country, his in town – to our careers. He asks me about my job and I tell him what it's like to teach chemistry to teenagers. He works in a bank but is hoping for a career change. 'I've applied for the police but my CV isn't up to scratch. Volunteer work helps.' He smiles. 'Hence the reason I'm one of Sharon's little helpers. I shepherd people in and out. Try to make sure no one feels uncomfortable.'

'That's why you spoke to me in the cafe?'

He nods. 'I'm glad you've not been put off therapy altogether. We all felt bad after the group meeting. I went back to the cafe but you'd already left and I was worried you'd be put off for life.'

'There was no need for you to worry. I was fine.'

'Well . . . It was insensitive of us. You didn't want to come and I think Trish, Pam and I more or less forced you.'

'You didn't.' I smile. 'But after I'd run out on the group, I couldn't stay in the cafe. I had visions of the whole class coming across to lend their support.'

'You have a point. But you know everyone means well?'

'I do. And I don't mean to sound ungrateful. I just don't like being the centre of attention.' I think for a moment. 'It was useful going that night, though. You remember the young girl, Gemma I think her name was?'

'The one whose house was burgled?'

'Yeah . . . well, something she said really struck me.' I remind him what she said about there being three types of people. 'I realised that over this last year I've become someone who lets life happen to me.'

He nods. 'We've all been there.'

'You seem pretty sorted to me,' I say. And then I

remember. *My name is Francis and someone tried to kill me.* I sit forward. 'Didn't you say at one of the meetings that someone tried to kill you?'

'Not quite. I was stabbed with a kitchen knife, four-inch-long blade.' He lifts up his shirt and I see he has a scar running at an angle across his side, between his ribcage and his pelvis.

'That's awful!' My hand goes up to my mouth. 'How did it happen?'

'I wasn't the intended victim. It was when I was in my first year at university. I was on a night out and was drunk. I'd gone outside to be sick and two men were fighting on the street. I ended up being caught up in their path and . . .' He shrugs. 'It's ancient history now but for a long time I was angry and I blamed myself. I had some medical complications so I spent several months in hospital. It was a difficult time.' He stands up. 'Okay if I use your loo?'

'Yes, it's just at the top of the stairs.'

While he's gone I take our mugs into the kitchen. I don't unplug the kettle but I do stare at it. Seventy-two minutes! A record. 'Congratulations, Ellen,' I say out loud. 'See? You really can do this.'

I'm enjoying spending time with Francis. Apart from anything else it's a relief for me to be myself. None of my family and friends know about my anxiety so talking about it, casually, normally, makes me feel as if I'm not such a lost cause after all. Ben is away with friends for a couple of days and I wonder whether to ask Francis to stay for tea, but I don't want to sound too needy so I decide not to.

'You're good with colour,' Francis says when he comes back into the living room. 'The red and the yellow in the bathroom, the greens in here – beautiful.'

'You're being generous.' I follow his eyes as he looks around the living room, crammed full of too much stuff, but I see what he means about colour – throws, curtains, the rug – livening up the dilapidated floor and walls. 'I've always loved colour. I used to have a garden and I grew all the flowers I could.' We both sit down again. 'I'm only renting here. I'm hoping the landlord might let me paint the walls at some point . . . if I'm here long enough.'

'In Sufi tradition, the three elements that make up the heart are yellow for joy, red for courage and green for compassion.' He smiles at me. 'You're all heart.'

I laugh. 'Oh no, I'm not.' I shake my head as I think about how much I hate Leila Henrikson and how happy I would be to see her suffer. How very happy indeed. 'I'm really not.'

'What makes you say that?'

'Well . . .' I hesitate for a second. 'I'm plotting revenge.'

'Against whom?'

'Against my ex-husband Tom and his new woman. They're in the family home and I want it back. So I'm talking to my solicitor and I'm planning on doing other stuff too.'

He raises his eyebrows, his interest piqued. I'm tempted to tell him exactly what I'm up to but then – what am I up to? I'm going to a therapist who has no idea that she's now living in my house with my husband. Apart from that, all I know is that I want my house back and I want to punish her.

'You're angry?' he says.

'I am.'

'With Tom or with the woman?'

'It varies. Both of them, but recently, more her. Tom is Tom. He's arrogant, up himself, bullish at times but we had almost thirty, mostly happy, years together and, like it or not, he is the father of my children. But her . . .' I shake my head. 'It's bad enough seducing another woman's husband – but moving into her home? Who does that?'

'Could Tom have told her you were happy to move out?'

'Who would believe that? She had to see how much effort I'd put into the place!'

'Maybe, but I guess what you don't know is how Tom has represented the facts.'

My temper surges up from the pit of my stomach. 'I know *this* for a fact. She's a *bitch*, Francis. She's conniving and complicit. And I'm not putting up with it any longer.'

Francis holds up his arms. 'Woah! I'm only playing devil's advocate.' He laughs. 'I surrender!'

'I'm sorry!' I laugh too. 'I just . . . She's a sore point.'

'No worries.' He stands up, glancing in the direction of the front door as if he's keen to be on his way. 'I should be off now. Thank you for the tea and the chat.'

I follow him to the door, feeling like I might have driven him out with my anger. 'Stop by again, won't you?' I say.

'I'd love to.'

'Next time you're visiting your mum.'

'Sure.' He walks off down the path, turning back to give me a quick wave.

I close the door behind him and go immediately into the kitchen. The fingers of my free hand reach towards the kettle plug, still in the socket.

Don't Ellen. *Don't.*

I snatch back my hand.

5. Leila

'Alex.' I'm standing over his bed. 'You need to get up now.' He's under the duvet and his jeans are on the floor, so he must have woken up at some point and put himself to bed. I shake his shoulders. 'Alex.' I rub his sternum with my knuckles. 'Alex!'

He raises himself up and shouts, 'Leave me the fuck alone!'

What's good enough for next door's cat is good enough for my son. When the bucket of water lands on top of him, he's out of his bed in an instant, shrieking, 'You cunt!' His arms and legs flail in front of me and then he tries to land a punch. It's a feeble attempt and his fist meets the air inches to the right of my head. I retaliate by shoving him hard against the wall and holding him there, my forearm lodged under his chin. He's four inches taller than me and undoubtedly stronger but he's caught unawares. When he tries to wrestle free, I tighten my hold so that he can barely take a breath. He stops struggling at once, the fire in his eyes dimmed by the onset of tears.

'Alex.' I pause until I'm sure I have his attention. 'I told you last year that I would have zero tolerance for further drug-taking. And I meant it.' I pause again to watch my words sink in. 'So now, you are going to have a shower. And then you are going to get dressed. And then I am taking you back to rehab.' I hear Gareth's oh-so-patient tone coming from my mouth and it makes me feel sick. I step away from Alex and he rubs his throat, his expression twisted. I can see fury in his eyes but it's tempered by fear.

'You're a bitch.' He spits the words at me. 'You're a psycho bitch. And I fuckin' hate you.'

'You are not spending the summer in this house drunk and drugged,' I tell him. 'I called the Bridge this morning and spoke to Mr Mooney. He's agreed you should come back in today. I've cancelled my clients so I can take you there.' I walk away from him and look back from the bedroom door. 'Pack a bag and be downstairs in thirty minutes.'

There's adrenaline in my veins and it propels me down the stairs in a flash. Violence excites me. I wish it didn't. I really wish it didn't. I know my weaknesses. I know them in the same way as a mother knows the intricate details of her new baby's face. There's a fine line between being a strong, uncompromising parent and being a bully. I crossed that line. Again.

I make myself a smoothie, my hands shaking as I take the ingredients from the fridge. I add raspberries and almond milk to the blender and then I drink it straight from the cup. Violence tastes metallic and I wash it away with the sweetness of fruit.

I can ignore Alex calling me names because it's important that he's able to express his feelings. But I won't ignore drug-taking and it's a welcome coincidence that being admitted to the Bridge will take him out of Edinburgh.

David.

David, David, David.

It's only a matter of time before he turns up at the front door. Our pattern over the years has been thus:

he gets in touch, wants my attention for an intense week or two, then heads off again. Usually, though, there's not too much talk about our upbringing. The only other time he became obsessed with revisiting our childhood I was living in Leeds. I hadn't heard from him for almost a year, and unbeknownst to me, he found out my address, and infiltrated my life. One evening I returned home from work to find him sitting in my front room, telling my then boyfriend far too many details of our shared past. Details I'd kept quiet for good reason. And what I choose to share, or not share, is nobody's business but mine. Contrary to popular belief, it isn't always good to talk.

Katarina comes into the kitchen with a duster and some polish in her hand. She has earphones in her ears and is humming along to the music. She doesn't notice me at first, and when she does she screams and drops the polish on the tiled floor where it bounces and rolls, coming to a stop next to my foot. 'I am jumping out of my skin!' she says, pulling the earphones out. 'This saying we learn last week. It is correct?'

'Yes.' I give her a quick smile and hand her the tin of polish. 'Katarina, I've cancelled my clients today and I'm driving Alex to Glasgow where he'll be staying for a week, perhaps longer.'

'Yes, I understand.' She thinks for a moment. 'I prepare food for Tom?'

'No. Tom will be home much later this evening, later than me. He has a work's dinner.'

A shadow falls across the kitchen floor. Alex is standing there, a holdall in his right hand. 'I'm hungry.'

'We'll stop and buy you something on the way.' I walk past him into the front hall and grab my bag and keys. 'Let's go.'

'You will be well, Alex,' Katarina says. She gives him a kiss on both cheeks and then he follows me out to the car, docile as a subdued dog. I don't expect this mood to last and it doesn't. We've barely left the city boundaries when he starts trying to goad me.

'I didn't get to say goodbye to barrister Tom. The man with an eye for a good arse, wouldn't you say?' I feel his breath on my cheek. 'You seen the way he looks at Katarina?'

'You didn't clean your teeth,' I say. 'Your breath is fetid.'

'Fetid!' He laughs. 'Tom would happily give her one . . . if he hasn't already, that is. Do you think he has? Do you think?' He pauses. 'And I bet she takes it up the arse, as well.' He leans into my cheek again. 'Although . . . hang on. That'll be the way you like it too, Leila, yeah? All the men you've had, you must have something going for you. Cos all I can see is a washed-out tart. Droopy tits. Flabby arse.' He keeps up with the insults for another couple of miles. 'Chloe, I could shag,' he says. 'I reckon she knows her way around a man's cock. Well, it wouldn't be incest, would it?'

I pull sharply into a lay-by and his head hits off the side window. 'Ow!'

'Out,' I say.

'What?' He's rubbing the side of his face.

'Get out of the car!'

'No! I'm not getting out.'

'Then you'll stop talking filth! Are we clear?'

'This could be classed as child abuse.' He's still rubbing his cheek, his expression aggrieved. 'I could report you.'

'Alex.' I sigh. 'You're not a child.'

He turns away, his body hunched against me. I drive another twenty miles before he speaks again. 'Maybe I can't help myself. There's a gene, you know? A gene for addiction. If I knew who my father was that might give me a clue.'

'Your father never took drugs,' I say.

'How can you be sure? Maybe he did. Before or after you met him.'

I can't tell him that I've kept track of his father all these years and that I'm sure drugs aren't his thing. I let him whinge on about his life and then he shifts his perspective wider. 'This is going to cost you thousands.'

'I'll find the money.'

'Will you ask Tom for it?'

'Maybe.' I leave the motorway and start to journey north.

'What have you told him?'

'Nothing as yet.'

'What if Tom finds out? What if he notices that I'm gone?'

'Of course he'll notice,' I say, not entirely believing it.

'What if he realises that your son's fucked up? What are you going to tell him – that you've sent me off Wwoofing? You like that sort of thing don't you? World wide organic farming. A nice, healthy pursuit for people like me.'

'I'm going to tell him the truth,' I say. 'I'm not ashamed of you, Alex. I want you to do better – I *know* you can do better – so I'm not always proud of you but that's not the same as being ashamed of you.'

'Sounds pretty fucking samey to me.'

'If you don't go back to rehab, you'll spend the summer falling deeper and deeper into drug-taking.'

'So you say.'

'You need to break the cycle. They're experts at the Bridge. You know that.'

'I'll be out of your way.'

'That's not what I want. Please stop seeing me as the enemy.' I point to a sign at the side of the road. 'Look! Hot food in fifty yards.' I indicate and pull into the lay-by, where food is being sold from a caravan. 'Fancy a bacon butty?'

He grudgingly agrees, hunger trumping moodiness.

We sit in the car in companionable silence eating our sandwiches, and then we continue on to the Bridge where we're met by Rob Mooney, who welcomes Alex like an old friend. 'Good to see you, Alex.' They shake hands and Rob claps Alex on the back, pulling him towards him. 'You've done the right thing by coming back. We'll get you settled in straight away and then you'll be in time for afternoon group work.'

'Anyone here I know?' Alex says.

'There will be a couple, I think.' Rob glances across at me. 'Now why don't you say goodbye to your mum? She has a fair old drive back to Edinburgh.'

Alex turns to hug me and Rob wanders out of earshot so that we can say our goodbyes in private. 'I know you're nervous, darling, but this really is for the best,' I say. This isn't what Alex wants to hear and he moves away from me to stare fixedly down at his shoes. 'You'll soon rediscover a more positive focus. The therapists will help you with that.' He hugs me again, tightly this time, then he slopes off, turning just the once to give me a surreptitious wave.

When he's through the door I go back to my car and sit with my eyes closed. Crying is not something I do. I used to, but I stopped when I was fourteen. On my fourteenth birthday to be exact. I stopped because it felt more powerful not to cry. I developed other ways to relieve pressure. Other ways to feel like I was coping.

Before I leave the car park I call Maurice. He is still my therapist – has been for twenty years now – and he is also my supervisor. I meet with him every month to discuss any concerns I have with my clients and I normally add on another hour for myself.

'Maurice? It's Leila.'

'Leila.' He pauses. I hear muffled noises in the background. 'How are you?'

'I know we're not due to meet for another couple of weeks but I need to see you.'

'I'm away at the moment, Leila, but I will be home next Monday. How about Tuesday evening?'

'That's . . .' My jaw tenses. 'That's six days away. I'm not . . .' I pull my spine straight. 'I really need to talk to you.'

'I'm sorry, Leila. You know I would see you sooner if I could.'

'I understand.' I look down at my free hand as it rests on the steering wheel, the same hand that pressed against my son's throat, preventing him from breathing. 'What time on Tuesday evening?'

'Shall we say seven?'

'Okay.'

'And, Leila?'

'Yes?'

'If you need to talk to me before that, call me, will you? I can always listen on the phone.'

'I will.'

I end the call and stare down at my hands, flex and extend the fingers, and try not to remember what they're capable of.

The radio blares on the drive home, filling my head with sound that doesn't allow me time to think. I bring the car to a stop in the driveway and at once Mrs Patterson appears. She's in her nineties, stick thin and gimlet-eyed. 'Leila!' She waves a blue-veined hand at me.

'Hello, Mrs Patterson.' I smile. 'How are we today?'

'Well, I don't know about you, my dear, but I'm feeling quite *spooked.*'

'And why is that?' I say.

'There's been a *man* hanging about. I noticed him yesterday along at the park but I thought nothing of it. Then *today* he was there again and he doesn't have a *dog.* Or a *child.*' She pauses to let this significant information sink in. 'And your young housekeeper let him in.' She pauses again, triumphant this time. 'And I'm not sure that's what you would want.' She leans on the front gate and the cat climbs up beside her. He fixes feline eyes on me, daring me to knock him off.

'Let me go inside and find out who he is,' I say.

'He's gone *now,*' Mrs Patterson says. 'But I thought you should know!' she shouts after me.

'Thank you!' I unlock the front door and close it firmly behind me before calling out, 'Katarina!'

'I am in here!' She's in the living room watching television. She stands up when I come in. 'It is only news. Good for English.'

'Yes, I know.' I smile, and register the falseness in my expression when I catch sight of my face in the mirror above the mantelpiece. 'I bumped into Mrs Patterson just now. Apparently she spied a man hanging about at the end of the street today and you let him into the house.'

'That is David!' Katarina says, smiling as she says his name, imagining that I'll be pleased.

'David?'

'Your brother.'

'Okay.' I hold up a finger. 'Did he touch anything? Did you leave him alone at any point? How long was he here for?'

Katarina's eyebrows collide and then she says, her tone a feeble whine, 'He is your brother.'

'I asked you three questions. Please answer them.'

'He was here ten minutes. He is alone when he go to toilet—'

'Are you an idiot?' I grab her shoulders to shake her but she instantly becomes a dead weight and I'm not strong enough to hold her upright. So I drop her. Her head catches on the edge of the coffee table and she lets out a wail. 'Never, I repeat, NEVER let anyone, especially my brother through my front door again. Do you understand me?' I'm towering over her and she stares up at me, quietly weeping. 'Do you understand me, Katarina?'

'You cannot treat me so bad!' she whimpers, her face a crumple of flesh.

'I can treat you however I like,' I say quietly. My right foot is inches from her head and it takes a supreme effort of will not to kick her, but then she's already down so why would I need to? Instead I squat down beside her. 'Do not tell Tom about this,' I say. Her eyes are wide and wet with tears. 'He doesn't know about my brother.' I stroke her hair back from her face. 'You understand, don't you?' She nods. 'Some things are better kept just between us.' My fingers are gentle as they circle the bump on her forehead but still I feel her shiver. 'You need to put some ice on your head.' I stand up. 'And there's some arnica cream in my bathroom cabinet. Help yourself.'

I go straight to the garden hut and smoke three roll-ups, one after the other. The early-evening air is damp and fresh. I breathe deeply and then cough as the air and cigarette smoke mingle and fight deep inside my lungs. David? . . . In my home? . . . My instincts were right but still, so soon? What the fuck does he expect from me? Haven't I given him enough already?

Thank Christ Alex is already at the Bridge, in an environment of no phone calls, no Internet access and no visitors. Who would have thought there'd be a silver lining to him taking drugs again?

There is a rustling in the bushes to my left and when I swivel round I see the cat, as bold as brass, casually grooming himself. 'You again,' I say out loud. He glances up at me and gives a soft meow before resuming his grooming. I swipe at him with my foot and he crawls under the bush. 'Fuck off and die,' I say. 'If you know what's good for you.'

I finish smoking and call David. He answers at once. 'Leila, I know what you're going to say.'

'You do?'

'I was passing and—'

'Were you passing yesterday too?' Silence. 'My neighbour is a watcher and she told me that you've been loitering, and if you do it again she'll call the police. But you won't be doing it again – why would you? – unless you want to aggravate me and why would you want to do that?'

'Leila—'

'Stay the fuck away from my house, David. I am warning you.'

I end the call and stand stock-still for a minute, thinking . . . thinking about the violence I witnessed as a child, and not all of it perpetrated by my stepfather. Some of the violence was mine. Some of it was David's. We were both capable of so much more than I care to remember. *Give as good as you get.* What could possibly be wrong with that? We were children: young, impressionable, mouldable children.

When I go back inside, Katarina is nowhere to be seen. I climb the stairs to my bedroom and open up the walk-in wardrobe where I keep the jewellery that used to be my mother's. She gave them to me 'to look after' when I was still a child. The set comprises earrings, a necklace and a bracelet – gold inlaid with precious stones, including sapphires and diamonds. I had the pieces valued a few years ago and they were worth over twenty thousand pounds. The design is dated, and I've never worn any of the pieces, but I've always kept them because they belonged to her. My father bought them for her. 'That was when I was at my happiest,' she told me and, true or not, I choose to believe her, hanging onto the fact of my DNA, my father a good man who died from a rogue cancer that stole him away from us before I was old enough to even make a memory of him.

Since I've been living with Tom, I store the set in a black lacquer box with several drawers and a lid that bends backwards at an angle to reveal a secret space in the base. The box and the rest of its contents must have belonged to Tom's mother, although I've never got round to asking him; it's not the sort of thing he's interested in, the minutiae of life bores him.

Tom and I have separate finances. With my university teaching and my therapy practice I earn a good salary, but not enough to afford Alex's treatment. Converting Tom's study into my practice room cost me a small fortune and I now regret insisting on paying for it myself. I have enough money saved to cover one treatment week but after that I'll need to come up with another plan.

I hold the necklace up to the light and watch the stones dance. I'm not sure I will be able to part with the pieces. My mum is long dead and most of the recollections I have of her are poor ones; this is one of the only positive memories that remains. However, while the thought of selling the pieces makes me feel disappointed, I'm not prone to sentimentality and if it's a case of making ends meet then so be it.

First, though, I'll ask Tom. If I catch him at the right moment and use all my powers of persuasion to make him understand how much I need the money, he might just come through for me. And for Alex.

We'll see.

6. Ellen

I wake up in the early hours of the morning, my pulse racing as it always does. I immediately get out of bed to do my checks. I begin at the front door: it's double-locked and the chain is firmly in place. The hallway has one double socket: empty. I walk through each of the three bedrooms, looking behind bedside tables and chairs. The kitchen preoccupies me for a while. I touch each of the knobs on the hob; they are firmly in the off position. The hob light is off and the rings aren't even remotely warm. The kettle, the toaster, the blender and the microwave are all unplugged. I've stopped using my tumble dryer – it's permanently unplugged – and I only use the washing machine if I'm in the house and able to watch it.

Fires caused by white goods: three and a half thousand last year. Deaths: twelve. I've become someone who googles – my searches stack up in my browsing history like prophecies of doom: causes of fires in the UK, death by fire, fire service reports, electrical fires, the overwhelming effects of smoke inhalation. The results both fan and dampen my obsession. Dampen because house fires are unusual and in our modern world of smoke alarms people rarely die. But my obsessive flames are fanned by bad-luck stories where, for example, a plumber uses his blowtorch to bend the pipes servicing a radiator and a spark from the blowtorch finds its way into the insulation between the plasterboard inside walls and the brick exterior. The house burns slowly, as the family sleeps, the fire smouldering inside the very skin of the building until the whole structure collapses inwards and ignites the bedsheets.

Over an hour has gone by when I climb back into bed. I've been there about three seconds when my feet hit the floor again and I recheck the front door. It's still reassuringly double-locked. I release the chain and redo it, sliding the metal along the bar until it connects with the round slot that keeps it anchored.

I'm wide awake now and I prop a couple of pillows up behind my head. Chloe bought me a Kindle for my last birthday and I like to keep up with the books she reads for her book club. I spend ten minutes trying to get into the novel she recommended to me, and despite normally preferring fact to fiction, I'm soon swept up in the story.

I read for an hour and then I retrace my steps through the house, checking and rechecking. When I turn off the light and rest my head on the pillow, I think back over my day and my thoughts settle on Francis, how easy he was to talk to and how refreshing it was for me to be myself. Perhaps I've cared too much about what people think of me. What's wrong with admitting I need help? What's wrong with friends and family knowing that I'm anxious? I haven't wanted them to worry; I've always protected them. I'm a mother and a daughter, a teacher who knows her subject inside out, a friend who is there in times of need. I've never been the one who needs help.

But now I do need help and next time Chloe comments on my behaviour I'm going to try to be honest with her, let her see me as I am. Not be afraid to be vulnerable.

I fall asleep around three, dozing on and off until eight thirty when the phone rings. It's Tom – he rarely calls me and I expect he's got wind of my meeting with my solicitor. I'm disinclined to speak to him but just in case it concerns Chloe or Ben, I answer. 'Tom.'

'Ellen.' He's straight to the point. 'I understand you're meeting your solicitor today. I was hoping for the agreement to be signed but when I called him just now he told me you want to renegotiate.'

'That's right.'

'Why?'

'I'm not happy with it.'

'So what's changed?'

'Hold on.' I cover the mouthpiece and breathe. The sound of his voice causes conflicting emotions inside me: fondness and suspicion, comfort and dread, a smile and a frown. 'I don't want to talk about it, Tom,' I say. 'My solicitor will be in touch with you after I've met him today.'

'Is that really necessary?' His tone is soft. 'Ellen, I know this last year has been hard on you. It's been hard on me too. Change is never easy—'

'How, Tom? How has this last year been hard on you?'

'I miss our family—'

'You broke our family.'

'Ellen. I think you and I both know it wasn't quite as simple as that.'

'Wasn't it? For six months you were leading a double life. You slept with another woman. You cheated, you lied, you left me.'

He sighs. The truth is always very tedious to Tom, especially when it shows him in a bad light. 'What is it you want, Ellen? Half my pension?'

'In the eyes of the law, I am entitled to it.'

'So you want more money?'

'You know what? Yes, I do. We were a team, Tom, you and I, and after twenty-eight years of marriage I'm pleased to say the law doesn't support your inclination to leave me with as little as you can get away with.'

'You agreed to the terms.'

'And you agreed to put our house on the market but instead you moved your woman in and have allowed her free rein.'

The phone goes dead. I punch the air with a soft fist and make breakfast, humming as I do so, pleased to have the upper hand.

I'm still feeling strong and determined when I meet with my solicitor, a grizzly man called Hamish who is close to retirement. 'I'm glad to see you've decided not to sign. He was getting away far too lightly.' He shakes his head. 'It was bothering me that we were giving in too easily and you would regret it down the line.'

'I want the house,' I say. I tell him that my dad is willing to sell up and come to live with me. 'I know they're making changes at Maybanks. They've already felled a one-hundred-year old tree. It was a beautiful feature in the garden. There was absolutely nothing wrong with it and in its place they've put a hot tub.'

He takes notes as I speak. 'How do you know this?'

'A neighbour told me,' I lie.

'There's no accounting for taste but the fact of the matter is that he shouldn't be making alterations to any of the marriage assets until he is sure they are part of his settlement.' He carries on writing as he speaks. 'What I will do is send him a letter telling him that circumstances have now changed. Your father is willing to sell his house, which means you can buy Tom out of

Maybanks. I also suggest we ask for half his pension and request that he declare any further assets.'

I nod. I haven't had the courage to do this up to now. Hamish had tried to persuade me to push for financial disclosure but I had resisted his advice because I was overwhelmed by the reality of divorce, never mind the division of the spoils. It hasn't felt real to me until now, until I went to Maybanks and saw that time had moved on and left me behind. I'm late to the party but I'm determined to catch up.

Hamish assures me he'll write to Tom at once and I come out into the sunshine to meet Chloe, Molly and my dad who are waiting for me in Princes Street Gardens. The castle looms large behind the strip of gardens, a once-upon-a-time moat. Chloe is sitting on a bench watching my dad and Molly, who are running up and down passing a miniature rugby ball. When Chloe sees me approaching she stands up. 'Did you do it?' she says.

'I did. Hamish is sending your dad a letter asking for the house as part of a renegotiation.'

'Oh my God! That's brilliant!' She hugs me and shouts, 'Granddad!'

'I'm a coming!' my dad calls back. He lifts Molly up over his shoulder, 'Fireman's lift!' and runs towards us, his jacket flapping and Molly's legs kicking.

He places her down on her feet in front of me and she catches onto my trousers as she balances herself. 'I'm going to find a squirrel now, Grannie,' she says and zigzags off along the path.

We follow behind her, walking more slowly, and I fill them in on what was said. 'I don't expect he'll just roll over and give it to you, Ellen,' my dad says. 'But stay strong, and in the meantime I'll get the house valued and ready to go on the market.'

'The uber-bitch won't want to leave the house,' Chloe says. 'Not now she's got her therapy practice there.'

'Well, it's not about what she wants,' I say. 'They both jumped the gun, what with moving Tom's study and chopping down the tree.'

Chloe looks at me sideways. 'How do you know about the tree?'

'Mrs Patterson,' I say quickly. 'I bumped into her.'

'Thank heavens you know! I wanted to tell you but I just couldn't. I was horrified when I saw it was gone.'

She tells my dad all about it and I watch his expression change from surprise to disgust and then disbelief. 'Why would they do that?' he says. 'There's plenty of room in the garden for a hot tub. They didn't need to take the tree down.'

'She likes order,' Chloe says. 'She's one of those women who values the neat and tidy over anything that might be natural and a bit messy. No wonder her son is so screwed up.'

'Is he?' I say.

'I think so. And so does Ben. He's not weird exactly, but he's awkward and he laughs in the wrong places, says inappropriate things. More like a fifteen- than a nineteen-year-old.'

'In a piranha-filled river the monkey drinks with a straw,' my dad says, tapping the side of his nose.

Chloe and I look at each other with questioning expressions. 'That one's lost on us, Dad,' I say.

'Just be careful, is all,' my dad says. He jogs off after Molly, who's balancing on the edge of the fountain, and shouts behind him, 'The battle is on, Ellen. You need to mind your back!'

Mind my back? . . . Leila's the one who needs to mind her back. The antipathy I feel towards her is crystallising inside me. I feel the rub of it against my sternum when I breathe in, reminding me of her existence, reminding me that she's a sitting duck.

Francis pops in again on his way back from the hospice and I'm more pleased to see him than seems right, considering that we've only recently met. 'I was worried you wouldn't come back,' I say. 'What with me moaning on about my husband and his new woman.'

'Everyone's entitled to a good moan,' he says.

We have a cup of tea and then I end up asking him to stay for something to eat. 'My son Ben is out this evening,' I tell him. 'And I'm not much good at cooking for one.'

'I'd love to stay,' he says. 'But let me go out and buy some wine or something.'

'Not necessary. Honestly. I have a couple of bottles waiting to be drunk.'

'Okay. Next time then,' he says, settling back on the sofa. My heart lifts at the mention of a next time because I'm lonely more often than I care to admit. I haven't acknowledged just how much in need of company I am, the right sort of company where I can be myself, be honest, no need to hide the truth.

We sit down to a meal of chicken and salad, and I listen to Francis talk about his mum, what a great friend and support she's been to him. 'I know she's eighty-five,' he says. 'But I just don't feel ready to lose her.'

'Grief is tough,' I say. 'I lost my mum about ten years ago now.'

'The death of a relationship can be almost as bad,' Francis says.

'That's true.' I pass him the serving dish of salad. 'It's taken me a full year to get used to the fact that Tom and I are now separated.'

'Is the therapy helping?'

'I've only been for one session so far but yes, I think it will help.' I smile and drink some wine. 'She seems very . . . good at her job. Her name's Leila Henrikson. Have you come across her?'

He shakes his head. 'Her name doesn't ring any bells.'

'Sharon recommended her.' I pour some more wine into Francis's glass and then mine. 'As well as the CBT, we'll be talking about how I'm handling the break-up.' I stare down into my glass. 'I went to see my solicitor and we're going through all the nitty-gritty of the divorce. I had agreed to let Tom have the house but now I want it back.' I explain about my dad's property. 'My dad could live in the annexe at the side of Maybanks. Of course Tom and his new woman don't want to leave. She has her . . .' I stop speaking – my mouth is running away with me and I'm about to say 'therapy rooms in there' but I stop myself because Francis doesn't know that Tom left me for a therapist, otherwise he might put two and two together and realise that Tom's therapist and my therapist are one and the same person. Being understanding of my OCD is one thing, being party to my deception is another. I don't want him thinking I'm the crazy, avenging ex-wife so I end the sentence with, '. . . own way a lot. So Chloe tells me.'

'You said before that you were plotting revenge.'

'Did I?' I give a short laugh. 'Wishful thinking.' All of a sudden I feel the onset of sadness and I blink away tears. Less than an hour ago I was feeling happy because I could be honest with Francis, and now here I am lying.

'Do you still love him?' Francis says. His hand reaches across the table to mine. He's concerned for me. He thinks my change in mood is because I'm thinking about how much I love Tom.

'No . . . yes.' I shrug. 'There's a side of me that will always love him but I know that we don't fit together any more. Like it or not, we've reached the end of the road. He's chosen someone else and I'm finding that time on my own is not so bad.' I smile.

Francis lets go my hand and raises his glass. 'Here's to you, Ellen.'

I raise my glass too and feel brave enough to hold his eyes, see kindness and warmth there and think that maybe, just maybe, I'll be able to be completely truthful with him. Not yet, though.

Not yet.

Tuesday, and I'm close to Maybanks when I catch sight of Mrs Patterson in the distance, her cat Bruiser following at her heels. I change direction and approach the house the long way round, my face averted. I'm through the front gate and down the side of the house, about to ring the bell to the annexe, when I hear the front door open and Tom's voice say, 'Honestly, darling, it's not worth worrying about.'

I press myself against the brick wall, holding my breath.

'I won't make any alternative plans yet then,' Leila replies.

Tom says something else that I can't make out but I can hear that his tone is gentle. And all I can do is keep quiet, screw my eyes up tight and pray. I anticipate a heavy hand on my shoulder. I'm fully expecting to be marched to the police station, or at the very least humiliated in the street, a freak show for passers-by, the ex-wife turning up as the spectre at the lovers' feast to cast her ugly spell.

I hear a vehicle pull up, and I open one eye to peer

along the edge of the wall. It's a black cab. Tom must be going to the airport.

'See you tomorrow,' I hear him say. He moves along the path towards the front gate and I glimpse the side of his body. He's wearing a navy suit and brown brogues and my attention is drawn to his hands, hands that held me and stroked me, and now they're stroking Leila. She's leaning into him, whispering something in his ear. Seeing them like this makes me feel sick but I am compelled to torture myself by watching them; I reach my head out a little bit further.

Tom laughs and pulls away from Leila, his eyes lingering on her cleavage before rising to her eyes. 'Hold that thought,' he says. He touches her face with his right hand, running the back of his hand over her cheekbone, and when it reaches her lips she kisses his fingers and takes his hand in hers, leading him to the cab door. I could be standing in the middle of the driveway and he still wouldn't see me because his focus is all for her.

The cab drives off and Leila stands on the pavement watching until it disappears round the corner. When she turns back towards the house, she spots me standing outside the annexe. 'Mary!' She walks towards me, smiling, and then her mobile goes off. She glances at the screen and frowns. 'I'll be with you directly, Mary.' She veers off the driveway and through the front door to take the phone call and I have time to process what I've just witnessed.

They are in love with each other. I suppose I should have known this but somehow it never occurred to me – I thought it was all about sex. I thought it was about lust and shagging and the hormonal rush of desire that fades within a year. I didn't need to witness the genuinely loving glance that passed from Tom to Leila. I didn't need to see their closeness, the held hands and the gentle touch. It has sucked all the good feeling out of me and left a bitter emptiness behind.

Frustrated with myself – my stupidity, my feelings still so open to being hurt – I stare around in anger, my eyes alighting on the hacked magnolia tree and the tamed flower border, and then, feeling reckless, I stare through the kitchen window. *My* kitchen, minus my display dishes and photographs but otherwise *my* kitchen. I experience a sharp pang of nostalgia for family times round the table: happy birthdays, epic family Christmases and the simple pleasure of everyday meals with my children.

I duck my head down when Leila walks into the kitchen and moments later she opens the door to the annexe and ushers me inside. 'Sorry about that.' She looks tired, harassed even. 'I was just seeing my partner off.'

'No problem,' I say, my smile false. *How can she not see what's going on here? How can she not sense how much I detest her? How much I want to see her fall?* 'Is he off somewhere nice?'

She ignores my question and points to the armchair. I expect there's some therapist's rule about boundaries, not allowing clients to become too close, not allowing clients to form attachments or find out about your personal circumstances. Well, it's a bit late for that, Leila Henrikson, UKCP accredited therapist. We have an attachment all right and it's not a healthy one. It began when you started an affair with a married man. My married man.

She begins by welcoming me back and then says, 'How has the last week been?' Her lipstick has been kissed off. There's a small ladder in her stocking – I expect she will be wearing stockings, not tights. Her cheeks are flushed. It's not difficult to surmise that they just had sex. Where, I wonder? On the bed that Tom and I bought in the new year sales five years ago? Or perhaps on the sofa in the living room where our children did their homework and watched *The Simpsons*? Or maybe they had sex standing up in the hallway, her back against the wallpaper that my dad and I hung one Christmas holiday?

How I want to slap her smug face, hard and fast so that she's knocked off her feet. But not now. Not yet. I'm going to be a good pupil. I'm going to play along. I'm going to tell her what she wants to hear in much the same way that teenagers in my class pretend to have completed the work I set them. So I tell her that I've been practising the exposure therapy exercise (I've only done it the once, when I didn't unplug the kettle and Francis knocked on the door to return my scarf) and know that it's helping me because I'm not so anxious (I'm not as anxious as I normally am because I spend a lot of my time being angry). 'It's a bit like the difference between loud noise and background noise,' I say. 'I know that the anxiety is still there but it's not so noticeable. The exercises are like a shield, almost, a way of taming the anxiety, if that makes sense.'

She says it does and congratulates me on my efforts so far. 'Habitual behaviour will kick in every now and then, so don't be disappointed with yourself when it does. Just sit it out.'

'I will.' I smile. 'I'm optimistic.'

'So let's talk about the second aspect to CBT, which is dealing with negative thought patterns.' She takes a breath and I do the same. 'You mentioned your recent separation and the fact that your husband was having an affair. How do you think this has impacted on your way of thinking?'

I consider this for a second. 'I felt like a failure.' I pause before adding, 'I felt ashamed and . . . hopeless, really. Like my life was out of control and everything that had gone before was now worthless. I put so much energy into my marriage and my children – yes, I'm a teacher, but I'm not career-minded. I'm all about family . . . and home.'

'Are you still living in your home?'

'No.'

'How does that make you feel?'

'My house has been sold.' I shrug. 'I'm living some-where smaller now and that's fine.' The lie slides effortlessly off my tongue. 'It was time for me to move on from there. But the woman?' I shake my head and stare through the window. I watch Bruiser stroll across the grass and find a space for himself under his favourite hydrangea bush, a bush he's been using as his resting spot for more than ten years. I wonder whether Leila's got into the habit of giving him extra snacks like I always did. I had a packet of cat treats just inside the kitchen door and when I was hanging out the washing he would circle my ankles until I fetched him a titbit.

'The woman,' I repeat. 'She makes me angry. Fucking angry, actually because I now realise that I've been too passive.' I laugh. 'Normally I don't swear much but then maybe it's time I did swear. I'm long overdue for some anger. I'm long overdue for putting me on centre stage. The woman—' I bite my tongue. I'm about to say 'is a lot like you, but it would give me away, surely?'

Leila allows the silence to expand around us for some time before she breaks it with, 'You say you felt like a failure and that you felt ashamed – using the past tense.'

'Yes.' I nod. This I can talk about. 'I've been thinking about my marriage and I've realised a lot, actually. My husband wasn't an easy man to live with. He isn't a family man, nor is he a team player, and I spent a lot of time making excuses for him. He loved the children and me, of course, but he was often moody and self-absorbed. Family life didn't suit him. He liked his own way and it's a relief not to have to pander to him any more.' I smile as the truth of this lightens the load on my chest.

'You had to manage his moods?'

'Yes, I did. And I've realised over this past year that I don't want him back. I would never be able to trust him again anyway,' I say. 'And surely the woman he left me for must know that what he did to me he could so easily do to her.'

'Does it matter what the woman thinks?'

'It matters to me that she thinks she's got away with it.'

'What has she got away with?'

'Ruining my life.' I feel defiant and I stare at Leila, waiting for her to defend this woman, defend herself. Leila holds my stare, her return gaze softer than mine. I can feel my defiance set hard in the line of my mouth and the length of my back.

'What would you like to say to this woman?' Leila asks me.

'I'd like to tell her that I'm going to get her back. I'm not sure how yet. But I will.' I gulp some air and smile. 'I will get her back.'

6. Leila

'Why are you sitting in the dark?'

Tom switches on the light and I squint against it. 'I was drifting off,' I say.

He bends down and kisses me. 'Busy day?'

I took Alex to rehab. That's what I should say.

Or maybe I should start with – Did I mention, Tom, that my son has a drug problem? And that just before I met you he was in rehab for a month. It cost me £25,000 and no end of worry. I hoped we would never go back there again. But we have. And I should also mention that my brother, who is on a mission to reconnect with our past, has been to our house. And no good can come of that. No good at all.

Except, I don't have to tell him about David because Mrs Patterson has beat me to it.

'Mrs Patterson hijacked me again.' He removes his tie and then begins to unbutton his shirt. His chest is completely hairless and it strikes me that I prefer men to have chest hair. 'She told me there's a man been loitering in the street and that Katarina let him in.' He throws his shirt into the linen basket. 'Is he her boyfriend?'

'No.'

'You've asked her then?'

'No.' I've forgotten that my mother's necklace is still on my knee and when I stand up it slides to the floor. 'He's not anyone.'

'How can he not be anyone?'

'Because Mrs Patterson is a lonely old lady with nothing better to do than spy on her neighbours.' I pick up the necklace and touch the stones with my fingers, sightlessly registering the shape of each stone before moving onto the next. 'One day she's going on about her cat, the next day it's a strange man.' I shrug. 'She seems to forget that clients are coming here all the time and sometimes they knock on the front door instead of the annexe.'

'So he was a client?'

'Yes. Probably.' Tom's persistence is beginning to irritate me, and tiredness makes me foolishly decide to compound my lies with more information. 'I think he was hoping for an extra session.'

'Why do you think that?'

'Because of what Katarina said.'

'What did she say?'

'Her English isn't great so I couldn't quite get the hang of it.' I rub my forehead. 'But it definitely sounded like he was a client.'

'And he couldn't have called you on the phone?' Tom has his trousers off by now and is standing in his boxers, not the baggy sort, the sort that hugs contours and leaves nothing to the imagination. His physique is sculpted by thrice-weekly body-work with his personal trainer. It's not just about health with Tom – he is vain. He needs to be the alpha male. And he needs other people to know it.

'Sometimes, in the early stages of therapy, clients become very dependent on their therapist.' I seem to be swaying on my feet. 'They see therapy as a safe zone.'

'Erotic transference?' he says.

'A little, maybe.'

'A downside to having your rooms at home. That was something I didn't consider.'

Julie Corbin

Like it was up to him. 'It's very common. It happens to therapists all the time. It's usually a passing . . .' I wave the necklace '. . . phase.'

'Are you drunk?'

'No, I'm not drunk.' I laugh. 'If anything, I could do with a drink.'

'What's wrong?' He places a steadying hand on my elbow. He is concerned, but underneath the concern is a kernel of impatience. He would have preferred me in a negligee, holding out his single malt, perfectly chilled in a crystal glass. (The glass is important.)

I feel emotionally drained and I'm tempted to brush it – him – off but when Tom is focused he's like a dog with a bone and so I give him something to chew on. 'I took my son to rehab today,' I say, following the words with a forced smile.

'What?'

'Alex has a drug problem,' I state. 'This is a matter of fact.'

He withdraws his hand and is silent for almost ten seconds as he thinks this through. All he can come up with is, 'I don't understand.' He frowns and shakes his head. 'Since when? Where has this come from? He's in *rehab*? Already? Is the problem so serious? How long has this been going on for? You can't get a place that quickly! Not for love nor—'

'Money? Yes, you can get a place that quickly if you can afford it – if you can call in a favour, as I am able to do, and if the client is already known to them.'

'He has an existing problem?'

'Yes.'

'And when were you going to tell me about that?' He looks hurt.

'Tom.' I stare down at the necklace. 'I've been a single

parent since Alex was born and so if it means that sometimes I forget to share information—' I shrug '—I'm sorry. I hoped that Alex was drug-free and would never take drugs again, but he's not, and he has, and it's been . . . a difficult day.'

He moves towards me and takes hold of my hands. 'You should have told me.'

'Would it have made a difference?'

'Of course!'

'In what way?'

'I would have helped you!' He half-shakes, half-hugs me. 'I would have come with you!'

'You're a criminal barrister and Alex is a drug-taker living in your home.'

'Our home, Leila! This is *our* home.'

It doesn't feel like that to me but then I have never felt a sense of home. I'm used to moving house, town, country even. I'm used to shifting sands, to rebalancing and recalibrating myself. 'Fear is at the root of everything,' I say quietly.

'For Alex? What's he afraid of?'

'Not just for Alex, for all of us.' I tug at the collar of my blouse and my fingers rest on the pulse in my neck. My pulse. My life. Life in all its fragile, bloody glory coursing through me. 'Fear is a driver for all of us.'

'Leila, please.' He takes me in his arms and starts to kiss me: my cheeks and my hair, my neck. 'I'm sorry. I can see you're upset. Why don't we get you to bed?'

'Yes.'

'I'm sorry darling, I haven't been much use to you lately, have I?'

It's true; Tom isn't much use. It was unlike me, but when we began our affair I had been cautiously optimistic. I hadn't just chosen Tom for myself – I'd chosen

him for Alex too. I knew that Tom was exactly the kind
of man Alex needed to spend time with. Human beings
rub off on one another and for all his faults, Tom is
nothing if not ambitious and purposeful. But Tom has
shown little interest in Alex up to now and that is disap-
pointing.

'How about we both go to see him at the weekend?'
he says.

'He's not allowed visitors.'

There's a darkness at the back of my skull. I rest my
forehead against Tom's shoulder because I want him to
stop talking now. He gets the message and starts to
undress me. I allow myself to become putty in his hands.
He peels off my clothes, item by item, kissing each part
of my skin as it's revealed to him. He's enjoying himself
– he has an erection to prove it. I feel almost nothing
but I go along with it because if I'm going to avoid
selling my mum's jewellery then I need to ask Tom to
lend me some money to pay for Alex's treatment.

Quid pro quo.

He takes me to bed and makes love to me, no effort
spared, and after a reasonable amount of time I fake an
orgasm and he falls asleep satisfied with his performance.

I'm exhausted but I don't fall asleep. I lie awake for
a while, thinking about David, about Alex, about myself.
And when my mind attempts to drill down into memory
and peer into the corners where my stepfather Gareth
lurks, I climb out of bed and go into the en suite bathroom, closing the door behind me. I stand in front of
the bathroom mirror and lean into the glass. I see weakness in my eyes and I don't like it. 'Where are you, Leila
Mae?' I whisper to my reflection. 'Where are you?' I
watch my expression flit from fear to neutral and then
to determined. The longer I stare the more I'm reassured.

Normally I prefer not to conjure up my teenage self because she doesn't sit well with the woman I've become but Leila Henrikson, the therapist, is a poor match for David.

When I find her, I breathe more easily. She's still in there, my teenage self, Leila Mae of the black eyes and the steady gaze. She is fearless. She is a survivor. She is me.

I swallow two sleeping pills before I go back to bed because I won't allow my mind to tempt me backwards in time. I won't think about Gareth. I never think about Gareth.

Tuesday comes round again and I'm feeling relieved because I've been counting the days until I can see Maurice, and at last it is today, this evening. I spend the morning catching up with admin and at midday I call the Bridge to see how Alex is doing.

'He's making progress,' Rob Mooney tells me. 'He has some unresolved issues but he's working through them.'

For five years Rob and I shared a therapy practice in Leeds and I know he is a master of understatement. The Bridge is a safe environment and I suspect Alex is kicking off. I can only imagine what he's saying about me – she expects too much, she always puts herself first, we've never been a proper family, she has boyfriends and then dumps them just as I'm getting to like them. And on top of all that, she says she loved my father but really he was just some guy she shagged and lost touch with. And she expects me to be moral.

On and on it will go.

David has been conspicuously quiet all week. I haven't spoken to him since last week when Katarina let him into the house. I wonder whether he's heard from John Lewis and whether he's got the job. It would be a departure from the norm as he usually works cash-in-hand jobs and it would make his stay in Edinburgh more permanent. He has always lived a nomadic lifestyle, picking up work here and there, never staying in one place for any length of time. So here I am daring to hope that he might have changed his mind about settling down to steady work and be planning his next trip abroad.

Tom has been working from home this morning and is flying to London mid-afternoon. He has been attentive and considerate all week and I feel myself softening towards him. Katarina is out shopping (I gave her a £100 bonus as way of apology for her banging her head. She's still wary of me but she couldn't say no to the money) and Tom joins me in the kitchen for lunch. I've made us both steak and chips and a green salad with a strong mustard dressing – his favourite. Throughout the meal he talks about his latest client and I'm able to ask the right questions, which encourages him to talk further. When we're finished I rinse the plates and he makes us both a coffee. We sit side by side on the sofa by the window that looks out into the back garden. The timing feels perfect.

'Tom,' I say. 'I wonder whether I could ask a favour of you.'

'Of course.' He takes my free hand onto his lap. 'What do you need?'

'I spoke to Rob Mooney at the Bridge this morning. Alex is doing well, but he does need to stay there for a further week, maybe two, depending on how he progresses, and I'm wondering whether you are able to lend me some money.'

He nods. 'How much?'

'It's expensive.' I widen my eyes. 'Ten thousand pounds.'

'Wow.' He pushes his breath out quickly. 'That really is expensive.'

'You don't get this sort of treatment on the NHS, or not until it's almost too late to make a difference. The therapists are experienced. The ratio of staff to clients is high and so the success rate is good.'

'How much did it cost you last time he was there?'

'It's five thousand pounds a week and he was there for five weeks.'

'I see.' We hold eye contact and I watch his thought processes. He's wondering how to let me down without it sounding like he's actually doing that. But the reasoning he comes up with is not what I expect. 'In principle, I want to be able to help, and I'm not saying I can't, but at the moment I'm having to deal with a financial issue myself.'

'Oh?'

'Ellen has now decided she isn't happy with the divorce agreement we've drawn up.'

'I thought it was all finalised. Wasn't she about to sign it?'

'She was but something has changed her mind. Her solicitor is now playing hardball, demanding that the marriage assets are frozen.' He waves his hand through the air in a circle. 'We're back to square one. We have a meeting scheduled for next week and I'll have to see what we can renegotiate.'

'Is she entitled to more?'

'In the eyes of the law, yes. She waived her rights to my pension and other monies we had saved. She didn't need to do that.' He sighs. 'She's now saying that she wants the house.'

'This house?'

'Yes.'

I stand up and move to the window. 'You told me she was happy to move out.'

'She was! She couldn't wait to get away from me.'

'But we've already started making the place our own.' I look at the extension and then at the spot where the oak tree once stood. Tom told me that for several years now he'd wanted the tree chopped down because its height and width dominated the space. The children had outgrown the tree house but Ellen loved it so it had stayed. I agreed that it was a light-stealer, and went along with Tom when he decided to have it felled. The hot tub wouldn't have been my first choice but I'd been persuaded that it was worth the expense and we'd enjoyed a couple of evenings under the stars with each other and a bottle of prosecco for company.

'I didn't tell you because I didn't want to worry you.' He stands behind me, wraps his arms round my waist. 'I'm not going to let her have the house but I might have to yield in other ways.'

'So this is the wrong time for me to be asking you to lend me money.' I lean back onto his chest. 'I'll apply for a loan . . .'

'Give me a couple of days,' he says. 'I'll see what I can do.'

I turn in his arms and kiss him on the lips. The kiss lights a fire inside us both and we have enough time for quick, hot sex on the sofa before I see him out the door and into the taxi. Mary McNeil has already arrived and I'm about to let her in when my mobile starts ringing. It's David. I ask Mary to wait a second and go back through the front door.

'David.'

'We need to meet,' he says.

'Why?'

'Say yes.' His voice shakes.

'David.'

'Say yes.'

Choice is often an illusion and I know that avoiding a meeting is not an option. He's already proved that he can find me and I don't want him bumping into Tom on the front path. 'Friday?'

'Okay.' He names a time and a place.

'I'll see you then.' I leave my mobile in the kitchen and open the door to Mary McNeil. I feel tense and tight-lipped but Mary is like a breath of fresh air. She has done well with her exposure therapy and is already noticing a reduction in her anxiety. Then we address her negative thought patterns. She talks frankly about her relationship with her husband and it becomes obvious to her that she is better off without him. She has feelings of anger towards the woman he left her for and I expect these feelings will need to be worked through, but we agree to leave that work for next week.

The fifty minutes with Mary pass quickly and before long Alison and Mark are in the room. Alison begins by telling me about an adoption party they attended over the weekend. The 'party' is for prospective parents to meet hard-to-place children, those who have been rejected on paper. 'It's the last chance for many of the children who then go on to long-term fostering,' Alison says. 'We were given a profile booklet to look through and we saw a couple of little girls we really liked.'

She stops talking and turns to Mark. He doesn't look back at her but continues staring ahead.

'Mark?' I say. 'Is there anything you would like to add?'

He shrugs. 'I have mixed feelings.'

'I knew it!' Alison says.

'Not about the adoption.' He gives her a scathing look. 'About those parties. It feels wrong.'

Alison sits back, folding her arms. 'I don't believe you.' Silence.

'Why do you say that, Alison?' I ask.

'I know him. I know how he thinks.' There follows twenty minutes of argument. Alison brings up everything she can think of – the fact that Mark once cheated on her, that he doesn't earn as much as her and that he drinks too much. 'A bottle of wine a night.' She points an accusing finger. '*That* makes you an alcoholic. And do I complain? Do I throw it in your face?'

'You're doing it now!'

'I'm not doing it now. I'm giving you an example of your faults so that you'll stop focusing on mine!'

The endless friction between the two of them begins to cramp my spine and I move around in my seat, my eyes flicking towards the clock on the wall.

'You wanted to come here!' Mark says.

'To make you see how selfish you are!' She goes on to cite more evidence – they always watch the programmes he likes on TV, they never eat pasta because he doesn't like it, he wants to go to the theatre so they go; she wants to go clubbing but they never go. I keep my mouth firmly shut, hoping she will burn herself out and we can spend the rest of the session in quiet reflection. No such luck.

'I don't understand why we have to keep talking about this stuff!' Mark shouts and both Alison and I jump. 'I just want to know whether we should adopt a baby, for fuck's sake!'

'Enough!' I yell, banging my fists on the arms of the

chair. 'When are you two going to realise that no two people see things exactly the same way? When are you going to give each other space to express feelings without judgement?' They both stare at me, stunned. 'And neither of you are willing to listen or to compromise. It has to stop!'

'The adoption?' Alison murmurs, wide-eyed.

'Do you believe you're ready to become parents?' I say. 'Honestly? Look at yourselves! Imagine a child in between you, listening to this, being pulled one way and then the other depending on your moods.' I pause to allow my temper to wane. I take several deep breaths, while Alison and Mark sit before me with their mouths open. 'You need to reflect.' My voice is quieter now but I know I'm hanging on by a thread. 'You need to decide whether you want to stay together and, God alone knows, you need to put some hard work into being a couple before you even consider becoming a family.'

I stand up and open the door. 'The session is over,' I say, and they scuttle off down the path, meek as mice. When they reach the end of the driveway they both look back, questioning. I'm standing with my arms crossed and my face reflecting everything I feel about the way they behave – self-indulgent, craven and cowardly complaining. I have no time for it. Not today. Alison grabs Mark's hand and they disappear along the pavement as if they're being pursued.

I close the door behind them and return to my consulting room knowing that I've crossed a line. I've shocked myself, never mind them. I have never before shouted at clients. No matter what I might have thought, I have always identified with their journey and, in doing so, kept my feelings to myself. I've been endlessly patient, relentlessly understanding.

This is a stress reaction. Everyone has a threshold and I have hit mine. And I know what happens next. Black. My head fills with a dense black cloud, like thick smoke, and then . . . and then.

'I need help, Maurice,' I say out loud, to the walls, to the windows and to the cloudy grey sky. 'Help me. Please.'

7. Ellen

If you take something back that's yours, is it stealing?

I've spent the morning sorting through a couple of the boxes in the hallway, and when I tipped out a plastic bag of odds and ends I found the key to Maybanks' back door. I sat down on the sofa and held the key in my hand contemplating whether or not I should use it. When I left the house a year ago I took most of my belongings with me, but I'd been rushing, because I wanted to be on my way before Tom came home from work, and so I forgot some of my things, the most important of which was the jewellery box from my bedroom. I realised my mistake almost at once and while I knew that I still had the back-door key in one of the boxes, I had never had the courage to even contemplate using it. I thought about asking Chloe or Ben to see whether they could fetch the box for me, but decided it wasn't fair to involve the children, so I emailed Tom. I emailed him twice. He told me he would drop it off. He didn't. I emailed him again and he said he'd pass it on to Ben or Chloe to give to me but he never did and I stopped asking.

The black lacquer box was my grandmother's and when she died she left the box and its contents to me. I'd played with the rings and brooches all through my childhood – it was part of a dressing-up game that I was so fond of – and for months I'd been hoping to get the box returned to me. It's not about the money or the sentiment, it's about a sense of continuity, a link with my past and with a woman who loved me.

I'm still holding the key and wrestling with the notion of housebreaking when Chloe pops in for a coffee. 'I smell baking!'

'Flapjacks.' I slip the key into my pocket.

'Beats the smell that's normally in here,' Chloe says. She glances into the kitchen. 'And still those black numbers on the sockets. The landlord hasn't been to sort the electricity out either then?'

I switch the kettle on and say, 'Not yet.'

It's my opportunity to confess that the numbers have nothing to do with the landlord and that I was the one who used the black marker pen. The words are on the tip of my tongue but before I can say them out loud I chicken out. I try to tell myself that it's because I'm optimistic that I'm gradually putting all this compulsion and anxiety behind me, but if I can't be honest with my daughter then the least I can do is be honest with myself: I don't tell her because, if I do, she won't let it go. (She has her father to thank for that personality trait.) She'll ask me to explain what's been happening, she'll want to know all the whys and the wherefores, she'll apply her nurse's knowledge and then she'll ask me what I'm doing about it, who I'm seeing. What therapist? What treatment? She'll probe and she'll pry until I end up telling her about Leila, and then what will she say?

I know my daughter and I'm sure she'll tell me to stop. She'll tell me it's beneath me and that I'll only get hurt. She'll tell me to keep her dad and Leila at arm's length and use legal means to secure a decent financial settlement. The house should be my focus, that's what she'll tell me. Keep your eye on the prize, Mum. Get the house back. That will be your revenge.

'Where's Molly?' I say, over the noise of the kettle boiling.

'Gymnastics. And Granddad has a plumber coming to fix one of the radiators. All part of getting the house ready to put on the market.' She hands me a couple of mugs and I add coffee and the boiled water. Chloe adds the milk. 'Have you heard back from your solicitor?'

I nod. 'Your dad and I are meeting this Friday.' I hold out the plate of flapjacks.

'They look delicious.' She takes a bite and briefly closes her eyes, savouring the taste. 'Just what I needed.' When she's finished the first one she helps herself to another and says, 'Mum, there's something I've been meaning to talk to you about.'

'Yeah?'

She takes a deep breath, her expression concerned. 'I worry that you and Dad wouldn't have separated if it hadn't been for me falling pregnant.'

'No, darling. Of course not.' I shake my head, frowning. 'Dad and I separating had nothing to do with that.'

'But Dad was so angry back then and you took my side. I know you stuck up for me; I heard you arguing.' She screws up her face. 'You argued a lot, Mum.'

'We did argue a lot but a mother should take her child's side – and so, for that matter, should a father.'

'Yes, but he blamed you for me falling pregnant.'

'It was almost seven years ago, Chloe.'

'Yes, but sometimes these things are a slow burn, aren't they? And when we were growing up, Dad was busy all the time and he expected a lot of you. You were the one who had to look after me and Ben. Keep the house quiet. Make sure everything ran smoothly. He did nothing that I can remember. So when I screwed up my chances of university you were blamed for it.'

'You went to university!'

'Later. Yeah. But you know what I'm saying, Mum.' She pierces me with determined eyes. 'You do, don't you?'

'Your dad did struggle with family dynamics,' I admit. 'Especially when he had a big case on, but we also had some great family times, didn't we?'

'With you and Grannie and Granddad. But not with Dad, not very often anyway.'

'That's harsh, Chloe. I remember lots of happy times with Dad.'

'Maybe, Mum. But you know I have a point?'

If anyone can say it like it is, it's Chloe and I shrug my acceptance before adding, 'It's not just about family, Chloe. I'm not convinced your dad even wants to be half of a couple.' Although when I think of the expression on his face when he was saying goodbye to Leila then perhaps that's no longer true.

'I just think that me falling pregnant was the final straw for him.' Her eyes are filling up. 'I've always felt guilty about it.'

'Chloe! Enough! Believe me, our marriage breakdown has got nothing to do with you or Ben.' I take hold of her upper arms and gently shake her. 'You are not the reason Dad and I separated. He wasn't getting the sort of devotion he wanted from me, and you know what? I wasn't getting much from him either but I had learned to live without attention. He needs an attentive wife; I don't need an attentive husband.' I can't help but smile. 'Although it is very nice when a man shows some interest.'

'What do you mean?' Chloe says.

'Well . . . I've made a new friend.' She lets out a scream and hugs me. 'Don't get carried away,' I say, holding up my hand. 'He's not interested in me like that but he's kind and he's a good listener.'

'I did think you were looking happier right enough!' She hugs me again. 'Happier than I've seen you in a while.'

'I am,' I admit, although it's more about seeing a way to get back at Tom and Leila than it is about Francis. 'As I say, it's not anything really. He's younger than me and he's very attractive and everything.'

'Mum, you're attractive!' Chloe says. 'And how much younger? A few years doesn't matter!'

'More than a few. And really.' I give her my serious face. 'There's nothing romantic between us but I feel like he's becoming a good friend to me. We seem to be on the same wavelength.'

She asks me his name and I tell her it's Francis and that I met him through a teacher at school. None of the family know that I was mugged and that I ended up going to group therapy and it feels too late to bring that up now. And even as I'm telling her about Francis I wonder whether it's all smacking of desperate middle-aged woman reading more into it than she should. He's popped in twice – twice! – and already I've turned him into a good friend. But I have to trust my intuition and my intuition is telling me that we are on the same wavelength and we could be significant to one another. Where Tom is now a closed door, with Francis I feel a sense of beginning.

But before I can concentrate on moving on, I need to be finished with Leila and Tom, and when Chloe leaves to collect Molly from gymnastics club I take

Maybanks' back-door key from my pocket and bury it
in my sock drawer. I might use it or I might not. God
knows I hate the woman but housebreaking is a whole
other level, isn't it? I'll wait and see how my next therapy
session goes. That will be the decider. We are set to
discuss my feelings towards the other woman. The other
woman? That'll be you then, Leila.

That'll be you.

Thursday dawns and I set off for my meeting with Tom
and the solicitors. I feel anxious (and that involves me
checking and rechecking) because I suppose there's a
chance that Leila will be there with Tom. And what will
I say if she is? Mary McNeil will be unmasked. I will
have to brazen it out. I'm past caring about what Tom
and Leila think of me, but I expect Hamish would find
my behaviour odd and that might knock my credibility
in his eyes. But more to the point, I want to reveal my
identity when I choose, not at a moment that's sprung
upon me.

I arrive before Tom and wait in the foyer. The New
Town office is ostentatiously plush, from the scarlet
embossed wallpaper to the huge chandelier that shim-
mers in ornate splendour above our heads. No wonder
the fees are so high. Hamish arrives next and he kisses
me on both cheeks, then says, 'Don't feel you have to
do any of the talking. I will speak for you unless you
particularly want to comment. I expect they'll begin with
a complaint because we're asking to make changes to
the agreement but remember that you're perfectly within
your rights, so don't feel even remotely bullied. I can
assure you I am relishing the opportunity to draw up a
fairer contract.'

The door opens and we both look round. It's Tom

and his solicitor and I'm relieved to see that there's no sign of Leila behind him. His solicitor is what my dad would describe as 'go-getting'. His name is Andre Rivoul and he has the eyes of a hawk, piercing and shrewd. I instantly decide that it's to my advantage never to catch his eye.

Both Tom and Andre are dressed in expensive, bespoke suits, while Hamish wears a more modest cloth and I'm in jeans. The last time I saw Tom was two days ago when I was lurking in the driveway of Maybanks, terrified of being caught out. But I needn't have worried because I was invisible to him, his eyes were all for Leila, and now he barely glances in my direction, nor me in his. Long gone are the days when our eyes lingered on one another and the brief glance I send his way reminds me that while there's no denying that he's handsome, there's a hardness to his stance and a meanness to his expression that I've never liked, and now those traits appear magnified. We say abrupt hellos and move into the meeting room.

The table is large and highly polished, the wood a reddish brown, I'm betting Canadian maple. We sit down, solicitor opposite solicitor, husband opposite wife. The solicitors lay out their papers while Tom and I wait, our postures mirroring each other, hands clasped on the table in front of us, eyes down.

Hamish guessed correctly as to how they would begin. 'Firstly, my client would like to register his disappointment,' Andre says. 'We have spent several months and several hundred pounds drawing up this agreement and Mrs Linford has waited until the eleventh hour to change her mind.' He pauses for effect, and I feel him staring at me. I look at Hamish and he gives me a small nod of support. Andre continues to talk, claiming his client's integrity and flexibility, and his client's wish to expedite the matter as soon as possible.

When he finally stops talking Hamish dives right in. 'As I stated in my letter, Mrs Linford is keen to move back into the family home. She is making arrangements to facilitate this and we would appreciate Mr Linford making way.' He goes through the finances while Tom and Andre share a rolling of eyes and frequent sighing as if it's all incredibly tiresome. When Hamish is finished, he looks at them both sternly, a headmaster to two indolent sixth-formers who have broken the rules one too many times. 'Perhaps you would be good enough to contact me again when you have read through our terms.' He slides two sheets of paper across the table and stands up. 'Ellen?' He turns to me and smiles. 'Shall we go?'

I'm on my feet at once. 'That was quick,' I say as we walk out together. 'Should we have given them the chance to reply?'

'Absolutely not. The less you let them talk the better. Solicitors of Rivoul's character should know better but it seems as if Tom is pulling the strings. Rivoul will know perfectly well that the law is on our side and I would have thought they'd want to avoid the expense of court.'

'I expect Tom will stop short of court,' I say. 'In principle, he doesn't like to waste money.'

'You might be surprised at how many otherwise sensible people lose their heads when it comes to divorce.'

'Ellen, wait!' We both turn and see Tom coming after us down the stone steps.

'You don't have to speak to him if you don't want to,' Hamish says into my ear.

'Thank you, Hamish, but I think I'm up for this.'

Tom is walking towards me, arms swinging, a frown

on his face. He stops in front of me, his stance wide, hands on hips. 'Are you planning on keeping this up?'

'What?'

'Maybanks.'

'I put body and soul into Maybanks, Tom. You know I did.'

'You moved out of Maybanks, Ellen.'

'You know why I had to do that. You were living there, in the spare room, happily planning the rest of your life.' I fold my arms. 'And when I left, you promised me you were putting the house on the market.'

'I made that promise in good faith,' he acknowledges. 'But circumstances changed, and now Leila and I are making a home there.'

'And what Leila and Tom want, Leila and Tom must have.'

His eyes narrow. 'So this is about spite? I find a way to keep the house and you don't like it?'

'You and Leila can live anywhere! It doesn't have to be in the home where we raised our family. I don't know why you can't see what a slap in the face that is for me, and for Ben and Chloe.' I shake my head at him. 'Just be generous for once!'

'Generous?' He laughs. 'Ellen, I'm a barrister.' He brings the flat of his hand to his chest. 'I could run rings around you. I could use the law to bury you in red tape that necessitates endless, expensive delays you could never afford to fight.' He gives me a tolerant look that raises the temperature of my blood. 'I am being more than generous with you, but, as ever, you are too blinded by your own self-importance to see that.'

'I'm sorry?' I try to breathe. 'What's that supposed to mean?'

'You have always sold yourself as the perfect home-maker, the perfect mother to our children, and yet Chloe was pregnant at eighteen. Our daughter *pregnant*.'

Chloe wasn't wrong when she brought this up with me a few days ago. Her pregnancy has always stuck in his throat as if it was a deliberate personal slight against him. 'And yet look how everything has turned out. Jack and Chloe are a loving couple and Molly is—' I pause to reflect on what my granddaughter brings into our lives. Words cannot do her justice and I settle for '—an absolute delight.'

'That's hardly the point.'

'So what *is* the point, Tom? Because it seems to me this is about *your* expectations, *your* judgemental attitude, your *ego*.' I move in closer and point my finger at his chest. 'Your ego squatted in the centre of our relationship, in the centre of our *family*, like a slimy, fat, greedy toad that needed to be constantly fed.' I drop my voice to a whisper so that only he can hear me. 'I want my home back. Do you hear me? I want it back. And I don't give a shit about what you and your new woman want.' I move in closer still until our faces are kissing distance apart. 'Fuck you, Tom Linford, and fuck her.' I hold his eyes for a couple of long, malevolent seconds, then I turn away. 'Hamish?' Hamish inclines his head and I take his arm. 'Let's go.'

If there was ever any doubt that I'm doing the right thing by fighting for the house, then it's well and truly gone. Tom has blown all my reservations out of the water. I'm not the one who's blinded by self-importance. He's talking about himself – and her. Always her.

I'm going after the house and I'm going after her.

7. Leila

Most people would look at Maurice and see him as a benign, avuncular figure. He's wearing a camel-coloured cardigan with a shawl collar and chunky brown buttons. He has a full head of white hair, half-moon specs and a walking stick. (He's awaiting a hip replacement.) Anyone foolish enough to judge him by his appearance would be surprised to discover an astuteness and attention to detail that is razor-sharp. He is already over eighty but he shows no signs of slowing down. Whenever I see him I feel my spirits lift because – to put it simply – he gets me. He is without doubt the most skilled therapist I have ever met.

His house is not dissimilar to Maybanks although it's situated in another part of town, south of the City with a view of the Pentland Hills. The room is larger and less modern than mine but the chair I sit in is deep and comfortable and, were I able to relax, it would hug me securely.

'Thank you for seeing me, Maurice.' I touch the back of my skull where the darkness lingers. 'I'm here because I'm afraid.'

He nods. 'Tell me what you're afraid of.'

'Alex is back in rehab,' I blurt out. 'I found him almost unconscious on his bed. I don't know what drugs he's been taking but I know he could end up hurting himself permanently.' I try to sink into the armchair but my body is unbending. 'I've tried my best with him. I've made sure he has everything he needs – a good education, opportunities, a home to invite friends to – I even chose Tom with Alex in mind. I hoped that they would bond but they haven't yet. They don't seem to like one another, or to be more accurate, Tom more or less ignores Alex, and Alex is scathing about Tom.' I pull my sleeves down over my hands. 'I don't know where to go from here. I've been feeling agitated and frustrated and just . . .' I trail off then catch hold of another thought. 'If there's one thing I'm normally sure of it's that I'm good at my job, and when everything else goes tits up at least I have my work, but now that's slipping too. I ended up shouting at Alison and Mark this afternoon.'

'The couple who are deciding whether or not to adopt?'

'Yes. I couldn't just sit there and listen to them complaining and moaning and missing the fucking point without wanting to smash their teeth in.'

I pull up my sleeves and scrutinise my nails. I don't speak for a full two minutes. It feels good to control the silence, to let it shorten and lengthen, swell and recede. Silence is more than just a lack of sound. Silence can speak volumes. Silence can inform and deceive. As a therapist it's important not to drift off when the client has lapsed into silence. It's important to remain engaged, to wait and to be attentive to what the client is trying to communicate. Therapy can be as much about what is not said as about what is said.

'Do you remember my brother?' I say at last. 'My family circumstances?'

'I remember.'

'He's in town. I've seen him a couple of times during the last few days and he calls me on my mobile, a lot, too much. He's been seeing a therapist himself – I don't know who; he wouldn't give me her name – and he wants to get everything out in the open.' I rub the base of my skull. 'And that begs the question – how does it make me feel? Well . . . when someone wants to kick me, I want to kick them right back. Harder. I can't help it. And I've been thinking – is it displacement? Or is it not?'

I glance up at Maurice. His eyes are with me.

'I don't know, Maurice. Maybe it is displacement. Maybe David wants to destroy me. Maybe I want to destroy him. Or maybe it's Gareth he really wants to destroy and I . . . I want to destroy my mother.' I look down at my shoes and see a tiny fleck of blood on the outside edge of my right shoe, close to the toe. Bird blood – Mrs Patterson's cat. Fucker.

'It's so much easier to sit in the therapist's chair,' I say. 'To understand what the client is experiencing and to feel a way forward for him or her, to listen and to guide.'

He nods. 'You have those skills. It's what makes you a very good therapist.'

'But with myself? I know . . . I think . . . I'm unable to bring that understanding into my own life.' My mouth is dry and I take a drink of water from the bottle next to me. I savour the liquid in my mouth, running it over my teeth, allowing it to pool in the spaces underneath my tongue before swallowing it. 'Gareth has come into my head again but there are holes punched in my memory. When I think about him, I can't really remember what he looks like. I can conjure up a fractured image – one grey eye, the tip of his ear, a dented cheekbone – but I can't see him clearly any more.'

'Do you want to see him clearly?'

'No, no. I don't. I really don't. But David has said he
wants to meet up with him. And I don't know why he
would want to. Why would he want to?' I laugh. 'The
man was a bastard to us. He effectively killed our mother
and he would have killed us too if he could have got
away with it. David wants everything to be transparent.
Everything out in the open.'

'Do you feel threatened by that?'

'I feel threatened . . . and afraid . . . and victimised,
but worse than that – I feel betrayed.'

'David putting his interests first betrays you?'

'Yes, exactly. That's what I feel. We had an agreement.
We promised each other that we'd never talk about what
we'd done, what we'd had to do for the sake of survival.
And he's breaking that promise.' I take a tissue from the
box on the table and spit on it, then try to clean the
blood off my shoe. The stain is stubborn and I have to
rub and rub before it's gone. 'I'm meeting him tomorrow
and I don't know what I'm going to say to him because
I've yet to work out how I can change his mind.' I sit
back in the chair and bite at the edges of my nails.

Maurice lets the silence grow for fifteen seconds. I
know this because I'm counting. I'd be doing the same
thing if I were him; allowing a significant pause before
responding. 'Perhaps it might be better not to try to
change David's mind,' he says slowly. 'Perhaps it might
be better to try to understand his motivation.'

That's exactly what I don't want to hear so I pretend
that it suddenly feels overwhelmingly important to share
my dreams. As a Jungian therapist Maurice will find this
hard to resist. 'I've been dreaming about David. These
past three nights have been all about David. He's at the
table with us having a family dinner. Tom is there and
Alex and myself. We're all talking and laughing, everything

is going well and then David announces why he's come to visit. I wake up at that point and I'm sweating, my pulse is racing. I feel like I'm in danger.'

Maurice nods slowly and I think he's taken the bait, but he hasn't. 'Imagine David is here now, Leila. What would you say to him?'

'I'd say – stop this! Forget about our childhood. Move on with your life. Be happy! There is nothing to be gained from dredging up all this stuff.'

'And what would Leila the therapist say?'

'She would say . . .' I try to breathe. 'She would say . . .' I shake my head. 'It's not relevant what she would say, and I'll tell you why.' I hold up my hand just in case he decides to speak. 'David's not motivated by his own growth and development as a person. David is doing this because he doesn't want me to be happy. He came to my house, you know? I was out, but Katarina let him in. He's only done that once before and that was when I'd been living with someone for a year.'

'Isn't it natural that he wants to come to your home? That he wants to meet the people who are important to you?'

'Yes, but he can't be part of my life. He knows this, Maurice. We agreed on it.'

'I understand.' He nods. 'I understand that as teenage brother and young adult sister you made a pact. But time has moved on and David wants to change the terms of that pact.' He nods again. 'And you are resisting him.'

'Too bloody right I'm resisting him because what he has to realise is that I have more to lose than he has. I've been lying – I admit that – and I'd be found out.'

'Found out by whom?'

'By Alex. By Tom.'

'Would it be so bad if they both knew about what had happened to you as a child and young adult?'

'Of course!' I let out some air; it sounds like a laugh but I have never felt less like laughing. 'Because then David would win, wouldn't he?' I hear myself say this and I'm shocked. Is this about winning? Is this about power? I thought it was about love and protection.

'David would win what?' Maurice says.

'Just stop this now, Maurice.' I frown at him. 'For fuck's sake. Why are you making me talk about David? I don't want to talk about David. I want to talk about Alex. I came here to talk about Alex.'

'All right, Leila.' Maurice sits back in his seat. 'Tell me about Alex.'

I talk about my son, about how much he means to me and about the hopes and dreams I have for his future. I hear myself talk and I know I'm being truthful, I know it's heartfelt. I also know it's a distraction from what I should be saying, what I really want to be saying. 'I can't force him to have a good life. I can't do that.' I pause. 'I don't blame Alex. I don't blame him at all. Blame is the language of children and politicians. Blame says – I'm unwilling to point the finger at myself so I'll point it elsewhere, at him or him or her . . .'

'Why would you blame him?'

I stare down at the bloody tissue in my hand. 'I could blame Alex for complicating my life. Lots of mothers would. And I could do that but I don't.' I glance at my watch. 'Fifty minutes.'

'Do you want to stay longer?'

'No.' I stand up. 'Thank you, Maurice. I should go now.'

'Before you do, Leila.' He gestures for me to sit down again. I don't sit down. I hold my ground, bracing myself in case he decides to be honest with me, to show me exactly what I'm refusing to see. He doesn't, of course. He rises slowly from his chair, leaning heavily on his stick until he finds his balance. 'I wonder whether you might cancel your clients for the next week.'

'Alison and Mark?' I move towards the waste bin and throw the tissue into it.

'Not just them. Perhaps you might give yourself a break from the needs of others and focus on your own needs.'

I feel my face redden. It's something that rarely happens to me. I touch my cheeks and the heat burns my fingers. 'I will.' I walk ahead of Maurice to the front door.

'I'm free at the same time tomorrow,' he says, his stick making rhythmic taps on the wooden flooring as he rushes to keep up with me.

'I should be fine, thank you.' The door is stiff and I have to pull it hard before it yields.

'Leila?' His voice is raised.

I turn to look at him. I'm squinting because eye contact feels painful. This is the man who sees right through me, past the woman I project to the world, past the person I want to be, right to my core, to the woman I am – and folks, she's not pretty. She is a fighter. She is selfish and cut-throat. She is out for her own survival, and if that involves lies and deceit she doesn't care. She does it anyway.

'Remember to breathe,' he says. His expression tells me he knows me, he understands me. He doesn't judge me. 'And call me.'

I nod my agreement and then say, 'I'm sorry for shouting and for swearing.'

'Emotions are running high. See them for what they are.'

'Fear?'

'Fear,' he affirms.

Maurice remains standing at the door. I start the engine and drive off. I look in my rearview mirror and see an old man, leaning on a stick. Appearances can be deceptive.

I spend the journey home visualising three – no four – roll-ups and an extra-large whisky. I burst through my own front door and tip the whisky into the first receptacle to hand – a mug that says 'Happy Father's Day'.

'You have a good evening?'

I turn round and see Katarina behind me, her smile faltering as it meets my frown. Her cheek is still bruised and it gives her the look of the downtrodden: the battered girlfriend, the homeless runaway, the refugee.

'You want a drink?' I hold the bottle out towards her. 'It'll do you good. It'll do us both good. We could bond – two women together.' I laugh at the ridiculousness of my suggestion. When have I ever done bonding with women? With anyone for that matter? 'What do you say?'

'No, thank you. I am on the medicine.' She takes a packet of painkillers out of her pocket. 'It says—'

'Suit yourself.' I wave her aside and leave the kitchen, hugging the mug of whisky and the bottle into my chest. The evening air is cool and sharp. A dog is barking a couple of gardens away and two seagulls are squawking on a rooftop. I smoke and I drink and I stare up at the sky. For once there is an absence of clouds, and the stars remind me of my own insignificance. The universe is huge, magnificent, boundless. My problem is a microscopic speck of dust on the spine of infinity.

'It's all good,' I say out loud. 'It's all well and good.'

A rustle in the bushes draws my attention away from

the sky and my eyes take a moment to refocus. I see a
rounded shape settling on the ground close to my feet.
Next door's cat – stupidly determined to roam where
he's unwelcome, forever in a garden other than his own.
'And you,' I say to him, nudging him with the tip of my
shoe. 'You're on your last warning.'

8. Ellen

Maybanks' back-door key is still hidden in my sock drawer but I think about it almost constantly. The idea of sneaking into the house when no one is there and seeing how Tom and Leila live together – the contents of their fridge, the bathroom cabinet, the bedside drawer – is an idea that has me hooked. I want to see what's changed and I want to see what's the same. And deep down, I think I want to know why he chose her over me. The kitchen and the bedroom are where the choices are made by men like Tom, aren't they? So what's she got that I haven't?

All that's stopping me using the key is the question of what happens if I'm caught? What would Chloe and Ben think? How would I justify it to them? Well, I think I'd justify it in two ways: firstly, legally the house is still partly mine and secondly, I asked Tom on several occasions to give my jewellery box back to me but he never did, so it's a case of taking matters into my own hands. And after the meeting at the solicitor's this morning, I know how good it feels to outsmart him, to stand toe to toe, eyeball to eyeball, and force him to see that he isn't the one holding all the cards.

I'm weighing up the pros and cons as I push my trolley up and down the aisles in the supermarket. My mobile rings. 'Mary? It's Leila.'

There's noise all around me. I stop pushing the trolley

and put a finger in my left ear, while pressing my mobile to my right.

'I'm ringing to let you know that I need to cancel our appointment on Tuesday,' she says. 'I'm taking next week off.'

'Oh? Oh, no. But why?' I say. This doesn't suit me at all. 'Have I done something wrong?'

'No, of course not. It's just that I need to recharge my batteries.'

'I . . .' I was looking forward to our next session. We're due to discuss the other woman and I can't wait to prick her conscience, to play with her, to chip away at the dividing wall between the professional and the personal until the truth of our connection is revealed to her. 'If possible, I'd really like to see you, Leila. I feel like I'm making progress. I don't want to pressure you.' I let my voice waver. 'I'm sorry, I . . . I was just hoping . . . you're helping me so much and—'

'You know, Mary. You're right.' I hear a smile in her tone. 'We are working well together so let's keep on going. I'm sorry to have disturbed you. I'll see you on Tuesday at 2 p.m. as usual.'

'Thank you, Leila,' I say. 'I really appreciate that.'

I end the call and stare at the handset, wondering whether I'm imagining things. With so much background noise I can't be sure but I think she sounded rattled. Has Tom told her about our meeting earlier today? Or is something else going on? Has she found out who I really am? I don't want that. I want the control, the advantage, to be with me not her.

There is a way for me to find out what the problem might be. Chloe hasn't been to visit Tom lately but Ben is back from his friend's and is going to visit his dad this evening. While Chloe is more circumspect, Ben is always open about what's happening in his dad's life. I won't even need to pry.

It's late evening and I've just finished a round of checks when Ben comes bouncing into the living room, looking glad to be home. 'You hungry, darling?' I ask him.

'No, I'm good, Mum, thanks.' He pats his stomach. 'Katarina made a meal this evening for the four of us. It was nicer than I thought it would be, beetroot soup with yoghurt and a stew type thing with beef and chilli.'

'Sounds good.'

'Okay if I grab a beer?'

'Sure. Get one for me too.' He comes across to the sofas with two beers. 'So you said there were four of you?'

'Leila, Dad, me and Katarina.' He opens both bottles and hands one to me.

'No Alex?'

'He's been sent to rehab.'

'Has he?' I start back in surprise. 'You were right about him having a problem, then?'

'Yeah, and Dad was like . . .' He trails off, shaking his head. 'He was being all supportive.'

'Oh?' I say, half casual. 'What happened?'

'Leila looked really tired and Dad was fussing over her. It was all a bit embarrassing.' He's pressing the button to turn on the TV but nothing happens because it isn't plugged in. 'Mum, what's going on with the plugs?' he says, bending down behind the TV to plug it back in again. 'It's the same whenever I go into my bedroom. My computer and my bedside light are unplugged.'

'I'm just a bit worried about the electricity,' I say. 'The landlord will get round to fixing it eventually but in the meantime we've just got to keep everything unplugged when we're not using it.'

'So that's what those numbers are on the sockets? He's replacing them?'

'Something like that.' I rub at my face.

'Fair enough.' He turns on the TV and begins to surf the channels, talking at the same time. 'Me and Angus bought our Interrail tickets this afternoon. We're going to start in Paris and end up in Bucharest.'

He tells me about the route they'll be taking and I listen to his plans. No more mention of his dad and Leila. He's moved on. And I do too. I'm relieved that Leila hasn't guessed who I am and so I don't return to the topic even though I'd like to ask more questions; it isn't fair to Ben and after all, I have the back-door key. I can find things out for myself.

I lie in bed and work through the logistics. According to her LinkedIn profile, Leila teaches a class at the university summer school, and when I check on the university website, I find out that the class takes place on Friday mornings. And on the first Friday of every month, come hell or high water, Tom plays golf with his cronies. Alex is in rehab so that only leaves Katarina. I don't expect Leila does her own food shopping, so that must mean Katarina goes out at some point. And if not for food then she must surely have made friends. I can't imagine she stays home all day.

Tomorrow is the first Friday of the month. If I'm going to do this then I need to strike fast.

I fall asleep, still in two minds and when I wake in the middle of the night I've been dreaming about Maybanks. It's a sunny day and Molly is a baby. She's crawling towards the hydrangea bushes because she's spotted Mrs

Patterson's cat sunning himself. When she reaches him she grabs a handful of the fur on his back and he raises his lazy head to stare at her, good-natured as ever. Chloe laughs and calls her daughter's name. She's barefoot and smiling, a long skirt swinging just above her ankles as she lifts Molly high up into the sky. Molly's legs kick and she gives loud, shocked giggles as Chloe throws her and then catches her, higher and higher, before finally pulling her close and kissing her pink cheeks.

Dreaming about my family and Maybanks is the nudge I need to make up my mind for me. I'm going back into my house today. I'm going to use the key and get the jewellery. I will get Maybanks back – I feel it in my bones – but in the meantime, I'm going to take back what's unequivocally mine.

And so by nine o'clock, I'm two streets away from my old home. Ben told me Katarina drives a Mini that was bought for Alex, but he's yet to pass his driving test. Tom still drives his Audi and I know that Leila has a BMW. All I have to do is keep my head down until all three cars have driven off. Easier said than done. School holidays means more people are around than usual. I approach Maybanks four times and then retrace my steps, walk down to the shore, along towards Newhaven and back. Several times I recognise neighbours up ahead – twice it's Mrs Patterson, who is wandering about in her slippers – and I do a U-turn before I'm seen.

I'm about fifty yards away when I see Tom leave the house. He throws his golf clubs into the boot, then drives off in the opposite direction to me. I walk around some more, down to the shore and back, and on my second pass I notice that Leila's car is gone. Two down and one to go. That's always assuming that Katarina will go out and that, if she does go out, she'll take the Mini.

Another hour goes by and I bump into one of my neighbours about a hundred yards from Maybanks. 'Ellen! Long time no see!' she says. 'I love your new hairstyle.'

'Thanks. I felt it was time for a change.'

'We keep hoping you'd move back into the street. It isn't the same without you.' We talk children and work and life in general and then she goes off to catch the bus. 'Let's meet for coffee soon!' she shouts back to me over her shoulder.

I wave in reply and continue along the street towards Maybanks. I'm worrying that I've missed my chance to get into the house when I spy Katarina coming out of the front door. She doesn't climb into the car; she walks off in the direction of town, a shopping bag over her arm.

I feel light-headed. My heart is drumming against my ribcage. I don't waste any time. I speed-walk along the pavement and turn into Maybanks' driveway. I slide the key into the lock at the back door and I'm inside the kitchen before I give myself time to think.

I close the door behind me and stand stock-still, listening. Apart from the fridge motor humming quietly to my left, I can't hear anything. I wait anyway and count slowly to a hundred. Still nothing so I start to move. By this time on a golfing Friday morning I'd have made a cooked breakfast and the kitchen would smell of bacon and eggs but there are no discernible cooking smells, not even toast, only the scent of sandalwood from perfumed sticks on the windowsill.

I look inside the fridge as I'm passing. It's full of the stuff of healthy eating: coconut water, mackerel, spinach and avocados. I'm surprised: Tom is every bit the meat and veg bloke – but perhaps he's changed. Perhaps he always wanted to eat like this. I don't know and I don't really care.

I tiptoe through the hallway and into the living room. Neither space has changed very much apart from the walls. I removed so many pictures and photographs when I left, exposing bare, rectangular patches, but most of them have already been covered with elegant prints and photographs. There are three photos of a smiling Tom and Leila: outside a restaurant, on a ski slope and on a beach. (They haven't wasted any time.) This I do care about and I feel the sharp stab of hurt feelings – Tom barely took any holidays when we were together and he certainly wouldn't have been willing to spend thousands on a ski holiday.

As I climb the stairs I see that there are several photographs of a boy growing into a young man, who I assume is Alex. He appears to be fun-loving, smiling at the photographer in an open manner, and I wonder about what took him down the drugs route. There isn't even one photograph of Ben and Chloe. Tom is someone who lives in the present or the future, so he was unconcerned when I removed the family photos but not to have wanted to keep one? Not one photograph of his own children. It beggars belief.

At the top of the stairs is Chloe's old bedroom. Gone is the wall design she loved so much – an expanse of musical notes, 'Amazing Grace', painted by a friend of mine who teaches music. There is nothing of Chloe left in here at all. Curtains, carpet, walls have all been revamped and a purpose-built wall cabinet runs the length of two walls and houses all of Tom's textbooks and files.

Ben's bedroom is as it was, although empty of his stuff as he brought it all to the rented house with me. The spare bedroom is sparse but lived in and I take it to be Alex's. There's an electric guitar in the corner and sheet music lying about the floor. The fifth bedroom is in the attic and Ben told me that Katarina sleeps up there.

I open the door to the conservatory that sits directly above the kitchen and am upset to see that most of the cacti have been removed. The room is almost completely empty apart from the odd plant and a couple of wicker chairs. I feel angry at the sight of it, all the love and effort that went into making a restful room wiped out by a few months of neglect.

I hesitate at the door to my bedroom, but only for a few seconds; then I turn the handle and force the door open. My insides lurch as if I'm riding on a rollercoaster. My bedroom no longer exists. The room has been completely revamped in much the same way as Tom's study has been. The king-size bed has been replaced with an extravagant four-poster affair that dominates the space. The carpet has been replaced with wooden flooring and the lush, velvet curtains have given way to airy muslins. (A pretty choice but not a practical one – the room will be freezing on winter evenings.)

The walk-in wardrobe has been fitted with drawers, shelves and rails, most of them commandeered by Leila's clothes, which hang neatly according to item and colour: silks and cashmere and merino wool, ranging from black and white to colourful blouses and tops. I touch each and every one of her items of clothing, enjoying the fact that I'm here, uninvited, and she'll never know.

As I thought, she wears stockings not tights, and silk underwear in black and red: basques, negligees, suspenders. She's spoilt for choice.

One drawer contains two types of vibrators, dildos, handcuffs and a selection of balls and plugs laid neatly in a row. I have never before considered myself naive or unadventurous but perhaps I am. I don't know whether to feel sad or foolish, so I close the drawer quickly and look for my black lacquer jewellery box. It's nowhere on display but it doesn't take me long to find it, inside the walk-in wardrobe on the floor behind Leila's shoes.

I slide the box inside my backpack and am about to leave when I have a thought that makes me stop. A sneaky, spiteful, naughty-child thought. *Why not, Ellen? Why not? Doesn't she deserve it? Hasn't she caused you more damage than you could ever cause her?*

Smiling to myself, I open the drawer of Tom's bedside cabinet and take out his nail scissors. I cut half a dozen small holes in Leila's cashmere jumpers and silk shirts, at the front of the shoulder where it can't go unnoticed. Then I hang them back up again as neatly as I found them. She has several pairs of expensive designer shoes and I scrape the scissors across the toe of two of the shoes from different pairs and cut the strap at the back of one of them. Then I replace the shoes and put the scissors in my pocket. Before I close the door, I have one last look at the room, deciding that as soon as I get my house back absolutely everything will be chucked out, preferably on a very large bonfire.

I'm on my way down the stairs when I hear a key going into the front-door lock. My body freezes while my mind quickly considers my options: to continue downstairs means I'll be seen at once; to go back upstairs means I might have a chance to leave when whoever has arrived home's back is turned. I choose the second option and go quickly upstairs and sidle into the conservatory, the best place to hide as clearly no one ever goes in here.

I wait, my eyes on stalks and my ears straining to hear

every small sound. I feel anxious but also excited. This is out of my comfort zone, no doubt about it, but it feels good to be behaving in a way I wouldn't normally. Women like Leila deserve to have the fight taken to them. She thinks her home is a place of safety? Not any more.

I hear a woman humming along to a tune and then she comes up the stairs – Katarina I presume. I see her retreating back as she climbs the stairs to the attic bedroom. I count to five and then I'm down the stairs like a shot. I dart through the kitchen, almost tripping over the shopping bags that Katarina has left there, and when I reach for the kitchen counter to steady myself I knock over a bowl, which falls to the floor with a loud clatter.

'Hello?' The voice is coming from the top of the stairs. 'Is someone here?'

I don't wait for her to appear. I'm straight out the back door. I creep slowly round the corner and along the driveway, hugging the wall and ducking under the kitchen window. As I pass the living room I make the mistake of glancing inside; Katarina is coming into the room and we immediately catch sight of one another. I see her green eyes, wide and surprised, and I know that she is seeing me as clearly as I see her.

Shit. Shit. Shit!

I jog along the street and within a hundred yards I'm onto a busy road. And then I slow down, looking guiltily over my shoulder several times to see whether she's followed me. She hasn't and I breathe a sigh of relief. Although why does it matter? After all, Maybanks is not Leila's house; it belongs as much to me as it does to Tom. I've damaged some clothing but otherwise I've only taken what's mine. And who would deny me that?

8. Leila

I spend the morning teaching my summer class and then arrive at the park-side cafe an hour before David. By the time I'm watching out for his arrival I have a third black coffee and a second shot of grappa on the table in front of me. This is my breakfast and my lunch: this and half a dozen cigarettes. The taste in my mouth is bitter with coffee and I can feel the pop of nicotine, caffeine and alcohol in my bloodstream.

When I first spot him he's about fifty yards away, weaving his way between pedestrians. I knock back the grappa in one shot, shudder and take a couple of long breaths. As I watch him I try to be objective and imagine how other people must view him. He's attractive in a rugged, unshaven way that would make some women push him into the chemist to buy a razor, while others would find his swarthiness attractive. He's wearing bargain-basement clothes that aren't in any way fashionable or flattering but because he's a good height, and slim without being skinny, he looks just about okay. If I was his mother I'd have a word, encourage him to smarten himself up a bit, see whether he could attract a woman worth keeping. But I'm not his mother – I'm his half-sister – and my love for him is neither endless nor unconditional.

He's about ten yards away when he sees me. His arm lifts in a wave and his mouth in a smile. At once I see the six-year-old boy who would wait for me after school and rush towards me at full pelt to seize my hand. 'What's for tea, Leila?' he'd say. Or, 'Leila, did you know that the moon makes the sea move?' Or, 'Leila, Mrs Williams says that there used to be wolves in England.' Talking and talking until we reached the front door and then he'd remember what was behind it. He'd go silent until the next day when we were free again.

'Hey, Sis.' He bends down and kisses my cheek. 'You want anything else?' He points to my drinks. 'Top-up?'

'I'm good, thanks.'

He signals to the waitress. 'A beer please.' He sits down and takes off his jacket, hanging it on the back of his chair. 'So what's new?' he says.

'Nothing much. You?'

'A bit, yeah.' He gives me a significant look. 'I spoke to Gareth.'

'Oh?'

'I've arranged to see him on Wednesday.' There's a beer mat on the table and he balances it on its end then spins it around. 'I'm hoping you'll come with me.'

I stare out over the beer garden. A mother and father and two small children are sitting in a circle on the grass playing clapping games. They are teaching each other the rhythm, and laughing. They practise over and over again but always someone goes wrong so they start from the beginning, full of good humour. I think about Alison and Mark and whether they will ever resolve their differences sufficiently to become parents. I'm still feeling concerned about myself for shouting at them and know that Maurice is right – I need to cancel all of my clients next week.

'Leila?'

I switch back to David. 'Is there a point?'

'Is there a point to seeing Gareth? Sure there is! It's obvious, isn't it? It's about returning to the scene of the crime, laying the ghost to rest so that we can move on.'

'I have moved on.'

'Maybe it's just me then.'

He gives me one of his appealing grins; I don't soften. 'There's no maybe about it.'

'Okay.' He sighs. 'So you're all sorted, but why won't you help me?'

I pretend to consider this and I even manage to make my tone regretful. 'Not at the expense of my own peace of mind.'

'Gareth's sick, Leila. He's in an old folks' home. I think it would do us both good to see him powerless.'

'Speak for yourself.'

'Okay – it would do *me* good.' He points his finger to his chest. 'Me, Leila. *Me*. Am I allowed to think about me occasionally or do all our conversations have to revolve around you?'

'David.' I look down at my hands. My fingers are interlocked, and that's good because my right hand wants to form a fist. 'Did you really speak to him?'

'No, but—' He holds up a finger '—I spoke to a care assistant and she said he'd be happy to see me . . . to see us.' The waitress brings his beer. He thanks her and takes a gulp. 'He doesn't get many visitors, that's what she said.'

'He doesn't get many? Or he doesn't get any?'

'One or the other. What difference does it make?'

'I'm just trying to form an accurate picture.'

'Okay, okay.' He drinks a mouthful of beer. 'I called the home. I spoke to a care assistant. She said he never gets any visitors. She thought he would be glad to see us.' A further few mouthfuls. 'And he's compos mentis.

I asked her that and she said he's of sound mind; it's his body that's fucked.'

'She said his body was fucked?'

'No, *I'm* saying his body is fucked. *She* said he'd had a stroke.' He shrugs his shoulders and makes a what's-with-you expression. 'Anything else you want to clarify?'

'If I come with you to see Gareth, will it stop there? Or do you want more? Do you want a piece of me? A piece of my life?' He laughs and shakes his head. I tap on the table in front of him. 'Answer me, please.'

'Sure, Leila.' He drains the glass and bangs it down on the table. 'I want a piece of your life.'

I hold his eyes and take a breath. 'Why?'

'Because you took a piece of mine.'

'And there we have it,' I say quietly.

'Can I get you anything else?' The waitress is back. She's young and sweet-looking with a bouncy ponytail. She's exactly the sort of girl I never was: trusting, smiley, with just the right amount of confidence.

I shake my head at her and David says, 'I'll have another.' He passes her the empty glass. 'And my sister will have . . .' He picks up my empty shot glass and smells it. 'What was this? Whisky?'

I don't reply. He looks up at the waitress and says, 'And a double whisky.'

Close relationships are so often about power. We think they're about love but, in my experience, it's more complex than that. They're about the constant give and take of power and influence. Love is proven when we relinquish our power and say, 'Okay, let's do it your way.' I love you enough to put you first. I love you enough to let you have centre stage while I stand in the wings. I love you enough to suffer for you.

'I'll come with you to see Gareth,' I say. 'I'll come with you against my better judgement because—' I give him a sad smile '—you're my brother and it's what you want.' He reaches across the table and tries to take my hand but I pull it out of his reach. 'I will go with you on the condition that afterwards you accept I'll need some time on my own.' I pause. 'There's a lot going on in my life at the moment, some of it challenging. I can't be at your beck and call.'

He nods several times as if he's taking my feelings on board. 'Firstly, thank you. I appreciate this, Leila. I know how hard it will be for you to see Gareth again. I know.' His expression is sincere. 'Secondly, is there anything I can do to help you?'

'No.' I gather my coat around me. 'My client base is growing and I need to give time and energy to that. But it's Tom, really. His divorce has hit a wall.'

'Alex is okay?'

'He is. He's signed up for an economics class this summer to give him a head start next term. He's an A student.' I nod, as if by nodding I will make it true. 'He's in with a great crowd.'

'That's good to hear.'

'Actually, I should go now.' I attempt to stand up but he pulls me back down again. 'Katarina is expecting me to help her with her English assignment.'

'Don't go. Your whisky hasn't arrived yet and you can't leave me to drink alone.'

I drop back into my seat. 'Just another ten minutes.'

'Tom home this evening?'

'Yes. We're having a late dinner together. I haven't seen him all week.' Tom is having dinner out with his golf partners, the grand finale to a day of male bonding. 'We have to talk about the terms of his divorce. His wife has decided she wants the house now, having moved out and been willing to sign off on it before.' I shrug. None of this bothers me that much, of course, but giving David information to feed on will keep his eye away from what is really bothering me. 'There's no telling where her head's at so it could drag on a while.'

'Have you met her?'

'No. I don't even really know what she looks like.'

'You haven't even looked her up on Facebook?' He snorts. 'You're not curious about what she looks like or where she works?'

'I know she's a teacher because Ben mentioned it once. And I also know she's a keen gardener but that's about it.'

'She'll be curious about you, I bet.' He starts to tell me about someone he knows whose divorce dragged on for four years and in that time the wife wreaked all sorts of revenge on the husband. I let him talk, listening attentively, laughing and sympathising in the right places. When his beer arrives, he downs it in five minutes and I urge him to drink the whisky as well.

He talks and talks. I listen, and I wait until there is a natural pause in his storytelling and then I take some money from my pocket and slide it under the ashtray. 'What time were you thinking of leaving on Wednesday?' He looks at me blankly. 'To visit Gareth,' I remind him.

'It's about an hour's drive from here so how about we meet after lunch?'

'We can go in my car.'

'I'll be at the end of your street for one o'clock.' His look dares me to say that's too close to home for me but I don't challenge him. I kiss his cheek and this time he lets me stand up. 'See you on Wednesday.'

* * *

I feel like I don't have a choice. I know what Maurice would say – he would tell me that of course I have a choice; this is an opportunity to be truthful and as soon as the words are spoken they will lose some of their power. I know this but I can't do it. I can't do it because I feel like my survival depends on protecting my life as it is. Who chooses to be exposed for the person they are? Underneath their career, the cashmere sweaters and comfortable home? Nobody I've ever met.

I should have another drink and go straight to bed but I choose not to. I'm in the garden next to the hut, smoking, feeling restless and afraid, but mostly angry. Without his big sister to care for him, David would have been neither fed nor cuddled. He would have been lucky to make it into his fifth year. And it didn't stop with childhood. I've given him money, thousands of pounds, more than I care to count. I've bailed him out of jail. I've dropped my life to rescue his.

And it's never enough.

I'm stubbing out my third cigarette on the paving slab when I hear a couple of meows. Mrs Patterson's cat is in one of his usual spots under the bush, licking his paws. He gives me a lazy sideways glance, then continues undaunted. He should be afraid of me, surely? I kicked him, I threw water over him but still he roams back into the garden. I shake my head up at the sky and bite my bottom lip. A blob of blood settles on my lip. I taste it, savour the rich, metallic taste and smile. Well puss . . . we're all punished for our inability to see what's coming next.

I deliberately let my shoulders drop to a more relaxed position, flex and extend my fingers until the muscles are warm and awake. I'm far enough back in the garden to be unseen from the upstairs windows of Maybanks or any of the neighbouring houses. The garden wall is high and the bushes are thick.

'Puss, puss,' I say softly. 'Puss, puss.' I approach him slowly. My feet make no sound as I cross the grass. The cat gives me another unconcerned backward glance and continues to groom himself. I'm gradually lowering my body towards the ground while keeping my voice gentle and kind. 'Come on then, puss,' I say. 'Come to Mama. Come for a cuddle.'

I'm down on the grass beside him, gaining his trust, quietly whispering, and then with a quick, confident motion I grab him. I have one hand wrapped round his jaw to hold it shut; the other captures his body and pulls it sharply under my arm. He gives a frantic squeal and then he fights, vicious, sharp claws dragging deep scratches down my forearm.

The sound of his neck as it breaks is a subtle, low-toned crack. His body stills instantly and drops in my arms, a dead weight. I stroke the fur once, then get down on my knees and push him under one of the bushes at the back of the garden. I force the body in as far as I can, close to the wall, at least an arm's length from the path, then I sit back on my heels and brush the earth off my palms. He will quietly decompose under there until his body is nothing more than a collection of tiny bones. There isn't enough heat to force rapid decomposition and any smell should dissipate in the air.

I stand up, my shoulders back, my lungs filling and emptying. I feel confident. I feel powerful. I've just wilfully taken a life and it makes me feel good. Better than good. Great. Taking a life makes me feel great. It releases an effervescent clarity inside me, a clarity that enables me to see several moves ahead. I feel my mind begin to circle a plan: a backup plan. After we visit

Gareth, if David decides he still wants more from me, then I know what I need to do.

I'm glad that Tom isn't home yet because it means I can riffle through the papers in his study without having to explain myself. I hear the squeak of floorboards above me as Katarina walks about, but it's already ten o'clock so she's not likely to come back down again and even if she did, I can silence her with a look. I remember, when we moved Tom's office from the annexe into the house, seeing a case file he was working on and a copy of some lab work that he was using in evidence. After ten minutes' searching I find what I'm after and run it through the printer, scanning a copy to my email address. I put the original back where I found it and sit on my bed with my laptop.

I copy and paste what I need and make a new document with the names and dates changed, then I'm back to Tom's study to print it out, using paper that's been in Tom's office for years but which he's incapable of throwing out 'in case it comes in useful'.

It has come in useful. This document needs to look as if it's been around a while, ten years to be exact. Fortunately the printer ink is low and so the whole effect is perfect. It could easily be a letter I received ten years ago. I fold it into three, then unfold it again. A few more times and I'm satisfied it will fool David.

I slide the letter under the mattress at my side of the bed and then I take a shower, cleaning the long cat scratches with soap until the painful sting brings tears to my eyes. When I lie down to sleep, I hear Leila Mae's voice inside me as clear as if it were still my own. 'You do what has to be done,' she tells me. 'You do it and then you move on.'

9. Ellen

When I arrive home, I lift the post off the doormat and leave the letters and my backpack in the living room before I begin my checks. Ben has some work at the local garden centre and has left a note on the fridge to say he's been called in at short notice. I'm horrified to see that he left his computer on and his bedside lamp plugged in. And he must have had a cup of coffee before he set off; the kettle is also plugged in. I think about what might have happened in my absence – a smouldering electrical fire that catches alight just as I'm leaving Maybanks, so that by the time I get back, the house is ablaze and I believe Ben is home, inside, unable to escape, disabled by smoke inhalation, lying on his bedroom floor dying.

I break out in a sweat and then I start to hyperventilate. Please, please, please – I've passed out before when I've had a panic attack and I don't want it to happen now, not when I need to check the rest of the house. I pace up and down, reasoning with myself, calming myself, my eyes closed and my mouth speaking words aloud: You're fine, Ellen. Everyone is fine. Ben is at the garden centre. Chloe, Molly and Dad – they're all well and happy. No one dies today, Ellen. Relax. No one dies today.

When I know I'm not going to faint I go to the front door and lock it. I unlock it and relock it. I move the safety chain into position and then out again, in and then out. I do this for a long time. The rhythmic slide of the bolt, the click as it lands inside the hollowed-out metal hole at the end, soothes me. The slide back again, as it connects with the opening, comforts me.

When the doorbell rings, it sounds like it's coming from far away and so I don't respond at once. The letter box is hip height and I feel something push against me. I catch hold of it – it's a DVD. I open the door. Francis is on the doorstep. He is handsome, I realise afresh. And he has kind eyes.

'You're home!' he says, smiling. And then, 'You look like you're in a trance. Are you okay? Has something happened?' He takes my arm. 'Ellen?'

'Sorry.' I try to smile but my face feels stiff. 'I got myself in a bit of a state. Just . . .'

'Do you want to talk about it?' He looks down the street. 'I'm off to visit my mum but I'm earlier than normal so I don't need to be there for a while.'

'No, you should go,' I say. I stare down at the DVD.

'It's the French film I was telling you about,' he says. 'The one where the man's in a wheelchair. It doesn't sound uplifting but it really is and it's based on a true story.'

'Yes, I remember you telling me.'

'We could watch it later?' he says.

'But you've already seen it.'

'I don't mind watching it again.' He gives me his uncomplicated smile. 'I could get us a carry-out on the way back from the hospice and we could watch it early evening if that suits you?'

'It does.' I smile properly now. 'It really does suit me.'

'Indian, Chinese or shall we go for the chippie?'

'I haven't had an Indian in a while. Butter chicken?'

'Butter chicken it is!' He walks backward along the path. 'See you about seven?'

'Perfect.'

It's not a date, I say to myself as I close the door. He's a friend. That's all.

I open my backpack and pull out the lacquer jewellery box. I place it on top of the dressing table and sit on the edge of my bed to look at it. I'm happy having it back where it belongs. It stayed on this dressing table for thirty years in my grandmother's house and then for another twenty years in mine, after she died and I inherited the dressing table and the box. I wonder whether Tom or Leila will even notice the box is gone. Well, I'm sure Tom won't but I suppose Leila might, although it shouldn't matter to her anyway.

But her clothes and shoes will matter. I still have the nail scissors in my pocket. It was a spiteful thing to do but I don't regret it. I could have trashed the place. I could have tipped paint over everything. I could have taken all their clothes out of the wardrobe and set fire to them in the garden.

And it makes no difference whether Katarina saw me or not. After my next therapy session, when we will be discussing my feelings towards the other woman, I don't intend to return to Maybanks. Not until I walk through the front door, with my own key, back home again for good.

I had expected days to pass before I heard from Tom's solicitor but I was wrong; when I open the thick envelope, I see it's from him. There's a terse covering letter and then form after form to complete. I call Hamish to discuss it.

'We're in for a battle but just remember that the prize

will be worth it, Ellen,' Hamish says. 'They're throwing a whole lot of silly nonsense our way, questions we've already answered but they're insisting we update them.'

'Do we have to update them?' I ask.

'I think it's in our best interest to do so because then we can insist on the same from them, and we both know that Tom has more assets than he declared on the first round of paperwork.'

'Ok*ay*.' I remember the conversation I had with him after the meeting where he insisted he was proving his generosity by not drowning me in documents. Maybe he changed his mind on that score. I say as much to Hamish but he's unperturbed.

'Let's answer the questions quickly and bat the ball back into their court.'

I agree to do my best and tackle several of the legal documents before my head feels too full of words and figures and I know I need a break. It'll be a couple of hours yet before Francis arrives so I go to visit my dad. There's already a for sale sign stuck in the ground at the front of his garden and I meet him coming out of the garage with a drill in his hand and his tool belt round his waist. 'I'm titivating the place up a bit,' he says, giving me a hug. 'It's often the wee things that make the difference.'

'The house looks great as it is, Dad, but in any case, I think the location alone will sell it. Don't tire yourself out.'

'I'm sure you're right but I'll make these repairs anyway.' He shows me his list. 'Don't want the buyers thinking I'm a lazy bugger.' I follow him into the kitchen.

'You really don't need to paint the downstairs loo,' I say, reading the list.

'I'll do it anyway. Might as well.' He stands on a chair and uses the drill to screw in the fixing for the blind that's been coming away at the wall. 'I can't believe I've gone for a year without fixing this,' he says. 'But what I really can't believe—' he turns round to look at me '—is that they chopped that beautiful oak tree down.'

'At Maybanks?'

'Where else?' He climbs down from the chair. 'When we get back into the house I thought I'd build a play-house for Molly where the oak tree used to stand. What do you think?'

'She'd love that, Dad. I was thinking the same thing myself. We're not there yet though. I have a ton of forms to fill in and a battle ahead, I think. Tom's not going to give up the house easily. And Leila's son is in rehab so Tom is being the ideal man and supporting her. That's what Ben tells me.'

'Well . . . you can't steal another woman's husband and expect everything to go smoothly.'

A husband or wife can't really be stolen; I know that – Tom must have been willing to go. He is a man who is decisive and sure of himself, not a man who is persuaded and led. After he confessed to the affair, he told me that he didn't feel we had a future. That he needed to feel more 'visible in the relationship', that he wanted the emphasis to move from 'family to couple'. I was at a loss to know why we couldn't have both family and couple. And as for him being visible – when was he ever not?

'I'm a great believer in do as you would be done by,' my dad's saying. He's on his hands and knees now and is using a Stanley knife to straighten the edge of the lino. 'Liars should expect to be lied to. Deceivers should expect to be deceived.'

When he says this I immediately think of Francis. It's been bothering me that I'm lying to him by omission. He knows I'm going to Leila Henrikson for therapy but what he doesn't know is that Leila is the woman my husband left me for. I'm going to have to speak to him because I'm worried that he'll find out by accident – chances are he'll meet Ben soon, maybe even this evening, and Ben might talk about Leila. Or I might let something slip – and I don't want him to find out that way. I have to tell him first. If he thinks less of me then there's nothing I can do about that but if I don't tell him, he's still bound to find out, and that will be worse.

When I get back home, I do my checks, then have another run at the financial documents, answering questions ranging from comprehensive details of my teacher's pension to shares I owned back in the nineties that I have long forgotten about. Tom has obviously decided to frustrate me into searching just in case I never sold them. Form-filling gives me a headache at the best of times and I'm pleased when Francis knocks on the front door just as I'm close to throwing the pages across the room. 'I haven't got the carry-out yet,' he says. 'I thought I'd be sure of your order then pop along to get it.' He follows me into the living room. 'What are you up to?' he asks me.

'Divorce.' I wave the sheets in the air. 'This is what it all boils down to.'

'He's burying you under a mountain of paperwork?'

'That's about the nub of it. He's not going to give up the house any time soon. Not now his new woman is ensconced in there.' I add, 'Bitch,' under my breath.

'Tackle the forms slowly,' Francis says. He gives me a rallying hug. 'It sounds like it could take a while but good things will happen en route, I'm sure.'

'You're such an optimist.'

'I'm more of a realist,' he says and I sense he's thinking of his mum.

'How's your mum today?'

'She's much the same. Holding on to life by a thread.'

'I'm sure she loves having you visiting every day.'

'She does. It's giving us a chance to say everything we need to say before she—' He hesitates before adding '—dies. Anyway!' He rubs his hands together. 'Let's get the order in.'

He pulls the menu out of his pocket and we decide what we're having. 'Will Ben be here too?' he asks me.

'No.' I've had a text from Ben to say he's staying out for a couple of nights at a friend's house, so that means it will just be the two of us. 'We can watch the film,' I say. 'Without being interrupted.' I try to give him the money to pay for the food but he insists on making it his treat and while he's off collecting it I do a round of checks and give the living room a quick tidy-up. I feel excited at what the evening might hold. Francis likes me – I can feel it – and I like him, so if he does make a move, what's to stop me?

The curry goes down well, as does the beers we drink with it. We sit on the sofa with plates on our laps in front of the film. Francis is right – despite the film's premise it is a feel-good movie and by the end I'm both crying and laughing.

'Good, isn't it?' Francis says, reaching across to take my hand.

'I loved it,' I say. Our eyes meet and hold. I don't breathe. He stands up and pulls me to my feet. My hipbones bump up against the tops of his thighs. He slides his hands into the back pockets of my jeans and pulls me in closer. 'I've been wanting to do this for a few days now,' he says.

I've lost the power of speech so I'm unable to reply.

He dips his head down and I bring my face up to meet his. I haven't been kissed for over a year. I haven't been kissed like this for over ten years. I let him kiss me and then I join in, matching and mirroring his moves, kissing and kissing until breathing becomes more important. I step away and smile across at him. 'That's—' I laugh. 'Lovely. Unexpected.' I'm nodding. 'It's been a while. I em—'

'I like you, Ellen,' he says, his expression sincere. 'I like your sense of humour and your kindness. I like your honesty—'

'Ah!' I hold up a finger. 'Well, there's the thing.' I try for a full breath but my chest feels tight so I only manage a shallow one. 'There's something I need to tell you, Francis, something important.'

'What?' He reaches for my hands, his smile faltering. 'What's going on?'

'I've been . . .' I sigh. 'I really hope you don't think less of me.'

'I couldn't think less of you.'

'I think you just might.' I feel nauseous and try to swallow the feeling down. It doesn't work but I press on anyway. 'You know how I'm going to therapy?' He nods. 'Well . . . Leila Henrikson, the therapist, is also the woman who is living with Tom, in my old house. Maybanks,' I add. 'The one I'm trying to get back.' He doesn't say anything but he does let go of my hand. 'None of my family know I'm going to therapy or that I've been back into my house. You're the only person who knows.' I clench my fists. 'It's deceitful and dishonest and I shouldn't be doing it but the temptation was irresistible.'

'Ellen, hang on!' Francis is shaking his head. 'If she's

the woman who's living with your husband then how come she hasn't recognised you?'

'I know. I really thought she would but she hasn't. I don't think she's even suspicious! I expected to be caught. I expected to be caught immediately and I'd decided I would give her a piece of my mind and then I'd leave but—' I throw my arms up in disbelief '—she welcomed me in! I'm going under my maiden name, Mary McNeil, and she seems none the wiser. She is a good therapist – I think she might actually help me if I let her – but all I can see is the woman who stole my life.' I wring my hands together. 'Ben told me that her son has a drug problem and is in rehab, so she doesn't have her troubles to seek, but the fact is that she is doing wrong, sitting pretty in my house.'

'Okay.' He steps away from me, obviously thinking. 'This is quite a . . .' He trails off.

'I've shocked you, haven't I?' I bring my hand up to my mouth. 'I know how it must sound and I would never normally behave this way but I—'

'When you spoke about revenge, this is what you meant?'

'Well . . . yes, because I'm getting inside information to give to my solicitor – for example, the oak tree's been chopped down.' I tell him about the tree house my dad built and how long the oak tree stood there and how it's been replaced by a hot tub. 'And then . . .' I hesitate, cover my face with my hands, then ram them into the pockets of my jeans.

'There's more?' Francis asks.

'There's more,' I say, his troubled expression knocking holes in my confidence. *You've lost him, Ellen. It's over before it's even begun.* 'If you give me a second I'll just get something.' I climb the stairs quickly, not allowing myself to think. I lift the black lacquer box off my dressing table and go back down to show it to Francis. 'I had kept the back-door key. I knew that she and Tom were going out this morning and I was banking on Katarina going out too, which she did, and so I went inside the house.'

'And you took this?' The tips of his fingers trace the mother-of-pearl inlay on the lid. 'It's beautiful.'

'It is mine,' I say. 'It was my grannie's. I forgot to bring it with me when I left. I asked Tom several times to give it to either Chloe or Ben but he didn't, so . . . yeah. I took it.' I keep going. 'And that's not all I did. I also cut holes in some of her clothes and scraped her designer shoes with a pair of scissors so that they are unwearable.'

He makes a face. 'I understand the need to get your own back, Ellen, but I'm not sure about this.' He gives a nervous laugh. 'I think that, in the long run, it might not be the best move.'

'I thought you'd be disappointed in me.' My shoulders deflate. 'But I couldn't not tell you.'

'Because deep down you are a good person.' He lays his hands on my shoulders and when he pulls me in to him, I close my eyes. 'With what you've been through this last year it's important not to be a victim, I can see that, and I understand that you need to seize back some control, but Ellen.' He stares down into my eyes. 'Promise me you'll stop now, because I just feel that . . .' He shrugs. 'It might not end well.'

'I will. I will,' I say. 'I only need to see her one last time.'

'And then you'll stop?'

'Yes, I will. I promise.'

I haven't been to bed with anyone since Tom left me. I haven't even imagined it because when I have, I haven't been able to get past the thought of taking off my clothes. But the alcohol and the kissing and the honesty have knocked my shyness into touch and when he starts kissing me again it isn't long before we're in the bedroom, helping each other to strip. I'm rushing, giggling, pleased that he hasn't rejected me. Francis slows us both down. His fingers are unhurried, more deliberate. He likes to see what he's getting. Every part of me is attended to. He has a lingering attention to detail and a tenderness that makes me feel like he's been thinking about this for a while and knows exactly what he wants to do to me. By the time he pulls me round on top of him and he's inside me, I take less than a minute to come and I gasp with the surprise of it. A few more thrusts, our eyes meet and hold, and he comes too.

I collapse onto his chest enjoying the lassitude that empties through me, spreading sweetness and warmth through every cell in my body.

After a few minutes I prop myself up onto my elbows and kiss beneath his ear. 'You are quite something,' I say softly. 'I haven't enjoyed sex this much for as long as I can remember.' Perhaps this is an exaggeration, but in the here and now it feels true. After a year without sex, the very existence of such pleasure feels extraordinary.

'Good news,' Francis says. He rolls me onto my back and reaches for the bottle of water on the bedside cabinet, takes a swig, then gives it to me. 'But I think we'll get better.'

I sit up and raise the water bottle in a toast. 'Here's to breaking records.'

I stroke his chest and down to his hip where my fingers trace the line of his scar. 'This must have hurt so much,' I say. 'Someone stabbing you, like that. You could have died.'

'It was difficult.' He brings my hand to his mouth and kisses my fingers. 'But it was a long time ago.'

'I'm so sorry.' I pull the duvet aside and kiss along the line of scar tissue. 'I feel for you.'

'It's not all bad.' He laughs. 'Look at the sympathy it's getting me.'

'I see.' I give him a scolding look. 'This is how you get women into bed?'

'I find it gets me what I want.'

'And what do you want?'

He whispers in my ear until he has my heart racing again.

The second time is even better and when he falls asleep with his head on my breasts, I don't move him off. I lie awake for what seems like ages, my hand stroking his hair.

9. Leila

It's true to say that, despite our efforts, past behaviour is usually the best predictor of future behaviour and so, although it's still days away, I'm nervous about going to see Gareth. Me, David and Gareth in a room alone together? I can only imagine what will happen. When we were children we called our stepfather by anything except his actual name – not to his face, of course, or at least not until we could fight back – shitbag, prick, fuckwit. In recent years when we've spoken about him we've only ever called him Gareth and that's quite possibly because he has lost his power over us. That's what I hope anyway.

I've cancelled almost all of my clients for next week as per Maurice's advice. All of them understood that I needed some time for myself – apart from Mary McNeil, whom I agreed to see after all, as she is at the beginning of the therapeutic process and needs the extra support. Mark and Alison were also reluctant to let go of me but I wouldn't give in to them.

'Is it just us that you're cancelling?' Mark says.

'No. I need to take a break for a week. I'm cancelling everyone.'

'I'm sorry about the way we behaved. We spoke about it afterwards and we realised how difficult we'd been.'

'As I said, Mark, I'm cancelling because I need a break, not because of anything you have or haven't done.'

I hear Alison's voice in the background and then she comes to the phone. 'Leila! We need to see you,' she says. 'What you said to us really helped and we want to talk about the promises we've made to each other.' I tell her she will have to save that for the following week. 'But please, we will try harder to listen.'

'I'll see you both soon,' I say and shut out her whining voice with the press of a button.

I haven't been back to see Maurice again because of the cat. Maurice has a sixth sense for what clients are keeping hidden and I don't want to talk about what I've done. It's two days since I broke the cat's neck and hid his body under the bushes. I've been down to the bottom of the garden for a smoke several times since and there's no smell as yet. Knowing the body is there, being eaten by grubs, his guts a nesting ground for blowflies, makes me feel powerful because I am the keeper of the secret. I am the queen of the castle. I am omnipotent.

Mrs Patterson has been wandering up and down the street calling for him and that should make me feel guilty but it doesn't. It makes me feel like I'm the winner and she's the loser. I'm in the know and she is out in the cold. Gareth always told me I was a psychopath – takes one to know one! I would shout back – but I'm not a psychopath or a sociopath. I'm simply acting out an old pattern, learned in childhood. Sometimes I let myself go there – as treat or punishment? I'm not really sure which. All I know is that it feels familiar and in that familiarity I find security.

Rob Mooney from the Bridge calls me to say that Alex is doing well and that he can have a visitor this weekend. The thought of visiting my son has me walking around the house with a smile on my face. I've missed him, not in an overt way, but in a subtle, discreet manner that no one else would notice. I don't tell Tom because I don't want him to come with me. I'm beginning to feel that my future lies elsewhere. I know he's trying hard to support me but I don't need a man making a meal of fussing over me. I need him to pay for Alex's treatment. And if he can't – or won't – do that then he's no use to me.

The scratch lines on my forearm are itchy. I'm wearing long sleeves to hide the marks. I've been wearing long sleeves for the past couple of days to hide the marks and have covered two areas of broken skin with small dressings. I pull them off now, quickly, wincing as I do so. Pus is leaking from one of the deeper scratches and I wash it with some antiseptic, then cover the same two areas up again. Gareth would tell me the reason the cat scratched me was because I was out of practice. It's my own fault for letting my skills slide. Skills I never wanted in the first place.

'Fuck you, Gareth,' I say quietly as I pull my blouse back on again. 'Fuck you.'

Alex. On the drive over to the Bridge I'm mindful of what he will be feeling. We've been through this before and last time neither of us got it right. We were both nervous and I made the mistake of asking questions that sent him into defensive mode. I decide that this time I won't risk that. This time I'll listen and encourage him. If I'm more therapist than mother then I should be able to hit the right note.

I park the car and have to stop myself running into the building, where I find him waiting for me in the foyer. 'Hi!' I hold my arms wide and walk towards him. He's bashful but grinning despite himself and we hold each other in a hug for twenty seconds or more. 'So good to see you!'

'Aye. You too, Mum. How's everything at home?'

'Good, yeah. Same old, same old.' I make a face. 'You know how it is.'

Rob Mooney is hovering in the background and he comes across to say hello. 'It's a good day to have a walk in the grounds or you can mosey into the village.'

'What would you like, Alex?' I say.

'Wouldn't mind a cheese toastie. They have a cafe in the village that's quite nice.'

'Village it is then! Let's go.'

I loop my arm through his and we walk the half mile into the wee village that comprises no more than a hundred homes, a pub, a cafe and a general store. As we leave the grounds I see a man standing beneath a tree but I don't think anything of it. We're settled in the cafe at a table by the window, with piles of food in front of us, when I catch sight of the man again, lurking outside, only about twenty yards away.

This time I am close enough to make out who it is – David. He knows I've seen him and he strides past the window, full of purpose.

For a split second, before the anger and fear kick in, I admire him. He's crafty, all right. Arguably craftier than me. I hadn't noticed him following me because it hadn't occurred to me that he would go further than Edinburgh city limits. Stupid mistake, Leila, I tell myself. He's perfectly capable of hiring a car and waiting at the end of the street for you to appear. You really can't afford to underestimate him.

'Do you remember Alistair, Mum?' Alex is saying. 'He was in the last time I was here. We're thinking of starting a band together.'

'That sounds like a good idea.'

'Put my bass guitar to good use.' He blows on the

hot string of cheese leaking out the side of his toastie. 'Alistair plays drums and he knows a lead guitarist who might be interested.'

'Where does Alistair live again?'

'The far side of Glasgow, close to Paisley.' He lays his toastie down on the plate and takes a breath, suddenly anxious. 'The thing is, Mum. Well . . . I don't think university suits me.' He watches my face to see my reaction to this bombshell but I'm far too preoccupied with what David is up to to be concerned by this news. 'Would you be bothered if I dropped out?'

'No, I wouldn't.' I smile at him. 'All I want, Alex, is for you to lead a happy life and for that you need a sense of purpose, passion if possible, and an eye to taking care of yourself.'

'Cheers, Mum.' He laughs. 'I thought you'd be mad.'

I am mad. I'm enraged, in fact. There's a fiery knot in my stomach that wants to burst out through my mouth, my fists and my feet. But I'm not angry with Alex. My brother, David, on the other hand – I would gladly stamp on his head right now. I wouldn't start with his head though; I'd begin with his ankles and his wrists, then feel the long bones in his limbs snap, and save the crack of his skull for last.

The doorbell tinkles and David comes into the cafe. I see him out of the corner of my eye but I don't look at him and neither does Alex, who is busy telling me about the group therapy and how much it's helping him. 'I feel more determined this time round, Mum. I'm not just saying that, I promise, I'm really not. Last time I kind of knew I'd do drugs again but this time I know I won't.'

'That's great news, darling.' I reach across the table and stroke his hair. 'I'm so proud of you.'

I'm able to inhabit two distinct identities simultaneously: I'm a mother who loves her son and is delighted and encouraged by his recovery and I'm a sister who is acutely aware of her brother's presence in the seat behind her and is contemplating taking hold of the dessert fork, reaching round and plunging it into his neck.

The waitress takes David's order: a cup of tea and poached eggs on toast. I can hear his speaking voice clearly, so I'm sure he can also hear Alex telling me about his plans for when he comes home. 'I'm going to help more. I know I haven't been pulling my weight. I think Tom would like that, wouldn't he?' I nod. 'I haven't been taking responsibility for myself. I'm only just beginning to understand what that means.'

While Alex talks, I make plans in my head. We'll move to Paisley. If that's where Alex would be happy then I'm willing to give it a go. We've only been in Edinburgh for two years; before that it was Manchester, before that Leeds, before that Guildford. Whenever we move on it takes David a while to find us again. He could contact Alex directly, through Facebook or Twitter, but he never has because his obsession is with me, not my son.

I'm going to sell the jewels our mother left me and then, when Alex is ready to leave the Bridge, we'll plan our move. It'll be a fresh start.

When I've eaten the little I can manage and Alex has hoovered up the rest, we leave the cafe and I drop him back. He gives me the sweetest smile as he goes off to his room and my heart swells with love and with pride. Perhaps I haven't been that bad a mother. Perhaps, at times, I've even done the right thing, the good thing.

As I walk back to my car I'm not surprised to see David leaning up against the driver's door. 'You didn't want to introduce me, then?' His expression is smug. He caught me off guard and he knows it.

'How did you know I was coming here? Was it Katarina? Did she tell you Alex was in rehab?'

He inclines his head. 'Wouldn't you like to know?'

'Could you move aside, please?'

He steps aside in an exaggerated manner, bowing as I open the car door. 'Your pleasure, oh queen,' he says. 'See you soon!'

I start the engine and drive off. My face is set firm the whole way home. My muscles are stiff with anger and concentrated thinking, and when I get through the front door I want nothing more than time to plan the rest of my and Alex's lives, but there is a melee in the front hall. Ben is there with Mrs Patterson and they're telling Tom something. 'Did you know Bruiser was missing?' Tom says to me.

'Who's Bruiser?'

'The cat.'

'We've made a flyer,' Ben says, waving a USB stick. 'We've come to borrow Dad's printer.'

'That's great!' I give a ridiculously wide, false smile. 'I'm just . . .' I point up the stairs '. . . going for a shower.'

When I'm inside my bedroom I close the door behind me and go into the walk-in wardrobe. I want to see my mother's jewellery to reassure myself that I have a way out of this. I reach behind my shoes for the lacquer box, feel along the floor with my hands, but it isn't there. I pull out three pairs of shoes and then I pull out all of my shoes, thirty pairs or more, and scatter them across the carpet. 'Where is it?' I shout. 'Where the fuck is it?'

And then an icy wind blows through me, settling in my skull like brain freeze: David's been in the house again, in my bedroom, going through my things. The realisation is a punch to my stomach and I have to lie on the rug clutching my middle for a few moments before I can sit up again. 'Fuck. Fuck!'

Tom opens the bedroom door, Katarina hovering behind him. 'Everything okay?' He stares at the shoes scattered across the floor. 'I thought I heard you shouting in here.'

'I was shouting.' I stand up slowly. 'I can't find the black lacquer box.'

'What box is that?' He starts picking up my shoes, laying them on the bed to pair them.

'The jewellery box. It was in the walk-in wardrobe. It must have been your mother's. I put some of my jewellery in it because . . . because it was there.'

'My mother's?' He frowns at me and then at my red stilettos. 'What's happened to your shoe?' He holds one of the stilettos up in front of my eyes. 'Look. There's a big scratch across the surface.'

'Jesus, Tom!' I shout, pushing him aside. 'I really don't care about the shoe! I want to know where the box is!'

There follows a bitter fight, when I say the box has been stolen and Tom insists that if it's true then it has to be Katarina who's taken it. Katarina is close to tears and mumbles something about some woman she noticed in the driveway yesterday. 'I see her and I think she is been in the house.'

'What woman? When was this?' Tom snaps. 'And if you thought she'd been in the house then why on earth didn't you tell us?'

Tom expects me to join in with this interrogation but I don't because I bloody well know it has to have been David and I'll get him back. By Christ I'll get him back. While Tom takes Katarina downstairs to enact her story, I check under the mattress to see whether David found

the letter I fabricated. It's a small measure of relief to
see that the letter is still there, silent as a sleeping bomb,
ready to detonate should I need to blow David's demands
to pieces.

Mrs Patterson listens to Tom and me shout at each
other until Ben has the flyers printed out and he leads
her away by the elbow. She goes reluctantly; she'll have
a lot to tell the neighbours. I expect it almost makes up
for the cat.

10. Ellen

I wake up in the early hours of the morning as I always do, and climb out of bed to do my checks. I'm walking across my bedroom floor when I sense a presence in the room and I tune in to the sound of breathing. Of course! Francis stayed the night, our second night together with Ben away. I feel the almost tangible pull of comfort and warmth and consider returning to bed and not doing my checks, but anxiety rumbles in my chest and I tell myself there's no point trying to walk before I can run. I didn't check the sockets before I fell asleep and I know I didn't lock the front door. Even people without a problem lock their front door.

It doesn't take me long because I really do want to get back to bed. I'm round the house in a jiffy and then I go round once more just to be sure. Francis is facing away from me when I snuggle into his back. His skin is soft and smells sweet and subtle like roses, the Golden Celebration rose in particular. I planted several bushes of those in my back garden and I wonder whether Leila has hauled them out or hacked them down too. My last thought as I drift off into sleep is how much I'll enjoy showing Francis Maybanks.

I don't wake again until seven in the morning. Francis is still asleep and I get up without disturbing him, shower and make us both some breakfast to take back to bed. I've already been in touch with Ben to make sure he won't return home and catch us in bed – I'm not ready for that and I don't suppose my son is either.

By ten o'clock we're surrounded by a mess of toast crumbs, empty coffee mugs and knives sticky with marmalade. It feels like just what the doctor ordered, a decadent and indulgent morning in bed, something I haven't done since I was newly married.

'What time is Ben due home?' Francis asks.

'In about an hour.'

'Better get cracking then,' he says. 'I'll take the dishes through to the kitchen.' He springs out of bed and I watch him, smiling at the joys of fancying a man who fancies me back, a man who seems to be mine at the moment – not that I'm projecting ahead; one night does not a relationship make. Still . . . his presence has given my battered self-esteem an adrenaline shot and I can't help but feel pleased, emboldened, strong.

'Would you like to meet Ben?' I ask Francis when we're both showered and dressed.

'Are you sure?'

'Yes, I think so.' I lean in and kiss him. 'I'll say you popped in this morning. I'm not sure I want him to know we've been to bed.'

'Might be a bit early for that,' Francis agrees. 'Where do we know each other from?'

'Well, I already told Chloe I met you through a teacher friend at school.'

'Chloe knows about me?' He laughs. 'So you were always going to seduce me. And there I was thinking I was calling the shots.'

When Ben comes through the front door we're both laughing, but if my son suspects we're closer than we make out then he doesn't show it. I introduce them to each other and then Ben throws himself onto the sofa and kicks off his trainers. 'Guess who I bumped into last night?'

'Who?' I say.

'Mrs Patterson. Bruiser's gone missing.'

'Oh, no!'

'She's really upset. He's been gone for four days.'

'Four days. That's longer than usual.' I turn to Francis and explain about Mrs Patterson and her cat. 'Bruiser's her whole life,' I say. 'He's quite a personality. Everyone knows him but he was especially fond of our garden. He must be ten or eleven now because she got him just before her husband died. He's been a bit of a wanderer in the past but he's never been gone for more than forty-eight hours.'

'I was round the corner visiting the Murrays,' Ben says. 'They send their love, by the way. And then when I was going to meet Archie at the pub, Mrs Patterson was on the corner by the park calling for him. She was in tears.'

'Poor love.'

'I took her home and said I'd help her make up some flyers to tape onto the lamp-posts. We had to go to Dad's to print them out and it was all kicking off again.'

'What was it about this time?' I say, not expecting what comes next.

'Apparently Leila couldn't find a box that has some jewellery in it.'

I stiffen and feel my face going a telltale red, so I bend down to the floor and neaten Ben's shoes at the side of the sofa.

'Dad didn't even seem to know what box she was talking about but Leila was positive it was in the walk-in wardrobe. She was in a right state about it.'

'I expect it will turn up,' Francis says, super-casual.

'Things always do.' The lacquer box is on the sideboard behind Ben's head and Francis leans across to cover it with a tea towel. I would give him a grateful glance but I am frozen with disbelief. The jewellery box wasn't hers and neither was the jewellery inside it! Why on earth would she make such a fuss?'

'Then it all went a bit Jeremy Kyle,' Ben says. 'Dad was convinced Katarina had stolen it but Leila was adamant it wasn't her.' Ben goes on to tell us that Leila refused to tell Tom who she thought it was and he kept pushing her to say that if it wasn't Katarina then it had to be some bloke who's been hanging around, a client of hers. 'Katarina told them she'd seen a woman in the driveway and Dad started to question her like she was a hostile witness. Mrs Patterson and I left them to it and went to put up the flyers. When we were outside she said to me, I don't want to speak ill of your dad but your mum really is better off without him.'

Ben stops talking at last, distracted by the mobile in his pocket. He jumps up and begins a lively conversation with the person on the other end, leaving the room as he does so.

I stare at Francis and Francis stares at me. 'What the hell?' I say. 'Francis, it's not her box! Nor is it her jewellery.'

'Sounds like there's more to the story than we know,' he says. 'I wouldn't worry about it.'

'Hang on!' I have a sudden light-bulb moment that makes my brain tingle. I didn't look in the secret drawer! Perhaps for some reason she put her jewellery in there. I throw the tea towel aside and press the hinge joint to pop open the drawer. My breath stops when I see what's inside. Unlike my jewels, these pieces are clearly worth money. There is a necklace, a bracelet and a pair of earrings. The gold is rich and mellow. The stones are precious: sapphires, some diamonds, aquamarines and others I don't know the names of.

'Look Francis!' I pass him the necklace and he holds it parallel to his face and watches as the stones catch the light and shimmer.

'Boy oh boy,' he says. 'This is worth something.'

'There's a bracelet and earrings as well.'

We both stare at the pieces. 'I can see why she was upset,' Francis says.

'I'll have to return them. I'll do what I did yesterday. I'll watch for them going out and then I'll put the pieces through the letter box.' My hand shakes as I take the necklace from him. 'It never even occurred to me that she might have put something of hers in there otherwise I would have checked before I left Maybanks.' My anxiety starts to build and I reach over to pull the kettle plug out of its socket. 'Sorry,' I say to Francis. 'This has got to me. I know how much I wanted my gran's jewellery back and now I've taken hers. It's probably her mother's.'

'Well . . . first of all,' Francis says. 'This can be put right.' I go to speak and he places a finger on my lips. 'And second of all, if you give me the address, I will drop the pieces off for you.'

'No . . . thank you. I don't want you to be implicated. What if you were caught?'

'It's unlikely I'd be caught. It would all be over in seconds.'

'That isn't fair on you. I did it; I need to put it right.'

'Your call,' he says, his expression serious. 'But the offer is there.' I can see that he's reached his threshold and I know I'm right when he says, 'I don't believe this is you, Ellen. I believe you're better than this.'

'You're right.' I nod.

He brings me in for a hug. 'I think you need to back-track before this gets out of hand. What if they get the police involved? What if Katarina is questioned and accused? How would you feel then?'

Francis is another Chloe – and that's no bad thing. He is decent and moral, and I can only agree that police involvement is not what I want. I will return the jewellery – but I'm not going to do it immediately because the temptation to make Leila suffer for that bit longer is irresistible. I want to go to my next appointment and see her rattled. I want to feel like I'm winning.

'I said I'd look after Molly for a couple of hours this morning and then I'll go to Maybanks to drop off the jewellery. I expect they'll go out for Sunday lunch. Tom always liked doing that.' I hug Francis's back as he finishes drying the dishes. His heart is close to my ear and I listen to its steady rhythm, knowing that I've just lied to him.

My dad is a member of a walking club and they've set off to walk along the cycle path from Leith to Colinton. He's taken his flask of tomato soup and his cheese and pickle sandwiches and waved goodbye. Molly and I weed the garden and plant some herbs, then we make a big pot of vegetable soup and read storybooks until Chloe and Jack come home. They went to brunch with Jack's new boss and expected to be back by one, but it's gone three by the time they get in.

'So sorry, Mum!' Chloe says, her cheeks flushed. 'But we all got on like a house on fire. Didn't we Jack?'

'We did.' Molly has already managed to climb onto her dad's shoulders and is covering his eyes with her hands. 'They're good people. And they have a munchkin like you, Molly moll.' He swings her round into his arms and she gives a shriek of pleasure.

'I'll be off then.' I do the round of kisses. It's great to see them so happy together but I'm keen to get going. I need to get down to Maybanks. I've no intention of giving back the jewellery yet but I feel drawn to the house – I'm pleased that Tom and Leila are at logger-heads. Will I be able to tell from the outside of the house that there is turmoil inside? 'Sorry to rush but I have people to see, dogs to buy.'

'I know the sort of dog you're talking about,' Chloe says, winking. 'Fabulous Francis.'

I laugh. 'I'm not seeing him until tomorrow.'

'You buying a dog, Grannie?' Molly shouts. 'Could you buy one for me too?'

'It's just an expression, Mol,' I hear Jack say as Chloe follows me outside to my car.

'Thanks for today, Mum.' She gives me a hug. 'And I'm really glad things are looking up for you. You deserve to be happy.'

She waves me off and I wave back, for all the world just like any other grandmother on her way home after babysitting. I drive down Hanover Street towards Trinity, making my mind up to be brazen and drive right past Maybanks, no hiding, no pretending, just a straightfor-ward drive-by. Unless Tom and Leila are standing in the front garden I should be able to get away with it. My heart is somersaulting as I turn into the road and I have to resist the urge to slump down in my seat and hold a hand up to the side of my face. I don't slow down. I continue at a steady twenty-five miles an hour, glancing briefly to my left when I pass Maybanks. The house looks exactly the same as it did yesterday and I feel the slump of disappointment. What was I expecting? A banner declaring the theft? I shake my head at my own childishness. I need to bide my time – just a little while longer. Tuesday is only two days away and I'm already counting the hours.

10. Leila

Tom was up and out of the house early this morning. I've no idea where he's gone and I'm not about to massage his inflated ego by calling him to find out. He hasn't spoken to me since last night when I discovered the jewellery box was missing. I know he's convinced I'm hiding something from him and he's right, I am; and I'll continue to do so because he's neither sympathetic nor empathetic and he'd never understand my relationship with David, no matter how hard I tried to explain it to him.

David has the jewellery – of that I am sure – and therefore he must be colluding with someone. It's not the first time he's found sneaky ways to infiltrate my life. Ten years ago when Alex and I were living on the outskirts of Leeds, he spent two months cultivating a friendship in order to have access to my flat. The flat was on the third floor of a converted flour mill in a beautiful setting close to the river. It was perfect for Alex because there was a comprehensive play area with tennis and basketball courts and there were several single parents living in the building so we were able to share childcare. David befriended the caretaker-cum-gardener over a game of poker in the local pub. Next thing, he was doing odd jobs for him and then before I knew it he was in my front room telling my boyfriend all about me. My boyfriend was called Mitchell and I distinctly remember his face as I entered the living room. He stared at me as if he literally didn't know who I was.

Aside from Tom and myself, there are only two people who could have told David about me visiting Alex in rehab and either let David into Maybanks or given him the jewellery: Katarina or Ben.

I find Katarina in the kitchen. 'I won't be angry with you,' I say, and at once she looks anxious.

'I am sorry. I clean the oven yesterday but—'

'It's not about the oven.'

'Tom is angry and I tell him—'

'It's not about Tom either. I simply need you to be honest.' I step towards her and her eyes widen. 'Have you seen my brother since you let him inside the house?'

'Yes. I see him but I do not talk to him.'

'Where was he?'

'Outside.'

'Did he ask you to get something for him?'

'No, no. I do not take jewels.' She is emphatic. 'I do not steal.' She stamps her foot. 'I do *not.*'

I believe her. She doesn't flinch from eye contact, and she's obviously insulted that I could consider her a thief. She might be a bit distant and dreamy sometimes but I have never suspected her of snooping or stealing.

'And you didn't tell him that I was visiting Alex yesterday?'

'No. Of course not. You tell me not talk to him.'

That only leaves Ben. He was in the house on Friday and could have taken the pieces then. I expect he'd be quite happy to make my life more difficult and I know that Chloe would be pleased with him. But there's nothing I can do about it at the moment.

Several of my sweaters and blouses have been cut with scissors, jagged holes that are impossible to repair. And my shoes. Three pairs ruined. I'm less concerned about replacing the clothes and shoes than I am about what this says about David's state of mind. This type of spiteful behaviour isn't like him and I'm unsure what to make of it. We're not due to meet until Wednesday when we go to visit Gareth, but I'll be on edge until then. After his stunt turning up at the Bridge yesterday, who knows where he will appear next.

I spend the afternoon tidying out my wardrobe, separating the damaged garments from the untouched. I still haven't heard from Tom so I decide not to make Sunday lunch but to take a bottle of wine upstairs and lie in the bath. It's something I almost never do but I need to do now: candles, warm bubbles, a glass of cold white wine.

I put the plug in the bath and run water over expensive bath oil that bubbles up, releasing the smell of roses into the bathroom. Me-time. That's what other women call it. Normal women. Women who don't have their past creeping up behind them, making ready to pounce, to smother them in a memory blanket.

I don't make it as far as the bath because as soon as I begin to undress I'm reminded of the scratches on my arm. They are almost but not quite healed. I touch the skin either side of the raised marks and I shiver. Why pretend, Leila? Why pretend? I turn off the water and sit down on the tiles, wedging myself between the bath and the toilet, and open the wine. I drink half of it, straight from the bottle. My stomach is empty and I feel the effect almost at once.

I close my eyes and give myself permission. *Relax. Remember. Conjure up Leila Mae. She might even be able to help you.*

My fourteenth birthday.

'How will you be celebrating your birthday, Leila?' Miss Tiptree asks me. She is a young, pretty teacher with big brown eyes and a small nose. She fusses about her wall displays, making neat little ribbon bows to pin beside the names of the children who are achieving well. She is my form teacher but she is utterly clueless about my life.

I arrive home from school to see David curled up on the armchair, legs and arms pulled into his body and his face hidden from view. Gareth is standing by the window and when I come into the room he turns towards me. He has the quality of a fairytale creature – the creature children are warned to avoid – rather than a human being. He has ash-grey eyes, the colour of incinerated bones. His hands are always damp with sweat as if he's just crawled out of a swamp. David and I imagine that he is really a lizard who's been given a man's body made from leftover bits that make him look almost, but not quite, human.

'I've been waiting for you, Leila Mae,' he says. 'I have a special surprise for you this evening.' David's body jerks as if he's falling into a deep sleep but I know that he isn't. He's been hoping for invisibility and now that I'm back he has it. Outside of home, he's often in trouble for picking fights and bullying other boys but when he comes through the front door, he shape-shifts from lion to lamb. 'Come with me.' Gareth holds out his hand and I step forward because the sooner we get this over with the sooner I'll be able to go to my room. I touch the base of my skull and sense a stirring inside the bone like the first small plumes of smoke from a newly made fire.

Gareth leads me to the top of the cellar steps. 'Are you ready for this?'

I haven't seen my mother for a couple of weeks now. I have heard her moving around in the bedroom and moaning in her sleep, and I hear her now: the scraping of a chair across the floor, a gurgling cough, a chink of glass. I briefly latch on to the thought that maybe if I call her she'll come downstairs and help me, maybe she's been getting well all this time, maybe she'll look like a normal mother and she'll hug me, order Gareth to pack his cases and get the fuck out of our house.

Gareth leads me down the steps. At first David and I believed him when he said he was a scientist. We would stand in front of his exhibits, wide-eyed and awestruck as he showed us furry bodies sliced through, skin pinned back on pieces of wood to reveal innards unravelling, miniature organs unpacked, white bone scraped of sinew. Over time we moved from spectators to assistants and were called upon to hold an animal still while Gareth performed his experiments.

He has captured next door's cat and she is in a cage in the corner, shivering. She hisses when we come close. She is an ordinary mongrel-cat with black fur and white patches scattered like snow across her chest. She's called Cheeky. I know this because she belongs to a girl my age who is in my class. On the school bus this morning she told me that Cheeky has been missing for a couple of days. 'You haven't seen her, have you?' she asked me. 'I'm worried that she might have been run over.'

She'll be my birthday present, then, that's what I thought. But I shook my head at the girl and said, 'I haven't seen her. I hope she comes back.'

Gareth is humming. He's excited – he always is just before the kill. My mouth is filling with bile and there are tap dancers banging out a beat behind my eyes. I touch the back of my head again, find comfort in the black space inside my skull. I know that if I concentrate on letting go then the darkness will weave through the particles of my brain until it obliterates every sight and sound, wrapping me up in a cloak of impenetrable smoke.

Gareth slips Cheeky a treat through the bars of the cage and the cat takes it because she's starving.

'Trust, Leila Mae,' Gareth says. 'Always important to gain the animal's trust.' More humming, more treats and then he opens the cage door. Cheeky is reluctant but she doesn't resist his touch beyond a cower and a half-hearted meow of protest when she is lifted out. 'You should hold her, Leila Mae. Today is your birthday, your special day. A special day for a special girl.'

I guessed a few months ago, from hints dropped here and there, that today was the day he would make me kill for the first time. 'There comes a threshold in every person's life when he or she must move from apprentice to master,' he said last week and David nudged me, his expression scared and questioning.

Gareth hands me the cat. 'Stroke her. Comfort her,' he says.

When I was ten I read that psychopaths begin their murderous habits by killing small animals and so I lived in constant terror of something triggering Gareth into murdering us all. Four years on, and I think that despite the threat of physical violence being ever present, like fumes in a crowded city, Gareth's game is not to progress to killing us but to corrupt David and myself. That is where his pleasure lies. His aim is to spoil our innocence. And he's succeeded.

I stroke Cheeky's fur and whisper words of comfort. 'There, there, puss. You're going to be just fine. Soon you'll be running free again.'

'Remember how to position your hands,' Gareth says, a rictus grin of excitement dominating his pale face.

When I was twelve I went through a phase of thinking that if I could understand Gareth's motivations then I could change him. I spent a lot of time in the library reading about dysfunctional families. I was sure that Gareth must have come from one and that this was his way of coping. I did my research. I found out where his parents lived and I went to see them. They were delighted that I had come to visit. 'We were hoping to meet you!' his mother exclaimed. 'We don't see much of Gareth. We know how busy he is with work. And how much time he spends caring he spends caring for your poor mum,' she said, her voice hushed. 'He's asked us not to pop round so we don't. We know how your mum needs her rest.'

I sat on the edge of their brown leather sofa and they fed me sandwiches and cake. When I had finished a glass of lemonade I asked for a tour of their bungalow. They showed me round with pride, pointing out Gareth's old room, Airfix aeroplanes hanging from the ceiling, and in the kitchen, the brand new fridge-freezer towering in the corner. Gareth's room was a non-event and the fridge-freezer was full of pre-packaged food – not even a sniff of animal organs. The house didn't have a cellar or even a garden hut. Nothing even remotely suspicious, nothing that indicated their son had developed his sadistic, twisted hobby in their home.

I left with a pound pocket money and a promise to return. Which I did. I even took David a couple of times. I began to believe that I could get them to adopt us but then Gareth's dad had a stroke and his mum started spending daylight hours at the hospital.

And as for Gareth's habits – I came to the conclusion that either he was adopted and 'genes will out' or he was simply an evil fuck, an aberration born of good people.

'Short, sharp break, Leila Mae,' Gareth says. 'We don't

want the animal to suffer. We're not about suffering. We are witnesses. Position her head so you can stare into her eyes when she dies.'

I do it. I can't feel anything and I can't see anything because I am lost in the blackness that has filled every space inside my head. Still I know it must be me who snaps her neck. It must be me who stares into her eyes. Because it is my hands that are holding her, my eyes that are looking.

'Are you watching, Leila Mae? Do you see the life leaving her body?' His excited tone changes to disappointment. 'You're not crying, Leila Mae? You should be crying.' Gareth is crying. Tears run down his face in a stream of perverted grief. 'You should be crying, Leila Mae. You hard-hearted girl. You evil little bitch.'

I lay Cheeky's body on Gareth's workbench and run upstairs to my room. Gareth won't follow me. He never does. He will stay downstairs and remove the cat's collar, hang it on a hook in the corner, another trophy to add to his growing collection. Then he'll dissect the body, emptying the furry carcass of everything that gave it life. He won't be happy, though. I have spoiled the kill for him and he'll be working out how to approach me next time, because no tears is a departure from the norm and he won't like that. He enjoys my distress. It's part of the ritual.

Not crying is my birthday present to myself – I'm not going to cry anymore because it's useless. A crying child should bring her mother running, a mother who says, 'What's wrong, darling? Let me help you.' I don't have one of those mothers so I'm fucked if I'm going to be a crybaby.

That night, I take my actions into my sleep and have dreams that are a jumble of sights and sounds, bloody fur and the snap of bone. When I wake, I feel an emotion that shames me, an emotion I could never share with anyone else – not even David, who is fast asleep beside me. Killing Cheeky made me feel powerful. I am a fourteen-year-old girl and I know what it feels like to callously, deliberately kill. I should be ashamed of myself but I'm not. I'm stronger for it.

11. Ellen

Tuesday comes round and so too the anticipated therapy session. I dress carefully in a sky-blue blouse that highlights my eyes. I wear make-up – the full works from foundation to mascara – and when I look at myself in the mirror I'm pleased with what I see. I expect that today will be the day I admit my real identity, because if the conversation goes the way I want it to go then she'll guess who I am. I take the jewellery with me and make my way to Maybanks, walking tall with the freedom of not caring whether I bump into anyone en route.

At exactly 2 p.m. I ring the doorbell. No answer, so I ring it again and then again. It's almost five minutes before the door opens and Leila is standing there. She is dressed in sweatpants and a loose jumper. 'I'm sorry, Mary. I'm suffering from a foul migraine.' She holds her hand up to shield her eyes against the light. 'Would you mind if we cancelled today?' Her speech is slurred. 'I should have called you. I won't charge you, of course.'

'You have a hole in your jumper,' I say, pointing to her right shoulder.

'Oh.' She feels the spot I've pointed out to her. 'Yes, I must have taken the jumper from the wrong pile. I was clearing out my wardrobe and . . .' Her attention drifts off. 'I'm sorry, Mary. I'm having a difficult week. I won't be any use to you today.'

'But we were going to talk about the other woman,' I say.

She frowns. 'What other woman?'

'The woman my husband left me for.'

She laughs. 'I wouldn't worry!' She waves a magnanimous hand. 'From what I know of you, and from what you've told me of him . . . well, you're better off without him.'

'But—'

'Just . . .' She closes her eyes. 'Let . . .' Her head drops to one side. 'It . . .' She giggles. 'Go . . .' She sways on her feet and I realise that she doesn't have a migraine. She's been drinking. She's properly plastered.

'Leila?' My tone is annoyed.

She opens her eyes and focuses on mine. Her pupils are dilated and I see my own reflection in the black of her eyes. My face moves closer to hers as if pulled by an invisible thread and my reflection increases in size until I see my own expression, wide-eyed and confused. Then Leila blinks and the spell is broken. 'Just go,' she says. 'Fuck right off!' Just before the door closes in my face I hear her say, 'Silly cow.'

'Bitch!' I say out loud. 'Some therapist you are!' The jewellery is heavy in my bag but I'm damned if I'm giving her it back now. I trudge home, feeling annoyed and let down. I find Francis waiting for me when I go inside.

'So what happened?' he says.

'We didn't have the session.' I throw my coat over the back of a chair. 'I feel really cheated.'

'Wasn't she there?'

'She was drunk!' I sit next to him on the sofa and tell him everything from start to finish. 'Her pupils were huge, black. I felt . . .' I shiver. 'I felt almost hypnotised by her.'

'Did you give her her jewellery back?'

'No. I . . .' His face says it all. 'I'm going to though. I really am.'

'Has it occurred to you that she might be drinking because the jewellery was stolen?'

'Yes . . . no.' I try to snuggle into him but he shifts his weight away from me. 'You're telling me this has gone far enough, aren't you?'

'Yes.'

'Tomorrow. I'll return the pieces tomorrow.'

'Why not now?' He stands up. 'We'll go together – or better still, let me do it for you. Let's put her out of her misery before the shit really hits the fan.'

'Please, Francis,' I say. 'Just bear with me for one more night.'

He sighs. 'All right, but really Ellen. This has to stop before someone gets hurt.'

'I know,' I say. 'I know.'

Next day I park a couple of hundred yards from my old house and set off along the street. My conscience – or maybe Francis's – has got the better of me and I'm taking the jewellery back. I'm halfway there when I hear a voice.

'Ellen! Ellen!' It's Mrs Patterson; she seems to appear out of nowhere. 'Have you seen Bruiser? He's missing, you know.'

'Ben told me,' I say. 'I'm so sorry.' I hug her tiny frame. 'You must be beside yourself.'

'I'm not sleeping. I'm not eating. My stomach is all churned up with acid and I know what some people around here are thinking, Ellen – He's only a cat. Why is she getting herself in such a state?'

'I'm not thinking that, Mrs Patterson.' I hold her hand in mine. 'Bruiser is no ordinary cat.'

'I knew you'd understand.' She gives a wistful sigh. 'I do miss you, my dear.' Her head drops to one side, then her face lights up and her head pops upright again. 'Will you come in and have a cup of tea? I've made scones.'

I can see Maybanks' drive from where we're standing. There are no cars in the driveway; it's the perfect time for me to drop the jewellery through the door.

'There was a dreadful fuss going on in there on Saturday,' Mrs Patterson says. She has her tiny hand in the crook of my arm and has started walking us towards her house. 'Did Ben tell you?'

'He did mention it, yes.'

'A great kerfuffle broke out because she couldn't find a box and when she described it, I thought to myself – that's Ellen's box! The lovely Chinese one that belonged to her grandma, with the mother-of-pearl inlay. I'm right, aren't I? And Tom was none the wiser – aren't men hopeless? That box only sat on your dressing table for ever and a day!'

I have to smile. Not much gets past Mrs Patterson. We're close to her house when she points out the flyer taped onto the lamp-post. 'Your boy was so kind, so very kind to me. He's put them up on the lamp-posts from here to the main road.'

'It's a great photo of Bruiser,' I say. 'Looks just like him.'

'I'm hoping. I'm really hoping,' she says, clutching at the string of beads round her neck. 'He's a bit silly about the traffic sometimes, that's my worry. He spies a patch of sunshine on the opposite side of the road and off he goes.'

'Let's get you indoors,' I say, looking skyward. 'The rain's on its way.'

'You come in for that cuppa,' she says, propelling me

along the drive ahead of her, surprisingly strong when she needs to be. 'I have *so* much to tell you. My loyalty will always be with you, Ellen.' She pats my hand and then unlocks her front door with a key from the chain she wears round her waist. 'Your secret is safe with me. If you came to get your lovely jewellery box back – and I'm not saying you did, mind – then who could blame you?' She's staring up at me without a trace of guile. Some people would intend this as a veiled threat but Mrs Patterson doesn't. 'I didn't tell Tom and Leila that I saw you from the window,' she adds. 'I wouldn't do that.'

'Thank you, Mrs Patterson.'

'Some people might not recognise you with your hair changed but I'd know you anywhere. That's Ellen,' I said to myself. 'And good luck to her.'

Mrs Patterson has four children and twelve grand-children and I catch up with all of their lives while we have afternoon tea in the front room. It's a surprisingly good spread for a lady who lives on her own and I would thoroughly enjoy it were the circumstances different. There are finger sandwiches with three fillings, scones with a perfect rise and blackberry jam made from the fruit from her garden. I manage to eat my share despite the fact that I'm itching to get next door.

Before too long her mind drifts back to Maybanks. 'There's something not right about that Leila. And I've seen a *man* hanging about, you know. Leila thinks it was him who took the box.'

'She said that?'

'Not exactly but she did say, "It's not Katarina. It's him! I know it's him!" But then she wouldn't explain herself any further and that made Tom angry. You know he had the oak tree chopped down?'

'Was it Tom who wanted it down?' I frown. 'I thought it might have been her.'

'He told me he wanted it down.' She thinks for a second. 'Perhaps he was just saying that, though?'

'Most of the cacti are gone too.'

'I noticed that. When we were upstairs – because Tom has his study in Chloe's room now, you know? – well, yes, I saw into the glasshouse and it was practically empty. So sad.' She shakes her head. 'So very sad. I asked Katarina about it and she said they took most of the cacti to the dump. I mean, why didn't they offer them to the neighbours?'

'Took me fifteen years to collect them all.'

'You won't be found out,' she says, her tone very definite. Her eyes meet mine. 'Katarina said she'd seen a woman but they took no notice of her. They were too busy arguing with each other.'

I nod my head, knowing there's no point pretending – or at least not with Mrs Patterson. 'You're right, I was here on Friday and I did take the box.'

'Ah . . .' Mrs Patterson gives a sigh of acknowledgement.

'I still have the back-door key and because the house isn't Tom's yet, I'm as entitled to be in there as he is.'

'Oh?' Mrs Patterson's face is a picture of interest.

'The problem is that she had put some jewellery in the box – I don't know why. You'd think she would have had something of her own to store it in.'

'Yes.' Mrs Patterson is gripped.

'It was probably her grandmother's or mother's or something,' I say, shaking my head. 'But regardless of who it used to belong to, it's clearly worth a lot of money and I will put it back.'

Mrs Patterson's face brightens. 'I can be your lookout!'

She catches her breath and then her expression clouds. 'Wait! Wait, Ellen. I've just remembered the important bit.' She thumps her thigh with a shaky fist. 'Silly old coot that I am.'

'Take your time,' I say. I have no idea what she's about to say. I feel like it could be anything from an important insight into Leila and Tom's relationship to an observation on myself – perhaps she's seen me sneak into therapy? If she has, I've a feeling I've no need to worry. In the parlance of buddy movies, Mrs Patterson has my back.

'Tom left first this morning, at about seven. Leila left next, just as I was having my constitutional. She stopped the car to pick up a man at the end of the street. And it was the very same man who has been hanging around.' She claps her hands. 'Very odd, I thought to myself. Very odd. And so what I did next was I tended to the front garden for a bit and out came Katarina. A sweet girl from the Czech Republic – Leila doesn't make it easy for her.' She shakes her head. 'There was some bruising on her face and I wouldn't be surprised if . . . well, I wouldn't be surprised if Leila has a temper.'

'You think she hit her?'

'I'm not sure, but anyway, I said to Katarina, I see that man's back. "What one?" she said and I said, the man who you let into the house the other night. Your boyfriend is he? "No!" she said. "He's Leila's brother David." And then she covered her mouth with her hand. "I'm not to say," she said, looking very guilty.' Mrs Patterson stops talking and leans back in her seat. 'What can it mean? Tom didn't know about this man. I know this because I've spoken to Tom about the man and he was adamant he didn't know who he was.'

'I don't know what it means, Mrs Patterson. I really

don't.' I stand up. 'But I do need to get going now.' I
pat my bag. 'I need to put these pieces back.'

'Lead on, MacDuff!' She rises to her feet, rubbing
her right hip. 'I'll be right behind you.'

I'm opening Mrs Patterson's gate, about to step onto
the pavement, when I see Francis coming along the
street. I automatically smile at the sight of him. He isn't
looking in my direction; his eyes are following the BMW
that is pulling into Maybanks' driveway. Leila is home.
I want to shout hello to Francis but I can't because Leila
will see me.

Mrs Patterson is at my elbow and she pulls me back
a few steps so that we are obscured by the honeysuckle.
'It's him,' Mrs Patterson whispers. 'The brother.'

'Where?' Leila climbs out of the car but there is no
one with her. 'I can't see him.'

'That man *there*,' Mrs Patterson says, pointing at
Francis.

'He's not Leila's brother. He's called Francis.' Even
as I'm saying this I'm faltering because Francis goes
straight up to Leila and speaks to her. I strain my ears
but his voice is too quiet for me to hear. Leila pushes
him hard in the chest and I hear Mrs Patterson gasp as
Francis reels backwards into the lupins.

'No love lost there,' Mrs Patterson whispers.

I don't know what to think. I don't know what to feel.
I watch Francis pull himself upright and follow Leila to
the front door. She slams it in his face and he holds his
finger on the bell. He lets it ring and ring and ring until
she opens the door and he goes inside.

'This isn't going to end well,' Mrs Patterson murmurs.

'I have to go.'

'Wait a second. Ellen! What about the jewellery?'

I take off at a run and don't stop until my face is so

wet with tears that the water is running down inside my T-shirt. If Francis is Leila's brother then I've lost my heart and my head to a liar. I've been played for a fool. By him. By her?

An intense anxiety starts up in my chest and my vision blurs. I lean on the garden wall next to me and try to think my way through this but I can't. I'm overbreathing, the rhythm builds and builds and I'm dragged along with it.

'Are you okay?' It's a woman's voice and I try to focus on her face but no amount of blinking makes the blurring recede. I'm lucky, because at the moment I feel myself pass out, she catches me, and the last thing I remember is her hand shielding my head before it hits the pavement.

11. Leila

I've had three drunken days. Three days of remembering. Three days of grabbing hold of what I need to keep and letting go of the rest. I'm dimly aware of answering the door at some point and Mary McNeil standing there, her expression as open and hopeful as a child arriving at a birthday party. I don't know what I say to her but her expression as I close the door stays with me. Angry. She was angry with me. Should I care? . . . Probably. But I don't.

On Wednesday, I reenter my life because today we visit Gareth. I collect David at the end of my road as arranged. I don't drive off immediately. I turn to face him but I don't speak; I simply stare at him. He is whistling through his teeth, pleased with himself. Gradually, as the silence grows, he becomes self-conscious and says to me, 'Everything okay?'

'Do you have anything to tell me?'

'Okay . . . so, I shouldn't have followed you on Saturday but it's not as if I spoke to Alex.'

'No, you shouldn't have followed me.' I look in my rearview mirror and see Mrs Patterson endlessly wandering the streets as she searches for her decomposing cat. I really must put her out of her misery. 'Do you have anything else to tell me?'

He shrugs. 'Not that I can think of.'

'Mum's jewellery?'

'What about it?'

'You took it.'

His eyes widen with exaggerated surprise. 'How could I do *that*?'

'I know you've taken it. I don't know how you got it but I will find out.'

'I haven't got it.' He frowns at me. 'Why do you always think the worst of me?'

'Because whatever we'd all like to believe, past behaviour is the best predictor of future behaviour.'

'People change!'

'People make small adjustments to their behaviour. And, over time, small adjustments can lead to substantial changes, but childhood patterns are hard to beat, especially when they are as ingrained as yours.' *And mine.*

'Harsh.' He laughs. 'Anyway, shouldn't that be ours? I don't believe you've escaped your childhood patterns.'

'Why don't you just forget the petty mind games, the clothes, the shoes, the taking Mum's jewellery and tell me what you're planning?'

'What I'm planning?' His expression is reflective as he stares straight ahead. 'I'm tired, Leila. I'm tired of being a loser and I'm tired of being an outsider. Sure I can play the game. I can pretend to be someone else. I can pretend to be the good guy, the guy who's well-adjusted, well-rounded, a modern man. But inside I'm fucked up because I'm never allowed to be honest and acknowledge my past.'

'And you blame me?'

'You're part of it.'

'Don't push me, David.' My tone is silky smooth. 'I mean it.'

'I know you, Leila.'

'Do you?' We're fully facing one another. 'Look at me closely and tell me what you see.'

'I see you, I see . . .' He trails off and I watch the confidence in his eyes flicker and then die. 'I see Leila Mae.' He drums his fists on his knees. 'Let's go, for fuck's sake.'

The care home Gareth is living in is situated close to a busy road on the outskirts of Dunfermline. The building is a modern design, built to the cheapest specifications, a long rectangular box with small, Lego-like windows placed halfway up the brickwork at regular intervals. The garden is small but neat, with one wooden bench cast adrift on a small hillock that faces the roaring traffic on the road.

'As a place to end your days this is about as uninspiring as it gets,' David says, climbing out of the car. 'But it's still more than Gareth deserves.'

I go round to the passenger side and take hold of his arm. I'm still angry with him but, if I can help it, I'd rather prevent him getting hurt and risk him spinning further out of my control. He's been agitated for the whole journey, humming, fiddling with the radio, the air conditioning and the knobs on his seat, like the nine-year-old boy he was. 'David, this isn't a good idea. You do know that, don't you?'

'Always so negative!' He gives me a playful punch on the shoulder. 'He can't hurt us now.'

'He can't hurt me, but I think he can still hurt you.' He begins to walk away from me and I grab his sleeve. 'Don't be imagining that you can goad him and get the better of him. It won't work.'

'Give over, Leila!' He shrugs me off. 'You're such a fucking killjoy. No wonder Alex takes drugs.'

'On your own head be it,' I say quietly and follow him into the building, where we're greeted by a nurse wearing a purple paper hat.

'We're celebrating a birthday,' she says, pointing to her head. 'We love a birthday here, don't we Agnes?' she shouts towards an old lady who's shuffling along the corridor close by. 'And who are you here to see?' she says to us.

'Gareth Thatcher,' I say.

'Oh . . . okay.' Her smile only wavers for a second.

'Does Gareth love a birthday?' David says.

'He didn't join us today,' the nurse admits. 'But we're always hopeful. We like to give our residents the option to take part but we don't force them.'

'Does he take part in many activities?' David asks.

'Well . . .' She smiles and rubs her right hand on the front of her tunic. 'I'm sorry but I don't think we've met. I'm Brenda.' She holds out her hand and we take turns to shake it.

'David.'

'Leila.'

'Lovely to meet you both. Are you related to Gareth?'

'His children,' David says.

'*Step*children,' I emphasise. 'He married our mother.'

'Has he never spoken of us?' David says.

'Not to my knowledge. He tends to keep himself to himself but perhaps your visit will be just what he needs.' She gives us an optimistic smile and we walk behind her along the corridor. Her frame is two sizes too large for her tunic and it rides up on her hips so that she has to pull it down every couple of steps. But what she loses in the body beautiful she clearly makes up for in kindness. She tells us about Gareth and the recovery he's made from the stroke he had a couple of years ago. 'His speech came back really quite quickly but he has a dense left-sided weakness that we're helping him with.'

'He won't be escaping any time soon then,' David says.

'We don't like to see ourselves as a prison,' Brenda says, gently censorious of his flippant tone.

'It certainly doesn't feel like a prison,' I say, glancing to my left where a group of old people are having a sing-song in the day room. 'It's obvious you deliver excellent care here.'

'We do our best.' She stops in front of a door and depresses the handle. 'Now, your stepfather can be a wee bit tetchy sometimes but we don't judge. It's not easy being dependent on others.'

'You're absolutely right,' I say.

'Here we are!' She breezes into the room. 'Gareth! Look who's here to see you!'

The smell in the room is a slap in the face, as if decay has already set in. Brenda must be smelling it too because the first thing she does is open the window. 'Aren't you lucky to have your children visiting?'

'*Stepchildren*,' I murmur. 'We're not linked by biology, only by my mother's poor choices.'

There's an old man sitting in a chair, his left side propped up with cushions. He's wearing navy trousers and a once-white shirt that has been washed grey. His slippers are brown moccasins and the left one is sliding off his foot. Brenda bends down to realign the slipper, then straightens both his feet. 'David and Leila,' she enunciates, smiling up into his face.

His head moves slowly as he turns his face our way. Mean, grey eyes focus on first David and then me. Gareth's eyes. It's him all right, and he observes us both with no surprise on his face, just a cool, blank stare. I sense David tense next to me and despite my anger with him I want to take his hand as a mark of solidarity, but he has moved away from me to pull up a chair.

'Isn't this lovely?' Brenda says and I have to stifle a laugh because it's anything but lovely. 'Whiling away a weekday afternoon with family. I'll leave the three of you to catch up.'

When the door closes behind Brenda, David places the chair in front of Gareth; I perch myself on the bed to the left of them both.

Gareth is the first person to speak. 'I knew that sooner or later you'd come.' His speech is slow but clear. 'David Francis and Leila Mae.' His grin reveals a row of yellowed teeth with two prominent gaps that make him look like he's been punched in the face.

David's left leg is restless. It's moving so intensely that I can feel the vibrations coming up through the floor into the soles of my feet. 'You haven't been cleaning your teeth, Gareth,' I say.

His grey eyes look up into mine. I feel a visceral revulsion but I'm able to hide it, an old skill not forgotten. 'What do you want?' he says.

'We want to see you, old man,' David says. 'Catch-up time.' He gives a hearty, patently false laugh and I watch the anxiety roll off him in waves. And if I can see it then so too can Gareth. 'We wanted to show you how successful we are. While you – look at you!' he scoffs. 'You're in here, crippled and pathetic. Your life is over. Won't be long before you're circling the drain, eh Gareth?'

Gareth gives a throaty cough. 'Coming back to Daddy.'

'You were no daddy to me,' David says and then he lets rip a torrent of painful memories: being denied food, being spied on in the shower, having to lie to everyone outside of our home, having to sleep in fear of being woken and dragged down to the cellar to witness the latest trapped animal's distress. It's a heartfelt outpouring. It's a weeping sore. It's fuel for Gareth.

All it does is strengthen him. I watch his back lengthen by two inches as he straightens himself up in the chair. Twice I nudge David's foot with mine but he takes no notice. He gets it all out. He thinks he's being assertive and strong but I know how Gareth is perceiving the outburst – as a sign of weakness and fear. And he's not wrong. You don't have to have an MA in psychology to understand human behaviour.

Finally David runs out of steam and he sits back, blinking rapidly, sweat breaking out on his forehead.

'Better now?' Gareth asks, smirking.

In a flash, David is on his feet and has his hands round Gareth's throat. Gareth makes loud throttling noises, his eyes wide open, lit up with what is at first a parody of fear, a pantomime actor. He's no match for David, the younger, stronger man, though, and I don't doubt that David will keep going until Gareth is dead, so after thirty seconds I intervene. I pull David away and hold him against the wall. 'Stop now,' I say quietly. 'Do you want to go to prison for this prick? Do you?' I reinforce my question with a sharp shove into the wall. 'Do you?'

'Let him do it,' Gareth shouts. His face has changed from grey to puce and his lips are a navy blue. 'Let him kill me, Leila Mae. He'll feel better for it.'

'We're going now,' I say to David and he nods, seemingly defeated. I push him ahead of me to the door but I'm unprepared for his final burst of determination; he sidesteps me to spit in Gareth's face.

Gareth laughs, delighted.

'Get out, David! Now!' I shout.

'Leila Mae!' Gareth's right hand reaches out and grabs me, his sinewy arm shaking with the exertion. 'I've kept your secret but I could tell the world if I wanted to. You remember that.'

'No one would believe you, Gareth,' I whisper into his ear. 'I'm a well-respected professional. I'm somebody. While you? You're just a pathetic old man who shits his pants.'

'Wait!' he shouts as I head for the door. 'Don't you dare walk away from me! Get back here you little bitch!'

I propel David ahead of me along the corridor. We don't see Brenda but we can hear her voice in the distance, 'Come on now, Jeanie! Let's have a knees-up!'

'If that nurse knew what he was really like,' David says, 'she'd let him lie in his own shit.'

Much as I agree with him I resist commenting. I want him in the car and I want to drive back to Edinburgh right now, to put as many miles between me and Gareth as I can. I bundle David into the passenger seat, start the engine and set off. We're about a mile along the road when he shouts, 'Stop! Stop the car!' I pull into the side of the road, both my indicators flashing. David throws himself out onto the grass verge and lands on his knees. He vomits onto the grass four or five times until his stomach has emptied. When he climbs back into the car I hand him some tissues and a bottle of water.

Neither of us speaks for the remainder of the journey. I'm aware of David sitting completely still, his chin dropping down onto his chest, his limbs motionless, as if he's had all of the energy sucked out of him. When we pass over the Forth Road Bridge, the clouds part and sunlight floods the car. David groans and covers his eyes with his forearms. I place a comforting hand on his knee but he jerks away from it, pulls up his legs and wraps his arms round his head as if protecting himself from an explosion.

'Don't put me out here,' he says when we reach the end of my street. 'Please.'

I don't answer. I'm angry because my head is full of Gareth. I knew I should never have gone to see him but I did it for David and what difference has it made? No difference at all. In fact, I'm afraid that the visit has made David worse.

I keep the engine running and wait. He starts fidgeting: legs shaking, hands pulling at his hair, his voice mumbling phrases that are mostly incoherent apart from the frequent use of 'fuck' and 'shit'.

After a while, when he sees I'm not giving in, he climbs out, slamming the door with a decisive bang. I drive off but watch him in my rearview mirror as he follows the car, jogging along the pavement, looking to the casual viewer like a normal man keen to get home.

When I pull into the driveway, he's already at the car door. 'I want to go back to see him again. I've thought of a better way.'

'Then you'll have to go alone,' I say.

'You never trust me, do you? You always think you know better. You should have let me kill him.' His expression twists. 'You always spoil everything. You're such a—'

I push him hard on the chest. His foot slips on the paving and he falls back into the flower border. By the time he's pulled himself upright, I'm inside the house with the door shut. He rings the bell, holding his finger on it, and when he stops pressing the bell he speaks into the space between the door and the wooden frame. 'Please, Leila. Just talk to me. I can get the jewellery back for you. I can! You know I can!'

I weigh up the pros and cons of letting him in. I need the jewellery but I don't want to give him any more attention. And then there's Tom. It's already late afternoon and he could potentially arrive home at any moment.

The bell keeps ringing and I'm pushed into a quick decision: Tom's opinion no longer matters and I need the jewellery.

I open the door to David and he comes inside, looking sheepish. 'Sorry. I didn't mean to call you names. I just think—'

'Don't,' I interrupt him. 'Please, just tell me where the jewellery is. I need it.'

'I didn't take it,' he says. 'I know who did, though.' He's looking on the floor and then on the hall table. 'She was going to put it back today. She had it in an envelope this morning and she was planning on pushing it through the letter box.'

'Who? Who is she?'

He lets out his breath. 'Tom's wife, Ellen.' He pauses, watching me while I try to process that.

'What? Why?' I say.

'The black lacquer box is hers. She didn't know you had jewellery in it.'

'Did Ben take it for her?' David laughs. 'Did he give it to her?' He walks into the kitchen and I follow him. 'Wait a minute, how do you know her?'

'And now the interrogation begins,' he says, throwing up his arms.

'Tell me.'

'Well, there's the thing, Leila. I don't have to tell you, because you already know who she is.'

'That doesn't mean I've met her.'

'But you have!' He points at me, laughing. 'You've spoken to her! At length.'

I'm not playing his game. I lean up against the counter and wait for him to grow tired of amusing himself.

'It's not often that you're caught behind the power curve, Sis.' He takes three apples from the fruit bowl and juggles with them. 'Oh what a tangled web we weave, when first we practise to deceive.' He puts the apples back and widens his eyes at me. 'Don't you think?'

'I'm not deceiving anyone.'

'Tom? Alex? Me?' He waits for my reply. I don't give him one. 'Ellen still has a key to the back door.' He comes to stand in front of me. 'She is one of your clients. She's using her middle and her maiden name.' He pauses for effect before saying, 'Ellen is Mary McNeil.'

12. Ellen

When I come round, I'm lying on my side and the woman who helped me is kneeling on the pavement next to me. 'I'm a first-aider,' she says. 'I think you were having a panic attack and then you fainted.'

'Yes.' I sit up slowly, rubbing my aching knees and elbows. 'Thank you for helping me.' She doesn't want to let me go but I convince her I'm fine and I leave for home. I walk quickly because I want to get home before I have another attack. I need time to think, to try to work everything out, because I'm struggling to believe it. I try to persuade myself that Mrs Patterson must be wrong. It could be that Francis had just met Leila – perhaps he meant to help me somehow? – and that he only resembles Leila's brother. Mrs Patterson is pushing ninety and her eyes might not be as good as she thinks they are. That has to be it. Nothing else makes any sense.

No need to panic. No need to feel betrayed. Just breathe, Ellen. Just breathe.

When I arrive home, I check all the sockets and I lock and relock the front door. I surrender to the compulsion because this is not the time for me to practise exposure therapy. I check the sockets again, I photograph them, I look at the photographs. I feel like I'm teetering on the brink of another panic attack and the way to prevent it is to check and keep checking until I'm pulled back from the edge.

It takes an hour for my anxiety to subside to a level that is closer to normal and then I remember I didn't walk to Maybanks, I drove there. I've left my car in a street about one hundred yards from the house. It's hardly a disaster – rationally, I know this – but I'll never be able to settle until the car is outside my front door, locked and with the handbrake on.

I take Leila's jewellery out of my backpack and consider putting it in the lacquer box, but I don't because it doesn't belong there. I hide it under my bed instead, inside a pair of winter boots, pushed right to the back where they're difficult to grab hold of.

It doesn't take me long to reach my car and I've just climbed into the driving seat when my mobile rings. It's Sharon, the police liaison officer. 'Hi, Ellen. I'm just checking in. How's everything going?'

'Good,' I say, almost choking on the word. 'Uh-huh.' I'm not always a spontaneous person but this is the perfect opportunity to find out some information about Francis. 'I'm glad you've called actually because—' I give a genuinely nervous laugh. 'This is a bit weird but you remember when you asked me whether you could give Francis my mobile number and I said no?'

'It wasn't Francis who asked for your number, it was Trish.'

'Trish. That's right and you said you'd post my scarf to me.'

'I did.'

'Well, Francis turned up at my front door with my scarf and—'

'He wasn't supposed to do that. I asked him to post it, not bring it round in person.'

'It's okay, it's just . . . he seems to want to go out with me.'

'I see.' She hears my silence. 'How do you feel about that?'

'Well . . . you know how it is when you lose your confidence.'

'Being mugged can do that to you, Ellen.'

'And so I thought you might be able to tell me a little bit about him. Just so I can be sure.'

'Of course. Yes, I can share some information with you. Let me see now.' There's a tap, tap of a keyboard. 'His full name is David Francis Morrison, although he told me he's always known as Francis.'

That's enough, really. That's all I need to know but I let her continue. She tells me he's unemployed and that he's been living in Edinburgh for only five months.

'He wants to join the police service, doesn't he?'

'Not that I know of,' she says.

'So how come he helps you out?'

'He volunteered himself, but it's not official. He just likes to help me put the chairs out etcetera.' Her tone changes. 'You will tell me if he causes you any problems, Ellen, won't you?'

'Of course.' I thank her and agree to keep in touch.

So many lies. I sit in my car, numb from head to foot, unable to move, unable to think clearly. This is a man I went to bed with. He's met Ben; Chloe knows about him. I thought we were heading into a relationship. I thought he cared for me. I really believed he cared for me.

I feel angry . . . hurt . . . confused. Each emotion pushes and shoves at the other and I'm pulled from wanting to cry to wanting to hit back at him. It makes no sense that he would target me like this. Is it some misguided notion about protecting his sister? Because Leila has never been in any real danger from me.

I drive back home and park the car just as Ben comes out of the house. 'Hi Mum, I let Francis in. Is that okay?'

My stomach does a double flip. 'You off out?'

'Yeah. And I'll probably stay over at Angus's tonight.'

'I'd rather you didn't,' I say quickly.

'Something wrong?' He comes across to stand beside me, his face concerned. 'You okay, Mum?'

I make a quick decision – whatever this is it doesn't involve Ben. I need to talk to Francis alone. I need to sort this out myself. Be brave, be strong.

'Just ignore me, darling,' I say. 'I would like you home for the night but text me when you're sure of your plans and then I'll know whether or not to expect you.' I stand on the step and watch him walk along the road towards town before I go inside. *Just play it cool, Ellen*. If you can go back to your own home and sit in front of your husband's mistress without blurting out the truth, then you can do this.

I come quietly into the house, closing the door soundlessly behind me. I stand completely still and tune in to all the sounds, upstairs and down. There's the normal gurgling in the pipes and hum of electricity. There's the faint sound of barking from the next-door neighbour's Jack Russell and a voice calling back to him.

And there's another sound. Francis is moving around in my bedroom. I can hear the creaking of floorboards and the opening and closing of drawers. I'm not sure I really want to catch him in the act of going through my things; looking for his sister's jewellery perhaps? It's enough for me to know that he's snooping.

I open the front door again and bang it this time, then shout, 'Hello? Anyone home?'

Almost at once Francis appears at the top of the stairs, rubbing his hair with a towel. 'Ellen! You're back.' He comes down in a rush, throws the towel to one side and pulls me towards him. 'I've missed you today.' He kisses my neck and my cheeks but I move my head to one side before he reaches my mouth.

'You okay?' He gives me a worried frown. 'You feel tense.'

'I'm just a bit anxious. It's been one of those days. I got delayed . . . It was all a bit hectic. And I haven't done my checks.'

'Poor you.' He turns me round and starts to knead my shoulders. 'Why don't I cook something for us both while you have a relaxing bath?'

'That sounds like a good idea,' I say, my tone completely even while my inner voice screams *Why? Why are you doing this?* I want to be able to say these words out loud but I can't. The reality of confronting him feels beyond me. 'There are some eggs and mushrooms in the fridge.'

'An omelette it is then.' He kisses my neck, from behind this time, and I shiver. How quickly I've moved from wanting him to touch me to being repulsed by him. He nudges me towards the stairs. 'Shall we say half an hour for the omelette?'

'Great.' I pick up the towel and climb the stairs. If not for the fact that I know he's been in my bedroom, I might not have noticed anything, but because I'm looking for signs of disturbance, I see them immediately: the duvet is doubled over at one of the edges as if someone lifted it up to look under the bed, my winter-jumper drawer is partly open and I know I haven't been in it for a couple of months and the black lacquer box is at an angle; I had left it straight.

I go into the bathroom and lock the door. I ask myself whether I think I'm in any danger from Francis. I have

what I consider to be a very good reason for misleading
Leila. What can Francis's reason be for deceiving me?
And would he ever physically hurt me? I remember my
dad's words when he was fixing the lino – do as you
would be done by. Liars should expect to be lied to.
Deceivers should expect to be deceived.

Maybe this is exactly what I deserve.

I decide that lying in the bath might make me too
vulnerable – it wouldn't take much more than a shoulder
push to break the bathroom lock – so I have a shower
instead, quickly and efficiently, then dress in underwear
and a pair of pyjamas. I listen in the hallway for sounds
of Francis approaching, and hear none, so I have a quick
look under the bed and can see that the boots are exactly
where I left them, the jewellery undisturbed.

Francis has set the table for two. He's turned off the
lights and lit two candles, which suits me perfectly; this
way it will be more difficult for him to see the expressions on my face. He hands me a glass of red wine and
urges me to sit down. Then he brings me a plate with
a perfectly cooked omelette and a side salad. I wait until
he's sitting opposite me before I begin to eat.

'So tell me,' he says. 'What happened today?'

'Solicitors and what not,' I lie. 'I spent far longer up
there than I expected to.' I take a sip of wine. 'It wouldn't
normally be a problem but I was—'

'Hoping to put the jewellery back,' he interrupts. He's
eating very quickly, almost shovelling the food in, as if
he's been denied food all day.

'That's right.' I find myself reacting to his speed by
eating more slowly than I normally would. 'And then
when I got down to Maybanks I was hijacked by Mrs
Patterson. She insisted I come for afternoon tea so that
we could discuss the mystery of the missing cat.'

'So you weren't able to take the jewellery back?' Francis has polished off his omelette and is eating the last of his salad.

My mouth is full and I finish chewing before I speak. 'By the time I left Mrs Patterson's, Leila's car was back and I didn't want to put the envelope through the door in case she caught me.'

Francis nods, and keeps nodding, staring first at his empty plate and then at me. 'I'm happy to help.'

'Thank you. I might take you up on that,' I lie. 'Anyway, enough about me.' My mouth moves in what, by candle-light, should look close enough to a smile. 'How's your mum today?' *If she even exists.*

He tells me about how they spent their time together, making a good job of describing a fun afternoon. A nurse called Brenda encourages those who are able to get up onto their feet for a 'knees-up'. 'The music was all from the sixties and seventies, catchy Cliff Richard numbers that everyone could sing along to.' He says his mum joined in from her chair while he danced with Brenda. 'She was wearing a purple paper hat. She's a good sport is Brenda.'

I don't believe a word. And the longer I sit there, the more freaked out I become. This man has been in my bed, in my body, in my heart and he is a liar. A considered, controlled, convincing liar.

I jump up, go into the kitchen and pull the plugs from the sockets. Francis is right behind me and he clasps my hand. 'Shall we talk through some exposure therapy?'

'Leila said this would happen, that I would slide back into obsessive behaviour and that it's nothing to worry about.' My voice shakes. 'Perfectly normal.' I take my hand away from his and lift it to my mouth. How can someone be so kind and caring on the surface and so utterly deceitful underneath? I don't like him touching me and I need him to leave, but I'm not sure how to engineer it without him questioning me. I could, of course, simply confront him and tell him what I know, but I don't feel brave enough. I'm a coward. Plain and simple. 'I think I need to go to bed,' I say. 'I've got myself overtired. I barely slept last night, what with the worrying about the jewellery.'

'I could drop it round now,' he says.

'Thank you, but let me deal with it.' I manage to lean into his chest and force myself to press a fleeting kiss to his lips. 'If I don't manage it tomorrow then I'll take you up on your kind offer.'

'You'd rather I went home tonight?'

'Well . . .' *Yes, yes, yes.* 'I'm sorry because you've come to see me after a busy day.' I snuggle into his neck. 'But I'm going to be no use to you tonight.'

'You don't have to be any use to me,' he says, his tone light. 'Is Ben coming back this evening?' He's kneading my shoulders again. 'I think it's better if you're not on your own.'

'He'll be back soon,' I say, crossing my fingers behind Francis's back.

'I'll tidy up the kitchen and stay until he arrives home, then.'

'You don't have to—'

'Ssh!' He puts a finger to my lips. 'You have to learn to accept help, Ellen.' He wishes me goodnight and stands at the bottom of the stairs while I go up. 'Call me if you need anything!'

'Will do.' There isn't a lock on my bedroom door so I take a chair and jam the back under the door handle, then I climb into bed and text Ben:

Have you decided whether you're coming home or not? It would be good if you could. I need you to come home tonight.

Sure, Mum. I'll be back just after eleven.

I breathe a sigh of relief and try to settle back on the pillow to wait for Ben, but within seconds I'm upright again. It's torture staying in bed because there's so much I want to do, not least checking the plugs throughout the house. But worse than my anxiety, I feel afraid. Just because he's a liar, that doesn't make him violent, the sensible voice inside my head reminds me. But my gut is telling me different. My gut says, there's a man in this house who can't be trusted. You shouldn't be on your own with him.

It's an hour later when I hear the front door open. I've been sitting bolt upright, staring at the door, and now I get quietly out of bed, move the chair aside and open the bedroom door a crack. I hear Ben hanging up his jacket and then Francis saying, 'Your mum's really tired so she's gone to bed already. I'll give her a call in the morning.'

'Cool,' Ben says. 'See you.'

The front door opens and closes again and I wait for a full twenty seconds before running downstairs. Ben is in the kitchen dropping two slices of bread into the toaster. I squeeze him tight and he laughs. 'Good to see you too, Mum,' he says. 'You okay?'

'I am now,' I say. 'It's always a relief to have you home.'

Ben is home, Francis is gone, and I feel like I've been given a sudden, very welcome reprieve. In this moment, all is right with the world.

Please let this be the end of it, I say to myself. I've learnt my lesson.

Really. I have.

12. Leila

Mary McNeil.

Mary McNeil, my client with OCD, is actually Ellen Linford, Tom's wife.

I walk around the kitchen shaking my head, more surprised than shocked. I never had one iota of suspicion that she was anyone other than who she said she was. But, at the same time, it makes complete sense. All that business about the other woman was directed at me. When I think of the courage it must have taken a woman of her character to do what she's done it makes me have a grudging respect for her. I think back to our sessions and the way she spoke about her husband – she's got him spot on. Tom is self-centred. He isn't a team player; he's a man who likes his own way. I can only imagine how unsupportive he was throughout their marriage.

'More fool you,' David says to me, and for once he is out of sync with my thoughts. 'Beware the ex-wife. Hell hath no fury and all that.'

'That explains the clothes and the shoes,' I say. 'It's more typical of a woman's idea of revenge than a man's.'

'She wanted you to see her as a living, breathing human being, rather than someone you haven't given a second thought to.' He has the fridge door open and is ferreting around. 'She wanted to shock you into seeing yourself the way she does. A husband-stealing bitch, a home-wrecker.'

I can't argue with that. 'We have a separate fridge for alcohol,' I tell him, pointing towards the pantry.

He fetches a beer, pops it open on the edge of the work surface and comes to stand in front of me. 'How could you not have known what she looks like? It's pretty shoddy, don't you think?'

'I've never been interested in the women who came before me, not with any of the men I've been with.'

'She doesn't want Tom back but she does want the house.'

I look around me, at the family kitchen leading into a garden that cries out for children – or did until we took the tree down. I think about Mary McNeil as I know her – a gentle, thoughtful woman who has given everything to her family. 'It's a lovely house and I can see why she wants it back. I know she put a lot of time and effort into the garden but maybe she put a lot of effort into the house too?'

'They bought it when it was run-down. Ellen and her father did most of the work on it.'

I incline my head. 'Perhaps I should have been more curious.'

'You're taking this well.'

He's disappointed. He likes nothing more than seeing me crushed and needy. I expect he wanted me to have a tantrum, shout and scream and bemoan the ex-wife who still has something to say for herself. The cheek of her! And when my tears stopped flowing, I'd be forced to lean on him, have him save me.

'You're not just going to give in to her?' His confidence is wavering.

'It's not up to me. Tom is fighting to keep the house.

But if the numbers don't add up he might suddenly decide to let her have it.'

'But surely he'll take your wishes into consideration?'

'Of course he will,' I lie. 'We're very close and truthfully? I'm attached to Tom, not this home. We're strong enough as a couple to weather a storm as minor as this.' I go to the fridge and bring out a bottle of white wine that still has a large glassful left in it. When I have it poured, I take a couple of sips before saying, 'Does Ellen really suffer from obsessive compulsion or was she faking it?'

'She does have it but she's getting better. She has respect for you as a therapist. She hates your guts for taking her husband and her house, though. That's pretty clear.' He enjoys saying this. He's in the know. He's one step ahead of me, and that makes him happy. It's a sibling rivalry that he should have grown out of years ago.

'How did you meet her?' I ask him.

'Chance. I volunteer with a victim support group and during one of the sessions she spoke about her husband and how she'd lost her house and I put two and two together.'

'Chance?' I'm sceptical. 'You didn't target her then, in the same way as you did Len, the caretaker in Leeds?'

'I had a choice of places I could volunteer and I chose the group she was going to.' He shrugs like it's all perfectly normal. 'I'm your brother. It's only natural that I should keep an eye on you.'

'By scheming? By lying?'

'It helps me when I'm able to see you through other people's eyes.'

'Helps you with what?'

'Helps me to understand you.' He pauses. 'You could say I'm protecting you by staying close to your enemies.'

'I don't believe Ellen is my enemy!' I shake my head. 'And even if she was it's no justification for your behaviour.'

'Well if I hadn't got close to Ellen you wouldn't know where the jewellery was, would you?'

'No, I wouldn't but that's hardly the point. What about Ellen's feelings in all of this?'

'Like you care?'

'Does she think you're genuine? Is she falling for you?'

'Why?' He laughs. 'Are you jealous?'

'You should leave her alone now,' I say.

'Why? She's nice to me. She's a good cook.' He drinks back some beer. 'She's boring but she's fine for the short term.'

'You've been sleeping with her?'

'Obviously.'

'And this is all about getting closer to me, is it?'

'I'm taking control of my life.'

Trying to take control of *my* life, more like, but I don't say this because I'd be wasting my breath. I know that my relationship with David is a map of blurred, intersecting lines; I only wish that he knew it too.

I persuade him out of the door with a promise that we'll meet very soon. 'I haven't forgotten about Gareth,' he says on his way down the path. 'I want us both to visit him again. I want to talk to him about Mum's death.'

I give a lying nod of agreement and off he goes, happy to have legitimately got into the house. He thinks he has his foot in the door now – he hasn't. And he thinks he has won my cooperation and that we'll go back to see Gareth together – we won't.

And we never will.

Next day, I wake up with Tom beside me in the bed. He's spent the last few days avoiding me and I have no idea when he came home last night, but none of it matters because I don't expect to be with him much longer. Until that time, though, I don't want him moping around making my life any more difficult than it already is, so I spoon into his back and rub myself against him. It's his favourite way to be woken up and it doesn't take him long to put his cock first and respond to my advances. It's not a pleasurable experience for me but it's not awful either. I'm perfectly prepared to use my body as a means to an end.

We finish up having sex and he rolls onto his back. 'So what have I missed?' he says.

'I found the jewellery box,' I say.

'Thank heavens! That was quite a scene you created.'

And you didn't make it worse by shouting at me? And shouting at Katarina? Accusing her of theft and of lying?

'I know. I'm sorry. It's just that I need to sell my mum's jewellery to pay for Alex's treatment. So when I couldn't find it I panicked.'

'Leila . . .'

'It's okay.' I stroke his upper arm and down to his wrist. 'I'll have the stones valued tomorrow and go for a quick sale.'

'I'm not sure . . .' My head is on his chest but I can hear him thinking. 'It's never good to part with family heirlooms. Why don't you have them send me the bill? I'll deal with it.'

'Would you?' I sit up and stare into his face, my expression girlishly grateful. I think I even manage some eyelid-batting. 'It's been such a worry for me.'

'Well, now it's taken care of.' His hand rests in the hollow of my spine. 'And how is Alex? We never talked about him when you came back on Saturday.'

'He's doing brilliantly.' At least this is true. I sit up

and smile at Tom. 'He really is. He should be coming home this week.'

'Then it's money well spent.'

I almost soften towards him but not quite, because I know that he would readily let me down again. He is a man who likes to be magnanimous when it suits him. That was one of the things Ellen said to me and I see exactly what she means. And now that I know Ellen has the jewellery, I know it will be returned to me and that makes me feel calm. I can stop worrying about it.

When Tom leaves for work, I give Maurice a call. The main reason Alex and I ended up moving to Edinburgh was because Maurice had moved up here from Manchester, a retirement that quickly became a semi-retirement, as clients like me found it impossible to let him go. In the past I've travelled over one hundred and fifty miles for my monthly sessions with him. Wherever I've been living, I've gravitated towards Maurice for support.

When I arrive at his door, he's waiting for me. 'I've been concerned for you, Leila,' he says. 'Come in now. Let's not waste any time.'

I have a lot to tell him. I start with the good news – the fact that Alex is so much better. 'The treatment has come at exactly the right time for him. He was like a different boy when I saw him on Saturday. I'm really hopeful, Maurice. I think we're through the worst.'

'That's wonderful news, Leila.' He smiles along with me and I want to kiss him for it.

I go on to tell him about David and how he followed me to the Bridge and then the business with the jewellery and Ellen.

'This behaviour is very concerning, is it not?' Maurice says.

'Ellen's?'

'No, David's. Manipulating Ellen, deceiving you both. What do think his motivations were?'

I shake my head. 'I don't know, Maurice. He loves to have control over me. He always has.' I shrug. 'Quite honestly, I'm past caring. I do feel for Ellen, though. She's a decent person who is way out of her depth with my brother. I should have given her more consideration than I did because then this could never have happened. I would have recognised her instantly and there would have been no fun in it for David.' I sit up straight and take a deep breath. 'I have something else to tell you.' I take another breath. 'I've made the decision to leave Tom. I know you probably saw this coming.' He has the grace to keep his face impassive. 'I didn't.' I raise my eyebrows at my own stupidity. 'Recent events have shown me that he's inflexible. He couldn't handle the real me. Even aspects of the superficial me, he struggles with. So we're going to leave Edinburgh.'

'You and Alex?'

'Yes. We'll most likely settle in Paisley. Alex has a good friend over there and I feel it's important for me to put him first.'

'And this is not about getting away from David?'

'I know what you're thinking,' I say and he gives me a gentle smile. 'You're thinking that one day I'll have to stop running, and you're right – just not now, not in Edinburgh.' And then I remember the cat. And that leads me to Gareth. I sit, unable to speak, knowing that I have to tell him because if I don't there's really no point in coming to therapy. It's with Maurice that I do my utmost to face myself. I can't always manage it but still I keep trying.

'I, em . . .' I swallow my nerves. 'I killed next door's cat.' I watch Maurice's face mirror my own regret. 'I'm sorry I did it.' I bite my lip, thinking of a way to lessen the crime. 'I didn't take the collar, though. Gareth always took the collar but I didn't.' Maurice's expression remains unchanged. 'Mrs Patterson has been looking for him but—' I make a gesture of hopelessness with my hands. 'She's not going to find him. I wonder whether I should buy her a kitten.'

'Do you think buying her a kitten is the answer?'

'I suppose it depends on the question,' I say flippantly, and immediately regret it. That's not what I'm here for. I stare down at my feet and listen to the ticking of the clock until I've counted to fifty. 'We went to see Gareth yesterday, me and David. It was a strange experience because I knew he'd lost his power over me but at the same time I was afraid he hadn't.' I stop my hands shaking by sitting on them. 'In the end, he didn't scare me at all and I spent the visit trying to protect David from himself. It didn't work and now he wants to go back.' I bite my lip. 'I don't care. He can go himself if he really wants to.'

'You don't care?' Maurice repeats.

'I really don't think I do.' This feels like a moment of epiphany and I smile. 'I spend my time thinking that David is the one who can't let go of me but I think I've been encouraging him. And now?' I pause to tune in to my feelings, and discover that what I feel is relief. The relief of a traveller at the end of a very long and stony road. 'It's over.' I sit back on the chair and let my words sink into me, trickle through arteries and veins, settle in bones and organs. 'Maurice!' I take deep replenishing breaths. 'You're a genius.' I stand up and kiss his cheek. 'I could never have got here without your help.' He hands me some water and I drink it down. 'You do know that, don't you?'

He acknowledges the compliment with a brief smile before saying, 'Leila, I hesitate to give you advice but I feel it's important to remind you not to expect too much too soon.' There is an edge of sadness to his tone. 'Sometimes we take two steps forward but that is immediately followed by—'

'A step backward.' I nod. 'I know.' His eyes are watching me, waiting for more. 'I'll be closing my practice,' I say in a rush. 'I'll speak to my clients this week and explain my decision to them.'

'You'll begin again in Paisley?'

'I'm not sure.' I shake my head. 'Actually, I really don't think I will. I need a break from listening to other people. I want to concentrate on Alex and myself. He'll be leading his own life soon. He'll find a girl, get married. I might even be a granny one day.' I smile. 'I know you don't have time for most of my clients, and there are plenty of therapists I can recommend, but I'm wondering whether you would be willing to see Tom's wife Ellen? I feel I owe it to her.'

'Of course.' He nods slowly. 'Give her my number.'

'I need to get going,' I say. 'Thank you for making time for me, Maurice.'

He walks me to the door and we shake hands. 'Don't be a stranger, now.'

'I'll be back,' I say, hugging him. 'You don't get rid of me that easily.'

He watches me drive off and I clock the expression on his face: he's worried for me. He doesn't believe me. He doesn't believe that I can change, that I can let go of David and move on. I get that. I understand his reservations. I'd feel the same if I were in his shoes.

No worries. I smile and wave in his direction. I'll just have to prove him wrong.

13. Ellen

Thursday, and Francis calls me at nine in the morning. 'Ellen! How are you? You feeling better?'

'Much better, thank you.'

'I was thinking about you last night. You're going to feel such a sense of relief when you've given the jewellery back to Leila.' I know what's coming next. 'Why don't you let me help you get it done?' He's nothing if not persistent.

'I've given it back,' I lie.

'You have?' He recovers well. 'That's great! Shall I pop in to see you after I've visited my mum?'

Are you really visiting your mum? Or is she a figment of your imagination? A convenient excuse to be in my neighbourhood? This is what I don't say. Instead I tell him that I'm taking my dad to Aberdeen to visit my uncle who is unwell. This is another lie, and I know I need to be less of a coward, but I feel like if I have a few days to think, to put the whole experience into some sort of context, then I'll be able to tell him to piss off and never darken my door again.

I've already done all of my checks for the morning but the sound of his voice means I have to do them all again, socket by socket, once, twice, three times, and then take photographs on my mobile as proof. It's time-consuming and utterly nonsensical but I'm past judging myself. The fact is that the checking makes me able to function and that's good enough for me. I've shelved any attempt at exposure therapy until such time as I can think straight, and at the moment, I feel as if that might be a while coming.

I pull out my boots from under the bed and tip the jewellery into my handbag, then I jump into the car and drive. I need to bolster my confidence, my sense of myself, so take the coast road down towards North Berwick, and as I grow closer I glance seawards, waiting for my first sight of the Bass Rock. When I was growing up, North Berwick caravan park was the destination for family holidays. And every summer we would set out in a fishing boat to watch and listen to tens of thousands of gannets flocking above our heads, cawing and diving, feeding and pooing and caring for their young, all of them nesting on the rock. It was my dad's favourite spot and his smile was never wider than when he was standing in the boat, staring up at the birds. 'All of nature!' he would shout to us kids. 'In action around us! Fantastic!'

I expect to find the sight of the rock comforting, and it is, but only for a couple of breaths. I park the car and wander around the small harbour, busy with colourful fishing boats, some of them not much bigger than a family car, and I sit down on a bench to let the sea air fill my nose and my lungs. When my mobile rings, I hesitate before taking the call because it's Leila. I wonder whether Francis is with her. Has he told her I have her jewellery? Could they be trying a two-pronged attack to get it back?

'Mary, it's Leila.' I don't speak. 'I'm sorry you encountered a drunken me on Tuesday.' I still don't speak. 'I know we didn't schedule a further appointment but I wondered whether you would be willing to come to see me today?'

I use a second or two of silence to digest her words. 'Why today?'

'Well . . . perhaps we could discuss that when you come to see me?'

'Are you on your own?'

She doesn't miss a beat. 'My brother isn't with me.'

'How do I know I can trust you?'

'Ellen,' she says, her tone significant. 'I'm not the one who has been using my maiden name to mislead you.'

'But you are the one who had a six-month affair with a married man before his wife found out.' It feels good to say this and I exhale a long-held breath.

'Fair point,' she says.

I have to hand it to her – she isn't easily fazed. 'I'm less than an hour away,' I say, glancing at my watch. 'I could be with you by two.'

'Perfect.' She pauses. 'And Ellen?'

'Yes?'

'I would be grateful if you could bring the jewellery with you. It was my mother's.'

I pretend I haven't heard that part and end the call. She'll get her jewellery, but I'm not going to be too much of a pushover. I'd like to say my piece first and on the return journey to Edinburgh I run through the salient points in my head and practise the words out loud. When I fuel the words with anger they sound justifiably formidable. I don't expect to shake her composure too much; I can't imagine she's a woman who is ever reduced to tears – but I will make my point.

I park my car directly outside Maybanks because there's really no need to pretend now, and when I ring the doorbell to the annexe, Leila opens the door at once. 'Come in, Ellen,' she says. 'It's good to see you.'

'Why is it good to see me? Because I have something you want?'

She looks at the floor as if chastened and then her eyes return to mine. 'I'm sorry you fell victim to my brother's games.'

'I think, on balance, I'm sorrier that I fell victim to yours,' I say forcefully. 'Because if you hadn't taken a fancy to my husband then I would never have met your lying, manipulative brother.'

She inclines her head as if she's taking this on board, then she sits down and gestures towards the chair opposite. 'Do take a seat, Ellen.'

'I'm not ready to sit down.' I stand in front of her and fold my arms. 'You wilfully took my husband and then you took my house. My children have lost their family home; my granddaughter has lost the garden she loved to play in.' I pause to gather my strength. 'I have OCD because of you. I am driven to distraction by my own anxiety and that is directly linked to you. I will be lucky if I can continue to hold down a job and I can trace all of this, *all of this*, back to you.'

'I'm so sorry, Ellen,' she says, her tone placatory. 'Please believe me when I say that I would never have continued my affair if I had known Tom was misleading me. He assured me his marriage was over and I believed him. I can see that I was wrong.'

'Why? Why did you believe him? You're astute – I know you are. You believed him because it was convenient.'

'Yes,' she admits. 'You're right.'

'You didn't even know what I looked like!' I shout. 'It was as if I didn't even exist! Who does that? Who behaves with such disregard? What is wrong with you?'

'What is wrong with me?' She gives me a sad look.

'I run away. I don't commit. I'm careless of other people's feelings. The only person I truly care about is my son.' She spreads her arms wide to include the house and the garden. 'This? It means almost nothing to me. You can get it all back.'

'I know. I'm fighting for it.'

'I don't think you'll need to fight.'

'And why is that?'

'I'm leaving Tom.'

'What?' I drop down backwards onto the seat. 'Already? Your relationship is over *already*?'

'I made a mistake. I thought Tom would be someone I could be with for the long term, the rest of my life even, but he's not.'

I laugh then because for some reason this strikes me as hilarious. She waits patiently while I vent my mirth and then, when I'm wiping my eyes with a tissue, she says, 'I completely understand why you hate me.'

'That's big of you.' I stare across at her. 'That's really, really big of you.' She is not as well groomed as normal and there are dark circles under her eyes. 'So what's put you off Tom?'

'He prefers his home life to be straightforward, doesn't he? And I don't think my life will ever be straightforward.'

She gives me a conspirator's smile and I'm not sure I like it. She's only known him for eighteen months. She's definitely not entitled to bond with me over his shortcomings even though I'm sure we could have an interesting time comparing notes. 'And does he know you're leaving?' I say.

'Not yet.'

I wonder whether to believe her. This is not at all what I expected. When I'd been practising my vitriol in the car I imagined that the therapist in her would let me speak, but then the woman in her, the one who loves Tom, would defend her position. I feel like my mood is a balloon that has a slow puncture. I'm gradually losing my anger and starting to feel, if not exactly a kinship with her, then an acceptance of her position. 'You're really leaving him?' I say quietly.

'Yes.'

'Poor Tom,' I say. 'I almost feel sorry for him.'

'I can't imagine he'll want to live here by himself, so I would have thought the timing would be perfect for you to get your home back.'

The light begins to dawn on me, slowly but surely, and it feels like a sunrise after a long, sleepless night. Perhaps I will get Maybanks back. If everything she's telling me is true, then I'm not going to have to battle for the house after all. It could all just fall back into my lap. As if it was meant to be all along.

'About my brother,' she says.

'Yes.' I feel the weight of emotion descend on me again. 'What's . . . Why did . . .' I try again. 'Did you know that he was leading me on?'

'No, I didn't. I only found out yesterday.'

'That's also when I found out. I was with Mrs Patterson and I saw you letting him into the house.' I reach for my handbag and tip the jewellery out onto my knee. 'He wanted me to give the pieces to him so that he could deliver them to you but—' I pass everything across to her '—I wanted to return them to you myself.'

'Thank you for that.' She looks relieved. 'He wouldn't have given them to me or, at least, not without me having to give him something in return.'

'I don't understand,' I shake my head. 'Perhaps I should ask him but . . .' I feel embarrassed as my eyes fill up with tears. 'I'd rather not see him again. I thought he genuinely liked me! I've been taken for a fool and I have no idea why.'

'David is complex,' she says. 'He had a difficult child-hood – we both did – but I was luckier, because I'm six years older than him.' Her expression is serious. 'We were everything to each other. Absolutely everything.' She stares out of the window. 'When you first came to see me, it was clear that you were someone who was suffering because your marriage had come to an end – but you're not damaged as such. You've been loved and cherished and you haven't suffered significant trauma as a child. I know the OCD feels overwhelming at the moment but I believe you have an excellent chance of making a full recovery.'

'Thank you.' I take a deep breath. 'That's good to hear.'

'But David and me, we have scars that run deep and will take years of therapy to heal. We bring our problems into every relationship we have and the result is—' she shrugs. 'Dysfunctional behaviour.'

'He's been visiting your mother in the hospice.'

'Our mother has been dead for almost twenty years.'

'I did wonder.' I shake my head. 'I believed him at the time, though. He's a really good liar.' I give a short laugh. 'I thought I was the one chasing him! We seemed to come together by accident. He brought my scarf back and I invited him in. Not the other way round.'

'He's clever,' Leila says. 'He should never be under-estimated.'

'So the scar he has just here.' I touch my side. 'He told me he was drunk and accidentally got in the way of two men who were fighting. Was that true?'

'He was stabbed,' she affirms. 'But not in the way he described it to you.' She leans forward in the chair. 'Ellen,

I don't expect you want to have anything else to do with my brother.'

'You're right, I don't.'

'Good.' She nods, reassured. 'You need to keep him out of your house. He is likely to be quite agitated when he discovers we have spoken to one another. He will perceive that we were going behind his back.'

'What if he does come to my house?'

'Lock your door and call the police.'

'You think he could be dangerous?' I say, recalling last night when I was in the house alone with him.

'It's possible. He has been violent in the past.'

'Bloody hell.' I stand up. 'This is just . . .' I shake my head, disbelieving. 'I've allowed a violent man into my house, into my life. 'I think I've had a lucky escape.'

'You have, but listen. Before you go.' She writes a mobile number on a scrap of paper and hands it to me. 'This is the number for Maurice van Burren. He's expecting your call. He's an expert therapist. I've been going to him for years.'

'And yet look at you,' I say, an edge of spite in my tone that I instantly regret because I can see that, despite appearances, she's a woman who's already on the ground. There's no need for me to keep kicking her.

'Touché.' She gives me a sad smile. 'I have a lot of wounding to work through, Ellen. And maybe I'm a slow learner.'

She sees me to the door and at the last second I turn back. I have to leave her with something true, something real and good from one human being to another. 'Leila, you really did help me you know,' I say. 'I think the exposure therapy will work.'

'It will work,' she affirms. 'Maurice will help you to keep going with it.'

'Good luck.' I reach out my hand and she shakes it. 'And I'm sorry about your clothes and shoes.'

'That's okay.' She laughs and shakes her head. 'It's the least of my worries.'

'And good luck to your son. Ben told me he had to go to rehab.'

She nods. 'Yes, he'll be home very soon, though.' Her face takes on an expression I haven't seen before. If I had to give it a name I would say it was an expression of hope.

I walk to my car and glance back just the once. She's standing in the doorway staring up at the sky but I've a feeling she's not really seeing the clouds. She's smiling as if her thoughts are happy ones and I'm glad for her.

I drive home thinking about our conversation. The whole thing bordered on surreal. By the sounds of it, this is a brother and sister who have a seriously unhealthy relationship. I'm still not entirely sure why Francis, or David as Leila calls him, decided to seduce me. To annoy his sister? As a warped kind of tit for tat – you got the husband, I get the wife? As a way of gaining insight into her life? Perhaps it's as simple as that. I have the feeling he isn't normally allowed over Leila's threshold. Could that be because he's prone to aggression? Mrs Patterson said he was hanging around outside, which isn't the way people normally treat their siblings. And I would bet that Tom doesn't even know he exists.

A strange business, but I'm sure I can live with never fully understanding either Leila or David, because Maybanks could soon be mine again and that's enough to banish all thoughts of the last few weeks. When I arrive home, I attach Maurice's number to the pinboard in the kitchen and tackle the financial forms with renewed enthusiasm. Poor Tom doesn't know what's about to hit him. His mistress is leaving him and his wife is odds-on favourite to get the house back. Serves him right. Sometimes there really is justice in the world.

I'm halfway through the forms when I get a text from Francis:

Hope everything's going well with your uncle. I'll pop round later this evening. X

I'm unsure whether it's best to ignore him or to answer him. I don't want him coming to the house and keeping his finger on the bell the way I saw him do at Maybanks yesterday. I think, on balance, it's best to keep him at bay until he's realised that I know exactly who he is and that I don't want to have anything more to do with him. So I text back:

I won't be home this evening and possibly not tomorrow either. Thanks for your concern.

I press send and remember Leila's advice about calling the police should he appear at my door. It's a sobering thought and one that I hope I don't have to confront any time soon.

13. Leila

September 1996

I'm in bed when I get the call.

'David Francis is in hospital,' Gareth says. 'Your mother wants you home.'

That's it. The line goes dead. I sit on the edge of the bed, naked and shivering. I'm not shivering because I'm cold; I'm shivering because my heart is afraid and, for me, being afraid turns me to ice. Fear freezes me until my limbs are rigid and my joints seize up and before long I won't be able to move.

'Come back to bed.' A warm hand lands on my back and burns me. I slap it away, stand up, feel my body stiff and complaining as I half-stumble, half-skid across the wooden floor to grab my belongings: underwear, jeans, sweatshirt, coat, backpack. I dress quickly, find my socks and boots at the door.

'You're not going, are you?' The hand's owner stands in front of me, smoothing back his hair, his semi-erect cock at eye level as I bend to pull on my boots.

I push past him and while I'm running down the stairs I make sure I have my purse, I have my keys, I have my pills.

'There's a bus leaving at midnight,' the sales clerk tells me. 'It'll get you into Dundee for 9.30 tomorrow morning; you'll have to change in Edinburgh.'

'I'll take it.' I spill money onto the counter between us.

'Single? Return?'

'Single.' He takes most of the money and passes me a ticket. 'Bus stop three.'

Antidepressants and lack of sleep is a paranoia cocktail, I know this, but it doesn't stop me thinking through a multiplicity of scenarios, from: David isn't in hospital, he's run away from home and Gareth has no one else to focus his particular brand of torture on (for some reason my mother is exempt – perhaps because she's already half-dead) so he's called me back to his lair, to: Gareth has killed David. With all the practice he's had on rodents, rabbits and cats, dogs and deer, it's come to the point where he just had to try his skills out on a human being and David was in the wrong place at the wrong time.

The journey is interminable. Headlights and rain, gear changes, the smell of other people's food, the sound of other people's chatter, breathing and snoring. I want to scream, to hurtle up and down the aisle, thumping my fellow travellers on the head until they *shut the fuck up*! Instead, I close my eyes and count down the miles, firstly to the Scottish border and then to Edinburgh itself.

The counting gets me there and when I alight from the bus, my brain punch-drunk with numbers, ice in my joints, my knees give way and I end up kneeling on the pavement like a supplicant who has just arrived from a foreign country and is grateful to touch the earth. I'm in the path of the other passengers and a couple of women step over me before one of them turns round to help me up. She doesn't look at me or speak to me but carries on talking to the woman she's with. I don't register what they're saying, just the tone, which is one of 'putting-the-world-to-rights'.

She has me on my feet and leant up against the bus stop before she walks off. I sway from left to right and practise moving my joints, bending and stretching knees, elbows and thighs, before I have the courage to set off and find the bus to Dundee. A shorter journey, this one, and when I get there I buy myself a coffee and swallow a couple of pills. I decide to go straight to Ninewells. If David is in hospital then that's where he'll be. I use the last of my cash to take a taxi and I'm at the reception for 10.30. 'David Francis Morrison,' I say to the receptionist. 'I think he was admitted last night. He's my brother.'

She runs her finger down a list in front of her, then she reaches for some papers to shuffle through, and then she makes a phone call. 'Your brother has been admitted,' she says at last. 'He's in one of our surgical wards.' She shows me the ward's whereabouts on a map. 'Visiting is between two and four, and then this evening, six thirty till eight.'

'Thank you.' I make towards the exit and then veer off along a corridor, following the signs for the surgical wing. Perhaps he's had his appendix removed or a small cyst or a lump cut out – something unimportant. Fingers crossed. Rabbits' feet and four-leaf clovers. Black cats crossing my path and straight into Gareth's hands. I shake that image out of my head.

This must be the one of the moments when people pray. I try for 'Please God, don't let it be serious. Please, please let him live. Please God, let him live', but it sounds trite, phoney, a cliché of wanting and hoping that is entirely without substance when it's coming from someone like me. And if God is the all-seeing eye then he'll be laughing into his celestial coffee.

I walk confidently onto the ward as if I'm meant to

be there and so no one challenges me. A group of doctors are off to one side discussing X-rays and I pass a physio helping a patient to walk. There is a mix of rooms, ranging from just one bed to six beds, and I glance into every one until I see my brother in a two-bedded room, propped up in bed with several pillows supporting his head, a drip going into his arm and a plastic tube clogged with what looks like pus and blood draining into a glass bottle on the floor.

His eyes are closed. I pull the curtains around us but he doesn't wake up so I take the opportunity to notice the changes in him. I haven't seen him for almost a year, three hundred and forty-three days to be exact, and in that time his jaw has grown squarer and his nose slightly thicker. I pull aside the covers to see where the drain is coming from and whether it will give me a clue as to why he's on a surgical ward. There's a large dressing covering the area above his hip and the plastic drainage tube appears from under the gauzy mass. It's too high to be the appendix. Could he have fallen on something?

'Excuse me. Can I help you?' A young nurse has arrived and she stands on the opposite side of the bed to me, beside David's head, as if protecting him.

The sound of her voice has roused him from sleep and he stares up at her. 'Is everything okay?' His voice is weak.

'David?' I say. He turns his head very slowly towards me. Our eyes meet and hold. A single tear slides down his cheek and then he smiles.

'I knew you would come,' he says.

'The wound was self-inflicted,' the doctor tells me. 'Your brother used a kitchen knife.'

He pauses while I take a startled breath. *David took*

a knife to himself? How desperate must he have been? How much of this is my fault? I swanned off down south and left David out of sight and out of mind.

Shame on me.

'He was extremely lucky not to puncture an artery,' the doctor says, and I nod, holding the back of my hand against my mouth in case I scream.

'He should make a full recovery but I am very concerned about his emotional and mental state. He has assured me, however, that this was not a suicide attempt.'

I remove my hand from my face and grip the edge of the seat. 'A cry for help,' I say.

The doctor nods. 'Does he have a history of self-harm?'

'No,' I lie. I can't get my head around this. David, my sweet, kind baby brother, stabbed himself. He plunged a knife into his own flesh. He could have died. I stand up and walk around the room while the doctor watches me, his expression sympathetic but weary. 'It was my fault. I shouldn't have left him alone in the house.'

'Alone?'

'Just with my stepfather.' I touch the base of my skull where the darkness waits. 'Apart from my mother but she doesn't really count.'

'And why is that?'

'She's bedridden.' I massage the back of my neck. 'David and my stepfather don't get on.'

The doctor sits forward. 'Is your stepfather ever violent towards him?'

'No. He's never hit either of us.'

The doctor nods, satisfied with this. 'Personality clashes can feel very intense for teenagers.'

I don't tell him that it's far worse than a clash of personalities; it's the atmosphere in the house that is the killer – the very air is infected with Gareth's obsession. Death is inhaled with every breath, stealing oxygen from your bloodstream until you're rendered breathless and afraid. It's like living in a grave. No wonder my mother is a walking corpse.

'I'll come back to Dundee,' I say. 'I'll look after my brother. He can go to school, do his Highers. I'll make sure he's safe and well-fed.'

The doctor looks doubtful. 'That would be quite a commitment for you, don't you think? How old are you?'

'Twenty-two. And I know it would be a commitment but he's always better off when he's with me.'

'Why don't we talk to your mother and stepfather?'

'I told you, my mother is an invalid, she won't come here.' I bring my hand away from my neck and back down to my side. 'And anyway, David turned sixteen last week so legally he can leave home, can't he?'

'Yes, he can,' the doctor agrees.

'Good.' I open the door. 'I'll be back later.'

I hitchhike back to where Gareth and my mother live. It's a semi-detached 1930s house, part of a rambling estate where Gareth is employed as the gamekeeper. He must have been waiting behind the net curtains, because as my finger stretches for the bell, the front door opens.

'Look who it is,' he says. 'The lovely Leila Mae.'

The house is divided into two sections. The front of the house is for visitors. There is a living room and a large kitchen, both sparsely but cleanly furnished. Gareth and my mother never entertain but there is the odd visit from the next-door neighbour to consider (she cleans up at the big house and mostly keeps herself to herself) and every now and then the owner from the big house might stop by to 'see how things are going'.

Keeping up appearances takes on a whole new meaning because, while the front of the house is bog-standard normal, the back of the house is where the living and the dying happens. There is a connecting door that I push open and then I walk along the hallway, squeezing past the tatty piles of newspapers lined up on both sides. The back two rooms are where the tokens and memorabilia of Gareth's obsessions are kept and they have multiplied in my absence: rows of tiny, and not so tiny, bleached animal bones; ugly wooden dolls with painted faces fixed in expressions of pain or violence; glass jars full of floating pieces of animal specimens; pile after pile of ghoulish photographs and drawings.

I stop in the centre of the room and wait for Gareth to follow me in. I avoid eye contact with him because the look in his eyes makes me feel as if insects are crawling under my skin and I automatically reach inside my sleeve to scratch myself. He's the least trustworthy-looking person I've ever met and I don't know why everyone can't see it. The irony is that he's never touched either of us physically, not once, but emotional abuse was a daily occurrence as he denied us everything that a child needs: love, security, nourishment, normality. And now he's driven David to attempted suicide.

I'd use a knife on Gareth if I could but a) I doubt I'd be quick enough, b) if I was quick enough, I don't believe he would die and c) if by some chance I was quick enough and he did die, I'm absolutely sure his cretin of a ghost would haunt me for the remainder of my days.

No, the way to beat him is to leave him, to take ourselves beyond his reach, to deny him our presence and show him that his habits don't live on in us – the ultimate fuck you.

I've done it for myself and I'll do it for David too.

'I've come for David's things,' I say. 'I'm taking him to live with me.'

'And where would that be?'

'None of your business.'

'It's not happening.'

'Still practising your secret experiments?' The grey of his eyes seems to swirl. 'If I ventured into the cellar, what would I find there?'

'Leila?' It's a voice from the hallway as wispy as smoke. Seconds later my mother comes into the room. Her skin is tight across her skeleton; her muscles are wasted. Her hair has fallen out and there is a weeping ulcer on one of her legs. If the spectrum of my hearing was wider I feel sure I'd be able to hear the sound of disease eating through her body like locusts swarming a cornfield.

'Mum.' My acknowledgement of her existence is enough to make her hobble towards me, to try to touch me with her witch's fingers. I can't let that happen and so I sidestep her. She stumbles and then falls over, grasping for the back of a chair but missing. 'I'm going to pack David's belongings,' I tell Gareth. 'Don't try to stop me.'

My mum whimpers and stretches out her hand from the floor like a beggar. 'Help me, Leila.'

Repulsed, I run upstairs to throw David's belongings into a couple of bin bags. Gareth stands at the door watching me, his dead eyes trying to pull me towards him. 'It doesn't work on me any more,' I say, ramming clothes into the bin bags. 'I'm not a child now.' I grab David's coat and shoes, pick up the bags – he has precious little to his name, so they aren't heavy – and go straight downstairs again, shouting behind me, 'Don't try to find us.'

My mother is waiting to ambush me. Her touch is like poison and I push her hard. 'Stay the fuck away from me!' I hear a crack as her head hits the door, but she rebounds back towards me and this time her emaciated body lines up with mine: hugging me, her mouth on my cheek, her limbs rubbing up against mine. A wave of revulsion empties right through me.

I welcome the darkness. I welcome the rush of oblivion as it fills my head. I don't know what I'm doing . . . I know what I'm doing. My hands are strong, sure and purposeful as they link around her skinny throat. It feels like it's been a long time coming and when she takes her last breath, my mouth smiles and my heart beats faster, like I've just seen a lover on the other side of the street and I'm crossing the road to kiss him.

I stop. She falls to the ground. My mother has looked like a corpse for so long that it never occurred to me she would actually *die* like normal people do. Dead. My mother, the endlessly moaning presence in the bedroom, is dead.

And I killed her.

This is too much even for Gareth. 'She fell down the stairs,' he tells me, a shake in his voice. 'That's what happened. She fell down the stairs.'

I lean into him and I say, 'You better watch out or you'll be next.'

I'm a hundred yards away before I retch at the roadside, my limbs shaking, my heart a jumble of pain and pleasure. I sit on the kerb and breathe the cool, fresh air of freedom. She's dead. My mother is dead. The noose round my neck is severed, the chains round my ankles cut away.

And I feel more alive than I've ever felt in my life.

I put the incident out of my mind. Literally. I am able to do that.

I rent a furnished, two-bed flat in Dundee town centre and four days later I bring David back to it. I'm proud of what I've managed to achieve in a week. I've scrubbed the rooms from floor to ceiling and scoured charity shops for cheap nick-nacks to add colour to the drab place.

'It's the only flat I could get at such short notice,' I tell David. 'But I think we can make it homely.'

'I love it.' His face is as pale as the wind, and tight with pain, but he manages a smile. 'You've made it really cosy.'

He refuses to attend the therapy session recommended by the hospital, and I don't force him. 'Exploring what I feel, Leila. Can you imagine?' He laughs. 'It would take them years to sort me out.'

'Tell me, then,' I say, settling down on the sofa beside him. 'Tell me why you stabbed yourself.'

He sighs and pulls at his hair before saying, 'He made me kill a dog, an Alsatian that he had trapped in the cellar, muzzled and starving for three weeks. He hammered nails through the dog's paws. I—' He stops talking and punches the side of his face. 'Too much, Leila. Too fucking much.'

We leave it there because I know those sorts of details and they don't get any easier with the telling. 'I'm going to call the police,' I say, suddenly fed-up with our continued childish silence. 'An anonymous tip-off.'

'We can't, Leila.' He grabs for my hand. 'What about Mum? He looks after her. Where would she live? How would she manage?'

'Okay,' I say, keeping his hand in mine. 'We'll say nothing.'

Should I feel guilty omitting to tell him that I killed our mother? No, because his attachment to her is imagined. She has never been a mother to him. And now she never will be. But more to the point, when I think it through, I know it would be foolish for me to involve the police because killing my mother has meant that Gareth now has more on me than I have on him. He'll keep the secret; I know he will. But there's no point pushing my luck.

We have several weeks of domestic harmony. I secure myself a psychology research post at the university and David is back at school studying for his Highers. Every evening I cook us a wholesome meal with protein and vegetables and complex carbohydrates. He eats two thirds of the food and grows stronger. By Christmas he's completely recovered and I encourage him to go out more.

'I'm worried about you not having a social life,' I say.

'I like it being just the two of us,' he tells me.

I don't like it being just the two of us. I'm twenty-two years old and I'm staying in every night watching television with my teenage brother, whom I'm beginning to realise is like a vine that's creeping around me, tentacle by sticky tentacle, tying me down. And once I've started to think like that I can't stop.

I feel restricted. I miss having a man in my bed. I know it's not David's fault – he didn't ask me to give up my life – and now I simply have to wean him off me; but I'm unsure how to go about it.

And then one evening I bring a bloke home with me. He's called Edward Trent and he's one of my fellow researchers. We've spent days flirting with each other and are at the point where we can't keep our hands to ourselves. We've been in my bedroom for half an hour when David walks in on us. I shout at him to get out, and he does, but not before he's taken in an eyeful: both of us naked and enjoying oral sex.

An hour later when Ed has gone home, I find David, all innocent, in the living room. 'What the hell was that? How dare you walk in on me! You knew Ed was in there.'

'I didn't.'

He holds a magazine up in front of his face because he daren't meet my eye. I grab it from his hand and toss it across the room. 'We don't own one another, David. I have friends through work and you need to make some friends through school, friends your own age who you can have fun with.'

His eyes meet mine for a guilty second and then his gaze shifts to the curtains. 'But I like being with you. We don't need anyone else. We're good together.'

'Do not come into my bedroom uninvited again,' I tell him. 'Consider yourself warned.'

That's not the end of it. The very next day he gets his own back. I come home from work to find Gareth sitting in the front room. The sight of him brings a blast of memory and I relive what I did – my expert, practised hands on my mother's neck, the sound of it breaking, her dropping to the ground, lifeless as a grotesque mannequin.

I flex and extend my fingers. I breathe. I stare at Gareth, who is watching my reaction and feeding off it. David is slumped in the seat opposite him. His spine has crumbled. And he is crying.

'Leila Mae, how wonderful to see you again so soon,' Gareth says, and then he treats me to his ghoulish smile. 'Your mother is dead,' he announces, still smiling. 'I thought you should know.'

Julie Corbin

So we're playing that game, are we? 'Did you kill her?' I say and David gasps. 'Have you taken her body down to the cellar? Are you planning on dissecting her too?'

'Leila!' David shouts, stricken. 'Stop it! Fuck! Mum is dead!' He sobs into his hand. 'I can't believe it.'

'You leaving is what killed her, Leila Mae.' He stands up and comes towards me. 'You and David Francis going off like that. How did you expect her to survive such a betrayal?'

'Get out.' I hold the door open for him. 'Go on. Fuck off!'

'You need me, little girl.'

'I've never needed you. You're a pathetic creep,' I say quietly. 'Now fuck off.'

'I'll keep your secret,' he whispers. 'Leila Mae—'

I find the courage to push him hard and then I slam the door behind him and slide down the back of it because my legs aren't going to hold me up.

'How did Gareth find us?' I say to David.

'I don't know.'

'You told him?'

'I didn't.' It's a feeble denial and I want to slap him and slap him and keep slapping him but he's already surrendered to a prolonged bout of sobbing, appearing to be genuinely upset that our mother is dead. If I attack him now, he'll only sink further into misery and I don't want to have to deal with that. I know how he gets when he's pushed to the brink.

'Mum's been dead for years, David,' I say. 'Get a fucking grip.' I find my emergency bottle of vodka that I've stashed in the back of the freezer. I sit on the sofa opposite David and swallow mouthful after frozen mouthful. 'Don't cry for her, David,' I say. 'She's not worth it. She hasn't been worth it for years.' If I close my eyes I can conjure up the sight of her face when she first met Mal and he would lift her up in the air and carry her upstairs, her arms tight around his neck, her smile wide and warm as sunshine.

'She did love us though, Leila.' He crawls across the carpet to lay his head on my knee. 'She did, didn't she?'

'Once, perhaps, maybe.' I stroke his hair. 'A long time ago.' Coming home from the hospital with David, kneeling down to show him to me, her eyes tired but shining with happiness. Look Leila Mae, she whispered. Look what we have. A baby to look after. Aren't we the two luckiest girls in the whole world?

More vodka, more memories: dancing in the kitchen, sledging downhill, giggling, shrieking, baking chocolate chip cookies and eating them all in her bed as she read me Dr Seuss. All of life's sugar packed into my first six years.

I drag myself to bed, bumping into walls on the way. David follows me into my bedroom. 'I can't sleep alone, Leila. Please don't make me.' He reaches out his arms like a child wanting to be hugged. 'Not tonight.'

I throw back the duvet cover and he comes into the bed, snuggling into my back. I close my eyes and my head spins. I open them again and feel David spoon behind me. It begins like this, with cuddling and comfort. I'm aware of his erection but I'm not shocked by it and I don't shy away from it. My mind has disengaged and so I respond to his advances with an instinctive willingness that is beyond reason – no part of me says *Stop! This is David, your brother. He shouldn't be touching you like this. You should be repulsed.*

I don't think anything. I simply feel, letting go to the desire of a man's body in synch with mine, and then I fall asleep.

$\star \quad \star \quad \star$

When I wake, winter sunlight floods the room with a shimmering, honey glow. David is lying beside me, wide awake and staring at me. I have a feeling he's been staring at me for some time. 'You look beautiful when you're asleep,' he says. He touches my breast, tentative at first, then confident. I assumed he was a virgin before last night but I must have been wrong because he's surprisingly adept and knowing.

I stop his hand before he can push his fingers inside me. 'No.' I say. 'No.'

Up to now I've been part-sister, part-mother and now, briefly, we have crossed a line and become lovers, but in the sober daylight I won't repeat it.

I find David a flatmate and I move back down south. He accuses me of abandoning him and I accuse him of taking advantage of me. I swear I'll have nothing more to do with him but even as I say it, I know I won't be able to make it true because we are pillars in each other's lives, the only allies to the dysfunction of our upbringing, and that makes him like a limb that I struggle to sever.

When I discover I'm pregnant, I plead with myself to have an abortion but I can't go through with it, because while I'm perfectly happy to kill a part of myself, I can't kill a part of David.

I don't tell him I'm pregnant. And when my son is born, I love him with a devotion that encompasses hope and courage and all things holy. Alexander. Baby Alex has all the smiles, all the potential, all the beauty of David and me. But none of the crazy.

I make one mistake. I am swimming in a sea of maternal hormones and I feel elated, weepy, lonely, proud. I call David. I tell him about Alex. I tell him that he is the father and he travels down to see us at once. Within ten hours he is standing by my bedside, ready to be a parent to Alex, ready for us to be a couple.

I'm actually a mother now. I'm not a sister playing at being a mother – I am a real, bona fide mother. David is a young man. He doesn't need my protection any more. He's six foot tall. He's handsome. He can read and write. He can confidently make love to a woman. He cooks; he can do his own washing.

'We need to make a pact, David,' I tell him. 'For the sake of our baby. We have to promise each other that we will stay apart. That we will allow one another to live separate lives.'

'What do you mean?' He slumps, disappointment written through his body language.

'We have to put the baby first and that means that he needs the best chance of a normal life.'

'Not a brother and sister for parents?'

'Exactly.'

'But no one needs to know!'

'People find out, David. People always find out.'

He's not buying this. 'Look at Gareth!' he says. 'No one has ever found out about him. We can keep a secret, Leila Mae. We can do that.'

It takes me over a week to persuade him to leave us. Every time I falter I focus on my baby's face and know he deserves the best this world has to offer him. I will not collapse. I will not shirk my responsibilities as a mother. I will be a tiger protecting my cub.

'It's time for you to go, David,' I say.

His lip trembles, his eyes fill.

I turn away.

I turn away from him and look towards my baby who has just fed and is flushed pink and contented. David's face recedes to the corner of my vision and then it fades out of shot altogether.

I bank on David forgetting about Alex and me. I'm optimistic that he'll meet a girl and move on. His sister with her fatherless baby will be a mild embarrassment to him and so we might see each other once in a blue moon, but no more than that because why would we want to? All we do is remind each other of things we'd rather forget.

14. Ellen

It's four days since I heard from Francis. I'm starting to hope he's given up and I feel the beginnings of relief lighten my step. The good times I had with him were short-lived and have been completely eclipsed by his lying. I still can't quite believe it and I am horrified and ashamed that I was so easily fooled. The whole romance was clearly too good to be true but I blindly went along with it anyway, imagining I was due some good luck and what could be better than the fizz and flight of a love affair?

Lesson learned.

I've begun to practise my exposure therapy again and it's tough. I spend an hour sitting on the sofa resisting the urge that tells me I have to pull the plugs from the sockets – I have to do it NOW or else the house will go on fire and Ben will die and I will die, firstly coughing and choking on the smoke and then the heat will build and our lungs will smoulder and there will be the smell of scorching, blistering flesh and then our bodies will be black, charred misshapen heaps of carbon.

And there will have been screaming. I will have heard the sound of my son screaming for his life. That, in fact, will be the last thing I hear as I die – Ben in total, appalling anguish.

I sit through all of these thoughts. The sights, the sounds, the smells – I feel as if they are real, and halfway through the hour my senses are exploding with panic-alarm bells, but I don't move. Somehow I manage to sit it out and the fear recedes and fades and then I'm just a woman, on a sofa, in a developed country where centuries of civilisation has meant decades of checks and balances to keep us all safe.

When I stand up I feel shaky but proud. I did it. It was tough but I didn't give in. This will be my life for the next few weeks and it will be hard work, but it means I'll be able to improve my mental health and resume a fuller life. Fingers crossed.

Ben gets out of bed at about ten o'clock and I make him some breakfast, then join him at the table with a coffee. 'You okay, Mum?' he asks. 'You look quite tired.'

'Well . . .' This is as good a time as any. 'Francis and I are not seeing each other anymore.'

'Oh, okay.' He takes a forkful of scrambled egg. 'Was it you or him?'

'Turns out he was lying to me.'

'Shit. What . . . is he married or something?'

It's on the tip of my tongue to tell him that Francis is really David, Leila's brother, when my mobile rings. It's Hamish's secretary to say that Hamish has asked to see me today.

'Good news, I hope?' I say to her.

'I know that Hamish received a letter from your husband's solicitor this morning. I'm not sure what it says but I can tell you that he came out of his office whistling just now.'

'Could be good news on the horizon,' I tell Ben when I've finished the call. 'I'm going up town now to see what Dad's solicitor has said.' I kiss him on the top of his head. 'Will you be home for tea?'

'Depends how late the football goes on for. And

Mum?' I look back at him. 'Don't let the Francis thing get you down.'

'I won't, darling. Thank you.'

Twenty minutes later I'm in Hamish's office and he gets straight to the point. 'Ellen, we've had word from Tom's solicitor.' He smiles. 'He's willing to do a turnaround on the house.'

It's what I've been expecting but still I can barely believe it and my eyes fill with tears. 'Thank you, Hamish. Thank you so much.'

'It's great news, Ellen.' He gives my hand a vigorous shake. 'Great news. I don't know exactly what's happened there but apparently Tom's circumstances have changed and he's now willing to move out.' He gives me the details of the deal, all of which sound financially manageable. 'Your father's house is on the market?'

'Yes, and there's already been a lot of interest.'

'Good. I need to thrash out some of the finer points with Tom's solicitor but I expect to have a deal on the table for you within the next couple of weeks.'

Maybanks will be mine again. I repeat this to myself several times and so I'm almost skipping as I leave the office to walk down Hanover Street to my dad's. It's late morning and the day is crisp and bright; a fresh wind has whipped the sky into a swirl of blue and white: a typical Edinburgh day minus the rain.

Leila was as good as her word; she really is leaving Tom, and I'll move back into my home. Life is looking up, up, up, and I'm in the mood to celebrate. When I arrive at my dad's, I say, 'Where's that bottle of champagne you've been keeping for Christmas?'

'Hiding in the back of the fridge,' he says. He's on his hands and knees again, clearing out moss between the stones in the pathway. 'Why?'

'Tom's done a U-turn on the house. He's willing to move out!'

'Well!' My dad rocks back on his heels. 'My flabber is well and truly gasted!' He gets to his feet and puts his arm through mine, swinging me around as he sings, 'Step we gaily on we go, heel for heel and toe for toe, arm in arm and row on row, all for Mairi's wedding.'

We reel and clap our way around the garden and into the kitchen until we're out of breath and we collapse on the sofa laughing. 'Who would have thought Tom would give in so easily?' my dad says. 'Not me, that's for sure.'

'I think . . . well . . .'

'Catch your breath,' my dad says.

It's not a lack of breath that makes me hesitate. I can't find the right words because I don't know how to begin to tell him about what's been going on.

'Let's crack open that bottle.' He staggers off to the fridge. 'That's set the joints complaining!' I hear the clink of glasses and then he's back in front of me. He hands me a glass, bubbly overflowing down the side, then holds up his own, saying, 'A toast.' He pauses. 'To my daughter, Ellen, who's made me prouder than any man deserves to be.'

'Cheers, Dad.' We clink glasses and make plans for when we're back in Maybanks. 'You should begin by living in the house and then we can convert the annexe when we have the time and money.'

'I don't want to be getting in your way.'

'Don't be daft.' I tip more champagne into my glass. 'As long as you don't cut your toenails in the living room we'll get along fine.'

'Does that mean I won't be allowed to hang my under-pants up to dry in the kitchen either?'

We both laugh and somehow we manage to drink our

way through the whole bottle, reminiscing about family occasions, about Mum and my grandparents and all the good things that create memories and encourage families to stay together.

'Come back for your tea,' he says a couple of hours later when he sees me to the door. 'I was round at the fishmongers this morning. Thought I'd make a fish pie. You know how Molly loves her mashed potatoes.'

I nod. 'I'll be back for six.'

'Bring Ben along.'

'I think he might be playing five-a-side football. I'll let you know.'

I walk off home and find myself smiling at everyone: old ladies who are holding up pedestrian traffic, fractious toddlers in buggies, surly teenagers. I feel generous and benevolent and my mood can't be dampened by any inconvenience or moodiness because I'm going to live in Maybanks again and that makes me feel like I'm floating on air.

I step into the house and hear a noise in the living room. 'You still here, Ben?' I shout. I leave my coat and shoes at the front door and walk towards him, champagne giggling in my bloodstream. 'You'll never guess—' I stop on the threshold. It's not Ben – it's Francis. I take a split second to register this thought and to remind myself of Leila's warning, and then I turn round and run towards the front door I have the door open and am outside on the step before he's caught up with me. He grabs hold of my hair with one hand and covers my mouth with the other. He hauls me back inside the house while I bite his hand and kick my feet against him.

'What's the matter?' He shakes me hard and I bite

the edge of his finger, so he slams my head against the wall. 'I only want to talk to you!'

I'm shaking with fear and frustration. I can feel that the back of my head is aching but I'm barely aware of any pain. Adrenaline pumps through me, dispelling the alcohol and sharpening my senses to pinpoints of clarity.

'I'm going to take my hand away,' he tells me. 'And you're not going to scream.'

I nod my head. My neighbours are all at work and he's just dragged me off the front step with no one to see me, so I know that screaming won't work. I'm going to have to try to reason with him even though I have nothing to bargain with. *Just listen to him, Ellen. Find out what he wants.*

When he takes his hand away from my mouth I notice a patch of blood on his sleeve. It's a stain the size of a baby's fist and the sight of it creates another level of dread inside me. He could have cut himself, but I don't see any signs of that – could it be Ben's blood? I take a surreptitious glance towards the front door and don't see Ben's sports bag there. He always dumps it by the door when he's going out to football, so he must have left already. Please God. Please.

Francis steps away from me and leans his back against the opposite wall. I don't speak or move apart from to breathe. He is shaking his head slowly as if he's listening to a mellow tune inside his head, but when he glances up at me, his expression is anything but mellow. 'You spoke to my sister,' he says. 'You went behind my back.' He wags a finger in front of my face. 'I know what you're thinking but you're wrong.'

He grabs my arm and drags me behind him into the living room. I'm tripping over my feet, knocking into the wall, and when my shin makes contact with one of the dining table legs, the skin tears and pain bites through to the bone.

'Sit down.'

I sit on the sofa, my back ramrod straight.

'Rescuer, victim, perpetrator – we all shift between these three roles but we tend to have a favourite.' He points at me. 'Take you, Ellen. I have been a rescuer to you, haven't I?' I nod. 'My sister has always bagged the rescuer role for herself but she's not the only one. No, no, no.' He bangs his fist against his chest. '*I* can also be the rescuer. I hope you told her that.' His face draws in close to mine. 'Did you? Did you tell her that?'

'I'm sorry.' I try not to shudder. 'I didn't.'

'Thought not.' He sits down opposite me and says nothing for a minute or more. His legs move up and down and every now and then his arms jerk outwards and fall back to his sides. I can see he's having an internal monologue with himself and then he says, 'I'm not mad. I know that's what you're thinking but I'm not mad. And now you're probably thinking it's only mad people who say they're not mad.' He gives a loud laugh. 'Damned if I do and damned if I don't. Story of my life.'

I don't want to speak but pressure is building inside me. I need to know how he got into the house. I need to know that he hasn't hurt Ben, that the blood on his sleeve isn't my son's.

'How did you get in here?' I say quietly, wincing as I speak because the waver in my voice is signalling my fear like a klaxon in a silent room and if I can hear it then so can he.

'When I was looking for the jewellery I found your spare key.' He points to the bureau. 'I was going to come back to look again but you'd already given the jewellery back to Leila.'

I nod, relieved that Ben was gone when Francis got here. I relax my back a little and wait. Francis has lapsed into silence again. His expression is pensive and then it clouds over with sadness. 'I have a son, you know,' he says. 'Did you know that?'

I shake my head. 'I didn't know that.' *Keep him talking. It might help.* 'Does he live in Edinburgh?'

'He does, but it might as well be Timbuktu because he doesn't know who I am. His mother told him that his father was some nobody from years ago.' He screws up his face. 'How would you feel if you were excluded from your child's life?'

'I'd hate it,' I say honestly.

'Exactly! But that's what's happened to me. The mother won't let me see him.'

'Couldn't you go to a solicitor?'

'I don't have the money. And . . .' His expression is pained. 'I don't want my son to get to know me that way, through a lawyer, with all the trouble they cause. I mean, she could just agree, couldn't she?' I nod. 'You think I'm right?'

'I do. A child needs two parents and you want to be a dad. I think that's admirable.' I believe what I'm saying although not where Francis is concerned. From what Leila told me and the way he's behaving now, I'm not surprised the mother is refusing to acknowledge him. Perhaps she tried to let him become involved in the child's life but he pulled a stunt not unlike this. I go along with him, though, because feeling as if he has me as an ally might help him to relax. 'How old is your son?'

'He's nineteen. Same as Ben.'

'He's an adult, then. I wonder whether you should approach him directly?'

'I wouldn't want to upset him. I feel it needs to go through the mother.'

'I understand that.'

'She makes it all about her.'

'When did you last speak to her about it?'

'Recently.' He smiles. 'He's called Alex.'

More silence. Time for me to think. Leila's son is called Alex. He is nineteen. I must be frowning as I make this connection because Francis says, 'What are you thinking?'

'I was just thinking that Leila's son is called Alex . . . and he's nineteen.'

The confusion must show on my face because he grows angry again, 'You see – this is what I'm up against! It disgusts you, doesn't it?'

I already know that their sibling relationship is dysfunctional but this is a giant step beyond what I imagined and I have no time to process it. 'I'm not judging you,' I say, sure that I mean it. 'It's just . . . it does take a bit of getting your head around.'

He throws his body towards me and pins me to the sofa, his weight heavy on my chest so that I can't breathe. 'You know nothing. Nothing about my life. Nothing about me. Nothing about my mother.'

I try to speak but there's no air in my mouth.

'I don't hate you, Ellen. But I'm pissed off with you.' His jaw tenses. 'Really pissed off with you because you should have given me the jewellery. That's why it's all gone wrong. Because of you.'

Tears are running down my face as I struggle for breath. All I can move is my lower legs and feet and I drum my heels on the floor in desperation.

'I'm not going to kill you,' he says, and suddenly he's standing up and I am gulping air. 'You're only a minor player in this story.'

'I . . .' I struggle to my feet, pain in my leg, in my head, in my ribcage. 'Francis, please. Please just go. I won't say anything. I won't do anything. We can forget this. I—'

I don't say any more because the front door opens and Molly's voice calls out, 'Grannie, it's me!'

Immediately, Francis's eyes scan the room as if for an exit or a hiding place.

'Hi, Mum!' Chloe shouts. The door closes with a bang and Molly runs into the living room.

'Molly!' I catch her in my arms as she barrels into the room. Pain bites inside my muscles and I cry out.

'Grannie.' Molly's smile fades, uncertain. 'What's wrong?'

'What's going on?' Chloe's eyes are worried as she stares at Francis and then me. 'Mum?'

'Are you all right?' Molly says to Francis, her expression serious. 'You have blood on you.' She points to his sleeve. 'Did you cut yourself?'

'It's not you I want,' Francis says to me.

'Please, Francis.' I hold Molly behind me. 'Please leave.'

'It's not you I want,' he repeats. He pushes past Chloe, walks along the hallway and out the front door. As it slams shut behind him my legs give way.

14. Leila

I have a busy week as I prepare for Alex and me to move on. The last sessions with my clients all go well, although Alison and Mark are convinced I'm leaving because of them.

'I know we've argued in here,' Alison says. 'But we've always seen it as a safe space and we thought you did too.'

'You told us that,' Mark says.

'And I meant it,' I say. 'I'd like to keep working with you but I'm moving away.'

'We can travel,' Alison says. 'We are committed to our therapy.'

It takes me a while, but I finally make them understand that another therapist will be able to help them just as much, if not more, than I have. They leave with her phone number, their expressions disbelieving and hurt as if I'm abandoning them, casting them out on the high seas with neither a paddle nor even a boat. I close the door behind them with a sigh of relief, realising that I no longer have the patience for clients like these who make problems where there aren't any. 'Try my life on for size!' I want to call after them. 'See what that feels like.'

I sell my mother's jewellery on Tuesday morning to a recommended dealer in Glasgow. 'Such pieces are unattractive to buyers in the current market,' he tells me.

'But the stones . . .' He screws up one eye to look through his eyeglass. 'The stones are impressive. Very, very impressive.'

I leave the dealer with a money transfer for more than twenty thousand pounds, enough to see us through the move and cover our costs for several months depending on how long it takes me to find another job. This is the first step completed and it bolsters me for what lies ahead. I know the conversation with Tom will not be an easy one – and it isn't.

I broach the subject on the Tuesday evening. We have just finished our meal and Tom is complaining about his wife again. He's going to have to reluctantly give far more ground than he's comfortable with. 'I always suspected she'd make trouble eventually,' he says.

I think of Ellen and the fact that, unlike Tom, she is almost completely without spite. She couldn't resist the temptation to spoil some of my clothes and shoes but she could easily have hung on to my mother's jewellery as payback and she didn't. 'I think you should let her have the house,' I say.

'What?' He pours himself another glass of red. 'This house?'

'Yes. She put all the effort into it. She loves Maybanks. She should have it.'

'Where on earth is this coming from?' he says, full of surprise and indignation. He drinks a mouthful of wine. 'We've made our home here!'

'Tom . . .' I take a breath. This part is never easy. I have left a good few men in my time and it's so much simpler to just pack a suitcase and be gone when they return home from their day's work. 'I don't think we're going to make it.'

'Make what?'

'I don't think we're good together,' I state. 'So, I'm going to leave before things go sour.'

His mouth hangs open. He's completely stunned. This sort of thing doesn't happen to Tom. Tom is the man in charge; the women in his life occupy a supporting role. He is the one who makes the life-changing decisions. 'You're leaving me? You're *leaving* me?'

'I am.'

'Why?'

'Because, as I said, I don't think we're good together.'

'Of course we're good together! Why else would I have given up my wife for you?'

'You told me your marriage was already over when we met.'

'It was.' He thinks for a second. 'Almost. And I broke up my family for you.'

'My children are grown up, you told me. I want another chance at happiness. That's what you said.'

'Darling, please.' He treats me to his most benevolent, winning smile and comes round to my side of the table to persuade me. 'Leila, let's talk about this sensibly. If there's something you need, then I will give it to you. I've already paid for Alex's therapy—'

'Thank you.' I stand up. 'I appreciate that.'

'I know you do.' He attempts to take my hand. 'I know—'

'There is nothing you can say, Tom,' I tell him, my tone emotionless. 'Please don't even try. You will only embarrass us both.'

He is stunned for all of five seconds and then he reaches for his glass of wine and throws it across the room. The glass hits one of the kitchen cupboards and smashes instantly, splattering red wine in an arc across the white units and splinters of glass in a wide radius.

And so begins a tirade of abuse: I'm a slut, a home-wrecker and a bad mother. I let people down. I'm selfish and hard-hearted. I'm completely to blame for my son's drug-taking.

While he shouts, I clean up the mess and after five minutes of hearing myself insulted in every which way possible, I stand in front of him and say loudly, 'That's enough! Go and be angry with someone else.'

He raises his hand and then stops it in mid-air, not willing to go as far as actually hitting me – he's not that man, which is just as well because I'm holding a knife in my hand and I am prepared to use it. He walks out of the kitchen and upstairs. I hear doors and drawers being slammed shut with temper and then five minutes later he's downstairs again with two packed suitcases and his brief-case in his hands. 'You don't have to leave,' I say. 'Alex and I will be out by the weekend.' I stand next to him as he grabs his keys and wallet from the hall table. 'Tom?'

He's unable to look at me.

'I'll take my car and all of my things,' I say. 'I'll leave the house keys and the diamond earrings you bought me for Christmas.'

He doesn't respond. His chin wobbles and his jaw tenses in response. He has become a wounded little boy and he needs to escape for a good cry, take himself off to another place where he won't be confronted with the reality of a woman who has rejected him.

I let him go and, sensing that Katarina must have heard most of this, I go into the living room. She looks up at me guiltily. 'I was not hearing. I am not listening.'

'Tom and I are not going to live together any more,' I say.

'I am sorry.' Her eyes fill with tears. 'I am not . . . this is not . . .' She shakes her head, unable to find the words.

'These things happen,' I say, with a businesslike tone. 'It's not for you to worry about.' I smile, but she still looks sad and I realise it's because she cares. She is a more sensitive soul than I have given her credit for. 'I'm going to be leaving over the weekend and I don't think you'll want to be here with Tom on your own.'

'He does not like me.'

'Don't take it personally.' I smile, but she is unable to respond. 'I'll give you three months' wages and buy you a return ticket to Prague if you want to go home immediately.'

'You will?'

'Of course. This is not your fault.'

'Yes!' She jumps up and throws her arms round me. 'I love go home. I have boyfriend and he is missing and I am missing.'

'That's good then!'

'Yes, that's good then!' She smiles and in that instant, her face is beautiful. It's the happiest I've seen her since she arrived. I know I haven't been kind enough to her and don't imagine she'll look back on her time in Scotland with any degree of fondness.

'Let's buy you that ticket.'

I log on to my laptop and she sits beside me, her legs moving up and down impatiently. 'I am sorry for you but I am excited for me.'

'You be happy, Katarina,' I say to her. 'You deserve to be happy. Don't forget that.' I print out her boarding card and hand it to her.

'Thank you!' She kisses the page then kisses my cheek. 'I pack!' She runs upstairs. 'I pack now!'

The next day when I drop Katarina at the airport, with more hugging and promises to stay in touch, promises

that I can't imagine we'll ever keep, Rob Mooney rings
– perfect timing – to tell me that Alex is ready to come
home. He gives me a progress report and I can tell that
Alex is in the right frame of mind to resist temptation
and put focus and effort into his future. 'The friend he's
made,' I say.

'Alistair?'

'That's right. They've been making music together.
Do you think it's a healthy, mutually supportive friendship?'

'I do,' Rob says. 'I know they're planning to meet up
and I think it will be good for both of them.'

'That's great news.' *Paisley here we come!* 'I could be
with you in just over an hour,' I say. 'Is that too soon?'

Rob assures me Alex will be ready and I set off,
planning as I drive, thinking about where I'll find work.
I have plenty of contacts in my current business but it
does make it easy for David to keep finding us, so I'm
contemplating a career change. I think of all the roads
not yet taken that still stretch out either side of me: I
could work on the land, learn to grow some vegetables,
make cheese even. (Well, why not?) I could train to be
a teacher. I could work in a local shop. In actual fact, it
doesn't really matter what I decide to do because the
job will be a means to an end. The next few years will
be about Alex, what's good for him and what brings us
closer, while at the same time preparing him for life as
an independent adult.

He's barely in the car when I say, 'How do you feel
about us moving closer to your friend Alistair?'

'He lives in Paisley.'

'I know.'

'What?' He stares at me, surprised. 'You mean move
to Paisley?'

'Yes.'

He smiles. 'Mum, I don't think Paisley would suit you and Tom.'

'It would just be you and me because, you see, well, I don't think it's working out with Tom.' I glance across at him to gauge his thoughts. 'I'm sorry, Alex. This isn't the first time I've left a man and we've upped sticks and gone to another city but I promise you it will be the last.'

'Shit! It's not because of me, is it? Was it because I had to go back to rehab?'

'No, no, no.' I briefly place my hand on his knee and he doesn't recoil. It makes my heart lift. 'It's me. I'm at fault. I don't think I'm meant to be the other half of a couple.' I glance across at him again. 'I'm sorry.'

'It's okay.' He shrugs, unconcerned. 'Tom and I don't really get along anyway. But Paisley, Mum? Are you sure?'

'Yes, I am sure. I'm absolutely sure.'

He's pensive for a bit. 'You can look at it in another way, Mum. You can say you're not afraid of change. You've always been able to recognise when something isn't right and move on. That's a good trait to have.'

I don't tell him that most of my moving on has been running away, because of my brother, his father and the secret I'm never willing to reveal. It's not that I don't think we would be unable to get past the fact of his conception, although I know that would take a good deal of working through; it's that I don't trust David. He has always been unpredictable and I won't subject Alex to that. Not now, not ever.

'I've not been much of a son recently but I'm going to make up for it, Mum, I really am. I'm going to get a job, carry on with my music. Become someone.'

His sincerity tugs at my heart and makes me feel proud of him. And perhaps proud of me too, and once more I let myself think that maybe I haven't made such a bad job of raising my son after all.

It's Friday and Alex has gone up town to say goodbye to some friends. We're leaving Edinburgh tomorrow. I've found us some temporary accommodation in Paisley for the next three months; we'll be able to seek out a better option once we're living there and we have more of an idea of the area of town that best suits us. I'm not a hoarder and have never been someone who has hung on to possessions just for the sake of it, so we haven't amassed a huge amount of stuff. The van will arrive at nine and I expect to be on the road by ten.

I'm ticking items off my list – van hire, registered change of address with the post office, letters to all my clients and to the university – when the doorbell goes. For a second I think it might be Tom, but he'd hardly ring his own doorbell and I don't expect to hear from him again. We had a stilted telephone conversation last night when he made an attempt to change my mind. 'I thought I'd give you a couple of days to cool off.' (I wasn't heated.) 'We both said things we didn't mean.' (I didn't.) 'Why don't we have a weekend away? Paris? Amsterdam? New York? You choose.' (I choose Paisley.)

'I'm sorry, Tom,' I interrupt him when he reminds me how good we are together. 'We're over. There is no us. Please don't contact me again.'

The doorbell sounds a third and then a fourth time. I hoped, I might have even prayed – but I didn't actually believe I'd get away without seeing David for one last time. And it will be the last time, because I'm going to do what I should have done years ago and put a stop to him bothering me.

He's standing on the doorstep. We look one another up and down. 'There's blood on your sleeve,' I say.

'You seem nervous,' he says.

'What do you want?'

'To talk to you. Please.' He smiles. It's the little-boy smile that I'm a sucker for, the smile that pulls me right back to his side. I'll give him an inch but no more than that.

'Five minutes,' I say. He follows me into the kitchen. 'Whose blood is on your sleeve?'

'No one's.' He widens his eyes. 'It's nothing.' He moves around the kitchen picking things up and putting them down again. I turn over the page on my notepad in case his eyes fall on my tick list and he works out that we're moving. 'Ellen found out who I was. Did you tell her?'

'I didn't need to. She saw you come in here.' I look through the window and down to the bottom of the garden. I can't see where I hid the cat but I know he's there, a quietly decomposing reminder of the power I hold in my hands. 'David, I have something to tell you. Something I should have admitted to you years ago. Wait here.' I go upstairs and bring the sheet of paper out from under the mattress, the one I copied and altered from the original in Tom's case files. 'Read this,' I say, handing it to him.

I watch his eyes as they move down the page. I see a shiver pass through him and then he shakes himself like a dog. 'You're trying to tell me that guy Ed is Alex's father?'

'I'm not trying to tell you anything. This is a DNA test. It states as a matter of fact that Edward Trent is 99.9% likely to be Alex's biological father.'

'The date on this is ten years ago.'

'That's right. I bumped into Ed in a pub and it was the opportunity I needed to ask him whether he'd be willing to take a DNA test. He said yes but he didn't want anything to do with Alex – he had just got married and his wife was expecting.' My lie sounds convincing even to myself. 'I said that didn't matter. I simply wanted to know for sure who Alex's father was because I had noticed something about his walk and the set of his mouth that reminded me of Ed.'

'You liar,' he says, a smile in his voice as he tries to laugh it off. 'The night Alex was born you called me. You said you saw me in the baby! My nose, my eyes.'

'I know I did. And I'm sorry for that but I was emotionally vulnerable, needy, very unlike myself.'

'Unlike yourself enough to be truthful.'

I shake my head. 'I had no birth partner and I wanted to speak to you, to make things better between us. I felt bad about our rift. I'd been given the gift of a baby and I wanted to share that gift with you. To heal us both.' I pause. 'Afterwards I realised it was only myself I was seeing in Alex. You and I have features in common after all and I was confused.'

The truth is this: I called David because I couldn't help myself, because I was misguided enough to believe, in that post-partum moment when there was a rush of hormones and my maternal love had been instantly activated, that David deserved to know the part he'd played in creating this beautiful, tiny, perfect human being. I didn't think about the consequences and I certainly didn't anticipate how much that decision would come to haunt me.

David takes a lighter from his pocket and sets fire to

the page. The flame flares up; the paper curls and blackens. He drops the burning remains into the sink.

'There's more than one copy.'

'I know this isn't true.' He is maintaining his position. 'You would have told me years ago.'

'When? When could I have told you? At what stage in your life would you have believed me?' He leaves these questions unanswered so I continue, sensing a chink of doubt. 'There's never been a right time, David. I thought that maybe if you met someone and married her then that might be an opportune moment but you haven't, and so that moment has never come, and now with all you have done these past few weeks I knew I couldn't delay any longer . . .' I trail off.

'You bitch!' He's shaking his head as if just realising he's been taken for a fool. 'You absolute bitch.'

'David, I think what you're conveniently forgetting is that you took advantage of me.'

'You were a slag! You slept with anyone.'

'I didn't sleep with anyone. I had sex with the men I wanted to have sex with. And I certainly did not want to have sex with my brother.' I move in close. 'You came into my bed when you knew I'd had too much to drink and you all but raped me.'

'You enjoyed it.'

'I was barely aware it was happening. While you were stone cold sober, entirely aware of what you were doing.'

He flexes and extends his fingers from fist to wide-open palm. It's an action I make myself. It's an action Gareth always made and I know what follows. 'I could contact Alex any time I want. Have you thought about that, Leila? I could blow your life sky-high.'

'And yet you haven't. And why is that?' I leave a space

for him to fill but he doesn't; he's busy watching his hands. 'I'll tell you why – because it's not about Alex; it's about me. It's about having power over me, owning me.'

'You can't own another human being.' His eyes flick briefly towards mine. 'Not while they're alive.'

I catch a look that I've seen before and I feel my joints stiffen. It's the dead-eyed expression that Gareth used to have when he came out of the cellar. 'You've had your five minutes, David.' My voice is strong. 'Please go now.' I glance at my watch. 'I have a client arriving in five minutes.'

He shakes his head. 'You want to know whose blood this is?'

'Tell me you haven't hurt Ellen,' I say quietly.

'Ellen? Why would I hurt Ellen? We only hurt those we love, don't we? Those we love – or in this case—' he brushes at the blood on his sleeve '—hate.' He holds out his hands palm-up, and moves them up and down as if weighing the emotions. 'Love, hate,' he repeats. 'What's worth more?'

'Love,' I say softly. 'Of course.'

'But hate feels so powerful.'

'So does love.' In the corner of my vision is the knife rack. I'm one step, one reach away from it. 'To be loved is what we all want.' I reposition my feet. 'You, me, everyone.'

He considers this. 'But, Leila Mae, can love exist where there are secrets?'

'There are no secrets between us, David. Not any more.'

'Oh yes, there is.' He throws his arms wide enough to encompass the whole room. 'There is one mammoth, fucking secret that you've kept from me for years but when Gareth told me—' he nods his head up and down, up and down '—When Gareth told me it made perfect sense because the night I fucked you, you talked in your sleep. You've always talked in your sleep. Do you know that about yourself, Leila Mae? Do you?' His face moves up close to mine, until our mouths are just inches from each other. 'I know you killed her.'

I hold his eyes, unflinching. Our mother. Always our mother. Back from the dead. Showing up in an Edinburgh kitchen, our eternal ghostly stalker. Should I deny that I took her life? Murdered her? (Because I did murder her, didn't I?) . . . I decide not. I won't deny my actions to David. Because of all the people in the world he should get it. 'Our walking dead of a mother?' I say. 'I didn't kill her.' My hand is in an awkward position behind my back but it's the only way to prevent David from seeing my fingers close round the handle of the knife. 'I took her life but I didn't kill her. Our mother was already dead. She died years before she stopped breathing.'

'You strangled her?'

'I did.' I nod. 'I really did.'

'Why?' He pulls at his hair with both his hands, maniacally, desperately, and then knocks his fists on his skull. 'Why would you do that?' he shouts. 'Why?'

'Because she opted out,' I say quietly. 'She should have protected us. She should have stopped him.'

'You. *You* should have told me.' He spits the words at me. 'Gareth knew. Fucking *Gareth* knew.' He pushes me hard against the counter and I grasp the knife more firmly.

'So that's your problem?' I laugh in his face. 'Gareth knew before you did?'

He's much stronger than I would have believed possible but when he grabs hold of my blouse I'm ready for him. It isn't easy to stab someone through a jacket, and the angle is awkward. The knife goes into his back just below the ribcage, deep enough to make him cry out but, not deep enough to completely disable him.

He has hold of my hair; I twist the knife deeper. He bangs my head on the worktop twice before I land a kick between his legs. I scratch down the side of his face, I bite the edge of his hand, and when my mobile rings, I grab for it, but awkwardly because David has stamped on my fingers and they feel broken. The name on the screen is Mary McNeil. 'My son.' That's all I say. I hope that's what I say. I can't be sure because my tongue seems to have doubled in size and is thick and cold in my mouth.

I want to fight him, I will keep fighting him, but there's an explosion in my head and I groan from deep inside my gut. I drop the phone and put my hand up to my head, where blood is running from my forehead, through my fingers, down my neck, my hands, my arms. I try to apply pressure to the wound but feel a piece of my skull move under my fingers. Fractured. My skull is fractured.

When I hit the floor, I groan again. And then I try to pull my limbs in close because I'm freezing. My insides are turning to ice. I'm back in the cellar and Gareth is standing before me. 'Stroke his fur, Leila Mae,' he says, holding a cat out in front of him. 'Look into his eyes as the heat drains from his body. That's what death is, Leila Mae. Death is cold.'

I don't want Gareth in my thoughts. I want Leila Mae with her black eyes and her surety. Her way of coping.

Her way of living. She wouldn't die like this. She would keep fighting to the end, the bitter end.

'Leila Mae.' It's David's voice. I feel his lips on my cheek. 'Sweet dreams.'

15. Ellen

It's not you I want. I've been lying on the sofa while Molly entertains me with her singing and Chloe makes some tea and sandwiches that we polish off in a rush of hunger. What Francis said as he left – *It's not you I want* – has stuck in my head and I have a moment of shock when I work out what it means.

'I have to warn Leila,' I say to Chloe, grabbing for my shoes, suddenly panicked. 'I should have realised sooner.' *Why didn't I realise sooner?* 'I thought he meant that he didn't want me for a girlfriend but now I've just worked it out – I think he means to hurt Leila.' I'm upending cushions as I search for my mobile. 'Call my mobile, Chloe, will you?'

'Leila? Why on earth would you warn her?'

She still doesn't know about the Francis Leila connection. All I've said up to now is that Francis and I had a falling-out and I felt threatened by him. 'Francis is Leila's brother,' I say.

'What? *What?*'

'Please, Chloe, I'll explain everything later. Just call my mobile. I have to let Leila know that he's on his way.' It doesn't take long to get from here to Maybanks, not if you have long legs and are fit like he is – fifteen minutes tops? 'He's probably there by now.' I swear under my breath. *Shit, shit, shit.* 'Please, Chloe, call me. Quickly! Chloe!'

'Okay! Okay!' She presses the screen on her mobile and seconds later I hear my ringtone. I follow the sound, sliding my hand down the side of the sofa to grab hold of my handset.

I call Leila at once and she answers after two rings, saying, 'My son—' and then there's a thumping sound and she groans, loudly, agonisingly, like an animal that's been shot.

'Leila? Leila?' I shout, frantic now. 'Please speak to me!'

'Too late.' It's Francis's voice. 'About five minutes too late.' The line goes dead.

'Fuck! Fuck!'

'Mum!' Chloe holds her hands over Molly's ears.

I immediately call 999 and when I'm put through to the police, I say, 'My friend is in danger.' I give them the address and they promise to send a car at once.

'Since when has Leila been your friend?' Chloe says, shaking her head at me.

'I'm going round there,' I tell her. 'You stay here with Molly.'

'Mum, you can't! Not if you really believe he's dangerous.'

'I have to do this.' I grab my car keys and run out the front door. 'I'll be okay.'

The short drive to Maybanks seems interminable. I sound my horn at one car and wave my fist at the driver of another, then pull up in front of the house and run up the path. I hear shouting, a man's voice calling for help. I burst through the front door and run into the kitchen. Leila is on the floor, blood pooling around her head. 'Please help my mum!' Alex shouts, leaning over her body, shaking her as if he thinks she's simply sleeping.

'Call an ambulance,' I tell him and I kneel on the

floor beside him, feeling for a pulse at Leila's throat. Nothing. Her face is chalk-white and her eyes are open but unseeing, so that she resembles a lifelike mannequin. I notice that an area of her skull about the size of a satsuma is caved in at one side. 'I'm going to try to resuscitate her.' I roll her onto her back and begin breaths and chest compressions. She feels cold, so cold, but I keep going. In between breaths I talk to her, 'Come on, Leila. Come on! Alex needs you. Please, please, come back to us.'

The police and the paramedics arrive simultaneously. One of the paramedics takes over from me while a policeman leads Alex and me into the living room. Alex is sobbing and I sit beside him on the sofa, holding his hand, while the paramedics try to save Leila and the police begin to question us.

Shock seeps into the very bones of me. I should have called her as soon as Francis left my house. She told me he was unpredictable and potentially violent. She warned me of the danger and if I had only alerted her to the fact that he was on his way then she would have had time to protect herself. There will never be any getting away from that. I had the power to save her life and instead I lay on the sofa drinking tea while I listened to my granddaughter sing.

Within an hour Maybanks is full of police and I'm taken into the annexe to give a statement.

'Is she dead?' My arms ache from Francis holding me down and from the chest compressions. I rub the muscles but it doesn't help. 'She is dead, isn't she?'

'Yes.' The policeman is about my age with greying hair and apple-green eyes. 'Can you talk me through what happened?'

I tell him about Francis's visit to me; I report that he

was agitated and aggressive. As I talk, my fingers feel the back of my head where he slammed me against the wall. The bruise is raw and brings tears to my eyes. 'He's Leila's brother but I hadn't realised how troubled he was until a few days ago when Leila told me they had a difficult relationship. I should have acted sooner and called her but I didn't,' I say to the policeman. The act of saying this out loud makes my mistake real and I begin to cry. 'I'm so, so sorry for that.'

'Take a moment,' the policeman says.

'I could have saved her.'

'You can't be sure of that. She may have invited her brother in anyway.'

I give the policeman Francis's description and he goes off to tell one of his colleagues. Alone with my thoughts, I rewind to the moment I came into the kitchen, the sight of her body, the brutality of her injury, Alex's distress as he tried to save his mum.

Leila is dead. For the last year she has been the woman I hated and if I'd heard of her death I would have thought 'Serves her right' or 'She probably deserved it'. Now though, I feel like I know her – I knew her. And while she made some bad choices, she wasn't the ruthless, conniving bitch I believed she was. She was just doing her best. Like we all are.

The parts of the puzzle come together with speed as the police trace Francis's movements on the day he killed his sister. At eight thirty, he caught the tram to the airport and hired a car then drove to the care home in Dunfermline. CCTV recorded him entering the premises by the tradesman's entrance and leaving almost thirty minutes later. During that time his stepfather was stabbed three times in the stomach and left to bleed to death.

When the nurse went into Gareth's room to give him his lunch he had been dead for almost an hour.

Francis's next stop was his visit to me and I tell the police almost everything I know about him. I confess to the fact of my own deceit – going to Leila for therapy, acting as if I'd never lived in Maybanks and had no connections to the man she was with. But what I don't tell them is the fact of Alex's parentage. I don't tell them about that because I'm worried the information might get back to Alex and he doesn't need any more confusion or grief in his life. He needs to remember his mother as someone who loved him and always put him first.

Before the day's end, a dog walker spots Francis's body on a piece of waste ground close to Crammond beach and calls the police. Francis has bled to death from a knife wound most probably inflicted by his sister as she fought for her life.

With no other relatives, I invite Alex to come and stay with us. He agrees at once because he tells me he can't stay in Maybanks – 'not when Mum died there'. Ben and I do our best to make him feel welcome although, understandably, the mood in the house is heavy.

My OCD is growing stronger and it scares me because I have no idea where it will end. Unless I complete thorough and repeated checks to sockets, locks, batteries and the handbrake, I'm fearful and jittery, my heart pounding with incipient dread. And I've begun to count. I count the steps I take from my bedroom to my bathroom, from the kitchen to the front door, from the car into the shops. If the number is even I have to repeat those steps, over and over again, until I count an odd number.

Chloe has noticed the counting. She thinks it's because of Francis and what I witnessed at Maybanks. 'It's post-traumatic stress, Mum,' she tells me. 'Don't worry, it's perfectly normal. None of this is your fault. The feelings will subside and you'll recover.' She hugs me. 'I promise.'

I give her a weak smile as if I believe her. She doesn't know the half of it and I'm too much of a coward to share the details with her.

I'm trying to take each day at a time and, as far as possible, to focus my attention on Alex who is often quiet, so that I worry he is withdrawing into himself. I speak to Rob Mooney at the Bridge, who assures me he will stay in regular touch, and he is as good as his word, calling every evening to check in on Alex, who takes the phone into another room and pours out his heart to him. He has a lot to say. At first he believed his mum was murdered by one of her clients but a couple of strokes of the keyboard and he's able to read an approximation of the truth. It took reporters less than twenty-four hours to link David Francis and Leila Mae as brother and sister. The media tells the story of a brother who murders their stepfather then hours later his sister, before dying himself of the wound inflicted by her as she fought to save herself. It's a ghoulish tale, bloody details relished by some journalists and commentators who speculate about family feuds and bitter arguments. But nowhere is there any suggestion that Alexander Henrikson is Leila and David's son and for that I'm grateful.

The police seem to share information on a need-to-know basis only, so Tom is none the wiser about my involvement with Francis and Leila, and has made the assumption that I was visiting Mrs Patterson and that's how I ended up hearing Alex calling for help. 'The house is yours now,' he tells me. 'I signed the papers this morning.'

He looks broken. He's unshaven and there are black circles under his eyes. I reach across and briefly squeeze his hand. 'I know you loved her, Tom. I'm sorry.'

'She was leaving me, you know?'

I stare down at my feet.

'I don't know why. I don't know what I did, or didn't do.' His voice cracks. 'You must think I deserved this.'

'No.' I hug him and hold him while he cries. 'No one deserves this.' I stroke his hair. 'No one.'

What price for Maybanks? A woman's life? Is Maybanks worth that?

No, never. Never that. At no point when I set out to get my petty revenge did I want Leila to actually die. To be ashamed and upset, yes, but never dead.

'And I'll pay for anything Alex needs,' Tom tells me, pulling away. 'It's the least I can do.'

'Thank you.'

'It's kind of you to take him in.' He shakes his head, perplexed. 'I know you have a good heart, Ellen, but this clearly goes beyond anything that would ever be expected of you.'

'Well, that, Tom, is the least that *I* can do.'

He doesn't know what I mean by that and I'm not about to explain it to him. It's simple really – I blame myself. I'm a grown woman who lost track of what's important. I shouldn't have been going to Leila for therapy. If I hadn't been her client then Francis would have had no reason to target me and so I would never have been involved on the day that Leila died. Perhaps she would have died anyway – we'll never know – but what I do know is that I had the chance to stop, to think, to talk to Chloe and allow her to make me see sense, but I didn't take that chance. I was too intent on looking for revenge.

I go to bed that night thinking about Francis's journey from Maybanks to the waste ground. It's a journey of almost three miles and I imagine him walking there, bleeding, in pain, knowing what he'd done and deciding that he would rather die than seek medical help. Perhaps he thought he deserved to die. I don't know and I try not to care, Leila's death being by far the greater tragedy.

Chapter closed, I think, although that thought is closely followed by doubt. Is any chapter ever closed?

The day of Leila's funeral I rise early and stand at the window, watching the horizon break open into a deep red seam like spilt blood. Rain is expected and that feels fitting for a funeral. I have spent the last week organising the details with Alex. He has chosen the music and the prayers and white roses to cover the coffin. Several of Leila's friends and clients have been in touch and there will be time for them to talk about what Leila meant to them.

'Lots of people have come,' Alex says to me as we arrive at the crematorium. Tom has bought him a new suit and I smooth the collar flat as we climb out of the car. There are at least a hundred people waiting to follow the coffin inside. 'My mum was really popular,' Alex says, crying and smiling at the same time. 'I never knew that.'

The eulogies are moving and I learn that, while Leila didn't have many close friends, she was well respected as a therapist. A couple called Mark and Alison step up to the podium together and talk about what she meant to them.

'Leila was always patient with us,' Mark says.

'No matter what,' Alison adds.

'She understood us.'

'And she helped us to understand one another.'

'She didn't judge us.'

'She was wise and forgiving.'

'We will never forget her, Alex,' Mark says, staring down to where Alex is seated in the front row next to me. He gives a formal little bow. 'Your mother was a wonderful woman.'

When we are leaving, I notice an elderly man standing slightly apart from the crowd, leaning on his stick. 'Do you need a lift back into town?' I ask him.

'I have a taxi booked,' he tells me.

'I'm Ellen Linford.' I hold out my hand.

'Maurice van Burren.'

He takes my hand and holds on to it. He's comfortable with eye contact too and as he looks at me I remember. 'Leila gave me your number.' I take a breath and seize the moment. 'I'm sorry to ask now . . . not the time and place but,' I wonder whether you might be able to take me on as a client?'

'Yes.' He smiles a sad but knowing smile. 'Why don't you call me this week and we can arrange a time?'

'I will. Thank you.'

He releases my hand and we both turn at the sound of an engine coming to stop at the pavement opposite. 'My taxi,' he says. I hold his stick as he settles himself in the seat and then step back as the cab drives off.

Alex, Ben and Chloe are standing about twenty yards away saying goodbye to the mourners. Ben has his hand on Alex's shoulder and Chloe is saying something that makes Alex smile; then she gives him a hug and I can see he feels supported, pleased to be part of a sibling group.

'We'll look after him, Leila,' I say quietly. 'We will get this right. I promise you.'

Epilogue – Four Months Later

We spend two weeks getting Maybanks ready to sell. Tom takes his share of the contents and I take the rest, most of it going into storage until I decide what to do with it. I scrub and dust every square inch of the place then I stand in the kitchen and stare at the floor tiles, moving my head right and left to catch every angle of light. I imagine I can still see a blood stain where Leila's head lay but, in truth, there's nothing there. For four days in a row I have washed the tiles with a weak solution of bleach and now all physical traces of Leila's death are gone.

Alex and Ben tackle the garden, going at it with great gusto, chopping back more foliage than I would normally allow, but I say nothing because Maybanks no longer feels like my home. While Leila's physical body is gone, her presence still lingers and I'm determined to try to move on. I'm still checking and counting and worrying about house fires but I think I'm over the worst. It's something I discuss with Maurice at my weekly sessions, sessions that I look forward to like a child looks forward to Christmas. He's helping me find a way through my anxiety and my compulsion, and I'm sure that my work with him will make my recovery possible.

'Mum!' Ben is at the back door, clippers in one hand and a water bottle in the other. 'Come and see.'

'What is it?'

'There's an animal skeleton under the big bush at the back.' He tips the bottle upside down and runs a stream of water into his mouth. 'It's wearing a red collar. I think it might be Bruiser.'

'Really?' I follow him to the bottom of the garden where Alex is on his hands and knees in front of a newly cleared area of ground.

'We cut the bush right back,' he says. 'And look what we found.'

'Oh my goodness!' There is a small animal skeleton about two feet long lying on the ground close to the back wall. I take one of the gardening gloves from the wheelbarrow and put it on before I feel around the top of the bones, prizing the collar out of the soft earth and wiping off the surface dirt. I show both boys the name engraved on the small metal tag.

'It is Bruiser,' Ben says, his eyes wide. 'Should we tell Mrs Patterson?'

'Yes, we must,' I say. 'Otherwise she'll always be waiting for him to come home.'

I wash the collar clean in the kitchen sink and then we go next door to break the news. 'But that wasn't his favourite bush,' Mrs Patterson says, tears forming in her eyes. 'It wasn't, was it?'

'No, you're right,' I agree, my arm around her shoulders. 'He preferred to lie further into the garden where it was sunny.'

'Perhaps he knew he was going to die,' Ben says. 'They say that animals know that sort of thing, don't they?'

Mrs Patterson nods her head and clutches the collar close to her chest. 'Well, thank you, my dears,' she says. 'Perhaps you can bring his bones to me?' A tear slides down her cheek. 'I'd like to bury him in my garden. I can chat to him then, you see.'

Alex is the least squeamish of the three of us so he gathers Bruiser's bones into a shoebox and we return next door to where Mrs Patterson is waiting for us with a couple of Bruiser's toys and his collar to add to the box. Both boys dig a hole in a sunny patch of garden and Mrs Patterson places the box inside it. When the earth has been put back, we all stand in a circle around the small mound and Mrs Patterson says a few words.

'Gone but not forgotten,' I say, hugging her as we leave.

I don't think anymore about it until a few days later when a courier delivers a solicitor's letter and a large cardboard box addressed to Alex. Ben is staying in university accommodation and Alex is out until around ten in the evening. When he comes home, he opens the letter.

'My mum's stepfather, Gareth Thatcher, has left me some stuff in his will,' he says, reading the letter. 'She would normally have inherited his things but because he was killed on the same day as she was everything comes to me.' He's silent as he reads the second page of the letter. 'I don't know why she never told me about him.' He glances up at me. 'And now I'm the last living relative.'

'Sometimes families lose touch,' I say, keeping my tone as light as I can. 'I'm sure your mum had her reasons.'

'I wonder what's inside here,' Alex says, lifting the end of tape that secures the packaging on the box. It comes off in one long strip and he screws it up in his hand then tosses it into the bin. He pulls back the cardboard flaps and we both look inside. The box is full of journals and drawings but what really draws my attention is a clear plastic bag full of animal collars, at least three dozen of them, far too many to belong to family pets.

My gut tells me that examining the contents of the box will not do Alex any favours. 'Why don't you go through these tomorrow?' I say.

'I'll just have a quick look.' I watch him skim through a couple of the journals, frowning as he sees the way each section is laid out: the date, a description of the animal, sometimes the animal's name – Cheeky, Buster, Poppy – and then a detailed drawing of the dissection, with notes in the margin.

The writing is straight and neat and my eyes are drawn to the title at the top of one of the pages: Leila's First Kill. That's what I think I see before Alex slams the book shut and puts it back in the box. I feel a chill inside my chest. 'I honestly think you'd be better off leaving these journals just now,' I say, reaching across to take the box from his hands.

'Will do.' He pulls the box across the table away from me. 'I'll take them up to my room.'

'You could leave the box down here?'

'I want to keep it in my room.'

'Alex, please. I'm not sure this is a good idea. Why don't you sleep on it and then we can go through the journals together?' I follow him up the stairs. 'Better still, why don't we call Rob?' He closes the bedroom door behind him. 'Alex, I really don't think you should be looking at this stuff on your own.' My heart is racing. *What happened in that house?* 'Please, Alex.'

'Just leave me alone, Ellen.' His tone is flat. 'I'm not going to look inside the box again. I'm tired.'

I hesitate, my hand resting on the door handle. 'Okay. But you won't upset yourself, will you?' I step back from the door and see the strip of light at the bottom go out. 'You're going to sleep now?'

'Yes,' he says. 'See you in the morning.'

I spend over an hour doing my checks trying to reassure myself that in the clear light of day everything will be manageable. Alex's light remains off and when I listen at the door I can hear the steady sound of his breathing. I go to bed and drift in and out of nightmares where Leila is crying for help and I try to reach her but every time I'm close enough to touch her the landscape changes and I'm further away than ever. And Francis is chasing me, his hands dripping with Leila's blood. When he catches up with me, his hands close around my throat, and that's the moment I wake up, gasping for breath, my heart racing like a runaway train.

The third time this happens I glance at my bedroom clock: 5:10. Not long until the morning, thank God. I get up and go to the loo and on the way back to bed I listen again at Alex's door. I need to take the box out of the room. He won't like me interfering but I'll tell him he can have it back when he's in Rob Mooney's company.

I turn the door handle ever so slowly and step into the bedroom. The bathroom light is still on and it illuminates enough of the space for me to make out shapes and shadows. In a split second I see that Alex isn't in the room. I snap on the light. Alex is gone; the cardboard box is empty.

'Alex?' I stand at the top of the stairs and call down into the darkness. 'Alex, are you there?'

He's not in the kitchen or the living room or anywhere else in the house. I call his mobile but there's no reply. I send messages to Ben, Chloe, my dad, Tom and Rob telling them that if they hear from Alex to please get in touch with me immediately. I'm teaching all day and in between lessons, I try his number, leaving frequent messages, 'Please get in touch' 'Please let me know you're safe' 'Alex, I'm really worried now. Please call me back.'

He doesn't call me back. And he hasn't contacted anyone in my family either.

My appointment with Maurice is at four and the first thing I say when I'm sitting in the chair is, 'Alex is gone.' I tell Maurice about the delivery and the contents of the box. Maurice's face normally gives very little away but now he sits forward, listening intently. 'He always answers his mobile. I'm worried he's upset, wandering the streets. Should I call the police?'

'Did he take the journals with him?'

'Yes. He left the animal collars, though.' I shake my head. 'I can't help thinking about Bruiser lying dead in the garden, right at the back, next to the wall.' I swallow but there's no saliva in my mouth and my throat hurts. 'Could Leila have killed him?' I say quietly. 'I mean, I know you're not allowed to break a confidence but . . .'

Maurice gets to his feet and crosses the room, his gait awkward. He stares through the window and then turns back towards me; his face is drained of colour. 'I would like to speak to Alex when he comes home,' he says. 'Would that be possible? Could you bring him to me?'

'You think he'll come home?' I say, not sure that I want that, realising in the space of one clear second that I could very easily be afraid of him. I think about Ben and Chloe and Molly and how important their safety is to me. I think about the violence perpetrated by Alex's mother and father. Expressions 'like father like son' 'genes will out' go off in my brain like tiny grenades.

'I'm going, Maurice,' I say. 'I think I should be at home just in case he turns up.'

Maurice accompanies me to the door. 'You must be careful, Ellen,' he says. 'I suggest you report Alex as a missing person.' He clears his throat. 'I also suggest that you are not in the house alone with him.' He raises a hand. 'I'm not suggesting he will harm you but I think that, bearing in mind what happened to his parents, you must err on the side of caution.'

'Thank you.' Our eyes meet and I sense that his anxiety is as urgent as my own. 'I'll be careful.'

When I return home there is still no sign of Alex. I spend two hours doing my checks, repeating them over and over again. The front door is locked and bolted. The downstairs windows are also locked and bolted. All the sockets are empty. The hob and the oven are off. I count the steps from bathroom to bedroom, from front door to kitchen, satisfied that the numbers are always the same. And always odd. They have to be odd.

Then I sit at the upstairs window and watch for him. Midnight comes and goes. One o'clock . . . two o'clock . . . I fall asleep in the chair, and when I wake at six, sunrise is still an hour away. My neck is stiff and my feet are cold; the street is eerily silent. I stare along the length of it and I imagine I see Alex coming towards the house, stealthily, moving through the shadows like a burglar. He has his hood up and he is wearing a heavy backpack. My breath falters when he stops in front of the house, directly underneath a street light. He removes his hood and looks up at the window. He can't see me because I'm sitting in the dark but still I pull back a little.

His eyes focus on mine. They are his mother's eyes, pupils dilated, blacker than the night sky. He holds me captive in his stare and then he smiles. It's not his smile. It's an imposter's smile: fake, taut and entirely without warmth.

I close my eyes tight and count to ten, my breath held.

When I open them again, there's no one there.

Acknowledgements

Much as I enjoy writing, I think I might give up but for the help of friends and family. During the writing of *What Goes Around* I owe a special thank you to the following people:

Stephen May, Emma Unsworth and my classmates on an Arvon course at Lumb Bank in Yorkshire: April, Beccy, Steph, Philippa, Lorraine, Ariela, Sophie, Emily, Carmen, Chloe, Shirley, Sharon, Tammy and Douglas.

My brother John and his wife Mags who left me alone in their house for two weeks so that I could wander the Edinburgh streets to find my setting.

My mum for making me meals and keeping me company.

Lottie for the supply of chocolate (!)

Regan and Gail Schreiber for their generosity (I will miss you!)

Cristina Thomas, therapist and friend, who read the first draft and kindly corrected my mistakes.

Neil and George for reading the early chapters and steering me in the right direction

Mel Parks, writer and friend, who is always there with a listening ear.

My editor at Hodder – Cicely Aspinall: patient and perceptive. I couldn't have asked for more.

My agent Euan Thorneycroft who blends encouragement with good sense.

My three sons, Mike, Sean and Matt. You make me happy. You make me proud. You mean the world to me.

If you were hooked on *What Goes Around*, why not try more of Julie Corbin's novels?

Tell Me No Secrets

They say that everybody has a secret. Mine lies underground. Her name was Rose and she was nine years old when she died . . .

Grace lives in a quiet, Scottish fishing village – the perfect place for bringing up her twin girls with her loving husband Paul. Life is good.

Until a phone call from her old best-friend, a woman Grace hasn't seen since her teens – and for good reason – threatens to destroy everything. Caught up in a manipulative and spiteful game that turns into an obsession, Grace is about to realise that some secrets can't stay buried forever.

For if Orla reveals what happened on that camping trip twenty-four years ago, she will take away all that Grace holds dear . . .

Out now in paperback and ebook.

HODDER

Do Me No Harm

When her teenage son Robbie's drink is spiked, Olivia
Somers is devastated. She has spent her adult life
trying to protect people and keep them safe – not
only as a mother, but also in her chosen profession as
a doctor.

So she tries to put it down to a horrible accident, in
spite of the evidence suggesting malicious intent, and
simply hopes no-one tries to endanger those she loves
again.

But someone from the past is after revenge.
Someone closer to her family than she could
possibly realise.
Someone who will stop at nothing until they get the
vengeance they crave.

And, as she and her family come under increasing
threat, the oath that Olivia took when she first became
a doctor – to do no harm to others – will be tested to
its very limits.

Out now in paperback and ebook.

HODDER

Where the Truth Lies

Claire's husband has been keeping secrets. About the whereabouts of the witness to the murder trial he's prosecuting. And about the letters he's been getting, threatening to kill their four-year-old, unless he tells the blackmailer where the witness is hiding.

With their daughter's life at stake, it is left to Claire to untangle the web of lies and half-truths and find out just who might be responsible. And to stop them. Before it's too late.

Out now in paperback and ebook.

HODDER

Now That You're Gone

Isla's brother, an ex-Marine and private investigator, has just been found drowned in the River Clyde. The coroner declares it an accidental death. The police are happy to close the case.

But Isla is convinced he was murdered.

Determined to find out what really happened the night Dougie died, and what he was doing in Glasgow, she starts looking into his unsolved cases.

What she finds will put her in grave danger and force her to question everything she thought she knew about those closest to her . . .

Out now in paperback and ebook.

HODDER

04 | 17

You've turned the last page.

But it doesn't have to end there . . .

If you're looking for more first-class, action-packed, nail-biting suspense, join us at **Facebook.com/ MulhollandUncovered** for news, competitions, and behind-the-scenes access to Mulholland Books.

For regular updates about our books and authors as well as what's going on in the world of crime and thrillers, follow us on **Twitter@MulhollandUK**.

There are many more twists to come.

MULHOLLAND:
You never know what's
coming around the curve.